SIX ISRAELI
NOVELLAS

I would like to extend my thanks to Nilli Cohen and Riva Hoch-
erman of the Institute for the Translation of Hebrew Literature, to
those friends whom I consulted about the selection, and especially
to the translators, who did such a marvelous job. My hope is that this
volume will fulfill its purpose by representing modern Israeli culture
at its finest.

G. S.
Jerusalem, 1998

collecting of small change is a ritual that gives his life its meaning, while to his daughter these coins become a symbolic asset that needs to be replaced. And yet, once she has tried to replace the father's symbolic potency (the coins) with a more authentic force, she punishes herself for attempting to sever the oedipal tie. After Shlezi's death, Rutschen fantasizes that he is still sitting in his usual place, counting out his small change night after night.

In its rich diversity, Israeli writing has tackled nearly every subject and form known in modern literature. The paranoia of the persecuted figure who is a victim of mysterious, impersonal circumstances has its roots in Kafka and occurs in the fiction of every nation and language. The repression of women and the social and psychological barriers to their independence is also a familiar theme in European and American fiction, from Virginia Woolf onward. Literature that pits passive against active natures, or that deals with the existential meaning of political activity, has its modern roots in Camus and Sartre and continues to play a significant role in European and American literature to this day. In many ways, Israeli fiction participates as fully as any other major literature in the themes and literary approaches that have shaped our age.

At the same time, the specific politics and geography of Israel give this literature a character all its own. In a country where life is lived on the razor's edge, at pressure-cooker intensity, all the elements present in world literature are radicalized and exacerbated. In addition, rapid changes in the country's demographic situation cause remarkably fast shifts in its literary influences and concerns. Consequently, what in other literatures plays itself out across lands and eras becomes more concentrated here, more compressed and compacted — but for that very reason, more intense. In the words of the poet Nathan Alterman, this literature presents "a whole world in a dewdrop."

★

of a woman named Nimra. Grossman successfully interlaces the peculiar atmosphere suffusing the last group of soldiers in the last desert outpost, with the complex relationship between the three protagonists. "Yani on the Mountain" explores the meaning and psychological rationalization of the political act and the effect of these acts on the private lives of young Israelis — an intermingling of existential factors and political circumstances that is characteristic of Grossman's early work.

"Shrinking" by Ruth Almog (1986) is a lyrical-impressionistic story based on a number of leitmotifs: cats, the neighbors, the disappointments of friendship, music, the main character's visits to her father, wanderings near the sea, chance meetings with other people, and most of all, loneliness. The recurring themes and atmospheric descriptions are distinct elements of impressionistic art.

Abigail, the asthmatic heroine of Almog's story, suffers psychosomatic reactions to her encounters with life and especially with Eli, her former pupil, who, lonely and abandoned as she, asks her to marry him. Almog suggests that Abigail's avoidance of intimate human contact is bound up in her oedipal bond to her father. Subjugated by this bond, unable to cope with him or, consequently, her own life, she can never achieve self-realization.

Family relations are also at the core of Yehudit Hendel's expressionistic story "Small Change" (1988) about the interaction between the paranoid experience of an Israeli woman in a foreign country and a complex relationship between father and daughter. Hendel is adept at describing the mentality of a community (in this case, German Jewry) without creating communal stereotypes by first sketching and endowing each family member with traits that are perhaps rooted in communal origins but transcend them: Shlezi, the father, is an obsessive, pathological, and destructive type who compulsively collects small change; Gerda, his wife, has an unhealthy attachment to her cats; their daughter, Rutschen, is a neurotic who suffers from traumatic guilt. On a surface level, the father's obsessive mental poet (in the sense Schiller would give the word) who draws on the fantastic, naturally prefers Uncle Peretz's fiery lover, Geula, to his placid, wretched wife, Yona, and he pities Peretz doubly because he is too good (or too weak) to breach the constraints imposed by his family life. The author's sympathy in this story belongs with the romantic Luftmensch, successor to the protagonists of Shalom Aleichem. Uncle Peretz is descended from the great Yiddish writer's Mottel the Cantor, Tevye the Milkman, and especially Menachem Mendel. In Shabtai, the melancholy humor and poetic spirit of the diaspora undergo a kind of dialectical resurrection.

A strange light is cast on Israeli provincialism and its impact on fraternal relations in Benjamin Tammuz's "My Brother," the main chapter of his broad, fragmentary novel The Chameleon and the Nightingale (1989). The story deals with the singular bond between two brothers, one active and the other passive: while the first makes every woman a conquest, the second spends his life dispassionately observing his brother's follies and triumphs. The author hints that the impassive observer who assumes an ascetic stance toward the world is perhaps committing a greater sin than the person who harms others but is ready to bear the weight of his misdeeds. This particular section of the novel may be read as an indictment of the artist's passive observation in peeping through the window of others' actions and enjoying their emotional experiences without taking responsibility for his own.

While Tammuz's novella takes as its setting the remote settlements of Palestine in the early part of the century, David Grossman anchors his in more recent history — in this case, the Yom Kippur War of 1973 and Israel's final withdrawal from the Sinai Peninsula several years later. In his novella "Yani on the Mountain" (1980), Grossman describes a crucial event in the withdrawal from Sinai: the army's demolition of a major intelligence station in 1979. Against this backdrop, a decisive, existentially significant encounter takes place between two friends, Elisha and Yani, both former lovers one hand, an awareness of its own ancient heritage, and on the other, a keen attention paid to modern Western writing. Almog, for example, is engaged in a dialogue with Virginia Woolf, and Appelfeld and A.B. Yehoshua with Kafka and S. Y. Agnon. Shabtai and Dan Benaya Seri veer toward the fantastic literature of South America (one thinks of García Marquez in particular), while Tammuz and Yitzhak Ben-Ner are not far from the symbolic realism of Max Frisch and the existentialist writings of Camus. Even David Grossman, whose novels are so imbued with postmodernism, shows his ties to European realism in the novella included here.

The influences are not direct and unequivocal. Hebrew literature has assimilated elements from an array of sources because the majority of the modernists read European languages (particularly English) and because the best of American and European — and more recently, Latin American — literature has been translated into Hebrew.

Although some of the concerns represented in these novellas are bound up with Israeli place and history, even these "local" materials are informed by universal themes.

Aharon Appelfeld's "In the Isles of St. George" (1965), for instance, transforms the image of the Holocaust survivor who, after enduring Europe and then Palestine, reaches the farthest outback of loneliness: he is a symbolic reincarnation of the mythological figure of Ahasuer, the Eternal Wandering Jew, who will never find rest or a place to call home. On a remote island, the character is presented with a bizarre opportunity to replace a solitary monk who is leaving for the Holy Land. It is a singularly Christian resolution to a Christian legend about the punishment given to Cain-Judas-Ahasuer, whom not even the purgatory of the death camps could redeem from the curse of eternal wandering.

A grotesque history of the Zionist dream is offered in Yaakov Shabtai's tale "Uncle Peretz Takes Flight" (1972). Shabtai, a senti-

INTRODUCTION:
A WHOLE WORLD IN A DEWDROP

Gershon Shaked

THESE SIX NOVELLAS, PUBLISHED between the mid-1960s and the late 1980s, were selected from a large number of works and authors. A previous collection, Eight Great Hebrew Novels (NAL, 1983), which I edited with Alan Lelchuk, featured works by Amos Oz, A.B. Yehoshua, and Yehoshua Kenaz, and so I chose not to include these authors in the present volume. Translation difficulties, the length and diversity of certain works, and their accessibility to foreign readers also affected the selection; a number of important writers, whose stature would otherwise dictate their inclusion, had to be omitted for these reasons.

As for the six authors represented here, I believe they show modern Israeli fiction at its richest and most diversified. The modern Israeli novella is not confined to a single literary school or style but, rather, extends across a broad spectrum: from the fantastic expressionism of Yehudit Hendel to Ruth Almog's lyrical impressionism and Aharon Appelfeld's symbolist impressionism; from the neorealism of David Grossman and Benjamin Tammuz to the fantastic realism of Yaakov Shabtai.

While to some extent the same claim could be made for any major national literature, the diversity of Israeli fiction is interesting in that so much of it derives from a particular duality: on the

CONTENTS

First published in 1999 by
DAVID R. GODINE, *Publisher*
Post Office Box 450
Jaffrey, New Hampshire 03452
www.godine.com

Library of Congress Cataloging-in-Publication Data

Six Israeli novellas / [by] Ruth Almog ... [et al.]; edited and with
an introduction by Gershon Shaked ; translated from the Hebrew
by Dalya Bilu, Philip Simpson, and Marganit Weinberger-Rotman.
p. cm. — (Verba Mundi)
I. Short stories, Israeli—Translations into English. I. Almog, Ruth.
II. Shaked, Gershon. III. Bilu, Dalya. IV. Simpson, Philip.
V. Weinberger-Rotman, Marganit. VI. Series.
PJ5059.E8S49 1998   98-34323 CIP

ISBN 1-56792-199-X

Text design by Mark Polizzotti

First softcover edition, 2003
Printed in Canada on acid-free paper

RUTH ALMOG · AHARON APPELFELD

DAVID GROSSMAN · YEHUDIT HENDEL

YAAKOV SHABTAI · BENJAMIN TAMMUZ

SIX ISRAELI
NOVELLAS

Edited and with an Introduction by Gershon Shaked

Translated from the Hebrew by Dalya Bilu,
Philip Simpson, and Marganit Weinberger-Rotman

VERBA MUNDI
David R. Godine · Publisher
BOSTON

SIX ISRAELI
NOVELLAS

SHRINKING

Ruth Almog

"WHY ARE YOU DOING this, Miss Abigail?" said Ida Rabinowitz.

Abigail, who was bending down, whispering, "Psst... psst..." and coaxing Goliath to come closer and take the chicken leg from her hand, straightened up and turned around.

The ground-floor neighbor was standing at the gate. She was a small, heavyset woman on high heels; the white flabby flesh of her double chin jiggled over her neck.

Abigail smiled at her and said, "What do you want, Ida?"

"*Ida?*" snapped Mrs. Rabinowitz. "Since when am I *Ida* to you?"

But Abigail only smiled and said nothing.

"Stop smiling like that."

"Forgive me, Mrs. Rabinowitz," Abigail said dispassionately.

"A thousand times I've told you to stop this!" she screeched.

"Stop what?" marveled Abigail.

"The cats! You bring cats to our yard from all over town."

"So what? Does it bother you?" asked Abigail.

"It's filthy."

"Nonsense. Cats are very neat animals."

"But Miss Abigail, I'm scared to go to the garbage cans. When I walk in there, they jump on me."

"That's because the neighbors never bother to close the door. It's not my fault."

"I hate them! I don't want them here!" retorted Mrs. Rabinowitz.

"Ida," said Abigail, "you know that there are a lot of rats here,

3

and you, who live on the ground floor, should be glad to have cats around. Imagine if the rats got into your apartment. Wouldn't you rather the cats ate them?"

Mrs. Rabinowitz looked at her with undisguised hatred and said slowly, "As long as you give them food, they don't eat rats. I will ask the municipality to come spray poison here. Your cats will die, too."

Abigail was taken aback and whispered, "No, Ida, please don't do that."

"Yes, tomorrow morning I'm going to city hall. You know, every night these cats howl and keep me awake?"

"That's a lie! A blatant lie! It isn't their mating season. They only howl when they're in rut."

"What's this 'in rut'?" Mrs. Rabinowitz asked nervously.

"In rut, Ida. Don't you know what it means? When it's their time to copulate. You know what 'copulate' means, don't you? To make love, Ida. It's pleasure. They howl out of pleasure."

Mrs. Rabinowitz was all flushed. It seemed to Abigail that even her short chubby arms had turned red. For a moment she thought she was going to have a stroke. But Mrs. Rabinowitz regained her composure. "You should be locked up in a loony bin, you fruitcake," and turned to leave.

"Hey, Ida, wait a minute," Abigail called after her, "I want to show you something."

Mrs. Rabinowitz hesitated for a moment, but her curiosity got the better of her; she turned around and looked at Abigail with an intense and truculent expectancy.

"What do you want?" she said.

"Look — do you see that beautiful black cat over there? He's the biggest tomcat in this neighborhood; his name is Goliath. Look what gorgeous fur he has. In the season of lovemaking, he drives away all the rivals from his territory. And look at that tiger cat over there. So sad. He's always so melancholy. His name is Job, and I like him a lot. And the gray one over there. She's such a coquette, so soft, so ingratiating. Aren't they adorable? And you want to kill them? All you can think of is killing. They don't harm anybody, Ida. They're not like people, you know."

Abigail, who got carried away by her emotions, knew she had been defeated. Mrs. Rabinowitz had not stayed around to hear her song of praise for the cats but had left in a deliberate show of rudeness, her small, heavy body wobbling on her short legs, tapping with her pointed high heels.

What a mean spirit, Abigail thought bitterly. She threw the cats the leftovers she had wrapped in a newspaper, then crumpled the paper into a little ball and dumped it in the garbage can. When she came up to the gate, she saw Mrs. Rabinowitz waiting for her. The little woman raised her hand at her, waving a menacing finger. "I'll report you to the Tenants' Committee, d'you hear me? You should be locked up in a loony bin, you fruitcake!"

Abigail stared at her and said, "You don't know how to put on rouge, Ida. You smeared it all over your face. You also put on too much powder."

"What?" Mrs. Rabinowitz recoiled. "What are you saying?"

"I'm saying you have to learn how to put on makeup. Your lipstick is disgusting."

On her way Abigail stopped at the grocery store to buy a few provisions. While standing in line at the checkout, she noticed a nice little container in the cart of the woman in front of her. She leaned forward and asked, " What's that? Something new?"

"Yes, it's a flavored cheese."

"Is it good?" asked Abigail.

"Depends on your taste," replied the woman.

Abigail asked the woman to keep an eye on her cart and went to pick up two containers of cheese. When she returned, she said to the woman, "I've decided to try it," but the woman did not respond.

From the grocery store she went to her father's house. She used her own key to open the door. From outside she could hear the television blaring. *Why does he turn it up so loud?* she thought irritably. *I can't stand that noise...*

In the hallway she was greeted by Rex, the German shepherd, who sniffed her basket.

"This isn't for you," she told him.

From inside the room she heard her father's voice calling, "Abigail?"

"Just a minute!" she called back, and went to the kitchen to unload her basket. Plates and glasses were heaped on the marble counter, and she thought, *What a mess! He always leaves all the work for me!*

She took the groceries out of the basket and opened the refrigerator. A foul smell filled the kitchen, and she hastened to put in the food and close the door. Then she washed the dishes and scoured the marble counter. The cleanser's acrid smell made her sneeze. She opened the window and gasped. *Everything is always closed here*, she thought. *How can he stand it?* She looked down at the floor and said to herself, *I'll wash the floor tomorrow, and defrost the fridge. It stinks inside.* When she entered the living room, her father said, "Shh . . . don't bother me."

He was sitting in his armchair in front of the blaring TV. Newspapers and magazines were scattered on the rug at his feet. Abigail bent down and picked them up.

"You're in the way," her father said. And then, when she was about to leave the room, he said, without taking his eyes off the screen, "Did you bring me the new issue of *Ha'olam Ha'ze?*"

"I'll get it later, when I take Rex out," she said.

"All right, all right. Be quiet now," he muttered impatiently.

Abigail took the papers into the kitchen, folded them carefully, and put them on top of a large stack. Then she went to the bathroom and started washing the sink. A bad odor permeated the bathroom. The cracks between the chipped tiles were black. She opened the window and sprayed the room with lavender-scented aerosol. But that made her cough, and she thought, *This isn't good for me.* She went out, closing the door behind her.

The dog followed her into the kitchen, wagging its tail and rubbing against her leg.

"You want out, eh?" she said to the dog. She fastened a collar and leash around his neck, peered into the living room and announced, "I'm taking Rex out."

"You're always bothering me," her father said. "And don't forget to bring me *Ha'olam Ha'ze*," he called after her.

Rex was old and heavy. He staggered at her side on his long, thin legs and panted incessantly. Abigail said to him, "Poor darling, summer doesn't agree with you, does it?"

Sadly she reflected on how old and sick he was, and that perhaps they would have to put him to sleep to end his suffering. On the way, she ran into Mr. Meir from her own building, who said, "Listen, Mrs. Rabinowitz has been complaining about you. About the cats, you know."

"So what do you suggest?" she said.

"I really don't know," he said uneasily. "I don't mind them myself, but you have to consider her."

"She's just a pain in the neck," Abigail said rudely. "Tell her to leave me alone."

Soon this vacation will be over, and then summer, then just one more year and I can retire. If I don't find a job at another school, I will retire. The new headmistress gets on my nerves. She doesn't know a thing about education. When she thought about this, Abigail felt stifled and stopped for a moment to breathe.

It was very hot, and the long summer days were unbearable.

When she got back, she made supper for her father and called him to the kitchen to eat. She poured some dog food into Rex's dish on the kitchen porch.

"Come to the table," she called out. "The flies are coming in."

Her father came into the kitchen. "How many times have I told you not to bother me when I'm watching television," he muttered. Abigail did not respond. She stood at the door watching him eat.

He chewed audibly and, when he was done, he started emitting a series of sucking noises. Abigail could not take it any more. "I'm leaving. Do you want grilled chicken tomorrow?"

"Whatever. It doesn't matter," he said.

"Don't forget to let Rex out before you go to sleep."

"Where are you going?"

"To a movie. At the museum. Do you want to come?"

"No. Can't stand the air-conditioning."

"Shall I get you a new book from the library?"

"I haven't finished the old one yet. Maybe tomorrow."

She walked to him, bent down to give him a kiss, but his smell repulsed her, and since he did not bother to raise his head, she hastened to straighten up, holding in the nausea that had seized her.

"Don't wear this shirt again," she said. "I'll take it tomorrow with the rest of the laundry."

"I stink, is that it?" he said, and a hint of mischief lurked in his eyes.

"A little bit," she said.

"It's old age that makes me stink, not sweat. You can't do anything about that."

"Take a shower," she said. "And you haven't shaved today. You look so seedy."

"Who should I wash and shower for? Who's got the energy?"

"You have to. You can't let yourself go like this."

"Who for? What for?"

"For me," she said. "Why not? I'm a human being, too."

Abigail remained in her seat for a few minutes after the lights came on in the little theater. Then she got up and wearily climbed the stairs to the lobby. Unlike the others, who lingered in the museum, she went straight out to the big square paved with large stone slabs. The harsh sunlight, which had washed over the white square during the day, was now transformed into the soft grayness of twilight; only the sky still retained a lingering, pale pink shimmer. The heat had abated a little and a light breeze was blowing, raking up trails of dust here and there. Abigail sat down on the low stone wall at the edge of the square. A man in red pants walked up to her; she heard him speak. She stared at him for a moment, then averted her eyes and gazed in the opposite direction. But the man stopped right in front of her, reciting some Russian verse. Her eyes turned toward him in spite of herself. His arms sliced through the air in sharp, aggressive gestures. *Maybe he's Pushkin,* she thought. The man had an aura of rage about him, and she was afraid to breathe.

When he finished, he stood on tiptoes, like a ballet dancer, and took a deep bow, with a wide gesture of his arms. Abigail clapped her hands as he staightened up and shouted "Bravo!" She thought to herself, *What am I doing? Am I out of my mind?*

But the man smiled at her innocently, and the aura of anger vanished. His face lit up, he took another bow and moved away, with a new recitation, toward two women who were coming out of the museum. They swerved and hastened to pass him by. The man turned around and punched a clenched fist in the air. The two women sat down on the stone wall, not far from Abigail.

"Crazy," one of them said, and the other added, "It's loneliness that makes people go out of their mind like that."

Abigail inched closer and closer, until she was quite near the two women. She listened to their conversation and said, "Wasn't that a remarkable movie?"

One of the women nodded, and the other, who was sitting next to Abigail, turned around, gave her a sharp look, then turned her back. To her friend she said, "The children's acting was wonderful."

Abigail said, "Did you notice how little dialogue there was in the movie? So few words and so much power…"

The woman who had turned her back did not bother to look, but the other one said, "Yes, now that you mention it…"

"Japanese cinema is great," Abigail said. "Kurosawa…" But the woman next to her was already on her feet. Her friend followed suit, and Abigail's words were left hanging in the air. She followed them with her eyes and noticed that they went to sit somewhere else.

On the steps of the nearby library, she saw a skinny young woman with a harried face, holding a tiny dog in her arms. Abigail's
eyes lit up, and she waved at the woman, signaling her to approach.
The skinny woman, who was wearing a long black dress, came up
to Abigail and said brightly, "Hello, how are you?"

"How cute," said Abigail. "Yorkshire?"

"Yes," said the woman and patted the dog. "A sweet and pam-
pered Yorkshire."

But when Abigail tried to pat the tiny dog with the pink velvet
bow pinned to its forehead, the woman recoiled and blurted out,
"No, no, he bites. He's mean-spirited and xenophobic."

"Like Heathcliff," said Abigail. "He was from Yorkshire, too. I
would like to visit there one day, to see the Brontë family home."

"Yes," said the skinny woman. "It's amazing, isn't it, what they
managed to produce out of their terrible loneliness, those sisters…
When you think of that godforsaken place, and how they grew up
in the shadow of death, and considering the conservative society
they lived in… It really is astounding."

Abigail nodded toward the dog and asked, "What's his name?"

"Iambus," said the skinny woman. Then she looked about her
and asked, "Have you seen my husband?"

"No," said Abigail, but at that moment her eyes lit on a tall, heavyset man in a white shirt and black tie who was approaching them
from the street. "There he is!" she cried, and pointed with her hand.

The man came over to them, greeted Abigail with a smile, and
hugged the woman. The skinny woman was almost engulfed by
him. When she released herself from his embrace, the dog cocked
its head toward the man and stretched its front legs to touch him.

"Look, look," Abigail exclaimed. "How he loves him! You must
have other dogs."

"Four more," the man said.

The dog wriggled in the skinny woman's arms and stretched
itself toward the man. The woman let go, and the man received the

dog with great affection, lifted it high, and kissed it on the mouth.

Abigail giggled.

"Come," the man said to the skinny woman. "I'm parked in a no standing zone."

The two turned toward the road, the man holding the dog in one hand, and the skinny woman with the other. Her long black dress trailed behind her. Abigail looked after them affectionately, almost longingly. *Like a skein of wool*, she said to herself. *I must buy a nice blue ribbon for it. Not velvet though, maybe twill…*

A young man was now approaching the museum from the street. He went past her, and Abigail looked after him in amazement. She wondered if it was indeed he and followed him with her eyes. The man walked to the box office, and Abigail thought to herself, *It's too late. The second show started a long time ago.* Then she saw him turn back. He was walking slowly, and when he came close, his eyes fell on her, and she said, "Eli?"

"Hello, Ma'am," he said, surprised.

"Hello, Eli, how are you?"

"Very well, Ma'am, thank you," he replied. "And how are you? I almost didn't recognize you."

"'Ma'am,' indeed!" Abigail blurted out disdainfully. "You must have grown children yourself by now. What is it? Have you forgotten my name?"

"Abigail," he said a little sheepishly.

"So what do you do?"

"I'm a lawyer. Until recently I worked for somebody else; now I've opened my own office."

"And how is it going?"

"Not bad. There's a lot of work. Maybe too much."

"And how many children do you have?" Abigail asked.

"None. I don't have a wife, either. I'm divorced."

"I'm sorry to hear that," said Abigail.

"Can I sit down for a moment?"

"Please, please do," she said in haste.

When he had seated himself next to her, he looked at her for a moment and then said, "Are you still teaching?"

"Well, yes. Do I have a choice?"

"Why? Don't you like your work?"

"As a matter of fact, I do. But it's not the same anymore. Everything has changed... These days you work only for the money and the vacations, not for love..."

"And you're here by yourself?"

"I went to the movie. An astonishing movie. You should see it. I'm thinking of going to see it again."

"I wanted to see it, but I was too late."

"Never mind, you can see it some other day."

"Perhaps you will join me?" he asked.

Abigail felt it coming, like the redolence of cheerful spring blossoms. Her throat closed-up, and she breathed heavily.

I can control it, she thought, *I only need to calm down and it will pass.*

The young man pressed her, "Well, what do you say?"

"We'll see. Maybe next week," she said with effort.

"Do you remember you used to like me then, when I was your student..." When she did not respond, he was taken aback, "At least that was my impression..."

Abigail did not answer. In her mind she could distinctly see the horrid picture of the beautiful Japanese woman lying naked on the bed in the cabin of the riverboat. *How gorgeous she was*, she thought.

"You know," she said, "almost nothing happens in this movie, yet you don't get bored for a minute. There's a kind of suspense in it..."

"How can you stand it living by yourself all these years?" he asked. "I find the loneliness so hard to bear."

Abigail looked at his hands, resting on his knees. The scars they bore looked white in the dark, and she said, "A minute ago it was light, and now it's completely dark. Night falls so abruptly."

"I got divorced two months ago," he said. "It's not such a long time to be by yourself, is it? But I find it very hard."

"Some Japanese are so good-looking," Abigail said. "That woman in the movie, I can't forget her face…"

"I go to the movies almost every night, so as not to sit alone at home. But I hate going by myself."

"You've got to see this movie. It's really stupendous," she said.

"Promise you'll come with me," he said, and smiled at her in the dark.

Abigail got up. "I have to go now. It's late."

"See you soon," he called after her. "And don't forget, next week."

When she turned to a street where she could no longer see him, she stopped and leaned against a tree. Her body was trembling, and her shrunken lungs were gasping in vain for air. She heard heavy footsteps behind her and hastily roused herself and moved away. Her hand fumbled in her bag until it found the inhaler that she put in her mouth, inhaling as she continued to walk. But she felt no relief and kept the inhaler in her mouth as she staggered all the way home. She stopped for a moment at the gate, then started climbing the stairs to her top-floor apartment.

It was hot and stifling; when she opened the door to her flat, a torrid gust of air leaped at her. Abigail did not turn on the light, but instead went out on the veranda and sat in her deck chair in the dark. Gradually her breathing relaxed and settled. She opened her eyes and looked at the squares of light on the building next door. In one square she saw people sitting and watching television. A bowl with black grapes was on the table. In another square she could distinguish only a flickering, piercing blue glow…

The house emits the heat it has absorbed the whole day, she thought. The roof should have been whitewashed…

After a while she entered the room and turned on the air-conditioning. When the room had cooled a little, she closed the doors and the windows and put on a record. She lay on the couch and closed her eyes. When the singer came to the verse, "Now I understand what you tried to say to me / How you suffered for your sanity… Vincent / The world was never meant for one as beautiful as you…" her eyes brimmed with tears, and she murmured, "How beautiful… how beautiful…"

When the song about Vincent was over, she got up, turned off the phonograph, returned the record to its sleeve and put it away. For a while she continued to hum the song to herself, repeating the tender and awesome words that always brought tears to her eyes. Finally, she got up, washed her face, and went out for a walk.

The streets were dark and deserted. A soldier walked by and stopped to look in a shop window. When she reached him, he started walking alongside her. He said something to her. He was speaking softly and she did not catch it. "Get lost!" she said. "Witch!" he called to her, almost spitting the word in her face. "You Cyclops," she retorted and smiled to herself, thinking that not an evening goes by without someone trying to accost her.

When she got back to her flat, she took out the big album in which she had glued all the class pictures. She did not have to look long. It was her first class, her first year as a teacher. In one of the suburbs. A neighborhood of red roofs and well-tended gardens, bordering on an immigrants' housing project. She stayed there for only one year. It was too much for her.

In the photo Eli looked all eyes. Black, wondering eyes. Abigail thought, *How wrong he was when he said that I used to like him. I had to restrain myself from hugging and kissing him.* But that pristine quality he had about him is almost all gone now. The tender, smooth and taut skin is now tinged with roughness. How handsome he was then, she thought, with those clever black eyes… that sweet innocence… Abigail reckoned he must be thirty-seven now. He looked much younger though…

She remembered when, after the holiday of Lag Ba'Omer, she had walked into the classroom and immediately observed that something was wrong. Eli's chair was empty, and the children's faces were grave. They were unusually quiet. "Sit down," she said and called the roll. When she came to Eli's name, toward the end (Sha'ar was his last name, Eli Sha'ar), Irit, his neighbor at whose house he ate lunch, raised her hand and said, "We were sitting around the bonfire when somebody said, 'Who has the guts to jump over the fire.' Nobody volunteered, they were all scared. Only Eli got up and tried. But he failed. He jumped right into the fire, Miss. He's in the hospital now, all covered with burns."

She sat by his bed in the hospital. If she had dared, she would have sat all night. Without him, the classroom was empty. His bandaged hands lay on the white sheet, his bandaged chest exposed. Abigail sat there trying to contain her tears.

His father said, "He won't be a violinist now. His hands are ruined."

Mr. Sha'ar's great dream. When she had called at his house he told her, "My Eli will be a second Paganini." The child played all the time — four, five hours a day. He played out of love for his father. Abigail remembered the essay he wrote for Mother's Day. She had tucked it away behind the class photo. Now she carefully took it out:

My mother is a physician. She is a very busy woman. She works hard at the hospital, and is often called on duty. I hardly ever see her. We have an arrangement with our neighbors. My father pays them so I can eat lunch with them. My father works very hard, too. He comes home in the evening. That's why I have to do all the shopping. Every day Father leaves me a list of groceries and some money. Father cooks the Sabbath meals. When my mother is not on duty, all three of us eat together, but that happens very seldom. Mother's Day is the saddest day of the year for me. I always make something for Mom, a little surprise, a picture or a present, but she is never home to receive it.

Abigail remembered how it tore her heart to read this essay. She did not know what grade to give it. How could she explain to him that she could not give him a grade? Her heart went out to the boy. She thought she could give him all the love he needed, but she knew it was not possible; she was only his teacher. That was the reason she made those house calls that year. True, the Ministry of

Education mandated them, but her colleagues laughed and told her, "You're a greenhorn."

Even though she made all those house calls only to get to Eli's house, she enjoyed them. They changed many things for her. The eighth-grade kids whom she taught science no longer waited for her on the path up the hill as she went home from school; before, they used to wait for her on the red loam wall, hurling obscenities and singing vulgar songs. She could never understand why they did it. She always wore the same coarse brown army sandals (which she still wore), a simple blue skirt and white blouse (which she still wore quite often). Occasionally, they even threw stones at her, though they never hit her. She knew they did not mean to hurt her, but she was scared. As she reminisced now, she could hear them shouting and singing. "In the middle of the night, when the stars are shining bright, Abigail and Moshe are f——". Moshe was the gym teacher and Abigail had nothing to do with him. She did not report it to the principal. She was ashamed. She had no doubt that it was her fault. Nor did she tell anyone that she was a failure as an eighth-grade science teacher. As soon as she entered the classroom, all hell broke loose. She would stand there, waiting for the students to settle down. She never raised her voice. Sometimes she would say quietly, "We have such an interesting topic today. Isn't it a pity to waste the lesson?" But after someone shouted, "We want sex education," she never said it again. When they finally sat at their desks — the big bully of the class would silence them and order them to sit down — they continued to make noise while she explained and drew at the board. But when she started making those house calls, the gang on the hill got smaller until it disappeared altogether, and she breathed a sigh of relief. The class, too, became more obedient. At last, there was only one rowdy boy whom she could not control, and when he entered the class one day with a stick in his hand and started whacking in all directions, she had to request that he be thrown out of school. "He's too dangerous," she told the principal ruefully.

★

As usual, her father was absorbed by the television. Abigail walked into the kitchen quietly and unloaded the groceries. The air in the kitchen was musty and heavy. She opened the window and the porch door and then peeked into the living room.

"Why do you always keep everything closed. You could suffocate in here," she said.

"Doesn't bother me," said her father.

Abigail walked in and started opening windows and drawing blinds, one by one, banging them angrily.

"Stop making noise," cried her father, and the dog seconded him with a short bark.

Abigail went back to the kitchen. She fried an omelet and made a salad. She cleaned the table and set it.

"Come to the table," she called.

"Don't bother me now. I'll eat later," he called back from the room.

Abigail stood at the door and said, "The flies will come in."

"Then cover it," he said irritably.

"The place needs fixing, Dad. It's awfully depressing," she said solicitously.

"After I die," he said.

Abigail cleaned the toilet and, when she came out, the smell of ammonia clung to her hands. She washed them several times with soap, but the smell stubbornly remained. "I'm leaving," she called from the hallway. "Don't forget to take Rex for a walk"

She was greeted by summer stench in the alley. It must be the dead rats, she thought to herself and quickened her step. When she reached the main street, the cars driving noisily through the filthy smog lunged at her with their flashing headlights, and when she waited at the pedestrian crossing, the buses belched their poisonous fumes in her face. Tears choked her when she said to herself, *An Inferno, a real Inferno.* She then decided to walk down to the promenade to breathe a little fresh air. She did not really like the sea air, but she preferred the silence, the darkness, and the light breeze to the din, stench, and crowds.

So Abigail headed for the beach. She used to go there quite often and stand for a long time facing the sea, her elbows resting on the wet rusty railing, watching the sinking sun, the bathers, the pink horizon. On the way to the beach she passed by the house of her old college mate, Rachel, and decided to drop in. But first she went into a nearby candy store and bought a few red candied roosters, chocolate cats' tongues, and a bag of mixed taffy. Rachel's children were always glad to see her, and Rachel herself welcomed her cheerfully. But this time she seemed a bit tense. "A friend is coming to take pictures of the kids," Rachel told her.

"How nice. Who is it?"

"Her name's Achsa. You don't know her. She's studying photography and wants to specialize in children's photos."

"Achsa?" Abigail said. "I knew an Achsa once. It was in the youth movement."

Achsa rushed into the house like a whirlwind, laden with various cameras, looking annoyed. When she had unpacked her gear, Rachel introduced the two of them.

Abigail beamed at Achsa, waved her hand, and cried out gleefully, "Long live progressive socialism!"

"Have you lost your mind?" Rachel asked.

"No way. Achsa knows exactly what I mean. What, don't you remember me? We were comrades sharing ideals and flag. Mooky was your leader, wasn't he? I never forget anything. A regular elephant. You were the prettiest girl in the movement, and you had a gorgeous embroidered Russian blouse. With an unusual name like yours, who could ignore you? Do you remember when we went to distribute posters all over town? Those were the days! Idealism, struggle, and fulfillment. Do you remember the grape harvest at Tel Yosef? Our hands were full of calluses. But not yours; you wiggled out of it. Your hands were too delicate. You went to graze the flock on Mount Gilboa with that handsome kibbutz member; Motke was his name. I never forget anything…"

Achsa looked at her coldly and impatiently. "I don't remember you. Sorry," she said.

"It doesn't matter. Who was I in those days? A scrawny little girl. But it's nice, after so many years, to meet a sister in arms. You were very active then, and afterwards, too. You joined the Pioneering Combatant Youth, didn't you? And when you came back to town, you continued to work in the commune. Do you remember the play at the Hanukkah Ball…"

Achsa cut her short. "Enough of this nostalgic drivel. I came here to work. I have no time for such nonsense. The past is gone and forgotten. Life has changed." And to Rachel she said, "Bring in the kids. I don't have much time."

Abigail said, "All right, all right. You needn't be so rude. I only thought…"

"Never mind what you thought. I'm in a hurry. I told you. I don't have time."

Rachel called the children, and Achsa yelled, "Bring some toys. Scatter them on the rug. Go ahead, play."

Both children brought in toy boxes and emptied their contents on the rug.

One child asked, "What do you want us to play?"

"Doesn't matter," she said, "Just play. Don't pay any attention to me."

"I thought…" Abigail said, and the unfinished sentence hung in the air, oppressively laden with disappointment. Abigail looked at Rachel, seeking some reassurance, but Rachel avoided her eyes.

Abigail started again, "What can I tell you? I always thought camaraderie was a lasting thing…"

"You won't let me concentrate," Achsa said. "Stand back, I don't want you in the frame."

"Why are you so edgy? One might think…"

"You can think whatever you want. I really don't care as long as you don't bother me here. I came here to work."

"Don't worry," Abigail said. "I'm leaving."

By the door she said to Rachel, "Just imagine! I would never have believed..."

"I'm sorry," Rachel told her. "We arranged to do this work, and she is under pressure."

"Pressure, eh?" Abigail said and turned to leave.

On her way down the stairs she remembered she hadn't given the children the candy she'd bought.

Abigail went to the promenade and, as was her wont, leaned against the railing and gazed at the sea. The metal pipe felt cold and sticky. In front of her stretched an endless undifferentiated expanse of darkness, and only on the horizon were the skies distinguishable and clear.

A man stood next to her, and Abigail said aloud, "Damn it! Can't a person be alone for one minute in this miserable city?"

The man did not reply, but he did not move away either.

"Go away," she said without turning to him. "I want to be alone."

"You can't tell me where to stand. This is not your private property."

"But there's so much room. Why here of all places?"

"I'll stand where I please," he said.

To hell with him, she said to herself and walked away. Abigail walked northward and, when she reached London Square, she climbed the stairs to Hayarkon Street. Two men were sitting on a bench under the street lamp, embracing. When she passed by them, she averted her eyes and walked very straight and erect. She was making her way up Hayarkon Street until she reached a posh new hotel. She deliberated for a moment, then went past the doorman, through heavy glass doors, and walked in. Red velvet couches dotted the spacious lobby, and showcases along its walls were filled with silver and ceramic artifacts. It felt cool inside, almost cold.

Tourists moved in and out, and girls in shorts or swimsuits stood
in a small group speaking loudly in English. Abigail sat on one of
the soft couches, took out her cigarettes, and rummaged in her bag
for a lighter. Her hand touched the smooth cellophane wrapping
of the chocolate cats' tongues, and she felt saddened for a moment.
She sat for a while, smoking. She saw a waiter pass by with a tray
full of bottles and tall shining glasses. "I'm thirsty," she thought. Suddenly she heard a man say, "Hey, what are you doing here?"

A teacher, a colleague. Abigail smiled at him and said, "Just sitting here. Fleeing from the heat. And you?"

"Looking for some relatives," he said, waving his hand as he
walked toward an elderly couple.

Abigail put out her cigarette in the tall metal ashtray that stood
at the side of the couch, got up, and left, passing again through the
tall heavy doors. The doorman nodded to her.

As usual, the oppressive heat had accumulated at the top of the
stairs and under the roof. Abigail turned on the air-conditioning and
sat outside in the dark, waiting for the room to cool off. In front of
her, in a square of light, people were sitting and watching television.
On the table stood a large bottle of Coca-Cola, glasses, and a bowl of
grapes. On the floor below, a blue light flickered inside a black square.

Abigail walked in, closed the windows and the doors and put on
a record. This time she chose Schubert's trio, Opus 100. She lay on
the couch and listened, waiting for the staccato that was her favorite. But suddenly the phone rang.

"You're never home," he said. "I've tried lots of times."

"Who is this?" she asked. Abigail did not recognize the voice.

"Eli. Eli Sha'ar. Have you forgotten your promise to go with me
to the film at the museum?"

"I never promised anything."

"So what do you say?"

"No, I don't feel like it. It's too fresh in my mind."

"Then let's go to another movie."

What does he want from me? she thought, and did not answer right away.

He said, "I'm dying to go to the movies, but I don't feel like going alone."

"No," said Abigail. "I'm busy."

"You're not busy. You're just looking for an excuse. You're not interested in seeing me."

Abigail fell into the trap. "No, not true. I'm really busy tonight. How about coming here for coffee tomorrow night?"

"What time?"

"Seven-thirty?"

"Seven-thirty, then."

When she hung up she wondered, *Why on earth did I invite him over?*

In the meantime she had missed her favorite staccato movement. She picked up the needle and turned off the record player. "Damn it!" she said.

She went to the bathroom and looked in the mirror. Wrinkles, she thought, I'm all wrinkles. She took her tweezers from the little drawer above the sink and started plucking her eyebrows. The tweezed area turned red and looked inflamed. Abigail put some cream on it. Then she plucked the hairs of her mustache. *Just look at me*, she thought. *Why did I invite him?* she asked herself again.

She read a little in her bed before falling asleep.

"Please come in, come in," she said, pointing with her hand to the living room.

Eli walked in and looked around. "You have a nice place," he said. "So many books! You even have a piano. Do you play?"

"Not any more. I used to."

Eli lifted the heavy lid and touched one key with a finger. "My father's dream was for me to become a second Paganini," he said and passed his palm on the keyboard, producing a grating glissando.

"I've always thought you jumped into that bonfire on purpose," Abigail said.

"There's something to that," Eli said. "At times I'm convinced of it myself."

"You didn't really want to be a violinist?"

"No. It was too hard. Day in, day out, practicing so many hours. I had a little talent…" Abigail remained silent, and he said, "He's dead, you know."

"Who?"

"My father. Two years ago. Cancer."

"I'm sorry," she said.

Abigail wanted to ask about his mother but did not dare.

"Play something for me," he said.

"Oh, no, I couldn't. The piano isn't tuned and some of the keys are broken… I haven't played for years."

"Pity…" he said.

"Let's go to the kitchen. I prepared a light supper."

His face brightened. "That's really very nice of you."

They ate in silence. Then suddenly he said, "My wife never made supper for me. Since I was a kid I always had to take care of myself. It's nice when someone does things for you."

He finished and lay the knife and fork diagonally on the plate.

"It's hot in here," she said. "Let's go in the living room."

When they had sat down, she asked, "Why did you get divorced?"

"It didn't work. I suppose I just don't have a model, you know what I mean?"

"No," she said. "I don't know what you mean."

"A model of marriage, I mean. You know that my mother left us."

"Altogether?"

"Yes, eventually she left altogether. Went to America. She wasn't happy here."

"And you haven't seen her since?"

"I went to see her several times. But she wasn't too eager to see me. She remarried and had children with him... I even took my wife once. I'm not sure why, really. It just didn't work. But it's still too raw, and sometimes I miss her. My wife, I mean."

"It's sad," she said.

Then he got up and said, "I'm going now." Almost fleeing. And she thought she must have disappointed him.

The Schubert record was still on the turntable. Abigail turned it on and laid on the needle gently. As always, she waited for her favorite movement. Those awful staccato notes. The anticipation that, transformed into music, filled her with intense pleasure. She lay down, her arms and legs very tense and her whole body permeated with immeasurable sweetness, almost too heavy to contain. Finally her favorite movement arrived, and she cried silently as the lump of pent-up sorrow gave way to the music and became one with it. Her whole body ached from the sudden loosening that followed her total capitulation to sorrow. Then there was one moment of terrible silence, immediately broken by the squeaking sound of the needle grinding the groove of the revolving record. The squeak jolted her nerves, and her tense body relaxed. Now she was able to retreat from the sorrow and hold it in again: a gun that could not shoot.

She continued lying there for a while, the squeaking needle scorching her empty brain, and when she felt she had regained her strength, she got up and turned off the phonograph. She went out on the darkened veranda, leaning on the railing that was damp from dew, and breathed deeply. But the air was murky and heavy.

She awoke with a start when the phone rang. She turned on the light and looked at the clock; it was two in the morning. She picked up the phone but did not say anything. Eli said, "I'm sorry I ran away like that. I want to apologize. Let's go to the movies tomorrow."

"You woke me up," she said.

"I'm sorry. I couldn't fall asleep. I had to talk to somebody."

"Okay," she said.

"It's a date then?"

"I don't know right now. Call me tomorrow, okay?"

"No, you're never home. I know you by now. You'll wiggle out. Let's decide now."

"Which show?"

"Second. I work late."

"All right. I'll wait for you downstairs at eight forty-five. Now good night," she said and hung up.

She lay awake for a long time. Before falling asleep she thought, *I'll go to the beauty parlor tomorrow.*

The beautician poured strips of molten wax on her legs. On her armpits, too. Hot steam from camomile extract opened the pores of her facial skin. Then a white mask. From there she went to the hairdresser, and from the hairdresser to a clothing store where she bought a flowery, youthful-looking dress. But when she looked at herself in the store mirror, she thought, *The dress is pretty, but I am not.* And when she finally went home to rest a little, she said to herself, *Nothing can help me now,* and she had to keep herself from scratching her face. For a moment she was seized by a great desire to tear up the new dress, to mess up her hairdo, to lash at her raging flesh. But she soon got hold of herself; she closed her eyes and listened to her own breathing until she regained the calm that was always her strongest suit.

At night, when he came toward her — she was standing under the street lamp allowing herself to feel a little like a high-school girl — he said, "You look great. You changed your hairstyle. It looks good on you."

Abigail found the movie boring. Despite the air-conditioning, she perspired continuously. She was afraid to lean her arm on the armrest and huddled in her seat. Gradually her lungs contracted, and she began to hyperventilate.

"I have to get out," she whispered to him, "I'm suffocating." She got up and squeezed herself between the rows, careful not to tread on people's feet, and stumbled in the dark until she came out. Outside, she took the inhaler out of her bag and put it in her mouth.

"Come," Eli said suddenly. "I'll take you to the hospital, to the emergency room."

She had not noticed him coming after her.

"There's no need," she said. "It'll soon pass."

Eli gave her a ride home in his car, and when she got out she said, "I'm sorry I spoiled your evening."

He did not come after her. He started the car and drove away.

She poured herself a glass of soda water in the kitchen and took a tranquilizer. Then she went to bed and fell asleep right away.

As usual, her father was watching television.

"I brought you grilled chicken for Sabbath," she said, peering inside the dark, stuffy living room. It was permeated by the usual stale smell.

"Shh… Don't bother me," he said.

"What's that? You're learning French?" she asked, amazed.

"Yes, sure. I'm learning all the time. Don't bother me."

Abigail put the chicken in the refrigerator. It emitted a bad odor, and she thought she ought to defrost it and clean it up, but did not feel like doing it right away.

"If you don't need me, I'm leaving," she said to her father.

"I don't need you. I don't need you," he muttered.

On the street, she picked some light purple vervain from a hedge. She went up to see her friend Stella and gave her the flowers.

Stella said, "Can't you ever come without bringing me something?"

Abigail grinned, "I just picked them off a hedge in the street."

Stella put the flowers in a vase and said, "I like their strong scent, but they wilt so fast."

"Do you have any interesting books for me?" Abigail asked.

"No," said Stella, "I don't have anything new. Let's go out and sit in a café."

"All right," Abigail agreed.

Stella went to take a shower and get dressed. When she came back, Abigail whistled and said, "What a stunner!"

"You should learn from me," Stella told her.

When they were sitting in the café, gazing at the passersby and sipping milkshakes through wide straws, they saw Abraham, Rachel's husband, go by with his children. Abigail called to them and gave them the red candied roosters. Abraham said, "Listen, I heard what happened. I'm sorry I wasn't there. I would have given her a piece of my mind."

"Nonsense," said Abigail. "I've already forgotten all about it."

Stella sat back in her chair, her long tanned legs stretched out in front of her. Abraham stared at them and said, "I can't stand that Achsa."

"I know, Rachel told me," Abigail said and noticed how Abraham's eyes were ogling Stella's body. Her blouse was cut open at the cleavage and her nipples stood out through the thin material.

"Keep in touch," said Abraham and walked quickly to catch up with his children.

"Achsa?" Stella asked. "The youth movement belle?"

"She's become a photographer in her old age," Abigail said. "She's a year older than me."

"Stop thinking of yourself as an old woman, and you won't look like one," said Stella. "Take a leaf from my book."

Abigail stared at her and said, "You have spunk. I'm different."

"Well, it's time you changed."

"What for?" asked Abigail.

"So you can catch a man."

"Not interested," said Abigail. "I don't need a man to snore next to me at night and stain my pillow with his oily hair."

"Well, you don't know what you're missing," Stella said.

"No," said Abigail emphatically. "I know what I'm gaining." And to herself she said that it had been two weeks since she went to the movies with Eli and he had not called. Somehow she knew that he had not forgiven her and was punishing her.

That night, it was three in the morning when he woke her up. "Did I wake you?" he asked.

"What do you think?"

"I can't fall asleep. I would come to you, but you probably won't let me in at such an hour."

"You're right." she said dryly.

"I'll come tomorrow then, okay? At eight in the evening."

What does he want from me? she thought. *I'll phone him tomorrow morning and call it off. I don't want him to come.*

Abigail went to a lot of trouble this time. She prepared three kinds of salads, and she bought Greek olives, pickles, and different cheeses at the market. Eli enjoyed the food and she was elated.

"What a pleasure," he said, and she felt so grateful that for a moment she laid her hand on his white scarred palm, but then withdrew it in alarm.

"Let's drive somewhere," he offered. "In summer I like to drive out of town at night."

Abigail was happy. She thought this was better than sitting and worrying all the time.

On the highway the car gathered speed, and Abigail noticed the needle reaching 90 KM. "Don't go so fast," she said.

"Scared?" he said laughingly and stepped on the gas.

"It's dangerous," she whispered, but he heard her and slowed down.

"I'm an excellent driver. You needn't worry," he said.

After a while, he went off the main road onto a dirt road leading to the beach. When they reached a low craggy plateau, he stopped the car. "Let's take a look at the sea," he said, and got out. Abigail went after him, her feet heavy with fear. She could not remember ever being so frightened. She took out the inhaler and put it in her mouth.

"What's the matter with you?" he asked.

"I'm asthmatic, don't you remember?"

He didn't reply, and she said, "Sea air doesn't agree with me."

"Then why do you live in Tel Aviv?" he asked rudely. "You should move to Arad. I'm sure they need teachers there."

"Because of my father," she said, all shrunken, her breathing sounding like water trickling.

Eli said, "Listen."

Abigail did not respond. She, too, heard the roaring sea, but could not enjoy it.

She wanted to get back in the car and go home but was afraid to offend him, so she kept quiet.

"How I love the sound of the sea," he said.

A slender crescent moon, cold and glittery, was hanging in the middle of the darkness.

Suddenly he touched her arm and said, "Let's go back."

All the way back she chatted compulsively, mainly about politics, protesting bitterly, inveighing against the government, members of Knesset, corruption, theft, and the appalling social conditions.

When she finally got home, she closed the door behind her and leaned against it, exhausted. She closed her eyes and started moaning loudly, vociferously. *I can't stand it any more*, she thought. *I don't want to see him again.*

"Take Rex out," her father said. "And on the way, stop at the library and get me a thriller. Spy novel if they have any."

When she got back, she gave Rex some dog food in his bowl on the veranda. Her father, who was watching television as usual, suddenly cried, "School starts tomorrow, doesn't it?"

Abigail said, "Yes, finally. Vacation is over."

"You should have gone abroad, like I told you. Then you wouldn't have been so bored."

"Who said I was bored?"

"All right, so you're not bored. Are you leaving already?" When she nodded, he said, "Then I wish you a happy and successful year."

Late that night, when she was preparing her plan for the first day of the new school year, Eli called.

"I wanted to wish you a happy school year," he said.

"Thank you," she said, surprised. "It's nice of you to have thought of it."

And then, almost against her will, she added, "I thought you had forgotten me."

"I was on reserve duty for three weeks," he said, yet in his voice she detected something that made her doubt his words.

"What are you doing?" he asked.

"Preparing my lessons for tomorrow."

"After so many years, you still have to prepare them?"

"You'd be surprised," she said.

The following day he called to ask how the first day had gone and said, "If you ask me for supper, I'll be happy to come."

"Please," she said, not knowing if she should be happy or upset. But when he showed up, she found it hard to contain the delight she felt.

She said to him, "I haven't had time to prepare anything. I had a busy day and I'm still not back in the swing. After school I went to see my father, and the time passed too quickly. Go sit in the living room and watch TV while I go to the kitchen. It won't take long."

At supper he said, "I don't like to eat by myself. At your place it's always so pleasant."

"You should find a girl and get married," Abigail said cheerily.

"Why don't you marry me? We'll have a good time together, I'm sure," he said and smiled.

Abigail said, "Please don't make fun of me."

"God forbid. I mean it seriously."

"Nonsense."

"No, you don't understand!" he cried. "I'm absolutely serious."

"I could be your mother," she said teasingly.

"So what? If anything, this is an argument for, not against."

"Eli, I don't have a sense of humor, so there's no point telling me jokes."

"Abigail, I'm absolutely serious."

Abigail got up and, standing very erect, said, "That's enough."

They watched a television movie together, and when it was over Abigail said, "It's getting late and I have to get up early."

She saw him to the door and on the threshold he said, "Thank you for the meal," and bent down and kissed her cheek. She almost closed her eyes to surrender herself to the sweetness and serenity that touched her but recovered just in time and told him, "Don't come any more."

"What?" he asked, alarmed.

"I said, don't come any more."

"If you give me a reason, I won't come."

"I can't give you a reason. Just like that."

"I won't accept such an answer."

"I don't owe you any explanation."

"I think you do. In the situation that has evolved, I think you definitely owe me some explanation."

"No situation has evolved."

"Aren't we friends, Abigail?"

Abigail hesitated. She wanted to say, "Not any more," but she couldn't lie.

"You needn't be afraid of me," he said and tried to embrace her, but Abigail evaded him and stubbornly said, "I'm asking you not to come again."

"Don't you like my company?" he asked, sounding offended.

Again she hesitated, and he said, "You can't fool me. I know you're attracted to me."

"No! That's not true!" Abigail cried. "Now go away, go and don't come back, do you hear?"

Eli turned away and started descending the stairs. When he was halfway down, he turned back and said wildly, "I will come again. I'll come and harass you until you tell me why not."

Abigail did not answer and slammed the door.

The next day, fearing he might show up, she went out with Stella and sat in a café. When Stella had gone home, she just walked and walked until she was exhausted.

When the doorbell rang, she did not respond. When he called her on the phone, she did not answer him and hung up as soon as she recognized his voice. But one day he waited for her by the gate, and when she passed by without stopping, he grabbed her arm and said, "Why are you acting like this?"

Abigail said, "You want to know? Then I'll tell you. I hate you. I hate you, and I never want to see you again."

From the corner of her eye, she saw Mrs. Rabinowitz standing on her veranda watching them. He was still holding her arm, glowering at her.

Abigail could not move and told him, "Leave me alone, please." But Eli did not let go of her arm and continued to glower at her. Abigail could not figure out what was in his mind, and suddenly she felt it coming on, like the redolence of cheery spring blossom. She started asphyxiating and hyperventilating. Eli noticed it and let go of her arm. Now she was obliged to take out the inhaler and put it in her mouth in front of him. But the attack was severe; her breathing sounded like the trickling of water.

"Take me to the hospital," she said, and when she collapsed next to him in the car, her head bent backwards, her lungs more shrunken than ever before, he said to her, "Calm down, Abigail. I won't come again. If this is what I'm causing you, I won't come again. I'm sorry, I didn't understand." And then, all at once, she felt better. Eli noticed it, stopped the car and parked on a street corner. He asked her, "Do you want to go home now?"

When they reached her home, he asked, "Would you let me see you upstairs to make sure everything is okay? I promise I won't come again. You needn't worry." Abigail whispered, "All right," and when they got out of the car, she noticed that Mrs. Rabinowitz was still standing on the veranda watching them.

Eli walked Abigail up to her flat, opened the door for her, and asked if she wanted anything. She told him where her medication was, and he brought it to her with a glass of water. She drank and swallowed the medication and sat down in an armchair, eyes closed.

After a while he asked, "Are you feeling better now?" Abigail nodded wearily.

"Before I go, I'd like to tell you something. I understand now that I really should not come any more, and I won't come. But I am sorry about it. And I'm even sorrier that we did not meet many years ago. Perhaps then I might have taught you to love yourself a little better. Now it's too late, and it's a great pity. You simply don't deserve this. And there's something else I want to say to you, something that I never said to you before. Those hours when you sat by my bed in the hospital, when I was a little kid, were some of the happiest hours of my life. I have never forgotten them." And then, when she had not responded, he added, "You gave me a lot of warmth that year."

"But apparently it wasn't enough for you, since you had to jump into the bonfire."

"That's right. It was not enough for me." He then got up and said, "I'm leaving now. Don't get up, I'll see myself out."

Abigail finished grading the exams and rose from her desk. She took chicken legs out of the refrigerator and wrapped them in newspaper. Downstairs in the yard, she stood and whispered, "Pssst... psst..." Right away the cats gathered around her. Goliath came close and rubbed against her leg. The contact of the fur against her naked leg gave her a pleasant sensation, and she told him, "You're so handsome, Goliath." She bent down and offered him a chicken leg. Goliath grabbed it and ran to a corner to eat it in peace. The other cats waited patiently, eyeing her eagerly. She tossed them whatever was left in the paper and crumpled it in her hand.

Mrs. Rabinowitz stood a distance away and watched her. When

Abigail made her way to the garbage cans, she called after her, "The young man doesn't come any more, eh?" But Abigail did not stop.

"I'll tell the municipality! D'you hear? I'll tell them to come and kill all your little pussycats."

When Abigail came out of the yard, Mrs. Rabinowitz was waiting for her. "Tomorrow I'm going to the city hall," she said and smiled.

"Go, Ida, go," Abigail responded, adding, "You smeared your whole face with rouge again."

On the way to her father's house, she met Rachel and the children.

"You haven't dropped by in a long time," Rachel said.

"I'm afraid of that friend of yours, Achsa," Abigail said.

"I'm sorry about the other day," Rachel said.

"Who wants a candy?" she asked the children cheerfully, taking out a bag of taffy from her handbag and offering it to the older child. "Share it," she said.

The children said thank you and the eldest tore the plastic bag and took out two candies.

"There's a trash can," Abigail told them. "Don't throw the wrappers on the street."

"Come and see us," Rachel said, and Abigail said, "Okay," and walked away.

When she stood at the door of the darkened room, her father said, "Shh... don't bother me."

"This time we'll go down the negative axis," Abigail heard the announcer say and she thought to herself, *So now he's studying mathematics...*

Abigail washed the dishes that had accumulated on the marble counter. From outside came a piercing sad howl. She looked out the window and saw a tomcat sinking its teeth into the neck of a female. On the veranda, Rex let out a furious bark, and the cat freed herself and escaped.

Fall is here, thought Abigail, and started singing to herself softly, "Now I understand what you tried to say to me, Vincent... The world was never meant for one as beautiful as you..."

translated by Marganit Weinberger-Rotman

YANI ON THE MOUNTAIN

✵

David Grossman

I

Ras Ajeh, Sinai. Sunday. Midnight.

The wind penetrated the mess hall. The iron handle of one of
the windows had fallen off the rotten wood, and the empty frame
— the pane had been smashed long ago — kept thudding loudly
against the wooden sill.

We sat around the only table left in the big hut. Six men in army
jackets, each of them huddled into himself, staring dully at the plastic cup in his hands. Steam from the cooling tea rose into the air.

There was a sound of pots crashing into the sink from the kitchen
and immediately afterward Peretz the cook cursing roundly. The
Norwegian opposite me, in blue overalls, with the UN symbol
printed in sky blue on his sleeves, his blue eyes lusterless even in
the bluish cloud of smoke permanently floating above his head,
cleared his throat emphatically, took his short-stemmed pipe from
his mouth, and with great force spat a heavy glob of spit. It rose
into the air and landed far away from where we were sitting on the
floor of the mess, which was covered with a layer of dirt and mud.

This was the silly competition with which we amused ourselves
in the apathy surrounding our lives here on the mountain, in the
slightly anarchic atmosphere of those last days. There was no way
— nor did I consider it reasonable to try — of imposing order and
discipline. And now too, although none of us had the least desire

to do so, we responded to the childish challenge. The plump orange parka with the thin brown hair and the perpetual grin on his face, the American member of the team supervising the demolition work, collected his saliva, red in the face, grinning even now with his mouth loaded, and spat — but nowhere near the Norwegian's glob. America had let its side down.

Now it was the turn of the engineering corps, and the oldest of the three strained his cheek muscles, narrowed his eyes, and sprayed between his front teeth — with consummate artistry — a rapid dancing jet that cleaved the air like a hissing snake, holding all our gazes, but falling, to our disappointment, short of the moist, rich stain on the floor.

It was the boy's turn now. He was an engineer too. He blushed, averted his eyes, and quickly collected a little spit, like one performing a disagreeable duty. It was evident that our little game was not to his liking, but he didn't have the guts to refuse. He wasn't like his dark, malevolent friend, the third of the engineers, the one with the amputated right thumb. With the sniggering obsequiousness typical of him he spat a shameful glob, which went no farther than his boot, and a thread of saliva now hung from his mouth to his trousers, glistening in the pale light. How he blushed. He blushed to the roots of his yellow hair.

And now — will the very thin, tall friend, black as a raven, do his bit? Certainly not. In all the time he has spent with us on top of the mountain, during all the final preparation for blowing up the military installation and the entire camp, he has not wiped the expression of bitter contempt from his face, nor has he spared us his snorts of scorn. Paldi, that was how he introduced himself to me when he arrived on the mountain with his friends ten days ago. And from then on he had not spoken a single word to me.

In which case, it's my turn. Stand up, clown. Amuse yourself. And I swell my chest, draw all my disgust and bile into my mouth — and suddenly stop, for he — is it possible? — now gets up provocatively, his face black and his hair black, his eyes smoldering fiercely, and he fixes them onto me more than anyone else, for he detests me more than any of the men assembled in the cold hut — in me, so I imagine, he sees the instigator of the anarchy reigning in the camp — and with a rapid movement he climbs the chair, and in front of everyone, with magnificent impudence, he opens his trouser buttons.

And now the Norwegian raises his eyebrows in astonishment, the American too, for he, Paldi, his eyes still fixed on me (why me of all people?), is pulling out his big, surpassingly pale penis, pressing his stump of a thumb on it, and spraying an accurate jet of piss far beyond the large stain sinking into the mud.

And again, at the sight of the yellowish jet, steaming slightly as it hits the floor, the obscure malice rises in me, dull and gloating, bursting to get out and stun the hut closing in on me, the people in it, and I stand up opposite him, silence any voice of protest inside me, and while his strong jet weakens and jerks over the dirt, drawing wet writhing snakes on it, I climb slowly onto my chair, take my penis out before the startled eyes — we've never gone so far before — and pee with all my might. Contract my stomach muscles until they hurt, eject the warm, steaming liquid, shooting power into it — and it lands, heavy, ripe, far beyond my mind's limits, raining to the floor and watering the dust.

And Jorn, the Norwegian, is on his feet already, clapping his big hands with slow enthusiasm, and the American is grinning, raising the jam-smeared bread in his hand like a glass of champagne.

I button up my trousers, feeling like an idiot standing on top of the chair, and sit down heavily.

Peretz comes in from the kitchen. His face is flushed. In his hand is a plateful of omelets. In the doorway he pauses for a moment, sniffing in surprise. The smell of the steaming urine is rising into the air, and Peretz shifts his astonished gaze from face to face, fixes his melancholy eyes on me, his admired commanding officer, and now, because of his embarrassment, my embarrassment, because of my spite and malice, the laughter bursts out of my mouth, and I let it crash over him without pity or joy.

Peretz, who never understands anything, smiles back at me with his groping smile, canine teeth exposed like an animal's fangs. "A little luxury, sir," he giggles nervously. "Omelets for your midnight meal," and he dishes them out with much ado.

The cold, oily omelet quivers on my plate. The smell of the urine mingles with the smell of the slippery yellow mess in front of me, and I purse my lips and push the omelet away. The American in the orange parka pounces on it and forks it up greedily.

The uniform murmur now heard in the hut is the whispering of the three engineers. They've been here for ten days already. As different from each other as it's possible for three men to be, and nevertheless sticking to each other like leeches all day long, scheming and plotting in whispers, drawing with the toes of their boots in the sand and gravel, arguing without enthusiasm, turning their backs on each other in despair and coming together again in the same despair, for the desert lying at the door of the mountain isn't easy on an individual, and the sand in their hourglass is running out. Competently, with dull precision, they glide over my mountain, planting stakes, skipping between the defense positions and the underground halls, making strange signs in yellow chalk on the walls, giving me looks of feigned apology when I pass, and getting right back to the job the minute my back is turned.

God, how I hate them! All their skill, all their efficiency, all their wishes are directed toward one object: finding the mountain's weak points, the locations of its soft underbelly, the place to hit with one blast of dynamite so that all the buildings still surviving here, all the installations, the strongholds, the underground halls and the fortified bunkers will collapse at once, cave in on themselves and turn to dust. The mountain is finished. All that's left is the dry hollow crunch of a plastic cup as it snaps in my hand.

And now the lukewarm transparent tea trickles onto my fingers and trousers, and the three owls of the engineering corps stop their whispering for a moment and look at me. The Norwegian, too, strong as a horse, his pipe glowing, looks at me with his dull eyes that never betray any expression and shakes his head in astonishment.

I get up, push the chair back, pull the sides of my army jacket together, and walk toward the door. Peretz comes running from the kitchen and trails behind me.

"When should I wake you, sir?"

"There's no need, cook. I wake up by myself."

"Still, maybe I should knock on your door at seven?"

"I told you — there's no need," I spit out at him, hunching my shoulders in anticipation of the blast of wind. To my surprise he follows me out. "What should I make for breakfast, sir?

I stop and look at him uncomprehendingly. How stupid he is. How can he not sense the danger radiating from me? Get away from me. Get away. The warning churns inside me. If only I could shoot words out of my elbows, my hot forehead. Look out, Peretz, beware.

"Sir, there's only enough food for three more days."

"We won't be here after Thursday, cook."

We stand facing each other in the roofed space, next to the entrance. Once this space was crowded with ravenous soldiers. I put my hand in his shoulder, flash him a cold smile, and crush his skinny shoulder bone. "Cook, I've already told you ten times to nail that window shut."

Peretz, tempted to believe my smile but already wincing under the pressure of my fingers, groans in pain, still smiling: "Tomorrow sir," he lies. "In any case, we're leaving here. What's the point — " and with these words all my rage evaporates.

In any case, we're leaving. What's the point? How much strength is still left in me, and at what moment will I burst like a bubble? There's no other possibility. This body is dying. Yani is dying on the mountain.

And he's still standing in front of me.

"What's the matter, cook?" I growl at him. "You want a good-

night kiss?" And I grab his collar, knot my hand and shoulder muscles, lift him up to me, light as a feather and kicking with both feet,
press my lips to the stubble on his sunken cheek, and print a warm,
slavering kiss on it, and then I throw him onto the door, and without looking back — so as not to give myself a chance to feel sorry
— I turn away, thrusting my hot forehead into the wind, as if to
butt it with my head. And I still feel no relief.

Now into the storm. To the narrow asphalt road that in the past,
only months ago, led between the officers' and soldiers' huts to a
hillock of earth hiding the underground halls where the intelligence information was received by attentive ears and eyes. From
there, I hunched my body against the wind cutting my face, kicking childishly at little stones driven onto the road, with jumps of
cold that anyone watching might have mistaken for jumps of joy,
between rectangular marks on the ground, memorials to the huts
that had once stood here but had now been uprooted and sent
north, then head on to the north gate, where a well wrapped up
soldier from a reserve unit shines his torch on me, and I hurry
away.

Next to one of the paths stands the last remaining barracks hut.
Its open doors bang violently; the panes in its little windows are
broken. I slip inside and stand in the bare room. In the light of my
torch one picture, a naked, big-breasted girl cut out of a magazine,
flutters half torn on the wall opposite me. Underneath it are a
name and a date: Raffi Mantzur. Discharge date 10/22/78.

Somewhere under the many layers of whitewash, my name too
is written and the date of my discharge from national conscript
service. Here, in this hut, I lived for twenty-one months. I was a
boy of nineteen when I came to the mountain. A young officer in
a two-year-old base. Eleven years have passed since then.

On the rotting floor are marks left by the legs of the heavy beds.
I bend down to look, but the darkness is dense and the torch light
dim. I can't see a thing, The winter nights this year are darker than

usual. And the days are no more than a pale flicker between the long-drawn-out nights.

The wind whistles in my ears, and I, on my knees on the floor, grope with the torch, ignoring the mocking voice inside me, the shame I don't feel anymore.

My search is rewarded: in a corner between the wall and the door, covered with dust, lies a green toothbrush. I remove the dust slowly, examine it by the light of my torch. Yes, yes, Watson, this toothbrush belongs to Mr. Mortimer Halberstam, a present from his friends in the hunting Club. Can't you see from the initials...

And now to the west gate, I run with my hands in my pockets, contracting my overly large body, avoiding the whirlwind of old newspapers with a practiced sidestep as they are borne by the wind, jumping over the open cesspit left exposed when they pulled down the lavatory shed, and onward to the electricity poles piled atop each other like elephants' legs, waiting to be carted away. On the dark horizon, the three engineers, dragged along by the wind like little birds, struggling against it, finally reach the building where they and the UN people sleep. I continue past the heap of stones that fly underfoot, in a gliding run that tries to be slow and graceful but is actually clumsy, over the communications trench — and here's the opening of the tunnel joining the two bunkers (one hundred quick steps in the dark), the trampled wire fence. I've arrived.

Here's the edge of the mountain. The craggy cliff looms up with a yawning power. It stretches toward the desert gaping at its feet, crashes down with the sudden fall of a rock, holds itself back with a strength it does not stop exerting for a minute, like a horse rearing backward. Such a posture fills me with actual physical excitement, for such unfinished movements, processes interrupted midway, have always made me feel uneasy, psychologically and physically, as if waiting for the continuation of the movements to be dragged out of me.

I turn away quickly from the edge of the cliff, toward my position set well back from the abyss. These days I'm not sufficiently sure of myself. I feel comfortable sitting on the damp ground between the disintegrating sandbags. The wind passes over my head; only its whistling penetrates my hiding place. I pull the damp plastic bag out of the pocket of my army jacket and light my flashlight. How it's shrunk. Lately I've been throwing away page after page. I won't leave anything behind me. The letters are hers, the ones I've kept on me all this time, the ones I've been casting day after day to the desert winds. How little she wrote me here. How her letters moved me. Always on pages torn hastily from a notebook, scribbled on the backs of pamphlets in a dozen different languages, nervous, jagged, unfeminine writing. Every letter separate, always written in passion, urgently, without humor. Always afraid she won't have time to do the right thing.

Take this one, for example.

From April 1976.

From London.

Something's happened at last. All the mental distress, the oppression weighing on her for so many months, ever since she arrived, is dissolving. It would be more correct to say, is taking on a clear direction, is opening itself some kind of liberating action. She can't go on living in this selfish inactivity any longer. Because — if you thought about it honestly — for the past year she's been leading the life of a leech. And now, finally, she's getting out of it. Now she realizes: staying in London, working in British television (however interesting), isn't the right thing. She's already bursting with the waves of energy flooding her. She'll be coming back home very soon, but she can't tell me yet what she's going to do here.

You know I've never been a big patriot (what a revolting word!) and my return to Israel has got nothing to do with love of country (what's that?) or what you call our 'vital interests,' but in the long run — it seems to me — they are important, and I believe in them. How strange that up to now I've never thought of doing anything in that

direction. Something active, I mean, not just venting impotent bitter-
ness among friends or at left-wing conferences, but here in London, of
all places (it seems we have to move away to see what's closest to us).
I met an Arab couple, a man and a woman who were born in Jaffa
(her) and Lydda (him), and up to two years ago lived in Nablus.
Today they're running a little bookstore for Arabic books. They told me
things I didn't know. That I didn't want to believe. That you'll prob-
ably dismiss out of hand (oof! I'm getting cross already)... Here
there were a few muddled lines, illegible or missing words, due
to the furious rapidity of her thoughts, then: *Oh, Yani, I'm*
choking on this inactivity, and counting the days left to the end of the
month, when I can leave my job — actually everybody's really nice to
me, understanding and considerate — and come home at last.

And at the end, the Cato-esque conclusion: "Yani, come down
from the mountain."

I hold the flimsy paper with its tattered edges in my hand and
loosen my fingers. Immediately, the wind comes and snatches it
away. It's gone. I'll never read it again. Her next letter was written
from France, a year later. What happened in all the months between the writing of the two letters, what made her leave Israel
again with so much bitterness? I'll probably never know, and anyway it's not important. She could never stay in one place for long.
She would have left sooner or later, regardless.

I go on lying there for a minute or two longer, and when a fine
drizzle begins blowing in I stand up, shove the flat plastic bag into
the pocket of my parka (there are only one or two letters left, and
I'm keeping them for the difficult moments still to come), zip up
the parka, and step out of the shelter of the stones and sandbags.

In the darkness the wind beats against the side of the mountain,
and now I can no longer resist the consolation contained in that
memory, and I hesitantly approach the edge of the cliff, opposite
the gaping desert.

Over there, in the gathering darkness of the abyss at my feet, amid the vegetation sprouting wildly over the camp's sewage pipe, an old trap lies waiting for me, and inside it the bait that is growing colder all the time.

The day after the Yom Kippur War ended I went out again to roam the wadis around the base, which had not yet been aired by the joy of those who have survived one more war. Without permission, ignoring the threats and warnings, the real and imaginary dangers they warned us of day and night, I stole out of the camp, which for the duration of the fighting had been sealed off, swarming with angry officers and frightened men. I burst into the wadi, laughing out loud to myself, reckless, opening the buttons of my stinking army shirt, pleasurably scratched by thorny branches, thudding into soft, fragrant tree trunks, clearing a path, beating down the tangled growth with my hands. And then, pushing aside a heavy, leafy branch, I found myself standing opposite an Egyptian Mig 21, resting there blackened and distorted, its nose poking between the tree trunks, and its wings spread quietly on the green ground. In the slightly crushed cabin sat a young man, his two charred hands clinging to the joystick.

At first I felt no fear. The scene was so unreal, almost innocent. In any case, it was too powerful for me to take in all at once. I stood there, still holding the branch that barred my way to the slightly absurd spectacle, and the only thing that kept echoing in my mind — the part of it that wasn't entirely frozen — was, *He's still growing his mustache.*

And in fact, there was a neat, narrow mustache growing on the man's upper lip. Carefully rounded at the tips, neatly trimmed, sticking up in jaunty, flirtatious maleness. Standing out in its impressive stylishness against the background of the sooty, fear-distorted face. You could imagine the man, in the air force club in Cairo or Luxor, narrowing his eyes as he passed the gleaming samovar, examining his gallant, dandyish reflection in its mirror-like surface, a little elongated, distorted, but nevertheless — there it was, the mustache!

I remember with surprising sharpness how with all my might I blotted out the torn plane, which had a straight line of little round holes stretching along its side, the strong smell that began rising in my nostrils, the sight of the black hands clinging to the joystick. Only the narrow mustache, only that expression of arrogance, that hopeful maleness bristling in the hairs.

After that came the shameful reactions.

I was twenty-three then, with a number of principles and expectations of myself. I struggled to toughen myself more and more. I sentenced myself to undergo daily trials of torture. I almost believed in my strength. And then, in the thicket of bushes, exposed to that sight, came the primal fear calling: *Run.*

But I went back. That same day, and on the following days too. A path began to appear in the thicket. I would sit, leaning against a clump of reeds, and look. Slowly the facial features and that narrow mustache disappeared; the blue uniform frayed, tore, and blew away in the wind; all the personal features were effaced, and only the suggested movement of the body remained, the forward crouch over the jammed joystick, the tense slope of the back, the strength in the shoulders. I saw all this in the painful way in which things become known to me when the information, which is too much to contain, explodes inside me and streams mercilessly into all the cells of understanding and feeling, leaving me exposed and helpless. Now too I bend forward, remembering the despair in the black, clutching fingers, the hollow stare fixed on the gay, green tendrils creeping over the nose of the plane.

For hours on end, almost every day, I would sit there, hidden from sight, hearing only the gurgle of the sewage streaming nearby, the distant voices overhead rolling toward me from the base on top of the cliff, and gaze hypnotically at the dead pilot, who was gradually shedding his human covering, his mustache and his uniform, keeping only the flow of the skeletal body, only the unknown, stubborn hunch over the controls.

Too quickly the creeping plants meshed over the body of the

plane. Each time I had to strain harder to make out the Arabic letters, the bullet holes. Then the branches broke into the cabin itself,
lapped up the man sitting there, surrounded him on every side.
Nature grew a fresh, green scab.

Moist and laden with scents, the wind whirls in the little lap on
the mountainside, spiraling upward to the edge of the rock where
I stand, hovering between heaven and earth. Another silly game,
the kind I have been playing for more than ten years; but now, in
my last days in this place, it no longer fills me with the familiar, tol-
erable fear but balls into a terror that is new for me, terror of the
strange tranquility and jubilation I feel here.

Four days left. Very soon I will have to decide.

Now, charging down the stony slope, feet thudding on the pit-
ted road, at a panting run over the guard-mounting square, where
a damp, torn flag flutters at the top of the pole, lonely and resent-
ful; onward, along the empty basketball field where two stumps of
posts sway in the wind (the nets have already been removed), and
from there, bowed against the gusts of the storm, to the trodden
dirt track, to my room, the base commander's room, remote from
all the remains of the buildings left here, three wooden steps over
which I glide, the concrete platform, the frozen metal of the door
handle, and the blast of heat from the electric heater, glowing in
the dark like the eye of an intelligent animal. Patient. The light
switch.

From a heap of blankets on the floor a vague mass looms up at me,
struggling between the blankets wound around him, writhing,
groaning, nearly choking, and in the end a bald egghead pokes up,
creased with sleep, blinking blindly in the harsh light, sending out a
long, white hand, which gropes on the floor, encounters a small blue
suitcase, two wet shoes, and at the end of its hesitant journey meets
a pair of glasses. (All this time I still haven't moved, paralyzed by
panic and astonishment.) The hand shakes the glasses slightly to
open them, returns with a rapid, economical movement to the

blinking face, puts them on at the third try, and only then my eyes focus, only then the face is illuminated in a flicker of memory and amazement, and the voice, that voice says, "Yani, Nimra's left me."

2

The night between Sunday and Monday.

I boil water with the electric plunger. Elisha takes one look at the oily spots floating on the surface of his coffee and pushes it away, talking all the while. He hasn't stopped talking since he woke up. His fingers rub the frayed threads of the army blanket, tie knots, untie them, draw nervous circles in the dust on the floor, little acts that drive me out of my mind.

Nimra came back to Israel two weeks ago. Elisha came back after her three days ago. There was no point to his life without her. He says these hard words with the casual haste of someone who is used to words and despises their power. He's working as a journal-ist in France, a reporter for a local paper in one of the provincial towns. (I didn't manage to understand exactly where: the stream of words was so muddled, so agitated.) It was Nimra who found the job for him. She worked for the same paper. She left Amnesty after that business with her old Argentinian. He himself, Elisha, covered health and sanitation in the town, had he told me already that they were living there together, he and Nimra, his book of poems in French was coming out soon, his first book, a friend who worked with him had translated them for him, it was Nimra herself who...

He talks, pouring out scraps of information that don't penetrate my mind, piling up details that don't connect with each other, as if, were he to stop talking, he'd have to look at me for the first time in seven years. From everything gushing out of him I manage to gather (to my surprise) that Nimra took my advice and called him to her in France when she sensed that her hold on life was slip-ping, and I even feel a flicker of jealousy: Nimra and Elisha. How many years he had waited to win her. Only later the happiness suddenly surges in me. Only later — I've already said I'm a little slow in such things — the amazement flares.

"Elisha, kid, what are you doing here?"

"In Israel? I've already told you, Nimra's left…"

"What are you doing here, in Sinai, in 'Levav'?"

Elisha is silent. He gathers his lanky legs, in their brown corduroy trousers, to his stomach, and his white calves are exposed. "I heard they're blowing it up."

"So what?"

"What do you mean, 'so what'?"

I understand. Now I understand. How beautiful. His eyes are fixed on mine with a stubbornness that doesn't suit him at all. How his appearance has changed. He grew up so quickly. His hair, which was thin enough when we served here together, has almost all fallen out. Only at the nape a few wispy curls are left. For the first time he looks older than I. His round spectacles add years to his age, too.

But now he sees me, and I tense under his wondering gaze and fix my eyes resolutely on a point in the bare wall in front of me. Let him look at me as long as he likes. Four more days. His eyes are on my filthy face, covered with heavy stubble, on my black, hairy hands. One blast of dynamite and the mountain will vanish into the sky. Now he's dropped his eyes, but he still steals glances.

"You, you've changed so much, Yani…" he whispers, looking a little downcast.

"We're getting old," I smile joylessly.

"It's not that," he says, "it's just that I didn't remember you so wide… so big…"

"Come off it, Elisha, I've always been this way. Maybe I put on ten kilos in all these years." Yani and a half, they called me.

"No, no… You were much less…how should I put it — you've thickened, you've grown into," he giggles, "a mountain of a man…"

and he glances around the room, to avoid looking at me, and he
doesn't say what he wants to say, what I know for myself, that I've
lost something of my human image on the top of this mountain, in
the seven years that have passed.

His look makes me angry too.

"You know you're not allowed in here."

"Nobody knows I'm here."

"I'm talking about the people on the base. What about Nimra?
Does she know?"

"I told you — Nimra's disappeared."

"What does that mean, 'disappeared'?"

"Disappeared. Packed her things and left for Israel. She said she
would be back in a week. After two weeks I began to worry, she's
not in such great…"

"Where did you look for her?" I interrupt him, not wanting to
hear what I'm afraid of hearing.

"All the hotels in Jerusalem, her father's flat — he didn't even
know she was in the country — and then in Tel Aviv, at Yair and
Anat's. She wasn't anywhere. She's disappeared."

"So you came here? You thought you'd find her here?"

"Hey, take it easy, Yan. I didn't come here because of her. You
know that."

I know. (The mere possibility of her coming here to me, to be
with me now, floods me with longing. And in this way, this round-
about way, I realize how weak I have become.)

"And you — do you intend staying here, in 'Levav'?"

He giggles. "Not forever. Just until they blow it up."

"You'll have to share the room with me. They've dismantled
almost all the other buildings."

"What do you know! I didn't see anything. I came in the dark."

"How?"

"With the guards' truck."

"And they didn't ask any questions?"

"No."

It's total anarchy. "They've taken everything away," I tell him, "the instruments and the antennae, the people, the huts."

"Who's left?" His voice too is very quiet.

"None of us," I reply. "No one from the old days. Me, the cook, the secretary the division commander lent me, and three guys from the engineering corps..."

"When's the explosion?"

"Another..." a hesitation, an elusive flicker I don't understand, "...few days. We don't know exactly. Thursday or Friday..." And I don't know why I lied, and what's being plotted inside me without my understanding it. Only inside my chest I feel my heart suddenly swelling in obscure excitement. A sign was given to me and then it vanished. Tentative joy and obscure dread. Elisha's here. Nimra's in Israel. Nimra's still alive. Me and my prophesies of doom. Look, the three of us are here again. And just like in the old days. How beautiful. How symbolic. Nimra who was my love, Nimra who Elisheva loved for so many silent years, Nimra for whose sake — for whose sake, too — I sentenced myself to this rocky exile. Seven years of exile, beginning in the childish taste of insult, because I had been abandoned here, betrayed by my friends, and later on, with the passing of the days, a new taste crept in, the taste of the desert surrounding me, and the taste of the young lives swarming here, on the cliff top, the hard work I took on myself, the slow, hypnotic sinking into another life, into a painless world, without demands or justifications. Will I ever see Nimra again to tell her this?

"Four, five days..." Elisha rolls the words around his tongue. Looks around dubiously at the walls of the little room.

"You thought you'd come, blow the place up and leave, eh?" I mock him, and he smiles an apologetic, shamefaced smile.

"You can stay here, in the room. I'll give you one of my mattresses."

"Isn't there — isn't there another room?" he asks weakly. Naturally: I'm not the most attractive roommate for such cramped quarters.

"They've taken everything. Anyway, we don't want them to know you're here, do we? It's strictly forbidden to let civilians in here, especially now, before they blow it up. If you show yourself outside," I grin maliciously, "you might get arrested, or shot."

"This is really crazy," he mutters to himself. "Four days ago I was still in Paris. Yesterday — in Beersheba. I wanted to go down to Eilat. She once mentioned having a friend who lived in Dahab. All of a sudden, at the bus station in Beersheba, I saw a newspaper: Explosion at Ras Ajleh this week." He smiles, showing his big rabbit's teeth, touching in their suggestion of weakness. "I said, this I have to see. After all — I spent two years here, and that does something to a person…"

His enthusiasm wanes. Again he looks around uneasily. Withdraws into himself in that movement of the soul that I once loved in him. But now it hurts me. It's me he's withdrawing from.

I see his distress. Four days shut up in this room with me. Why doesn't he get up? Why doesn't he relieve himself by walking briskly from wall to wall, by kicking the tin cupboard?

His bowed posture, the soft lines he draws in the dust — he hasn't learned a thing. Already I'm filled with rage; but no, I mustn't frighten him. I want him here. God, how I want him here. Seven years I've been waiting until one of them came back and was trapped. Now I need cunning. The cunning of the spider.

"You can go out at night," I encourage him. "We'll go for walks together, to the cliff, to position four. Even our hut, number seven, is still here. I wouldn't let them take it. Imagine. They won't take all that. It'll go with the mountain."

He smiles at me. "And the mountain. Sky-high, eh?"

He draws a big mushroom with his hands. Then he stands up, kicks the blankets clinging to his feet — he nearly falls — pours a little water from the kettle into a glass, shakes it with precise, economical movements and throws the contents into the plastic bin in the corner. Then he fills the glass with water again, takes a green pouch out of his case, rummages inside it (I'm still watching the small, quick movements, fascinated). With a quick flick of his hand he pops something into his mouth, swallows it with water in one rapid gulp, tossing his head back.

"Blood pressure," he explains.

Already? And he's so young. Not yet even thirty. Now he takes a tour of the room. He opens the door of the little fridge, smiles at the can of concentrated fruit juice inside it, passes a finger over the dusty table, spends a long time inspecting my webbing equipment hanging over the bed.

From the expression on his face it's evident: he doesn't like the room. Naturally. From Paris to here, to this monkish cell, which hasn't a single picture to charm the eye, not a single book. In despair he collapses onto the pile of blankets and gives me a baffled look.

"Let's work it out. We finished our national service at the beginning of '73, so you've been here six — no, seven years..." The last words come out in a whisper; he looks at me in astonishment, almost fear. Maybe he's begun to understand.

"At least" — he tries to cover up his too obvious astonishment — "at least you got some satisfaction here, right? I heard that in the war it was on the front line, you were under air attack..."

"It was rough. They brought down a few Migs here." But I don't tell him, of course. (For a few weeks the army combed the desert searching for the vanished Mig. During the entire war I wasn't as tense as I was in those days of baffled, confused searching. There was no point in telling them. They would have come and taken him out of there with a crane, and ground the metal down into scrap iron. I imagine that even for the dead man it was more comfortable the way he was. I would have felt comfortable there, if I were in his place.)

"And you're already a — what have you got there on your shoulder, I've already forgotten those games — what is it? Lieutenant colonel?"

"Major." Even when he was a soldier he had never grasped the insignia of all the ranks. Nimra would scoff at him because of it, but it seems to me that this kind of thing endeared him to her. The army always seemed to him an amusement for childish men. He would split his sides laughing when we drilled. I liked the drill, the military language, the strict, ritual nature of military life. In that regard, I preferred Nimra's lack of humor. She would express her revulsion at the army and the uniforms in short, blunt sentences that infuriated me, but that I could at least deal with.

Seven years had passed. Now the only way I can see it all is through his eyes. But of course I don't tell him that.

"And what will you do," he asks, "after... after it goes up in smoke?"

He, too, I discover, finds it hard to say. "They'll put me into some office at headquarters, I suppose."

"Look how we've been flung all over the world," he marvels. "Me and Nimra in France, Hanoch in Cambridge, doing a doctorate on raptors or something like that, Yair a lawyer..."

And he goes on listing the names of the boys and girls, the finest years of my life, all those who have been dispersed like dandelion seeds, and I no longer remember for sure what the glue was that kept us together in those months we spent here. Perhaps it was only the hostile desert lying all around us, and the fear of the unseen enemy, that kept us together with a false patina of friendship; perhaps it was nothing but an illusion that I continue to cherish as if to convince myself.

Suddenly he's optimistic. "Never mind. I'll stay here. We'll talk, we'll cross swords. We've got a lot to catch up on after seven years. You never answered my letters once..."

"And when will you look for Nimra?"

He thought for a minute. "When it's all over here. Maybe she'll calm down by then and come back by herself. It won't be the first time. You don't know anything yet..."

"Yes, yes, and when do you have to go back?"

"In another — ten days at least. I didn't even tell them where I was going. I went to the editor, told him I was taking a vacation. I had a vacation coming to me from way back, from the scoop about the rats. Have I told you about that yet?"

I smile. A new ease spreads through my body. How much peacefulness there is in the sight of Elisha in my room. As if time has stood still. True, we're still a little apprehensive — so it seems — of the moments of silence that fall between us, not like in the past, when the silences were only a pause to cool our blood, seething in the ardor of the talk and the affection, but there are four days ahead of us, four days and four nights, and we've got so many things to say to each other.

I smile again. "No, you haven't told me yet."

"Never mind. It'll wait. In four days you'll know all there is to know about me." And we both laugh in relief.

"Hey, have I shown you this yet?" And he pulls a slim white booklet out of the suitcase, his poems. "In a hundred years this will be worth millions," he giggles and flourishes it extravagantly. "The original manuscript! Listen, listen to this. You deserve a little choice culture."

"My French is lousy," I apologize.

"Mine too. The main thing is the soul. Listen."

At three o'clock in the morning he falls asleep. I make a comfortable bed for him between the table and the cupboard, cover him with two army blankets and go out to the concrete platform. For the first time in years — ever since the war, in fact — I feel a powerful need to smoke. With all my heart I long to know what Nimra called "the right thing." There is too much hanging on too thin a thread, and I am not strong enough to decide.

The wind has calmed down a little, but it is still cold and wet. I can feel the drops condensing as they touch my face. I'm burning. Almost level with my eyes, the great night mists roll slowly past, making everything hazy. Against the background of this decor, anything could happen. Even Elisha's arrival at my nest on the

mountain peak, four days before the end. Even Nimra might mate-
rialize out of one of those soft, foamy clouds and step toward me.
For a moment, in the grip of that old fear, I can see her, brisk and
solid, separating herself in furious complaint from the flimsy cloud
in which I have located her, stepping toward me with her firm gait,
in her eyes that worried, somewhat defiant look; now she's seen me,
now she's heading in my direction, standing opposite me, and slapping me, hard, her hand flat on my forehead, hey, you're dreaming
again.

In those days, after she had left me in that burst of resolute con-
viction, invulnerable to argument, leaving me alone on the mountain, a little lost (there was no hint in our relationship, no logical
reason for anything like this to happen; she simply got up and removed herself from my life), spinning down without understanding
what it was that had hit me so hard; in those days, when I still had a
glimmer of hope that the same outburst that had torn her from me
would bring her back, I would conduct long, stubborn arguments
with her. I would climb to my position on the cliff, hidden from
sight on the sandy ground, and talk to her. To the memory of the
sound of her voice, the gesture of her hand. At first soundlessly, with
only the facial expressions that slipped out of my control, with
clenched fists, in an inner whisper, and later on, the closer I approached the regions of the pain, actual roars would break from my
mouth, and then the words, the pleas. How I hated myself. I would
sit there, a defeated clown, hating her, loving her, looking for signs
in clouds, in columns of ants, torturing myself with her memory,
castigating myself with her harsh criticisms ("You've turned your
weaknesses, your fears and anxieties, into an ideology; you enjoy
feeling like a freak of nature, but in fact you're banal. A god full of
self-pity." And more: "I'm not prepared to understand that you love
only me and loathe the rest of the world. That story would have
flattered me when I was sixteen. Today it makes me sick.") and
answering her with the so logical, well-formulated arguments that

I was already sick of, that didn't even convince me, that I could only impress Elisha with — and afterward even that was taken from me.

On the platform, in the cold wind, in the darkly rolling night mists, I am suddenly seized with longing for that pain. The taste of the jealousy and insult is already long faded. Even the love has subsided. Only the stern concern, the responsibility for her fate that I've imposed on myself remains. Now, for a stinging second, it hurts me faintly ("your processed feelings").

And now: Elisha.

How am I going to hide him here in the coming days? What good will come of having the scatterbrained Elisha here to upset the routine of my last days on the mountain, when I have to work on such a strict schedule?

Nonsense. I have no schedule at all. Others determine the sequence of events, and others carry them out. I have been left here because I demanded it. Any low-ranking officer could have supervised the final arrangements. All I am now is a walking nuisance. I can see the eyes of the engineers. The quiet, slightly mocking look of the Norwegian. If Elisha stayed, perhaps he would relieve the boredom.

And not only that: I can trust him. He felt the place as I did. Still from then, from the days when we were young soldiers here, when we combed all the low sand hills, when we escaped from the camp and hiked to Refidim to visit Nimra who was incarcerated there, even before we grew heavy and cynical, when I met him sleeping in the cave of the doves, his hand under his head, his gaping mouth revealing his big teeth, and afterwards — when together we studied the birds and the herbs of the surrounding mountainsides. The roads we forged through the tangled growth of the wadi, the talks through the night, the chess games, Nimra, Nimra...

He can stay, I decide. No one will know. I'll make his stay pleasant. I won't get on his nerves. He can write his poems to his heart's content. If he wants to, we'll talk. If he doesn't, we can be silent. That too is possible.

Full of energy and enthusiasm I return to the warm room. There, on the floor, curled up in his blankets, he's asleep. His feet are sticking out. In the days of our youth we would wrap wet towels around his long feet as he slept, dip his toes in water. Smiling I lumber to my bed. A hair's breadth separates me from the deed. But I know Elisha wouldn't understand. Too many things have happened to him. He has lived his life. Maybe at the end of these days he will understand.

For a long time I toss and turn on my bed. My back needs two mattresses at least. Otherwise it hurts. Anyway, I haven't been sleeping lately. Sometimes it seems to me that it's been months since I closed my eyes. That it's only thanks to that fire that I keep on running.

In the end I give up. I switch on the reading lamp and look at him. For some reason, I feel full of pity for him. He's so gawky, so helpless in his sleep, without his glasses, his moon face gleaming in the dark, his smooth, too-long legs. What did she see in him?

A spasm crosses his face, twitches a muscle in his cheek. I switch off the light. I feel a great responsibility for the man lying there, completely at my mercy. Now as then.

3

Monday. Morning.

I love my camp in the mornings. This morning, too — windswept, the sky blue and clear. Only in the afternoon will its color dull and all at once gloom will descend on this fenced-in square of land. For the moment, the brown mountains still stand out sharp and clear against the sky, and dozens of black crows flock in ritual formation from the four corners of heaven to the *high blue eye*: the rush of black wings cleaving the air, for a single moment — eye meets eye, a hoarse, mocking cry, and once more they are dispersed to edges of the sky, where the blue is still white and gray.

Elisha is sleeping, huddled up on the mattress; I close the door gently, bound over the three wooden steps, and hurry to the rock.

The rock is only a massive lump, the biggest I have ever seen, of brown-red limestone crouching behind my hut, far taller than I am, netted with deep fissures, huge humps, stubborn bushes that have taken hold on it, rising far beyond the barbed-wire fence surrounding the base, half within the area of the camp and half without, facing the desert.

I climb a step in the rock, cling to protuberances with my hands, maneuver acrobatically between the familiar cracks. The ascent has to be accomplished in a certain way, and this is the way.

And then, muscles trembling with the effort and the morning chill, happy to be here again, as I was yesterday and the day before and all the other days, I pause for a moment and perform the morning ritual.

First the powerful, quivering stretch, touching the sky above and the earth below, the roar of a yawn flung in the direction of the desert — ah, what a mighty lion cub is waking to his day — and then: the avid gulp of fresh air that hurts the lungs, the brisk, ruthless rubbing of the scalp, the genial pee, the steaming arc spraying from the heights of the rock to the gaping depths of the wadi. I'm still here.

On my way down from the rock, depression is already stealing back. Maybe because the moments of drowsiness and faintness have passed, maybe because the descent is slow and hesitant, lacking the excitement that I find in climbing the rock. One day I'll probably find myself on top of a high tree, without understanding how I got there, too frightened to come down.

In the mess hall Peretz is waiting for me, beaming with happiness. He has made semolina porridge this morning, to alleviate the cold. Now, with only the two of us in the big hut, he allows himself to show his love for me openly. Ready to serve, dancing attendance, simpering, removing an imaginary stain from my filthy parka, setting before me with a flourish the steaming bowl containing the whitish paste. Sitting opposite me, his hands covering his mouth, his eyes shining with excitement. Waiting for my verdict.

But I'm in no hurry, for suddenly I realize that the face of my cook, who has been with me for four years now, looks very strange. Something has happened to his face, and I look at it closely. I don't understand, and an old revulsion stirs inside me.

Nimra always complained that I took no notice of the people around me. That I was too absorbed in myself. "You see other people as shifting scenery, and nothing else," she said. I didn't like it when she said that, but she was right. It sometimes happened that only after many years I discovered the face of the person who had been living right next to me. I'm not at all unperceptive, and I'd like to believe that I possess a certain degree of sensitivity; still, only at some specific moment would all the features of a face, all the tiny lines, the pale spots where the hair sprouted from the scalp, the slope of the eye, the curve of the nose, all those dozens of details — only at a specific moment would they suddenly crystallize, surging into one vivid, living entity before my eyes.

This happened very rarely, and always in relation to people who meant nothing to me. I can never understand why they were singled out. I never knew in what circumstances it would happen. And I couldn't predict it in advance. I hated those moments. I would be shaken by their advent, when, as in the moment when a photograph is developed, a sharp image would suddenly emerge from the routine dullness, cracking open in front of me, powerfully revealing itself and leaving me astonished, alien to myself.

"Is anything wrong, sir?"

He leaned toward me. His face was too close. Now I saw.

"No, cook. Everything's all right. I was mistaken. A false alarm."

And indeed, it was just a mistake. I'm so shaky. It's nothing but an external change in him after all. My senses are deceiving me. "What have you done to your eyebrows, cook?"

Shyly his fingers feel the exposed bones of his eye sockets, jutting out grotesquely.

"They...they shaved them off."

"Who?"

"It doesn't matter, sir. It was only for fun, really."

"Cook."

He squirms in his chair. Sniggers. Mumbles. From his story I understand how hard his life is here. Living in the same room with the engineers and the two foreigners. No, they don't torment him, God forbid, just have their bit of fun — in a joke, like, throw him between them like a ball, slap him around in a friendly way, make him dance for them, tie him to the bed with belts when he's sleeping, all in good humor, sir. Yesterday, while he was asleep, they shaved off his eyebrows.

"Did it hurt?"

"A bit. They're already growing back."

I should have gone around to their room occasionally. I'm the base commander, after all. I'll go around there today. Peretz fixes his eyes on me. He thinks my silence stems from my concern for him.

"There are lumps in the porridge, cook."

His face falls. "I'll get you another plate, sir, from the bottom of the pot." And he hurries to the kitchen.

Peretz spends all day in the kitchen. In the empty mess hall. From morning to midnight he fusses with the pots. And there are so few mouths to feed. Why doesn't he ever go outside in the sun?

He shrugs his shoulders. My interest makes him uncomfortable. He likes it in the kitchen, sir, and what's there to do outside, who's there to talk to?

I look at him, at his fingers gripping each other, his moist eyes staring at me. I see his concern for me, his eagerness to be close to me, and I know he's as full of dread as I am. Only he has a support and a consolation: me. That's why he looks after me so devotedly, feeds me, pads my body with his cooking. He has expectations of me, and already I know how much he'll hate me when I fail. Poor Peretz. How long are you going to go on kidding yourself? There's no hope for the mountain.

And I push away the second plate of porridge he brought me, ignore his stung look, and head for the door. When I reach it I remember Elisha sleeping in my room and order him to make three sandwiches for me.

"With white cheese and tomato? Maybe yellow cheese?" The spark has returned to his eyes.

"No. Just jam."

Peretz stares at me in astonishment. The only one who touches that mess is the American. But a moment later the three sandwiches are in my hands. For the first time Peretz gives me a sullen look. His professional pride is hurt, and I am glad of this rebelliousness.

On my way out I bump into them, all of them. First the three engineers, surrounding me and barring my way for an embarrassing moment. Paldi and the old one with the peaked cap pulled down to his eyes don't even look at me. The youngster is the only one who smiles. When I extricate myself from the tangle of their bodies I meet the Norwegian, who nods at me affectionately, with a mischievous narrowing of his eyes. I like watching him move. There's a broadness in his shoulders and his back; he moves like a big, calm fish. And when I encounter the American, who always walks with his head bowed, grinning to himself, I thrust one of the sandwiches into his hand, God knows why, and hurry off.

Two sandwiches will be enough for Elisha.

Not even the two sandwiches succeed in spoiling his good mood. His face is pressed against the windowpane, where he has cleared a field of vision for himself in the dust. He devours the view of the bare, distant mountains, the calm expanses of desert. His fingers crumble the bread absentmindedly.

"Like a prisoner," he laughs, happy, gesturing toward his meal, the high mountains.

I smile politely.

"What's this? Isn't there anything to eat on your base, Yani?"

"And what did you expect? In five days' time we're getting out of here. We've been eating bread and jam for a week…"

His face falls a little. A moment later he's exuberant again. "I didn't sleep all night" he tells me. "Well, not exactly all night but… Anyway, all the time I was thinking of the old days, you know. We've already lived together before, for nearly two years… Actually, when you come to think of it — ever since then I've never been in such close, intensive contact with anybody…"

… And how we once painted the room bright red, just to annoy Nimra, and the soup we cooked on winter nights (once there was such a cold winter and we didn't have a stove, we had to heat the room with the toaster), and the runs around the base — you wanted to toughen me up, remember? — and the talks at night in the room, in the position on the cliff: mutual character building, we called it. Oh, Yani, what a child you were, how can we have been such children? And the books we devoured, hundreds of books. I've never read so many books in my life (Ayn Rand and Hermann Hesse, it horrifies me today to remember how we admired them — and you discovered *Zarathustra*, too). And your electric shaver that I ruined, and I never even had a beard. I just wanted to try it, and I ruined your old Remington. Ah, the cookies my mother sent once a month, like clockwork (I've been on bad terms with the old folks for a year now, ever since I followed Nimra to France), and that crazy running off to Refidim, to the women's prison…

I let him wander down memory lane. Roam through the garden of my life with impunity, even though I don't like hearing about these things. The darkness of memory is the right place for them. Exposure to the air spoils them.

Suddenly I get excited. "Why don't you write something, a poem, or…"

"A poem? What about?"

"About…well, everything. The base."

"A requiem?" He laughs but refuses. He can't write like that, to order. It has to come from within; it has to burn like a fire in his bones.

"But one day maybe I'll write it. Maybe the explosion'll do it," he laughs.

His Adam's apple jumps rapidly up and down. He's finished the sandwiches. "I'll die of hunger by lunchtime," he grumbles, wipes the crumbs from his mouth with his hand, looks at me for a minute, and crams them in his mouth.

"Don't expect too much from lunch," I answer him resentfully.

"When do the newspapers come?"

"There aren't any newspapers here."

Where did it come from, my enjoyment in frustrating his little hopes? Where did the hostility come from, trembling inside me? And he isn't being too friendly to me, either. This isn't the way I wanted it.

Elisha takes his poems out of the suitcase. "At least there's something to read here," he mutters. Yesterday, for a few embarrassing minutes, he read his poetry to me. I don't understand French well. In the end he gave up and put the booklet away. Now he's taken it out again. He sits on my bed and reads with concentration. Let him.

I get up without saying anything to him and go out.

Outside now, to the breathing space between barbed wire and barbed wire. In the past, two years ago, you could still slip through the fence and go down to the green wadi, to the birds' nests and their mating flights, to the sharp-nosed fennecs' holes, to the jackals' lairs. Then they laid mines around the fences, and as for getting out — go flap your wings.

What remained was the path to the generator shed, which now consists of nothing but four iron poles sticking up to the sky, the ground between them black with oil and petrol, whose smell still lingered on a month after the barrels had been removed — and from there, go down, slither down the steep slope to the gaping north gate, to the tangled barbed wire swaying in the wind, to the giant wooden wheel around which the telephone wires were once coiled, to the subterranean halls where once upon a time the intelligence work was done and now a great beam of wood bars the door. Not even I am allowed to go in to the linoleum-covered corridors and the flights of stairs and the halls themselves, for the dynamite is already there, ready and waiting. I kick the heavy door with a mule kick, and a dull pain in my heel accompanies the sharp, hollow sound, thudding against the corridors in the bowels of the earth.

Run. Go on. Farther, to the high sand hills where stubborn desert bushes cling, to the now empty vehicle bunkers facing the desert, painted in soft camouflage colors, but — what's this? Two of the engineers, the boy and the old man, are busy there, without their jackets, strenuously carrying a long, green, obviously heavy sack, which they put down with gentle care next to the bunker wall.

From my distant vantage point, hidden behind a tall rock, I look at them, at their brows knit with strained concentration, at the deliberate movements of their hands. The old guy — he must be fifty — with his eternal peaked cap, short and vigorous, running between the bunker walls, surveying his handiwork, hurrying over to the sack, fixing its position, and once again, like a busy sparrow, stepping back, tilting his head — I too, from my hiding place, wait in suspense for his verdict — now he clicks his fingers approvingly and clucks his tongue at his yellow-haired companion as a signal to bring another sack from the pickup standing behind the bunker.

When they disappear I emerge from hiding and slip quickly into a bunker. The heavy sack, lying there fresh and green, focusing all the rays of the desert sun, draws me to it. I bend over it, touch it with my finger, am surprised at how flimsy it feels.

They're back too soon. Panting and sweating, with another sack in their hands. Now they've seen me. Now they're looking at each other hesitantly, lowering the sack to their feet, straightening their pained backs, smiling at me with a sigh.

With a single movement — as if one string is pulling them both — they brush their hands over their pockets, take out their cigarettes, shelter the white sticks with their palms against the malevolent wind — and the bluish smoke spirals upward.

"That's it," says the old man, pushing the cap out of his eyes with his finger and wiping the sweat off his forehead with his sleeve. I wonder: fire next to the dynamite?

"Hard work?" I make my voice smile, cold in the pit of my stomach.

"Not too bad. Tomorrow or the next day we'll finish the lot."

"What is it? TNT?"

Now their eyes light up gleefully. "TNT flakes. Every sack like this weighs fifty kilos."

Paldi appears from behind the bunker wall, sullen and impatient. His soft tread, the stealthy way he slinks into the bunker, make me feel uneasy. "What's up with you two, how much time...? Oh."

He falls silent, leans against one of the walls, far away from where we're standing. I can't help respecting him. I can't help hating him. It seems to me that he can see right through me. If he said one word, if he came to my room one night and said, "Talk, I'm listening," I would put myself in his hands. Because he's close to me, closer than any of the others on the mountain. There's a fire consuming him too, and it doesn't matter where it comes from, but he's still got the strength in his hands to restrain his hatred, it still hasn't risen up inside him uncontrollably. If he came, I could tell him a thing or two myself.

But he's too proud.

And they explain to him. This and that, in two days' time they'll connect the detonators to the explosives, connect the detonating cord, the central cord, to the two detonators, which will activate the detonating cord, which will set off the...

Their voices fill with excitement. Their words run into each other; they tear the air with their hands, full of warmth and friendly apology, gentle and polite, but my eyes are fixed on his. What do I want? Someone to talk to, that's all. But I know he won't step out of his circle. In the midst of their excitement, I turn away and walk off. In any case, the morning is spoiled. For a moment longer I stand in the center of the camp, at the place where all the roads meet, and then I rush off, never mind where, wherever my feet carry me, and the thudding of my army boots on the asphalt paths gives me back the courage I lost for a moment.

In my caravan office I find Rinat, my secretary. A nice girl, lent me by the division commander, always full of cheerful optimism, vigorously shaking the dusty, unimportant files, paper leftovers of thirteen years of my life in the camp. From the Six-Day War to now: December 1979.

"Hi, Yan," she smiles, dimpling her cheeks.

"Hi, Rinat. What's happening?"

"Dovik got in touch. To tell me that when we're finished here, I'm being transferred to Haifa. Close to home. Isn't that great?"

"If you say so."

No one leaves any messages for me in my office. Only my secretary gets messages. It's hot in the caravan, thick with dust. I don't like being here. I never did. I flounder between the furniture piled with papers, climb onto a chair and page through a thick volume of military law. Before my eyes is a big, bloated spider, all the threads of a dense web joining in his body — he doesn't even tremble when I blow at him belligerently. I touch him — he's dead. Down below, Rinat babbles gaily. Now that's she going to be in Haifa, she's going to sign up for some courses. Art — that's her ambition. Has she ever shown me her charcoal sketches?

It's hot in the caravan, and humid. My back hurts from standing hunched on the chair. In this heat, I work up a lust for the little girl at my feet, for her alert young body. And while she's standing with her back to me, piling up papers, I jump off the chair, like a big, wicked cat, grab hold of her shoulders, turn her slender body to face me — I regret it already — and cup her childish chin in my hand.

Rinat's face goes blank with fear. "Hey, Yani, stop it," and her voice is weak, choked. But I kiss-bite the thin lips without desire, scratching the delicate skin with the stubble of my beard, and only when all of a sudden — through the dull emptiness between us — I feel the alert little tongue responding to me, the slackening lips, the deepening breath, I wake up, and angrily, as if deceived, I fling the small body away, and it thuds against the tin cupboard.

And now: the dishevelled, panting shirt, the collar climbing to the chin, the low whimpers, the flood of tears. Put out your hand. Outline the trembling lips with your finger. You can't leave it like this. But I don't move.

And she weeps. A long wailing sound comes out of her little mouth. Torrents pour from her nose and mouth. Her whole body shakes. And then, the rage rising against me. The sobs distort the words. They told her about me, what I was like, like a wild animal, that I've forgotten how to behave like a human being, and the meaning of civilization, and consideration, and altogether — I should have shut myself up in one of the caves around here and stayed there after the explosion too, alone with the crows and the jackals, which were obviously the most suitable companions for me...

And I don't say a word. There's still today and tonight. There's still tomorrow. I get up and walk out.

The position on the cliff.

The desert — purple in the pale sunlight, full of shadows, humping, gaping, streaming continuously toward the horizon, toward the two blue gleams: the bitter lakes.

I collapse on the damp sandbags. I wallow in the tiny grains, I smell their smell, stretch my legs far behind me, dirty my face with the earth. If only I knew the secret — I would sob. If only I could go down to the wadi again, forge my way there, to the leaning dead man. Six years have passed since then. Perhaps all my stubborn hanging on here was a mistake. People live with each other. Mark Daniel was murdered, but people live with each other. Elisha's still alive. Elisha will live forever. Nimra won't be able to stand it. She should have come here. Asked me to give her a hand. She'll never do it. I'll never talk to Paldi. What's the point of going down to the dead man in the wadi? The living don't help the living, why should they help the dead?

Six months I was alone here, on the mountain, without a friend or a kindred soul, until both of them arrived, almost at the same time: Nimra and Elisha.

First — Elisha.

He came with a big group of recruits. Tall and skinny. White-skinned and thin-haired. I was put in charge of the group. (I took on the task of my own free will, just as I took on other tasks.) A bunch of whining sissies, and Elisha among them. But I found him one evening in the tangled growth of the wadi bed, excitedly watching the mating flight of a male falcon, and afterwards, in the cave of the doves — which was secret and hidden from all eyes but mine — I found him sleeping, his hands under his head, and his mouth slightly open in that innocent, trusting expression.

Elisha didn't notice me on either occasion. I never told him. (Strange: we told each other so many things, and I never knew how to tell him why I chose him out of all that noisy crowd.) In those days I got him out of a court martial — the base commander was a softhearted man and under my influence — I drew him into quick-witted exchanges of repartee on our chance meetings on the base, I co-opted him onto my detail on the nights of the ambushes. I lay in wait for him. I wanted a friend. Someone to talk to.

When he arrived on "Levav" I was already a "mountain veteran." Soldiers came and went; they begged to leave the rocky cliff, loathed the mountain and everything on it, counted the passing days on tables and charts.

And I — I gave all I had here. When my turn came I didn't apply for transfer to a more convenient urban base. I remember long months when I didn't take the leave due me. (I broke off relations with my father shortly after I arrived here: suddenly I realized that the gulf was unbridgeable. I wonder how much the desert had to do with it.) I knew all the secrets of the mountain, the steep crevices, the crows' nests in the bushes, the vipers' paths, and the marks etched by the wind in the rocks.

I was nine years younger then. Full of astounding ideas about my life, and especially my death, crude and blunt and very romantic. Alone on the basketball field, I would hurl the ball against the wooden backboard, one hundred, two hundred, five hundred, a thousand times, from midnight to daybreak, three, four, five hours, until I fell dazed and sweating on my bed, and still I felt no release. I went out every day for private target practice with my revolver. I shot dozens of lead bullets into cardboard men, riddled them with neat round holes from their heads to their hips; I squeezed the trigger with my right hand and my left, I shot from the hip, from eye level, from behind my head, and I felt no relief. Every evening I ran five kilometers around the base, easily beating anyone who tried to join in. I deliberately provoked all the tough guys on the base — and still I didn't calm down.

I didn't like the soldiers of my own age that I had to live with. I hated their laxity. I imposed penances on myself: no smoking for six months (that's how I stopped smoking), abstention from meat for months on end, sleeping without blankets, weeks-long silences, hopeless, unfair bets I took against myself, as a result of which I spent many nights on guard duty, and worse: in one of the caves in the wadi.

But I was crazy for company. Whenever I saw a spark of understanding in the eyes — usually hostile — facing me, I was overjoyed, ready to melt silently away, always waking up, too late, to the shattering of the illusion.

And only Elisha — perhaps because he was so delicate, and afraid of hurting me, bowed himself and moved in the storm I blew up, and gradually straightened himself again; but by then we were already together, amazingly strong in our own eyes. And only Nimra, who was as sturdy as the cliff itself, only she, with that calm dryness of hers, knew how to guide the torrent seething inside me with a practiced hand into dams, and into narrower and narrower canals — until I found relief, until my days began to go forward in a way that I can cope with, under her wise eyes.

And now that I'm thinking about Nimra, I can no longer restrain myself. Though I know it's still too soon, that I'm frivolously wasting the strength saved up in my pocket, I hurry to rummage in my parka and pull out the plastic bag, still damp from yesterday's rain. Now, in the pale light of the sick sun, I raise to my eyes the big, blue sheet of office paper with the words "Amnesty International, France" printed in French and English in the top left-hand corner, and immediately, eagerly, I plunge into the crooked, untidy lines, Nimra's sinewy handwriting. My other world, here on the mountain top.

How bitter this letter is. How much pain there is in the simple words. It seems that the activities she was enthused into undertaking by her pair of Arab friends in London were not a success. No, she doesn't want to bore me with the details, the wounds have not yet healed: "At moments like these, Yani — only at moments like these — I can understand your staying there, on top of the mountain, far away from everything, and see another side to it, more persuasive than the 'hedgehog ideology,' but no, I take that back, because..."

Because a new loophole of hope has opened up, a fresh channel of feverish activity, in which she can immerse herself to the point of oblivion, which will swallow up the craving inside her.

"And so — and I haven't taken it in yet — I'm in the race again. I feel better now (at least, enough to write to you), and the days are a little brighter, for there's hope, Yani, and there's a chance, and the world's still worthwhile."

Hector is his name, and he too is a fighter. Hector comes from Argentina: the Argentina of 1977, groaning under the military regime.

Hector is only a boy, twenty-four years old, and already the leader of a cell of "brothers" in the "Montaneros," the Marxist guerrilla army fighting the violent regime with mosquito bites. Hector is small, she writes, black-haired and bespectacled, and he has grown a scanty beard over the past year. "He's all energetic quicksilver," a fiery speaker, a witty journalist, a stubborn fighter for freedom, handy with both words and bombs, ah, how many words Nimra lavished on him, and she hadn't ever seen him face-to-face. Only his photograph standing on the desk of her office in the amnesty office in Paris, only the thick, closely written document in her hand, telling her his life history, the history of his double life — underground and public — the gist of his articles and broadsheets, which his followers paste up at night on the walls of the houses, the details of his wounding on the night of the abortive attack on the government prison where dozens of his comrades were incarcerated, the secret of his miraculous escape from his pursuers.

Hector Gabriel Nestor is in great danger: all the sensitive feelers spread by the junta are closing in on him, and he is oblivious to the danger. Anonymous people, incredibly courageous, emissaries of Amnesty in Paris, succeeded in reaching him, spoke to him at length, tried to persuade him to leave the country that was digging his grave — but to no avail. He lives in a circle of fervor and faith, which he doesn't want — is unable, they think — to break out of. What kind of a life would he have in the soft countries they want to take him to? So he said to them as he escorted them to the door, and what would he tell his children in years to come, and what would he say to his conscience.

And Nimra, watching from a distance the hunt whose outcome is so clear, is infected with the paralyzing anxiety, hovering like a cloud over the head of the Argentine boy, and at the same time, in embarrassing contradiction to her will and logic, finds herself fascinated by him, by his courage, his defiant indifference, his pride. These are things worth living for, Yan, and you can call it dime-novel romanticism if you like.

No, I too am infected by her emotion. How moved I was when this letter reached me in April 1977. I saw emptiness in everything then: in my passivity sitting here, in my insignificant activities, my inability to break out of the circle I had drawn around myself.

Hector, hundreds of kilometers away from me, as foreign to me as two people can be foreign to each other, hypnotizing the tense attention of so many people, touching life and death, swept me away too, shot spurts of hope and strength into my life, returned me to the yearning I had found in the eternally soaring figure of the dead man at the bottom of the wadi.

Despite the very real dangers, Nimra ends her letter with characteristic hope: her emissaries have met Hector's father too (his name is Mark Daniel Nestor, "a wise, wonderful man, who looks exactly like Gepetto") — a lecturer in Russian literature at the University of Buenos Aires. Like his son, he is a stubborn fighter for human freedom, but since he is an immigrant who came from far away, since he is twenty-five years older than Hector, since he is a father, he was prepared to pay attention to the fears of the emissaries, and his face darkened — so they reported to her — when he saw the conclusive proofs they showed him, and he said — "not very firmly, to be sure" — that he would speak to his son, his Hector, even though, and he had to say this to them, in these matters he had little influence over his son, as they would surely understand for themselves.

But for Nimra this faint promise is enough. The hoped-for happiness has already installed itself in her life. I even detect a hint of transparent, childish cunning in her letter. She's already rented a small flat for Hector Gabriel in a quiet quarter of Paris where the emissaries will smuggle him. She's already registered him — without his knowledge — for an M.A. in philosophy at the Sorbonne (he is a philosophy student in his country); she's already found a job for him in the Argentine information and cultural center in France, a place already populated with a number of men and women who have escaped from Argentina. She has accomplished all this with ease and speed, schemed, planned, pulled strings, and all she can do now is wait: Will the emissaries succeed in persuading the ardent young man at their next meeting (there's no doubt he'll be persuaded, one glance at the documents they managed to get hold of recently will be enough)? Will they succeed in getting him out through the traditional escape route? Will he want to live in France, without tension or responsibility? And one more question that is left unasked, but that I can read between the lines: Will he fall in love with the good-looking young woman (taller than he is, apparently) whose expression is so mature and serious? Will he appreciate the stubborn, long-distance battle she has waged on his behalf?

And again, the blue page, with the words piling closely on top of each other toward the end, trembles in my hand, alive and pulsing and throbbing with desire, and I loosen my grip on it, and it's snatched away, whirled wildly upward, by the quick, clever wind, which carries it off, with everything in it, to the desert.

4

Monday. Afternoon.

I think a lot about growing up.

The thought of growing up, that mysterious process that one becomes aware of only after it has taken place, has been buzzing at the back of my mind for many years now.

I was four years old. I remember it was evening. My parents' house. There were a lot of guests. They clinked glasses, talked to each other standing up. My mother was still alive. It was the last year of her life, and she didn't know it. I don't remember much of that evening.

I see myself, moving clumsily over the flowered carpet, struggling between the knees and thighs looming high above me, listening to the roar of unintelligible words rolling over me, repeatedly shaken by the sound of the volleys of hoarse, nasty laughter (it's me they're laughing at), bombarded with slippery-shimmery sensations, none of which I can take hold of, half choking from lack of air, giddily trapped in the labyrinth drawn on the carpet, lost between the thicket of legs, shoes, the body smells and perfumes, when suddenly I was clutched by the bitter, surprisingly adult knowledge: one day I would die.

I don't know what it was that flashed this certainty into my mind. Perhaps it was a word pronounced in the thicket of heads-eye-glasses-beards-makeup-bald-pates above me; perhaps it was only a momentary illumination, due to the fear of choking that suddenly seized me between the tree-trunk legs.

One day I would die. Like Grandpa, who died last year. I would not be alive any more. Of course — first I would have to grow up (although children died, too: rumors of this had reached my ears), become as tall as these people whose faces I couldn't see, know how to talk like them, to say the words they say, put on a beard and a bald head and eyeglasses, and after that, without anyone asking me if I wanted to or not, I would die.

I was still standing there, eternally maimed, without a chance of recovery, when another, no less terrible thought struck me: everyone would die. My father and mother (I didn't know how close I was to the truth in her case), my granny, my friends, the kindergarten teacher, the scary old woman who smelled of rotten potatoes and lay in wait for me every day in the park, my cousin, Aya... I went on, paralyzed with dread and remorse, reviewing the list of my dead, feeling that every time I remembered a particular person I was immediately pronouncing his death sentence (if I didn't remember him he would manage to escape somehow), and at the same time unable to stop, and I came to the definite conclusion that everyone — except, perhaps, for a child in my kindergarten who had shown me a secret magic green bottle someone had given him, which I assumed would be able to save him — was soon going to disappear.

I was so alarmed that I burst into tears. My mother comforted me. She made me promises.

My thoughts about my maturity change from day to day. They always grow up before me. I'll never catch up with them. When I was sixteen I went to bed with a woman for the first time. I was sure: this was it. When I was nineteen and a half I broke off relations with my father, gave myself a new name. I knew — this was maturity, and now: go out and live.

I was nineteen when I arrived here. I tasted military life that leaves no room for doubts. They put their faith in me, they entrusted men's lives to me. I came to know the mountain and I immersed myself in it. I knew with absolute clarity — this was the way.

And then I discovered that it wasn't the way. There was Elisha, who was weak and cynical, and not in the least "military," and Nimra who detested both cynicism and military obtuseness, and who threw herself with brave seriousness into anything that captured her heart. I studied both of them and I thought, "that's what I want to be like. A little cynical, a little enthusiastic. Sometimes a man of compromise, and sometimes positive and cruel. Loving and scornful at once. A cedar and a reed."

And they went away. Both of them. They left the mountain. They left me all by myself. They mocked my dreams (I wanted them both to volunteer for the regular army, like me, and go on serving on the mountain); they shattered the foundations I had built for myself.

I think a lot about growing up. I'm a man of thirty who weighs two hundred pounds and who everyone's afraid of, while he himself is afraid of doing things that everyone else does without a second thought. I'm afraid of the life waiting for me down below, after I come down from here; I'm afraid of going back to my empty flat in Ramat Gan. The explosion about to take place paralyzes me with dread. Elisha, who's sleeping in my room now, his hidden thoughts, the need to talk — they frighten me.

For some reason I feel profoundly cheated. Someone took advantage of a single moment, when I was asleep, to utterly change the world around me. No wonder I don't know what to do after I come down from here; I don't understand the life down there, I can't come to terms with the kind of world where people murder Mark Daniel and make his son disappear forever. I'm still despairingly trudging around the brightly colored labyrinth on the carpet.

And now I have to get up from where I'm sitting at the bottom of the position, and go back to him, to Elisha, who by now must be starving and wondering where I am.

I don't go yet.

In three days' time, on Thursday morning, they're going to blow up the mountain, and I have to do something. If only I knew what. Man, I say to myself, they're hurting you, blowing your home sky-high. Protest, chain yourself to the rocks, don't let them. Oh, you romantic child, Nimra smiles, you're still spellbound by your childish dreams. There are so many baobab trees to uproot. Stop making a fool of yourself, kicking your legs like an insulted, cheated child. You've lost nine years of your life, wasted them here, can't you see, this is the moment to do the right thing, Yani, come down from the mountain...

In my room, Elisha's lying on my bed. His hands are under his head and his eyes are staring at the ceiling. When I come in, he jumps up, eyes glittering with rage. He's sick of it. Sick of lying here all day shut up between four walls, without a book, without a newspaper, without anyone to talk to, never mind the hunger! Why haven't I brought him anything to eat since lunchtime? What's the matter with you, Yan? Look at yourself in the mirror, you're filthy as an animal. Ever since I came here you haven't looked me in the eyes once, as if you're hiding some lie from me; all you do is rush restlessly around the room, growling to yourself, oozing hostile drops of sweat, and in addition to everything else you don't talk to me, you don't do anything to make things easier for me here, you're like a stranger, worse — an enemy. Go, go already, go back

to your important business — or better still, go get me something
to eat for supper. Go!

"Nimra phoned," I lie calmly, floating in that pleasant fog again.
If only she *had* phoned.

He stands rooted to the spot, his words frozen in his throat. The
skin on his forehead stretches, as if some invisible hand is pulling it
back. His eyes bulge out of their sockets, and his eyelashes flutter at
the lenses of his glasses.

"She phoned? Nimra? Where to?"

"My office. Via the army exchanges."

"Did she say where she was?"

"No. She just asked permission to come here before the explosion."

"What for? Why, Yani?"

Ah, his fallen face, his twining fingers.

"Did she say anything about me?"

"No. Just that there were a few problems in France. That she
feels better now."

"That's what she said?"

Oh, my cynical game. His pain. The happiness bubbling in me.

"When will she come?"

"Tomorrow, the next day. She couldn't say exactly."

"Did you tell her I was here?"

"No. We'll give her a surprise."

Elisha leaps out of bed. One minute to his suitcase, the next to
the door. Like a trapped rabbit. I gloat.

"Stay here. Where are you running to? You wanted to find her,
didn't you?"

"No! Not like this!" He shouts hoarsely, and I hush him. Remember: nobody's supposed to know there's a stranger in the room.

"Calm down, kid," I tease him, "think logically for a minute.
This is a heaven-sent opportunity. We'll sit here together, the three
of us, we'll talk, we'll try to understand. We've swept so many
things under the carpet…"

He drops onto the mattress, limp as a rag. His glasses fall to the floor. He crawls on all fours and searches for them: now he's found them. But what's this? One of the lenses has come out. The frame has loosened, come undone. For a moment he sniffs around close to the green linoleum, his hands trembling, sieving the dust, the shed hairs, a filthy Band-Aid, bits of paper. Here, he's found something, his fingers close tightly around it, he holds it out to me triumphantly, imploringly: a tiny screw, like a pin's head. He wants me to screw it into the loose frame. He himself can't do it now, in his blindness.

I struggle with a miniature screwdriver, trying to tighten the tiny screw back into place; like a speck of dust, it drops from my fingers without making a sound, and disappears.

"You…you…on purpose…" His stammering words, his flushed face, his hatred for me is beginning to erupt. It's an improvement on our silences.

And again he's on the floor, at my feet, peering with his purblind eyes, gasping in the dust, sneezing, despairing, collapsing on the mattress, holding his head in his hands. Now I see the booklet of poems lying at his side. Between the typed lines I notice a lot of new corrections, words added in ink, a whole verse crossed out. I wonder what's going on.

Elisha raises his eyes to me. Shakes his head in disbelief. "Don't you understand?" he asks quietly, patiently, as if speaking to a small child. "I'm lost without my glasses."

I hold out the dismantled pieces in my hand. The blind, lensless frame, the stem, the dirty lens. But no expression of sorrow crosses my face, even though I try. My facial muscles refuse to respond. They've frozen in their hard bristliness.

"I'll go and get some supper."

Elisha doesn't answer. He just stretches his long body out on the mattress and wraps himself in the blanket. As he does this, a light cloud of dust rises in the room, caught in the last sunbeam of the day.

★

I hurry out of the dim room. Ostensibly in remorse, but actually full of glee, which propels me in childish hops and skips to the mess hall, to the sweating, glittering-eyed Peretz, who proudly serves me a veal cutlet with mushrooms. Jorn, the Norwegian, and Jordash, the American, had received their monthly rations early, in honor of the approaching Christmas holiday. Now there would be plenty of food for everyone during the days that remained. The fridge is crammed full again with frozen meat and pâtés from abroad.

How happy Peretz is. How tall he stands.

For four years now Peretz has been with me on the "Levav" base. He had even sent his parents to visit me when I was in Tel-Hashomer Hospital with an ulcer. (They came from one of the cooperative agricultural villages in the Sharon. Small, wrinkled, very dark skinned, tiptoeing in their shabby coats, they showered me with food and an outpouring of embarrassing concern. I didn't know how to get rid of them.) Peretz, whom I had rescued twice from jail, who came into my room one night, whimpering like a puppy, called me "father" — I'm one year older than he is — and insisted in his distress on telling me all the troubles of his life.

"Not bad, cook," I say to him, and he beams. How easy it is to make him happy. I'll speak to the unit commander, make sure he's transferred from here to a comfortable base. If only I remember. But I'll probably forget. These days everything slips through me. My mind's like a sieve, and I prefer it that way. I like this feeling of lassitude in the forgiving fog that encompasses me, that will go on encompassing me until I leave this place, until the violent rending comes.

"Cook, two jam sandwiches. And an omelette."

"There's another portion of veal left, sir…"

"With jam. Two. And bring me a hammer, you idiot. How many times have I told you to fix the window?"

"But in any case on Thursday it's going to be…"

"A hammer, cook."

And while the insulted Peretz is busy preparing the sandwiches and the omelette, I kneel down in the thick layer of mud covering the mess hall floor and nail the rotten wood of the window frame into the wall. The heavy hammer blows make the whole hut shake, and my own body with it, as I pound in one nail after the other.

Monday. Evening.

At this hour, when the sunset burns in the sky like the bloody eye of a dead fish, Elisha and I, each leaning against his own wall, are a little distant. There's still some tension between us, but already the bitter knowledge that we've failed in our attempt to mend the torn years between us, already the nimbus of the dusk, already his weakening, dispiriting hunger have relaxed the hostility a little.

He tells me about Nimra. About his love for her when she was his, about his hurt, because of course she had never seen him as a man to share her life with. Even as a silent admirer, a distant lover, she didn't want him.

But one night ("a night when I had the distinct feeling that something was going to happen"), when he returned from the Lydda airport after seeing his parents off ("Hey, we haven't said anything about my folks yet!," "Never mind, later…"), he had stopped his car at the gate for a tall girl with a big backpack — and it was Nimra. ("When exactly, Elisha?" — "About December '76, why?" — "Because I'm missing a year and a half of hers, from about that period.") She had just returned from London, where she had been working for British television. For a whole year she'd worked there. She'd even edited a program that had been awarded a prize by the BBC. And then (you know her), at the height of her success, when the tempting offers began pouring in, she fell into one of her fits of restlessness and depression, and with her characteristic impetuosity, with that physical revulsion against hesitation, she packed her few belongings, resigned from her job, and came back to Israel — straight into my car.

★

Elisha talks, and I barely listen. I hear only the sound of her name, see only the girl standing with the pack on her back, fearlessly, on the side of the road at night.

Again and again, like pictures from an endlessly repeating movie, I see her long legs folding into the car, her Botticelli Venus hair wound around her mouth in the wind, her intelligent eyes widening in astonishment as she recognizes him. How her joy overflowed. "...She didn't have an apartment in Jerusalem," he continues, "and she didn't want to stay with her father, and since my parents were out of the country... Well, you know, little by little..."

In the evening she washes the dishes; in the morning he shaves at the basin, while she brushes her hair behind him, here a button comes off, there a nail needs hammering in, a glass breaks, and a family joke, a zipper to close, one thing leads to the other...and he titters.

And all that time I was here. On top of the mountain.

"But she's not all right," he adds gravely, "she hasn't got her feet on the ground. Sometimes she gets so depressed for no reason. There were weeks when it was impossible to talk to her. Sometimes she disappeared for days on end, without saying where. She got all kinds of ideas into her head. She met a couple of Arab intellectuals in London, you know? She didn't tell me much. She's not right now either. You don't know anything yet, Yan, wait till I tell you, I'm worried about her. If I wasn't I wouldn't have come..."

Enough. I don't want to hear any more. Come on, Elisha, it's already dark outside, we can go out for a little walk.

Outside, in the darkness, I match my steps to his. I feel the fetters of his weakness on my feet. In the dark, without his glasses, he's completely blind. From time to time he takes hold of my shoulder, gropes ahead with his feet, and I, with my new malice, lead him precisely to the stone-piled escarpment, to the gaping communications trenches, to the trampled-down barbed-wire fence, and he's already bruised and scratched and bleeding, but the night smell of my camp is in his nostrils, and so is a west wind blowing from the Suez Canal and the Bitter Lake. Even a blind man can sense the marvelous open spaces here.

Elisha is as excited as a child: "Look, this is here and that's there," and how I love him, what I had loved once upon a time, in those nocturnal moments; how glad I am that his eyes are blind to the white patches left by the uprooted huts on the bare ground. I see the camp with his eyes. Everything's fine. Everything's as usual, and everyone's only sleeping.

Afterward, at the edge of the escarpment on top of the cliff, he wanders happily, oblivious of the danger gaping at his feet. One rash step would be enough to send him crashing onto the rocks below, into the lap of the mountain where the wind whirls; and I, from where I'm standing, too far away to give him my hand, watch him with tense, precise attention, relax my straining limbs. Even if he falls, he'll be swallowed up in the dense thickets below. Nobody will see him, and the sound of his cry will go unheard. He'll fall softly toward the dead man, waiting in tense anticipation in the darkness of the thicket. My double secret at the foot of the mountain. Nobody knows that he came here, to Ras Ajleh, not in France and not in Israel, either.

And I still didn't understand what I already knew. There was that flicker, and there was a great radiance. I hurry to Elisha cavorting on the sides of the position, and I remove him from the danger.

Tuesday. Morning.

I didn't close my eyes all night. I was still wrapped in that dulling fog, but I was already readying myself for the knowledge, which shone at me through all the screens.

Early in the morning both of us are already awake. He stirs slowly in the tangle of his blankets. His eyelids are heavy, and his cheeks are creased with sleep.

I watch him stealthily as he eats his meager, jam-smeared bread, as he drinks his oily coffee; I sense his hunger, the weakness in his limbs, and my heart goes out to him. Since yesterday something's happened to me. There's still today and tonight, still the next day and the next night...

When I interrupt my roaming around the camp and drop into the room for a moment, I find him in my bed, reading his poems for the thousandth time, his face distorted. "They're not worth a damn," he whispers to me in despair. "These poems, no, this isn't what I wanted to say, and I've only realized it now, only here, on the mountain, reading and rereading them, it's all a lie, a lie and a fake, and she told me so, and I didn't want to hear her. How can anyone write this stuff?" And he begins poring over the pages again, which are already ragged, shaping the words with his lips, shaking his head, no, no, and I slip outside again.

In the office caravan, Rinat hands me a message. Journalists will be arriving to cover the explosion of the base. They'll arrive at Ras Ajleh on Thursday at eleven zero zero hours. A light lunch with the O.C. Southern Command and the division commander, and afterwards, in vehicles belonging to the Southern Command, to "Etrog Hill," from where the explosives will be activated by the outstanding student of the last demolitions course. Shooting angles have already been planned and tested for the press and TV cameramen, and telephone lines have been laid down for on-the-spot radio reporting.

"And apart from that — "

"Yes, Rinat?"

"I've got permission from the division commander to leave here today."

In other words, she's already told him.

"Okay."

And I turn around and walk out.

★

Outside clouds are already darkening the sun, and I push my hands into my pockets and stroll slowly along the paths. The hectic ferment inside me has disappeared. Now only intelligent weariness guides my steps. I just have to do it. Not think about it, not cast doubts. Only concentrate all my attention on the relief that the news has brought me. It seems there is no need even to plan. Everything will proceed of its own accord. All I have to do is keep the secret from him, get up on Thursday morning as usual, take my leave of the base along my regular walking route, promise him I'll be back at lunchtime — why should he suspect anything, he knows my habits already; and the silence, the stillness of death that will reign here, that too is not unfamiliar to him — and afterwards, on to the "light refreshments," to the reporters and hollow jokes; and from there to "Etrog Hill," to the tense and already superfluous activity of the engineers, the broadcasters' phrases, the smiles of nervous anticipation on the faces of the men of words, a promising young second lieutenant, astonishingly young, as I was when I came here, goes up to the switch closing the electric circuit.

The moment of stillness.

I watch the days of my life going up in the mushroom of smoke, which rises higher, curling in on itself. I see them borne upward in the dense fog that does not look harmful and destructive. I hear the surprised sighs of relief — "Is that all?" — suddenly interrupted, when the slow thunder comes rolling toward us, pregnant with disaster in its amplitude, and only now — as it falls onto them, heavy and inevitable — are their minds penetrated by the consciousness of the power collapsing there, defeated. Now, for a minute at least, the smiles will be wiped off their faces, their bodies will be shaken like hollow reeds in the crashing thunder.

But already the empty words are flowing again like water from a riddled jar; already the terrible truth is fenced in and channeled into banality, and the smiles — a little nervous still — are emerging from their lairs. We've survived this, too. It didn't even hurt...

And only I, slapped half-jokingly on the back in all directions (perhaps some glib journalist will even crown me with one of his corny cliches), turning away from them, stoically enduring their torrents of words, sensing the mushroom of boundless joy soaring inside me, for I am leaving a secret behind me on the caved-in mountain, fragments of life merging with the earth and the sky, melting into the rock and the molten iron, hanging here like a cloud, my continuing life, the world is still worthwhile.

My feet carry me to the shooting range. To the green, man-shaped targets, riddled with hundreds of holes, to the pot-bellied sandbags on which the shooters leaned. Blackened cartridges lie scattered over the ground, oil-soaked rags cling to the thorns. From the edge of the field a red, dirty bandage flutters toward me, borne on the blustering wind, swept along on the currents of air, gliding over the barbed-wire fence, spinning wildly in the gray sky, and escaping into the desert.

I hurry back to him, lying underneath the blanket now, his head under another blanket, and the booklet of poems thrown under the table, bedraggled and unraveled, like a dead, white bird.

"Hey, kid," I burst into the silence. "What's up?"

He extricates his head from the blankets. How he's changed. His face is so pale, his eyes staring.

"Elisha, what's wrong?"

His voice is quiet and calm. He can't go on like this. He feels like a prisoner. And the whole thing's ridiculous: he's supposed to be on holiday, and instead of enjoying himself and tanning himself in the sun, he's lying here, trapped in a dark narrow room, his head spinning with prolonged hunger, his weak eyes hurting, even his poems, his hope, transformed into an empty pile of words...

I encourage him. Tomorrow or the next day Nimra will come, we'll sit and talk, like then, we'll remove the barriers, we'll straighten things out. Maybe she'll even be reconciled with him, because they didn't part in anger after all, only because of mental distress — temporary, no doubt — and now, in this peaceful place, free of all human schemes and spitefulness, perhaps she would find it in her heart to return to him, and who would welcome it more than I, because there was no chance of anything between her and me anymore, we had drifted too far apart, and it was better this way.

And Elisha listens and is tempted to believe. He is so weak and naive, which is precisely what Nimra loved in him, his childish, almost simpleminded innocence, which he tried to hide behind a clumsy, harmless sarcasm, his unconflicted soul, his ever ready forgiveness.

Now too he is easily encouraged. Spellbound by my words, tempted, pleased. Gradually he leans against the wall, stretches his limp body, hiccups, raises his head to the naked light bulb, and of his own accord, without my asking him to, he begins telling me about her again.

For an entire year they lived like that in his parents' house in Jerusalem. He never made any demands of her, and she let him live with her like man and wife. They lived quietly, but without serenity. Nimra's behavior was strange and disturbing. Sometimes she disappeared for days on end. He never asked her where she'd been. (Once, when he dared to, she looked at him so imploringly, that he vowed never to question her again.) But he heard rumors. Someone had seen her in Nablus, with a crowd of local youths, talking to them vehemently; other people told him that she was mixing with extreme left-wing circles. Accusations she hurled at him when she lost her temper ("Not with me, I never gave her any cause to be angry with me") confirmed his suspicions.

One evening she brought home an Arab of about thirty, a tall man with a mustache and asked Elisha's permission to put him up for a few days. He was in danger, she explained. This time too Elisha didn't ask any questions. They put the man in one of the rooms, and he never came out. Nimra took him everything he needed. For hours on end the two of them secluded themselves in the room, while Elisha, in the other rooms, worried.

Men and women he didn't know now came to his house, looked

at him with unconcealed suspicion, greeted him curtly, and hurried into the room, with its tormenting secret.

There were days when he felt he couldn't take it any longer. His hand would hover nervously around the handle of the door to the room. Throw them out, they're taking advantage of you, maybe even endangering you, he protested; stop smiling sweetly — but he never did anything.

Nimra was frantic in those days. She hardly spoke to him. Only apologized to him over and over, for the unhappiness she was causing him, for upsetting his life like this, but very soon, even sooner than he thought, she would be leaving, and she would stop torturing him, but in the meantime — he was her home and her bed, and she begged him to remember the charity of her youth, when she walked with him in the wilderness.

And he told her the truth, that he didn't care, even if all these friends of hers, the stern-eyed men and the martyred-looking women with their slovenly clothes and vein-knotted hands, even if all these secretive Arabs and Jews went on prowling around his house, dropping cigarette ash on his mother's carpets, falling asleep with their shoes on the armchairs in the living room, he didn't care, as long as she was there, to come creeping into his bed at night, smelling of cigarette smoke and sweat, and to fall asleep immediately in utter exhaustion, snoring with her mouth defiantly open.

"And him — the Arab?"

"The Arab was an Arab." He never exchanged a single word with him. He never even knew his name. Sometimes, late at night, he thought he heard footsteps in the house. Brisk, vigorous footsteps. To and fro. But he wasn't sure. One evening — Nimra had been away for several days — the Arab came and sat opposite the TV set, and Elisha observed him. They still hadn't spoken to each other. Elisha was uneasy. He kept looking at him out of the corner of his eye. He saw a lot of tense alertness; he saw a strong man, bursting with the fullness of his power, suffocating in his enforced idleness and imprisonment. The whole room bristled.

It was during this period that Elisha began to write. He wrote poems, stories, even a couple of acts of a play, and he felt that he had found the right thing to do. He had never had to worry about earning a living. His father gave him a generous allowance, and so he could spend his days bowed over his notebooks. At first he was ashamed. He was like a boy discovering his lust. Then he got carried away, began showing his writing to other people; he even sent things to literary journals, was politely rejected, and sent them again.

"I never became a great writer," he giggles, "but I do write for newspapers. When I was still living in Israel I wrote too, for a local paper in Jerusalem. You know — characters from the marketplace, neighborhoods with an 'angle,' humorous pieces here and there, and so, when I came to France, I already had a profession. Did I tell you about my scoop on the rats?"

"You mentioned something."

He falls silent, disconsolate. "I wrote to you here. All the time. You never answered."

I shrug my shoulders.

"Every month, like clockwork, I wrote to you. Every time I thought, this time he'll answer, what's he got to do up there that keeps him so busy? In the end I despaired of you."

"You never mentioned Nimra in your letters. You never told me you were living together."

"I didn't want to hurt you. From a distance things seem different from what they are in reality."

In the tin cupboard, behind the pile of filthy underclothes, in a swollen brown paper packet, lie their letters. The letters they all sent here. Elisha, Giddy, Hanoch, Papush. A packet full of puzzled questions. How long was I going to go on sitting here, on top of the mountain, when was I going to come down, stop playing childish games, and do something with my life. Mild rebukes, hints of envy, perhaps even longing, faint stings winging toward me from all over the world, Cambridge, Jerusalem, Paris. I was their silent line of communication on the heights of the mountain. They wrote to themselves, to each other, and to who they were once upon a time, and I gathered all their words inside me and never wrote back. The only time I broke my silence was when Nimra wrote her last letter from Paris, when in panic-stricken haste I wrote one line: Send for Elisha, I wrote to her, and that was all.

And one day — Elisha goes on with his story, his eyes closed — it was all over. I still don't know exactly what happened. It seems that one of the group was caught with explosives on him. He was a terrorist. Maybe it was the man who was already staying permanently in my house, maybe one of the others. A girl was arrested with him too. They arrested them on the university campus in Jerusalem.

The house emptied out in one minute flat. It was all over — the whispering in the locked room, the password knocks on the front door, the worried phone calls in the middle of the night, the cans of glue and paint brushes in the hall.

They left the apartment, looking at me sadly, shrugging their shoulders. And I was sad, too. In an instant my life was empty — you might even say strange. An Israeli, a sabra, like me, a soldier in the intelligence corps, an innocent, a stay-at-home, even a self-declared coward, aiding and abetting secret, shady gatherings, giving shelter to an anonymous Arab. But you understand, of course: Nimra.

And that was the hardest of all: Nimra had been deceived. That same evening she told me everything. Or almost everything. That was the only time I ever saw her cry. ("Nimra?" — "Yes, yes, Nimra!," with suppressed pride in his voice. I'd never seen her cry.) She, who had gone with them all the way, faced all the dangers, given them her money, her strength, shelter, a meeting place, walked around in their rags, spoken to people in darkened rooms, in refugee camps, in the corners of shady cafés, who had risked her life — and submitted to ugly insults and suspicions too — had done all this on one explicit condition, and the condition had been broken, and she couldn't understand it at all. They had promised her, they had sworn: only in peaceful ways, only with words, and all of a sudden — explosives, a whole network of carefully planned actions, in which she, Nimra, was only an innocent courier to be exploited to the full.

A few days later she left him. She returned to London, to lose herself in the excitement of the big city. But she didn't go back to working in television. She decided she'd had enough of reporting on other people's activities. It was time to act. She found her way into Amnesty, the organization that fights for political prisoners all over the world, for citizens deprived of their rights, for people living under occupation. And in the course of an in-depth investigation into the military regime in Argentina, she ended up in France, where the incident with Mark Daniel Nestor happened, but that's a long story…

For the last few minutes I have stopped listening to him. The pieces of the distant mosaic are coming closer and fitting together. Her distant life, the blow, the new hope, her worldwide activities, my passive solitude here, my continuing impotence, the right thing. Where is she, where is she now, the tall girl with the thick, assertive brows, the long, fine fingers, strong and dry as earth? Where is she?

And suddenly, I hush Elisha and sit up alertly. I hear sounds outside the room. Strange noises, thorn-trampling steps, an engine throbbing, a stifled cough. And full of dread that my secret will be discovered, the secret of Elisha in my room, I burst outside, huge and mighty against anyone who dares upset my hopes and cast me back into the fog of weakness and impotence, but there, on the rocky ground surrounding my concrete building, at the foot of the giant rock, the yellow pickup is parked, and it's only the three engineers hurrying in an endless relay race to the pickup and back, carrying the green sacks, leaning them against my walls.

In a minute, in vast relief, I'm with them. Hoisting a sack onto my shoulders and running behind them. Strength pours into my legs and my aching back. Joy surges in me as I lay the sack next to the wall, as I charge back to the pickup, faster than all three of them, more powerful than all of them put together. The deed is being done.

The green pile mounts around the four sides of the building, surrounding the grey walls containing Elisha, the unwitting captive, brilliant in its vivid green, like a fresh lawn basking in the sun.

We work in silence. Breathing heavily, sweating, we pass each other. They can't understand the change that has come over me, and how can I explain it to them? I am even stronger than Paldi. I no longer need him. And so I can afford to smile at him.

And then, surprisingly, the work is done. So quickly. The three of them turn to go. The short, old guy winks at me, the young one blinks at me, and Paldi raises his amputated finger in a victory salute. I see a new look in his eyes.

And I, worn out, sour with sweat, flushed with the agonizing heat of an excitement too great to bear, brimming over with my new happiness, return to my room, to my innocent prisoner, but — what's this? He's already asleep, slack and limp, huddled into himself, with a thread of saliva dribbling onto the blanket from his gaping mouth.

Tuesday. Afternoon, evening.

In the afternoon his temperature suddenly shoots up and he has an attack of the shivers. I pile blankets on top of him, force him to swallow two dusty pills that I find in my cupboard, but he goes on shivering, huddled up, his teeth chattering.

For a while I sit opposite him and watch him anxiously. Then I hurry to the mess hall and ask Peretz to make me two meat sandwiches and a vegetable salad.

Peretz doesn't look at me. Ever since yesterday he's been acting with chilly hostility. Maybe my new eating habits annoy him, and maybe he's finally realized that even I can't stop the march of time toward that moment.

But what's he to me?

Proudly I lay my booty before Elisha. He doesn't react. His lids droop over his eyes. He gestures aimlessly. He has no appetite.

At my wit's end I crouch down next to him, put my hand on his hot forehead, smell the odor of the sweat rising from his burning body. I try to soothe him, cool him down a little, but he eludes my hand, huddles into his blanket, and turns his face to the wall.

Not like this, I think as I emerge into the darkening evening sky, as I sit down on the concrete platform, I don't want him like this. Weak and limp — yes. But with all his wits about him, awake and alert, with his hair on end, even before he knows why, and then, at the sound of the dull echo booming in the bowels of the earth, underneath his feet, to grasp with a thousand senses, with every nerve end in his body, the act, the full force of his isolation here, the hopelessness of his situation.

And while I'm sitting there Peretz appears, urgent and alarmed. A fight's broken out in the dorm. Come quickly, sir.

When I open the door I can't understand what's in front of my eyes: a tangle of bodies, a strong smell of male sweat, and not a sound to be heard, apart from harsh, strenuous breathing. It's impossible to tell who's hitting whom.

The American, fat and hairy, is lying half naked on the floor, his right hand crushed under Paldi's knee, while he, with bloodshot eyes and both hands hanging onto the short man's scanty hair, is banging his head again and again, with a dull thudding sound, on the floor. Jorn, the Norwegian, with the permanently reflective expression on his face, the top half of his body bare and bronzed with a golden fuzz, glittering with sweat, is pressing the yellow-haired young soldier into the corner between the cupboard and the wall, punching him mercilessly with his huge fists, beating all the life out of the slender body, the muscles on his back rippling in coordination with his blows. The old engineer, obviously exhausted, keeps coming back and clinging with tired stubbornness to the Norwegian's back, hatred in his eyes and great weariness in his arms, pushed off, casually, again and again, by the powerful hand, hurled against the cupboard and the legs of the beds, only to get up and grope his way blindly back to the nexus of the violent commotion, and be hurled away again.

And then I'm in the middle of it, too.

In my attempts to rescue the fainting youth from Jorn's pounding fists, I get caught up in the blows. Still on my guard against the temptation of those lakes of rage penned up in my body for so many days, seething in anticipation, I submit to the rhythmic blows, trying with all my strength to pull the lifeless body from the trap of the cupboard and the wall, but something seems to have gone wrong, and my intention to have been misunderstood, for in an instant the whole room turns into a boiling sea of hostility, a tide rising in everyone's eyes and fists. Inspired with a new strength, from the four corners of the room they rise, the beaters and the beaten, and turn to face me.

Why all this happens, I don't know. Perhaps because of our prolonged isolation on the mountain top, perhaps because the silence and the boredom have become unbearable: a spark of life has been ignited in them, and I am trapped.

They fall on me with their fists and feet, hammer my head against the iron frames of the beds, roll me in suffocating blankets, until my mind clouds, I choke on my own blood, and my hands and feet flail desperately in all directions, refusing to obey me.

Like a limp sack I absorb the blows, which no longer hurt me, are only a tiresome nuisance. I hear — as if from a great distance — the sound of their rasping breath, the groans as they sink all their strength into me. Paldi's figure — sweating, black, red-eyed, exuding hatred — dances before my eyes. I see only him. Feel only his blows. I can't be angry with him.

Suddenly, a cold, wet shock: Peretz throws a bucket of water on us, and like fighting dogs we are separated, peel off each other, and drop to the floor.

★

In my room, Elisha is awake. Lying with his eyes open, looking at the ceiling. The shivering has passed, and all he feels now is weakness. Perhaps he won't be able to come for a walk with me tonight. His legs can't hold him up. When he turns toward me, he sees my face, the bleeding pulp, and he stares.

Afterward we spend a long time cleaning the wounds, wiping the dried blood, dressing the deep cuts. Elisha, despite his weakness, gets out of bed to take care of me. His face is close to mine.

When I tell him what happened, his face does not betray his feelings, but I know how much he shrinks from any manifestation of violence. Even the sight of the blood is hard for him.

To cheer him up, I promise that even if his legs fail him we'll go for our nightly walk, even if I have to carry him on my back. And he laughs. So many times I've carried him on my back, when he couldn't keep up on our exhausting marches along the wadi beds, in the tough training programs I subjected my body to, and in which he — so enthused at first by my cruelty to myself — insisted on participating. I was like his big brother, after all.

Yes, yes, he exults, we were good friends, it's obviously a question of age. Today I can't open up to people like that, I haven't got the strength to make the effort, yes, yes, that's the way of the world. What plans we had, what faith in our unlimited strength, our unshakable integrity. How we despised our parents, the distorted truths they taught us. How sure we were that we would never be like them — suspicious, telling half-truths. And the only one who managed to escape was Nimra, and we got stuck somewhere in the middle. She was the only one, both when she was with us and when she was far away, who transcended all that, and that's why we loved her, if you'll allow me to put it like that, Yan, and that's why we'll never stop searching for her wherever we go, and if you'll bring me my case, Yan, I'll show you something, and he pulls two photographs of her out of the pile of clothes, and we pore over them eagerly.

One is a passport photo, which I know very well. She gave me one just like it, after a lot of coaxing. She was seventeen, and even then she made sure not to smile at the photographer.

The other one was a newspaper clipping in French, and although it was very worn and creased, you can still see her: Nimra, in a long coat, her hand clutching her throat, leaning over, her whole body straining forward, her eyes fixed on an invisible point, which is absorbing all her attention, all her strength. The look in her staring eyes is illuminated by many camera flashes. In the background is a large crowd, an ambulance, a few uniformed people. They're all standing around her, surrounding her, and at the same time she is very alone, untouchably apart.

Elisha wants to go on telling me about her, about her fiery life, but I don't let him and draw him away from there to our own days, the hundreds of days and nights, the guards together under the pure summer sky, the absorbing intelligence work, the "Fishinger" cakes that Giddy, the kibbutznik, brought from home, the Friday CO's parades, the slap in the face Nimra gave one of the officers for hurting her roommate and insulting her in front of everyone, our night flight from the base to the army town of Refidim, to the women's prison, where we visited the jailed Nimra, whom we found miserable, beaten, dirty, and so humiliated…

Thus, little by little, I draw him into those distant days, testing his memory with descriptions of the birds living in the wadi, encouraging him to smell the herbs we picked on our walks, from which we brewed a hundred kinds of tea, playing all the strings with calculated precision, and he — innocent, loving creature that he is, infected with my happiness, his enthusiasm exceeding my own, tears of merriment in his eyes — gives me a lot of enjoyment in return, whose likes I shall not see again; reminds me of things I've forgotten, nicknames we gave our friends, boys and girls who were once here, loves, hates, small joys.

And then he falls silent and stares at me, surprised at the intensity of my happiness. "You're playing a strange game here, Yani," he says, and doesn't elaborate. Afterward, he continues quietly, "And in one week's time, I'll be in Paris, in Lyons, and all this time here will seem like a strange, unreal dream. You understand, in one more week I'll be back in the rat race."

"And will you take Nimra with you?"

"Can anyone take Nimra anywhere?" he laughs. "If she wants to — she'll come." And after a pause, he adds, "I don't know, I don't know if living with her is good for me. She's not right in the head, Yani. You'll see, when she comes here you'll sense it at once, something inside her's shifted since they killed that Argentine of hers, something…"

"Aren't you hungry?" I ask, noticing that he hasn't touched the sandwiches I brought him. "They're with meat. We got new battle rations today."

He pulls a face. He's not hungry. "It's peculiar. My stomach seems to have stopped working. But actually I don't feel bad. On the contrary. I feel clean. Like after fasting on Yom Kippur. You know, Yani, now I think that in spite of everything it's a good thing I came."

At midnight we go out for our nightly walk. Elisha leans on me with the full weight of his body. He's weak and limp. His legs buckle with every step he takes, and I have to support him. We proceed at a gentle pace, very peaceful and serene. We don't talk, because it's hard for him to talk, and the wind snatches the words from our mouths, and we feel good.

5

Wednesday. Morning.

There's today, and tonight. And then tomorrow morning.

At breakfast the Norwegian looks at me, appalled. Yesterday, after the storm subsided, when we were lying there dazed and sweating, Jorn was the first to recover. He gave me his hand, helped me up, pulled the others to their feet, lent me a handkerchief to staunch the blood flowing from my ears and nose, and asked me to forgive him. Afterwards the others dared too. They came up to me, slightly stunned, shamefaced, muttering apologies through split lips, lowering eyes that were turning blue from punches.

Now too, during breakfast, Jorn can't control his feelings. Agitated, he puts out his hand, like a child, to touch the gaping cut on my forehead, and strokes it gently, like a healer. This is his apology this morning, and it suits me better than the hastily stammered apologies of my countrymen.

Everyone circles me on tiptoe, pitying, knowing how it hurts me to be uprooted from this place; they've seen me wandering around endlessly all day long, heard rumors about my life here. But I don't need pity now.

Peretz outdoes himself this morning. Ever since Jorn and the American donated their Christmas rations to us, our table has been groaning under the load of canned meat and chicken, slices of pineapple and melon, exotic spreads. "Like breakfast in a five-star hotel, cook," I pat him on the shoulder, and the three engineers laugh loudly and diligently.

In my room Elisha has just woken up. His face is yellow, and his cheekbones are very prominent. There's blood trickling from his nose, and when I arrive he's busy stuffing cotton wool up his nostrils. His movements are slow and uncertain. His eyes are half closed as he raises his head to the ceiling.

One more day, he says to me, and one more night, and a day. This evening or tomorrow Nimra will be here, and her presence will make him better. And afterwards, when he leaves here, he'll go straight to Jerusalem, and his mother will take care of him. She'll give him chicken livers to eat. The miracle cure.

"And I don't take care of you?" I'm almost insulted.

He laughs softly. As if he knows, as if he entrusted himself to me knowingly. Slowly he gets up and changes his clothes. Throws his creased trousers and sweaty shirt onto the floor, and threads his thin body, swaying like a reed, into white trousers and a light-colored shirt, an operation that tires him so much that he collapses onto the bed again, and I have to give him warm water to drink from the cup in my hand.

Afterwards he stretches out his legs. A long, white smudge on my bed. White spots peep out of his nose, too: the cotton wool. Yesterday, he tells me with his eyes closed, he was still suffering from bad headaches, because of the hunger and the loss of his glasses, but now, miraculously, this too has gone. He feels no pain at all — on the contrary, it's as if all the sights and smells have become more vivid. With a golden glow. And his thoughts well up pleasantly inside him.

Ever since the end of 1978 he's been living in France, and don't ask how he ended up there. There must be some higher power that guides people and leads them toward each other. If not, how can you explain the fact that all of a sudden, more than a year after her disappearance from his parents' home in Jerusalem, he received a letter from her in France?

Come, she wrote to him, and he — "Did I have a choice? I would have followed her to the moon" — packed his case, the same one lying here, and went. His parents were furious. They said terrible things to him. You're ruining your life for the sake of a crazy girl, they said, who's been playing fast and loose with you for five years now, who's never loved you, only taken advantage of your weakness and your soft heart.

His father even said that if he went to her he would stop supporting him. But Elisha didn't care. He left his unhappy parents and flew to her, in France.

There, in Lyons, he didn't find what he was looking for. Not a woman pining away for love of him, but a broken reed. Nimra, beaten to the roots of her soul, mourning the destruction of her dream and her love.

In those days she decided to leave her job in Amnesty. The people she worked with in the organization understood. (One of them, whom Elisha talked to once, told him that she had "crossed the thin line between helping others and harming herself. Our conscience wouldn't have allowed us to go on employing her. She isn't cut out for the work. We should have seen it coming.")

So Nimra joined the staff of one of the local papers. The affair in which she had been involved, and recommendations from Amnesty, paved the way for her. Joylessly and painlessly she did her job. "You wouldn't have recognized her. Quiet, subdued. Where was the Nimra temperament, the enthusiasm and the bursts of rage? Even her walk had become heavy…"

Nimra was living in a fog, in a truce between the times. Recovering from the chronic terror that had scarred her, listless, sleeping a lot, sinking deeper, and Elisha was unable to save her.

With her recommendation, and thanks to his previous experience in Jerusalem, he, too, joined the staff of the paper. "Our health correspondent" said the byline with his name; "the sewage man," his friends on the paper nicknamed him, because the first — and so far the last — scoop that had come his way, thanks to a leak at a bargain price, was an exposé of shocking fraud, as a result of which the lower levels of the city sewage system were infested with thousands of rats.

Hey, he hadn't told me about the ceremony yet.

Down there, in the labyrinth of the underground city, between the canals of churning filth, the gray concrete walls lit up by glaring floodlights, in the miasma of the permanent stench, a group of people gathered: the new official in charge of the city's sanitation, reporters, the sanitation workers in their big boots, and Nimra, who had agreed to come with him.

From now on, the new appointee promised, everything would be different. Our city and our souls will be purer, and all thanks to our guest of honor, the courageous and honest reporter who exposed the "Watergate" of Lyons.

The workers sniggered loudly, and the cameras flashed. It was a ghastly scene. The glare of the floodlights on the concrete walls, the dark, streaming water, the handful of people huddled together in muffled, secret, fear, the gleaming eyes of the rats. For they were indeed there — hundreds of thousands of them, vast, silent families.

Eyes, eyes are staring at me, Nimra hissed in his ear and clutched his arm in terror. Take me away, she breathed heavily, get me out of here. But before they had taken a dozen steps she bent over the railing of one of canals, and her vomit was borne away on the dark stream.

"That was only the beginning," he went on, as he changed the blood-soaked cotton wool. "Afterward it was impossible to reach her. She sank and sank. She got ideas into her head. She said terrible things. Later on, she didn't even want to talk to me. She said we were too different, that I'd never understood. Sometimes she spoke about you. I think she may have still loved you. But she was falling fast. She hardly went to work, she didn't eat a thing for days on end. She grew pale — almost transparent. When I begged her to take pity on me, to take care of herself, she would smile at me, a faint remnant of the Nimra laugh, and draw a line on my lips with her finger. She was so sorry to cause me pain, but just a little patience, soon, sooner than I thought, it would all pass, everything would be for the best, and don't take any notice of me..."

"And one day she got up and left. She went away." I interrupt his sigh, his attempt to gather his straying thoughts. He nods weakly. Nimra disappeared.

And I too am dissolving, disappearing, because I know. I know her. Nimra would not come back, not to me, and not to him either. She had gone to die by herself, in a corner of her forest. And I was only sorry, so very sorry, that she hadn't come to me, to cling to me in the death of our dreams, in our fall from the mountain peaks.

Suddenly he rouses himself. "Enough," he says. "That's enough about me and her. You haven't talked about yourself at all. All the time I've been shut up here you haven't said a word about yourself. You've grown so silent. I don't remember you like this."

"What? Yes. Not like this. People change." And I hurry to get up, put on the clumsy parka. "It's lunchtime," I say to him, "and me —

I'm like Pavlov's dogs: half past twelve comes, and I'm hungry. Over here, in this place, you hang onto islands of routine. What would you like me to bring you? You haven't eaten anything since the day before yesterday. You haven't even touched the bread..."

"You rush off to your meals as if they're serving delicacies there, not dry bread," and again he laughs his new laugh, a silent laugh, and I hurry out. I don't like this laugh.

Outside the wind is gathering force. As if it's collecting its tides and currents from the four corners of the desert and assembling them here, in preparation for tomorrow. Columns of dust dance in front of me, and I bury my mouth in the collar of my jacket. Through my half-closed lids I see them: black snakes, writhing, bursting from their coils, covering the eye of the earth in a sinister vortex. The electric wires, waiting to conduct the spark to the dynamite. Glittering in the sun, crawling to the plump green sacks, seductive, clinging to each other, stretching to the top of the hill, to the north gate, to the edge of the cliff, to the subterranean halls, a dense black net, the legs of a gigantic spider, quivering in anticipation.

In the mess hall, gloom reigns. It seems that even they, the engineers, are sorry for what they are about to do. There is no joy in their voices when they tell me that they have already connected the fuses and the detonators to the dynamite.

Now all that remains is the slow counting of the hours. Only remorse toward the mountain beneath our feet, which trusts us so blindly, oblivious to our treachery, the treachery of the grasshoppers who have been stepping on its surface for all these years, and that tomorrow — at an appointed hour in the morning, an hour that is indistinguishable from all the hundreds of thousands of other hours that have passed over it and vanished into the eternal desert — will suddenly feel a heavy lump condensing inside it, tearing its guts apart, spraying it in all directions.

And this, perhaps, is the reason behind the silence in the empty hut. Peretz serves the good food without uttering a sound, and we chew in silence. The Norwegian sitting opposite me looks worried, even a little frightened. He nods stiffly, frequently and nervously, and his pipe flickers like a warning signal. Son of a people that knows the darkness, the other creatures who live in and around us, that respects the forces of nature. The deed is not to his liking. I sense his fear, and I have greater respect for him this morning.

Wednesday. Afternoon.

The sky is darkening now. An obscure anxiety stirs in the clouds gathering silently from all corners of the horizon, in the uprooted thorn bushes rolling over the grounds of the camp, escaping over the barbed-wire fences, floating aimlessly over the desert and the abyss.

Even the big agamas, with their sand-colored eyes, hurry down from the rocks where they bask and bow their endless bows. Even they, these giant lizards, are escaping in all directions, in haste and great confusion, their tails dragging behind them and drawing lines in the sand, and their faces — their grinning monster faces — are grim.

I notice them today between the holes in the stone fences, in the communications trenches, circling each other clumsily. From time to time a mysterious distress overwhelms them, and then they attack each other furiously, their yellow mouths gape, emitting a hoarse, menacing whisper.

Geckos and spiders, beetles and jerboas, a countless multitude of tiny creatures is swarming everywhere today. The sand beneath my feet is full of activity. The birds of prey — the buzzards and the hawks — circle the sky expectantly, gather in their wings and claws, swoop again and again, bringing a swift death to these little denizens of the dark, which some mysterious force has banished from their usual haunts and sent scurrying into the sunlight.

And I don't go into my room, to the hollow body lying there in the semidarkness, whitening in its pallor.

I stroll through the fields, among stones and fences, hitting the

empty garbage cans with a broken branch, trying to revive the happiness, that sense of streaming light, and make it infuse me with
strength and decisive confidence in the deed, but something's going
wrong, and the vistas opening up only yesterday are now closing before my eyes. And what's the point, I torture myself with questions,
what's the point: a childish, insignificant act of protest? Perhaps a
debt I owe someone? Who? No, no. Something's out of joint. In my
eagerness to push the thought of the deed out of my mind, I clutch
at it again, torment myself with it. This isn't how I meant it to be.

And I go on walking with heavy feet, sullenly and listlessly hitting the hollow cans, the stones. Not like this, not like this.

In December 1978 — one year ago exactly — I received the last
letter. This time too from France. A few dozen lines in a devastated
handwriting, tumbling onto one another, struggling with one other.
In one burst the words erupted from the pen, past mixed up with
present, details I didn't know, and others she had mentioned again
and again, nervous jumps from one thought to another, and then —
abruptly, the sudden, lopped-off end, which exploded my anxiety
for her and made me send her my immediate reply. My first and
last letter from here. To what she had written in her letter I did not
react at all. For what can I say to her? I was as stunned as she was.
I only asked her to send for Elisha, her ever willing, easy-to-please
lover, who brought with him serenity and gentleness, which she
needed so desperately now.

Mark Daniel Nestor was a doctor of Russian literature at the
University of Buenos Aires. (The place: again, the west cliff position, sitting on two damp, unraveled sandbags, protected from the
wind and the drizzling rain.) The son of well-off immigrants from
Czechoslovakia, blind from birth in one eye, honorary editor of
the arts faculty journal, member of writers' committees, philo-
sophical societies, Spanish translator of *The Great Russian Reader*.
And most important of all, of course, Hector's father.

Hector about whom, she thinks, she has already written to me.

And she repeated the things she had written in her previous letter. So far Nimra transmitted the facts and impressions as they were, in her usual condensed, dry manner. From here on everything became confused, unintelligible: had Nimra transferred her love for the son — Hector, whom she had never met — to the father, Dr. Daniel Nestor, who was twenty-five years older than she was? Or perhaps it was only his pain and impotence in the face of the hostile, tyrannical power blocking the movement of his life, only his stubborn fight, which drew her to him with a force she can not resist — and who can understand this better than I? I don't know. But it isn't important. I tried to discuss it with Elisha twice in the past few days, but as soon as he started talking about it, I cut him off. I still prefer her frightened vagueness to his lengthy, obscure interpretations, for he was so moved by her summons, so tender and concerned, that he didn't demand explanations of her. From what he told me yesterday and today, and especially from what he didn't say, I understood: there are a lot of things he doesn't know.

Desaparecidos — that's what they call them in Argentina: the disappeared. The ones who are suddenly torn away from their homes and lives, between one act and another. A faint ripple stirs in the gaping hole — the anxiety of relatives, a wife or mother gone mad with worry, and it's over. They are never seen again.

Fifteen thousand of them have been counted in the past two years. The prey of the military junta, which decides human fates. Men and women of all ages and classes, housewives, students, workers, intellectuals. All of them snatched away. A loud knocking on the door at night, a swift, brutal abduction in a crowded street, a mysterious summons to a meeting at the dead of night in an out-of-the-way place — there was once a man, and he is no more. Woe to the protester. Woe to the mourner of his dead. And it happened to Hector. Hector — whom Nimra had never seen in her life, and only his photograph stood on her office desk in Paris, the ardent Hector, "all energetic quicksilver," she wrote to me then, whom the best people of her organization managed somehow to track down, to show incontrovertible evidence of the great danger he was in, to demand that he allow them to rescue him, and he refused...

They took him at noon. From the crowded university library, working on the editorial for his newspaper. He didn't see them coming, but some of the others sitting in the big hall saw them climbing the lofty staircase, calm and efficient, faceless in their leather coats.

Hector was sitting with his back to them (eyewitnesses told his father afterwards), but the stir of excitement that ran through the hall tensed his body. He took off his glasses and, by putting the carbon paper behind the lenses, turned them into a mirror. The two men knew exactly where to go. (The same eyewitness said that in some strange way everyone in the hall knew who would be caught in their sensitive feelers. Many of them looked at Hector even before the men directed their steps toward him.) As they came up to him from behind, Hector dropped the carbon paper, wiped his glasses and put them on. There was no tension visible in his body now.

The two men stationed themselves on either side of him, and without a word being said he got up and stood between them. He was crushed between their hefty bodies. None of the people sitting at the tables dared to raise their eyes. In step the two men descended the staircase, holding Hector under the armpits, with his legs in the air. For a moment he looked back at the hall, but he didn't say a word. Nor did the expression on his face betray his thoughts.

Hector's notebook, stained with blood and feces, was thrown by a nameless person, not one of the students, in the middle of a lecture on Russian literature, into the face of the lecturer, Mark Daniel Nestor. (The notebook thrower stood up and left the crowded hall with a slow, arrogant step. Nobody stopped him.) That same week Mark Nestor was fired from his post "for inciting his students to take part in negative political activity, and exploiting his position as a platform for Marxist propaganda."

This is more or less how things happened: telephone threats in the middle of the night, anonymous letters, a violent assault by a "drunk" in the street, slashed tires, a dead rat thrown onto his door-step from the window of a passing car. And all because Mark Daniel didn't keep quiet, and wrote letters to heads of governments and journalists and intellectuals of his acquaintance all over the world. Human beings don't "disappear," he wrote to them, they are ab-ducted and tortured, they are poisoned with curare which causes convulsive choking, they are dropped from airplanes into swamps that swallow them up, they are given the *submarino* treatment and submerged in barrels of water until they lose consciousness; they do not — on any account — vanish into thin air. Someone does it. Someone sets up the death camps in the jungles. There is a guiding hand, and this hand, while one finger points accusingly at freedom lovers, the others point at it.

And so, with the stubbornness of a man with justice on his side, a man so beaten that blows no longer hold any fear for him, Mark Daniel went on sending his letters — which he knew would never reach their destination — and demonstrating, and protesting, and time after time they summoned him to one or another office, and men of his own age, natives of the country, mustached and grave and concerned, men with nice families who only wanted what was best for everyone, but whose hands hovered constantly over the swelling on the side of their trousers, told him, "Keep quiet. Don't tempt fate, don't tighten the noose. You know how easy it would be for us."

And the people who loved him were horrified at his rashness, and implored him to stop, and he — whose life was not worth liv-ing without his son, the son who debated with him so passionately on their evening walks in the modest neighborhood, who grew so heated during their long arguments about the future developments of Marxism, about the way of the dead revolutionary Che; without his child, whom he loved like his soul — would go on beating his head against a stone wall, and go to stand with the "madwomen of

the Plaza de Mayo," the women whose loved ones had "disappeared" during those black years.

With them he stood and faced the blank walls of the Presiden-
tial Palace, moved slowly in the gray wind, as if praying, full of dread
in the grim, obdurate despair surrounding them and the handful
of men standing there with them, giving himself over to his pain,
to his weak revenge. Together they stood there, those who were
already beyond fear.

And now the falling rain twists and turns in little rivulets, penetrat-
ing the position and turning the sky gray. In the distance — faint
cries rise and are flung by the wind into the abyss, far from here.
A whole year has passed since she sent the letter, and this is the first
time I have read it again. I have been saving it for this moment.
The pale blue pages flap about in my hands, and I let them go, but
wet with rain, they do not fly up. They fall around me in the mud,
cling to me, and turn little by little into a soggy blue mess. Slowly
evening comes.

And then, the turning-point: Amnesty, in co-operation with the
Human Rights Committee of the American States, sent a second
delegation to Mark Daniel Nestor. A year before, Nimra's friends
had met him and asked him to persuade his son to escape from the
country that was trying to kill him. Now he himself was the object
of their concern. So great was the danger hanging over his head that
they almost forced him to escape from Argentina. They smuggled
him into France. There he was met by Nimra, who was responsible
for looking after him.

And thus the father stepped into the concern and sympathy
yawning inside her for the son. Thus she mingled his life with hers,
fought his war with him, infected by his fear, his despair, his passing
hopes. Thus she learned to love Hector through his eyes, grew
familiar with the poets he loved, tasted the dishes that his father, and

only his father, knew how to prepare for him. Thus the two of them fought with all the means at their disposal to denounce the conspiracy of silence and fear. To break through the curtain covering the abomination. Gradually they grew closer. The elderly teacher of Russian literature, the determined girl from Jerusalem, carried away by the ardor of her eager, generous faith.

From then on things happened quickly. (Nimra's words too sped from her pen in panic-stricken haste.) One day — a few months after they began living together in a rented house in Lyons — while she was sitting in a café, waiting for him, Nimra was approached by a short young man with a mustache and a South American accent. He said that he knew where Hector was but that he was allowed only to give the information to Hector's father, to Mark Daniel. Nimra was agitated and suspicious, but the young man made light of her fears. He was genial and smiling, very keen to help. It was evident that he wanted to tell Nimra everything he knew, in order to reassure her, but that he was obliged to obey his superiors. When Mark Daniel ("the dear doctor" he called him, with undisguised admiration and respect) came this evening, at eight o'clock, to the meeting place in the park on the main *avenida* of the town, he would tell him everything. He would remove a stone from his heart. In any case — she managed to get one thing out of him, against his will: Hector was still alive, and their efforts, the storm they had stirred up with their protests, had borne fruit. You are not alone, he said to her before he left.

Mark Daniel was surprisingly calm when he heard the news. And in the evening too, when he put on his suit, and combed his beard, he showed no signs of excitement. Nimra can not get anything out of him. She herself was very tense. Suddenly Mark Daniel had become remote from her, and she could not reach him.

She led him with her arm linked in his (the blindness in his one eye made it difficult for him to see at night) down the long avenue, on the way to the little rose garden.

An electrical pole suddenly separated from itself. A tall, strong man, with a grotesque mask on his face, peeled it off, whispered something, a kind of slogan, and fired one bullet into Mark's chest.

And afterward, the wailing of the sirens, the press photographers, the milling crowd.

Only at home, their home, after the initial interrogation was over (the young policewoman took her blood-stained coat from her, and covered her with a kind of yellow, shining cape), did Nimra find the letter. Mark Daniel knew what was waiting for him. From the minute Nimra told him about the youth — he knew. How painful: he wanted it. An end to the hopeless struggle. He grieved for her. This world was not worthy of her.

That same night, huddled up in the shining cape, trembling with fear and rage (not a single tear — so she said), she wrote me this letter, because she knew — only I would understand.

And I, here, on the mountaintop, like a balloon pricked with a pin, in a pain I didn't know I was capable of, sank again into my apathy and my resignation. Although I wrote to her, and asked her to send for Elisha, although I hoped that he would go to her, I already knew, from the tone of her words, from her beaten spirit, I knew — he would not be able to save her. And I too had nothing left to look forward to now.

The last page, which I held for a long time in my hand, whose ink was dissolving in the rain and blotting out the lines, was snatched away by the wind. For a moment it flew high, fluttered over me like a blue, living bird, flapping its wings — and the next, a shower of heavy drops ripped through it and dragged it down into the mud.

I rose quickly to my feet, packed with frantic energy again, roaring with the immense power gathering inside me, violent and raging. The moment had come.

I ran to my room in the pouring rain, under the suddenly darkening sky, all alone on the mountain range. Again I was a male cub erupting from the earth. Now time pressed.

★

I burst tempestuously into the room, but Elisha barely reacts. Only his lids flicker for a moment. His pallor and apathy stun me. How thin he has grown, how he has sunk into himself in the past three days. When he arrived he was full of life and high spirits, and now...

Anger rises in me at the body that refuses to rebel, to cling to life. How can he give up so easily, allow his weary soul to make him suffer so? But I say nothing.

Outside it's already dark. I bend over Elisha and lift him effortlessly in my arms. His knees and head drop lifelessly. Carefully I leave the room, grope my way down the three steps, and begin to run.

The cold air, the pelting rain, beat against my burning face, strike the light body in my arms, staining his white clothes with damp spots. All Elisha's strength is now gathered in his right arm clinging to my neck. His head sways in time to my running. For a moment he raises it, his blind eyes look at me in astonishment, but without resistance. There is a kind of smile in his eyes, and once again I am flooded by a wave of joy, streaming new strength into my body.

Now, running rhythmically, breathing slowly, along the narrow road, charging toward the escarpment, toward the artificial sand hill, and already my destination is taking shape in the darkness opposite me, the subterranean halls are right in front of me. But suddenly, in a flash of insight, I know what I have to do for him, and immediately — even without his asking me — I turn toward the cliff.

There's still a lot of strength in my arms and legs, and this is just as well, since it will make it easier for me to lead Elisha down all the paths of the camp, to reach all the places and the scents for the last time. My farewell present.

And I run.

On the stone escarpment, above the communications trenches, between the twisted black snakes, to the walled positions, to the concrete platforms bearing the giant antennae, to the top of the cliff, facing the abyss.

There I stand for a moment, sweating and panting. I hold his body over the abyss, for him to feel — he can no longer see — the wind as it rises from the depths, the smell of the dense, damp vegetation, the secret lying there among the tangled branches.

But I linger no more. I run on, onward from there. To the north gate, to the barbed-wire fences, between the white patches on the earth, to the gasoline smells of the generator shed. And from there to the CO's caravan, the basketball field, past the deserted canteen and the fortified bunkers. And everywhere we go I talk to him, whisper forgotten things in his ear, living moments, names and acts, our high-spirited pranks, our love, our high hopes for the days to come, the days in which we are now sinking and joylessly capering.

And only the strength of the grip on my neck tells me that he understands, that he is awake.

And thus we reach the gates to the subterranean halls, and I lay my limp bundle on the damp floor, between the rivers of mud, and with a strength I didn't imagine I had in me, I remove the heavy wooden beam barring the gates, and the huge doors open with a creak. I pick Elisha up in my arms again, and together we go inside.

Here a new blow is awaiting me, which — if I had been an imaginative man — I could have avoided. For I could surely, in all these weeks, have imagined the sight of the long, empty corridors winding in the darkness, the silent stairs descending into the dim, dark, bare-walled halls themselves, packed with green sacks.

"Ha…" Elisha in my arms raises his head with an effort, surveys his surroundings. Then he looks at me, and I see that he too is stunned.

There's no point in trying to explain.

Only someone who spent thousands of crowded hours here, in the hum of the instruments, the commotion and the excitement, the tapping of the typewriters, the transmitters and telephones; only someone who experienced the anxiety of responsibility and difficult decisions here, the flushed young faces, the tremendous ferment of energy that assumed so many forms, of effort, and love, of quick, nervous repartee, of youthful hopes, anxieties and suffering, only someone who was here during days of peace and war, who experienced that strained, tense attention, would understand my devastation. My helplessness now, facing the ghastly silence filling the air, dense and crumbling.

I let Elisha slide from my grip and collapse next to him on the linoleum floor. Again I am a child of four without hope. Knowing all the answers. Now all my enthusiasm melts away. The feverish agitation that has been burning in my body since morning begins to exhaust me.

"They're killing you with this," says Elisha. I nod speechlessly. The sights I see out of the corners of my eyes disturb me. It is as if there, in the recesses of the hall, the darkness is alternately thickening and dissipating. The walls move slowly around in a circle, closing in on me. My arms and legs tremble with the effort of the running.

"Funny how you get attached to a place like this," he says. "A few tons of iron, prefabs, electric wires, antennas. Such a cold, ugly agglomeration. It could have been on any other mountain, anywhere else, you know."

I know. I look at him wonderingly. He is lying on his back, where I have dropped him, his hand under his head. It was just like this, in this position, so open, that I once found him in the cave of the doves. The memory sears me again. Ten years have passed since then.

"Thousands of soldiers have passed through this place. Sometimes I ask myself why you out of all of them stayed behind."

I smile weakly. I don't know.

"Everyone hated the mountain," he goes on talking in his mild way, sending the words into the air like delicate soap bubbles. "The food was lousy, the work was hard, it was always cold, there was nowhere to go to have a good time, and this terrible desert."

"I had nowhere to go on to from here."

"That's not true. They made you fantastic offers then. I remember."

"Are you hinting that I'm sorry for myself?"

"Maybe. Actually — yes. I think that's it. I know you, Yan, and don't forget — we were friends."

"That's over."

"Again that tone of voice. You're still a child, you really are — no, let me talk," he chuckles: that quiet, maddening chuckle again. "I've waited three days to talk to you. Let me talk."

He shifts in his place. Raises his hand in front of his eyes and squints at it, pondering. The silence.

"When we met, we were about twenty. But you were older than I, than all of us, by decades. You knew everything. You knew how to do things. There were times when I felt uncomfortable in your company. And not because I didn't like and admire you; on the contrary — I felt as if I was cheating — that you gave me a lot more than I could give you in return." He fell silent and turned his face toward me. "Do you understand what I'm saying at all?"

I understand. Where did he get this sudden strength from, this flow of words?

"I never imagined we would reach the stage when I would say all this to you, Yan. Such things are spoiled by exposure to the air."

A silence falls between us again. It's cold in the hall, and steam escapes from our mouths as we talk. My mind is like an open wound. The words lash at it, scar it. How long can I stand this? Please, Elisha, stop.

"You taught me new things. You showed me what friendship can be. You took all this for granted, but I discovered a new world. For me, 'friends in the army' meant wisecracks and a laugh in the canteen, and sitting around getting weak and bored, and talking about girls, passing the unavoidable time as painlessly as possible. And then you came, so mature, so knowing and full of scorn, and you — forgive me for putting it this way, but since we're already talking — you simply chose me. That's what I felt then: you lifted me out of the circle I was living in. Remember?"

I remember. The feverish heat now gives way to frequent, prolonged waves of cold. I shiver and hug my knees. His enthusiasm, his eloquence make me feel uneasy one moment, and the next — alert and deeply, irrationally anxious.

"…And I worshiped you, Yan. Actually worshiped you. We were twenty years old. You had such amazing strength — destructive strength. You were even destroying yourself, and it fascinated me. It had something to do with our age, I guess. Nimra used to say that people were afraid of you, not because you trod on corpses, but because you trod on your own corpse. That's what she said."

I say between pursed lips, "And what else did she say about me?"

"Come on, Yan. Don't let it get to you now. She said a lot of things. We were often together, and you were with us all the time. You were the glue and the wedge. I gave up the battle in advance. But I couldn't always take it. There were times when I hated you. A petty, vengeful hatred. Do you ever have feelings like that at all, over here by yourself?"

I do. You don't need people around you to have those kind of feelings.

"Of course you do," he says firmly. "We're almost thirty. If I was introduced to the twenty-year-old Yani now, I would laugh. I would say there's no such animal." He raises himself on his elbows with effort and looks at me. How his eyes glitter in the darkness.

"Nimra's speaking through your mouth," I tell him. "I can hear her saying these things to you." I see that I've hurt him, and I enjoy it. "She never understood. Neither she nor you are capable of understanding what it means to live here on top of a random mountain, knowing all the time just how random it is, and to live alone, in the greatest possible loneliness, even if you're surrounded by hundreds of your kind, to live in despair, when the closest thing to you is a memory of ancient hopes growing fainter all the time, and the constant nagging feeling of having missed out, and a desire that drives you crazy for something that you can't define, that only the dead man in the bushes has any clue what it is." I am raging, shivering with waves of chills, and I let slip things that I shouldn't, but I don't think he understands. "Neither you nor she can understand the daily struggle with the kind of life I lead."

Now I shake his arm hard. I sense that I am hurting him, but I have to inflict this pain on him. "I'm talking about alienation, Elisha. About the fact that thousands of soldiers came and went, and didn't leave anything here. And even I, who once had a friend and a girl here, and a few desires and hopes and heartaches and little joys — I won't leave anything here either, and nothing's left in me. Everything's dying. Even my best memories, my love for Nimra, my days with you. Everything vanishes quickly in this place. Sometimes I think it's something in the climate here. I fight against this annihilation. I fight it tooth and nail, because I'm afraid, afraid, of that casual army camaraderie, of the 'wisecracking in the canteen,' because 'being a soldier' means being alienated. Alienated from the weapons they push into your hands, a friend-within-limits to the men sharing your tent, or your tank, until you part, until you go your separate ways, and when you meet again you won't have anything to say to each other. And alienated from yourself, because you're nothing but an object, for them to do what they like with. And so — if you want to preserve your sanity, be alienated, contemptuous, detached from the pain of transience, protect yourself. It's war — no, don't interrupt me now, I listened to you..."

"But I can't listen to you talking like this," he says angrily. "You're getting carried away in your bubble. You forget there's another side, too — there's alienation everywhere. I know that feeling as well as you do, and I lived among people." Now he sits up with a groan. We lean opposite one another, two islands of human warmth and sweat in the heart of the cold, empty hall. Our voices echo between the walls, thud down the corridors and return to us after a long time, distorted. I feel tremendous excitement, as if I am about to be smashed against the walls into thousands of pieces.

"Your fear is childish," he says to me, "and so is your reaction to it, this weird punishment you've imposed on yourself. An insignificant cry of defiance against an indifferent world. You've shut yourself up here on the mountain — fine! You've grown rough and prickly, grunting instead of talking, bitter, filthy — fine! What good does it do? Who does it help? What's it supposed to mean, for God's sake?"

I rise quickly to my feet. I explode upward, seething with fury, giddy from the rapid movement, trembling and swaying. "Don't judge me! Not you! Don't you dare judge me!"

He is hurt. He was always quick to take offense. From the heights of my upright position, I see his head shrink between his shoulders, as if to defend himself. He was lying: he hasn't changed very much in all these years. Only added extra shells.

"Maybe you're right." His voice is very quiet. I sit down heavily. I want to comfort him. To touch his shoulder. But we are estranged and remote, the dead embryo of an old love. "But I got out of here," he adds, as if talking to himself. "With my fear and my weakness. I'm a coward, Yan. A terrible coward. And you're more of a coward than I am." He laughs. "How amazed I was when she said that to me. Yan — so big, enormous, a mountain of a man, brave, an outstanding officer — and afraid as a child. Hiding up here on the mountain, wrapping himself in layers of flesh and uniforms, armoring himself with hostility and contempt. Afraid, afraid."

I don't answer. What can I say?

"I've known it for a long time, Yan. For a long time I suspected that all your talk about the 'eternal youth' here was a lie. That phony yearning, the sentimental inflation of every banal memory. I saw you in those days, how your eyes caressed every stone, every empty trash can. The love that poured out of you. Wasted love, I thought to myself, love for dead things, narcissistic love. There's no relation, Yan, between the reality that existed here and your sentimental memories, and suddenly — in a flash of illumination — I saw you, your wasted life, the child incapable of growing up, the adult clinging to the child that was. How I pity you, Yan, because there's no truth and no life in the world you've created for yourself here, because you came up here as a boy of twenty and you're leaving as a defeated old man. Without any faith, cynical and alone. Even the two friends you once had — you've lost."

He pronounces the words one by one. I sink into my apathy. And he becomes filled with strength. We are like two communicating vessels. Has it always been like this?

"Nimra..." I whisper weakly. "Nimra will come."

"Nimra won't come," he says curtly, mockingly, with a nastiness I have never known in him. "That's part of your childish game, too." He sniggers nastily again, demolishing me in my weakness.

"Why...why do you think so?" My voice, what is the matter with my voice? It's like a child's voice.

"Because Nimra's gone. Nimra's dead," he says without emphasis, and my heart freezes within me. I knew it. "You don't have to be a genius to work it out," he says. "She spoke about it herself several times. That business with the Arab who was caught with explosives, in Jerusalem. And then Mark Daniel. That was too much, even for her." He is silent for a moment. He draws lines in the dust with his finger. "That's the trouble with you," he says in the end, "with both of you. You set your sights too high. You play for the highest stakes. The alternative is very cruel in such cases."

"I lied to you about Nimra," I say. I no longer care about anything. I want to stay here until I am orphaned. Until I vanish with the mountain. To lean against the green sacks, and cease to be.

"You lied. I knew it. I had a lot of time to think about it, Yan. Three whole days. When you don't eat, strange things happen. At first there's a terrible weakness, and headaches and giddiness. And then suddenly everything becomes light. Radiant. Everything looks sharper. Your senses open. The hunger stops bothering you, and you feel a kind of purity. You're clean and whole. I thought a lot in the past few days, Yan. About you and me, and about her. At first I hated you. You've been tormenting me, and I don't even know why, no — don't deny it now, you kept me in a strange kind of prison, you starved me — no, Yan, don't protest. I know there's no shortage of food on the base. Haim came into the room this evening. He came to call you, and he saw me. He told me."

"Haim? Who the hell is that?"

"Your cook. Peretz. His first name's Haim." He snickers. "And you wanted to fight alienation here?"

I keep quiet. Now I am in his hands. A great fear descends on me. The shards of all my miseries come and surround me. The walls begin to revolve in their strange, slow dance again. Only now do I realize what a fool I have made of myself.

"I've hated you these past days," Elisha continues, and I can hardly hear him, for I have neither the strength nor the will. I know for certain that I will never be able to get out of here to the surface of the earth and the night sky. "And I despised you. Suddenly that marvelous legend, Yani, the prophet of wrath on the mountain peak, who people talk about at reunions in awed, respectful whispers…" He falls silent again and breathes deeply. Then he says, "I can't even be angry with you. I've got a rotten character. I'm always prepared to accept a good excuse. Just say something to me, and I'll buy it."

I shrug my shoulders.

"You know, I could have escaped from here yesterday. I almost did. But I wanted to stay with you, because I don't want you to harm yourself. Because I know that Yani tendency to sink into gloom and despondency, to reject the outstretched hand…"

"Go away, Elisha. Leave me now. Go up. I want to be alone."

He smiles. He lays his hand on my shoulder. "You know," he says, "you saw us as traitors. Me and Nimra and the others. And for a while — when we were discharged from the army, and we came down from the mountain, and you were the only one who stayed here — we really did feel like traitors. Empty. We envied your faith. On the rare occasions when we met we would talk nostalgically about 'Levav' and the good old times, and it was only Nimra, when she came back into my life, who opened my eyes, who showed me how hollow that nostalgia was. Because what did we actually have here? Hard living conditions, boredom and degeneration, and a longing to get out of here. How unjust it is, Yani, for young men and women to rejoice in every day of their lives that's past and gone. 'Another day over,' we would congratulate each other, and we weren't even twenty years old. People our age all over the world were living full, complete lives during those wonderful years, while we were here in the sandstorms, and the thunderstorms, always half starved, afraid of unseen enemies, wasting our lives away in coffee drinking, idle chatter — look, I'm getting angry again just thinking about it…"

"But there was something about it, Elisha," I answer weakly, "something beautiful. If only because it was innocent, it's worth missing."

"Missing, yes. Not wallowing, not addiction." He is quiet for a moment. "You went overboard, Yani. You always get carried away and go too far. You're like Nimra, except that your directions are different."

I chuckle bitterly to myself. In a certain sense, both of us have reached the same place. I lie on my back, my hands at my sides, and stare at the ceiling. Elisha. Nimra. Me. It was all pointless. Even his harsh words no longer hurt me. I listen to the play of the echoes in the long hallways. In twelve hours' time everything will be over for me. Here I will lie until the saving blast comes. I won't move from my place.

But I don't believe that either. I no longer feel in control of my fate, and I don't care. I am weak. How comfortable it feels.

"Come on, Yan. Let's go. It's depressing here."

I open my eyes and look at him. Very heavily Elisha stands up. He raises himself to his knees, then to his feet. He sways slightly, turning white in the darkness. "Elisha," I whisper to him, and he leans over me. His moonface has lost its anger, regained its placidity.

"You've gone bald," I chuckle softly.

"Remember what happens to those who mock Elisha's baldness."

I smile. The hint of a smile.

"Leave me alone, Elisha. What do you care? No one will know."

"Why? To exhaust the process to the full?"

"That sounds like a quote from Nimra."

"Right. Come on, Yan. There's nothing more for us here."

"Nor outside either."

"The game's outside, you fool."

"I wasn't born for this life."

"You're a freak of nature." He laughs and bends over me, takes hold of my arm. "Get up."

"You're quoting her again," I complain.

His hands reach for my armpits, and I stop him for a moment. "Elisha."

"Yes?"

"What happened here? What happened to us?"

He's embarrassed. He averts his eyes.

"Come on, I hate moments like this. Come on."

[1980]   *translated by Dalya Bilu*

UNCLE PERETZ
TAKES FLIGHT

Yaakov Shabtai

UNCLE PERETZ WASN'T AN UNCLE. He was a Communist, and apart from my grandmother everyone predicted he would come to a bad end. His father turned his back on him in anger and disappointment, and the rest of the family too wanted nothing to do with him. If only they could have shut him up in a dark room and forgotten he existed.

Uncle Peretz took no notice of them. He wanted to redeem the world. His brother, Akiva, tried on a number of occasions to talk him out of it but to no avail. He was firm as a rock in his faith, and all the discussions ended in quarrels.

For the sake of the salvation of the world he sacrificed himself with exalted ruthlessness. From the day of his conversion, his warm voice, which once had tenderly sung "Over the ocean and far away/ Tell me, birds, do you know the way?" grew silent. He no longer danced, barefoot and bathed in sweat, at the Working Youth meetings, and he stopped going down to the beach and wandering aimlessly amid the sand dunes and vineyards. He became gloomy and severe, sunk in mysterious activity and angry arguments. With fanatical zeal and hostility, he frequently held forth on the revolution and the freedom of mankind. Only his broad stride and the look of boyish innocence in his blue eyes remained the same, and in the early evening he would still stand on the roof of his house, gazing far into the distance.

He was tall and gaunt, and his hair, which was prematurely gray at the temples, would stand up straight in the wind like a hoopoe's crest. His face was tanned and his fingers brown with nicotine.

As he stood there, intent and defiant and exuding an ineffable air of superiority, it seemed as if he was about to take flight and soar over the roofs of the houses and the Persian lilac and the tops of the sycamore trees into the blue of the sky, where he would perform some great deed.

He remained standing, casting a thin lizard's shadow on the roof tiles while his decapitated head rested on the sand of the yard not far from the dovecote, whose few remaining doves were looked after by my cool-cheeked grandmother. She performed this chore without enjoyment, filling in for my dead grandfather until he came back, even though, for all her purehearted faith, she knew very well that he would not.

When darkness fell Uncle Peretz would climb down from the roof and go inside. The light of the kerosene lamp would fill the little entrance and the room with a shifting, wintry shadow. The shadow stretched over the floor, clung to the furniture and corners and climbed the wooden walls, from which the faces of Marx, Engels, and Lenin looked down severely. Their writings filled the shelves of the bookcase to overflowing, along with other socialist tracts and various propaganda pamphlets published by the Party. They were shrouded in a yellowish brown gloom and looked like tomes written by rabbis or sorcerers. Books and pamphlets also lay on the square table, in the wavering circle of light, and sometimes on the wide iron bed, heaped with two pillows and a thick feather quilt and covered with a blue velvet bedspread.

And in the middle of all this, surrounded by the smell of books and bed linens and the hot smell of the lamp was his wife, Aunt Yona, and she wasn't an aunt, either, but a small, fragile woman put together from slender bones and a melancholy moon-face.

At first her future seemed promising. She knew English and worked as an accountant with good chances of promotion at the exclusive Spinney's food store, where the officials of the British Mandate did their shopping. Her cheeks were rosy and her soft, black eyes behind their long lashes concealed a lively, intelligent smile that only rarely spread and lit up her whole face. She was tender and pure. But from the moment Uncle Peretz decided to redeem the world her future collapsed, and she became a seamstress. All day long she sat bowed over the old Singer sewing machine standing in the corner of the room, a bit of thread between her teeth and the tape measure hanging around her neck.

When he walked in, the house would fill with subdued commotion, as of angels and seraphim racing behind an invisible screen. All her muffled hopes revived, and she was full of fear. To and fro she rushed, handing him a clean towel, a pair of socks, or an ironed shirt, putting away his heavy boots, preparing supper. She did everything with exaggerated caution, fearful of every step, as if one reckless movement or jarring sound might destroy everything on the brink of coming into being again.

Actually, her behavior aroused Uncle Peretz's resentment, but he suffered it in silence and resigned himself to his fate. He did not want to hurt her feelings.

They ate supper in the white kitchen. They sat facing each other with the oil lamp between them. On the table, on plates and in bowls, were fruits and vegetables, various leaves, nuts, raisins and seeds, as well as marmalade or strawberry jam that Aunt Yona made herself. She was a vegetarian, and he had adapted in order to make things easier for her and also to make her happy.

After supper Uncle Peretz usually went to committee meetings. When he had no meeting to go to, he would sit at the table and immerse himself in one of the Party pamphlets or in a work by some socialist philosopher. His face and his callused hands were illuminated, but his back and the rest of his body were in darkness

and the shadow of his head hung high above him, floating somewhere in the corner of the ceiling.

Aunt Yona sat in her usual place on the end of the bed. She
would embroider or do the "finishing off" on her sewing, looking
at him out of the corner of her eye with silent expectation. If only
she had tied a pretty scarf around her neck, she thought to herself,
or worn a necklace like Geula, maybe he would have favored her
with a glance. But once upon a time he would have taken her head
in his hands and kissed her on the eyes without any incentive at all.

Afterwards, when the lamplight began to dim, they would drink
a glass of cold milk and go to bed.

Friday night and Saturday morning were devoted to the Party.
Uncle Peretz would go to public meetings and demonstrations and
come home exhausted and excited. Sometimes a few of his friends
would come around on Saturday mornings for consultations. For
hours they would sit debating with each other in a dense cloud of
cigarette smoke: they would denounce evil, calculate the time table
of redemption, and search for ways and means of expediting the end
and ushering in the brave new world. Yona would bring them bis-
cuits and tea in big china cups, close the door carefully and go sit
in the kitchen.

Outside, on the other side of the flimsy veil separating her from
the world like a white mist, the days passed by like a caravan of ca-
mels. Only the castor oil plant would bloom before her eyes with
bright, purple flowers, produce its fruit, and let it drop to the
ground. And the Persian lilac in Friedman's yard, too, whose scent
would give rise in her to secret longings, and in whose shade she
wished that she could lie down, imagining the pleasant coolness,
the freshness and delight this shade would bestow upon her. If only
she had once said something beautiful, she thought, perhaps everything would have gone back to what it was before and been good
again. And when she thought this, she had in mind the third day
of Passover, which had been a mild day full of dry scents of blos-

soming, and she and Peretz had strolled through the vineyards and the virgin fields to Sharona and beyond. Everything was so alive and benign, and afterwards they had climbed a sycamore tree and as she was climbing down again she had been seized by fear, and Peretz had held her in his strong hands, swept her up and put her down in front of him and laughed.

"Like a crocodile's skin," said Peretz and stroked the bark of the sycamore tree with his hand. Behind his head, through the green foliage, she saw little scraps of sky-blue and trembling yellow sun spots that slowly misted and dissolved, and she closed her eyes.

That was a long time ago, even before their marriage, but she remembered everything: the good smell of his sweat, the hard stubble of his beard, the little patch on the blue shirt he was wearing, the Arab who rode past on a donkey, the embarrassment.

On their way home they met David Roizman. He called them from a distance and afterward he embraced Peretz and invited them to go down to the beach with him. She didn't say anything, but readily Peretz agreed, and she was annoyed.

"And where's Raya?" asked Peretz.

"The parcel's come undone," Roizman replied with a shrug. "The wine's been drunk and the bottle's empty," he added with a wink, and he slapped Peretz on the back and laughed.

Peretz laughed too, but he sounded embarrassed, and she could feel how he was avoiding her eyes. Afterwards there was a silence and suddenly Peretz began to sing in Polish and David Roizman joined in, but her mood was already spoiled. When they approached her parents' house she stopped and said that she was tired and was going home. She expected Peretz to accompany her or at least coax her to come with them. But he only touched her shoulder and said, "Be seeing you," and the two of them turned away and walked down Bograshov Street, singing in Polish.

This episode, together with the feeling of insult and despair that overcame her when she was left alone, she tried to efface from her memory. But they kept coming back of their own accord — when she was sitting like this in the kitchen, for example, listening to Peretz's voice blend with the others behind the closed door. She was sorry, as sorry as she had been immediately after the incident occurred, for not having gone with them, and she reproached herself bitterly for trying to force him to choose between her and David Roizman. That had been a big mistake.

At noon the door would finally open, and they would emerge from the room looking tired and serious, leaving crumbs, pamphlets, pieces of paper, and cups full of ash and cigarette stubs behind them. Uncle Peretz would accompany them into the yard, where he would sometimes linger with them a while before going back inside.

But early in the evening, after a heavy afternoon sleep, a great calm would descend on Uncle Peretz and he would seem like a different person. What he liked best then was to go out for an aimless walk. Taking broad strides, he would lope through the sand with his hands clasped behind his back. Aunt Yona would follow a few steps behind him, dressed in a black pinafore. Sometimes Uncle Peretz would break into a whistle as he walked, as in bygone days. His whistle was as clear and fluting as the warbling of the birds in the woods, and Aunt Yona would look at his straight back and listen proudly and gratefully.

At regular intervals they would visit Grandmother. Uncle Peretz loved her, and so did Aunt Yona. And on the Saturday after she turned seventy they came early.

Grandmother's room, which was shrouded in perpetual gloom, had an air of melancholy and smelled of velvet, mothballs, and featherbeds. The Sabbath was departing, and its departure left an oppressive feeling of emptiness behind it. Grandfather's dark picture hung in the center of the wall, which was painted a ghostly white.

"Good Sabbath and *Mazel tov,*" Uncle Peretz proclaimed in his warm voice and smiled.

"Good Sabbath," Aunt Yona chimed in like a hasty echo and placed her home-baked cake on the oval table. Uncle Peretz set a bottle of wine down beside it.

"Good Sabbath," responded Grandmother and her eyes shone. She thanked them for the wine and cake but only after expressing disapproval at the unnecessary and exaggerated expense.

They drank a toast with Grandmother's raisin wine, and Aunt Yona exclaimed "May you live to a hundred and twenty!" to which Grandmother replied, "Amen, and the same to you," adding, "In good health and with a sound mind and strong heart."

The wine made Uncle Peretz jolly. He poured himself a glass and another glass and began to sing "Purify our hearts to worship thee truly," drumming his fingers on the table as he did so. Afterward Aunt Yona asked Grandmother how she was feeling and what the news from her son in America was, and after Grandmother had replied she sat still and silent as a snail in its shell listening to the conversation between her and Uncle Peretz.

The conversation flowed quietly and calmly. They spoke of health matters and money matters and current affairs in the Yishuv.★ Grandmother served tea and cut slices of cake. She listened quietly and gave her opinion quietly, smoothing out invisible wrinkles in the tablecloth with her thick, brown carpenter's hand as she did so. One thing led to another and in the end Uncle Peretz got onto the subject of the British rulers and the corrupt leaders of the Yishuv and the proletarian revolution that was going to save the world. Grandmother tried to change the subject, but he would not let her. Flooded by a wave of fanaticism, he gripped his glass of tea in one hand while the other waved up and down, one finger pointed threateningly at her.

"Leave off. Leave all that to the goyim," Grandmother interrupted him in Yiddish. "Better you should enjoy yourself in life. Go to the cinema."

"The revolution *is* my life," replied Uncle Peretz sternly, and a vein throbbed in his temple.

Grandmother made a despairing gesture with her hand and shook

★ The Jewish population of Palestine before the State of Israel was established in 1948. [Trans.]

her head with a smile. She was a shrewd woman, skeptical about all forms of extremism. Suffering and poverty had taught her good and bad, and in her own attitudes she kept deliberately to the golden mean. Even in her attitude toward God, in whom she believed unquestioningly, and whose precepts she observed, there was a healthy dose of moderation and consideration for herself.

"Why are you killing yourself, Peretz? All this isn't for you."

"I'm not killing myself. I know what I want and I know what I'm doing. I'm a free man."

"Then do what's good for you," said Grandmother quietly and almost compassionately. "Why do you have to climb up the walls?"

"This is what's good for me!" said Peretz angrily. "The world's rotten. It has to be changed!"

"Are you responsible for the world? Leave it alone. God will take care of it."

"There is no God!" retorted Uncle Peretz nastily. "There is no God!"

"Good, good," said Grandmother, who wanted to put an end to the argument, a faint blush covering her cheeks. "Leave Him alone. At least on the Sabbath let Him rest."

But Uncle Peretz would not agree to "leave Him alone." He stuck to his guns and angrily listed all the evils that religion and its priests had brought upon the world — stupidity, hypocrisy, decadence, and subjugation — and announced that religion was the root of all evil and nothing but the "opium of the masses" and an instrument that served the interests of the ruling classes. In the end he referred her, with more than a hint of arrogance, to the works of Marx, Lenin, and Plekhanov.

"Good, good," Grandmother repeated almost soundlessly, smiling and overlooking the insult until he calmed down.

Grandmother did not consult the works of Marx and Lenin. She felt no need at all to change her views, even if they seemed old-fashioned to some. She was a free woman in her own world. Besides, she was far too busy. Her legs were heavy now and her movements slow. Her days were full. She cooked for herself, went out to do her shopping and visit her friends, cleaned her house, fed the doves with birdseed and breadcrumbs soaked in milk, and prayed.

Aunt Yona was not conversant with the works of Lenin, either, but she did try. Many times, when Uncle Peretz was not at home, she took one or another of his works from the bookcase and tried to read them, anxiety and breathless hope fluttering in her breast. She soon despaired of the attempt. The strangeness and boredom seemed to petrify her brain, and she could not take anything in. Marx, Engels, Lenin, Plekhanov — more than arousing her hostility they filled her with fear and a sense of miserable inadequacy. She was fading away, dying for a single token of affection.

Uncle Peretz calmed down. He ran his fingers through his mane of hair and smiled a winsome, boyish smile. As usual, he swore that he would never get into an argument about these matters with Grandmother again. Grandmother asked him not to swear, since he was unable to control himself in any case. But Uncle Peretz insisted on swearing again and gave Grandmother a hug. A spirit of reconciliation descended on everybody and he began to sing "The Temple will be rebuilt."

Outside it was already dark. And inside the room too. The Sabbath had departed, but its memory remained like a pale square on the wall where a picture had previously hung. Grandmother waited a while and then lit the lamp. Uncle Peretz lit a cigarette and smoked it with enjoyment, after which he stood up and took his leave, and Aunt Yona made haste to stand up with him.

And on their way home, in this empty hour between the Sabbath and the working week, he was seized, as usual, by a feeling of depression as heavy as remorse, a feeling of suffocation, as if he had wearied of all his battles and wanted to rest and be consoled. Now everything seemed exhausting and futile, and for a moment he longed to lay his hand on Aunt Yona's neck and draw her lovingly closer. If only she would bend her head slightly toward him. But she walked next to him wordlessly, afraid of spoiling the mood.

Slowly they approached the dark house. When they passed the mulberry tree he felt an urge to turn around and keep walking for a while. But he did not do so. He continued on beside her, sunk in thought, and by the time they opened the door his heart was already locked up again.

For fourteen years Uncle Peretz devoted himself to redeeming the world, but the world remained as sinful as ever. Only the lines on his face deepened and the books and pamphlets cramming the bookcase multiplied. And then Geula Apter arrived on the scene.

Geula was more than ten years younger than he. After graduating from the Teachers Training College, she spent one year teaching. In the middle of the second year she left her job and went to work as a tile-layer and packer, and after that as a waitress in the Workers' Canteen. For four years she was married to David Roizman, and then they suddenly separated. He went to Alexandria and she stayed behind. Uncle Peretz was attracted to her and intrigued by her. Occasionally he tried to approach her or get into conversation with her, but he never succeeded in exchanging more than a few clumsy sentences with her, and once she appeared to him in a dream.

In his dream they had gone together to see his mother, who was living in a house in Dizengoff Street. It was a fine, warm winter day with a blue sky and a yellow sun, and they were in high spirits. As they approached they saw that the house was gone. On the plot, which was covered with fresh weeds after the rain, all that remained was a concrete platform and a bit of yellow-painted wall. Under the window, which was set in the wall, hung a tin mug. This was the mug used by his father for the ritual washing of hands, and it filled him with aversion. On the platform itself stood a rusty iron bed. He stepped onto the platform and approached the bed, while Geula remained standing behind him. She was playing with a gold coin and waiting. To his amazement it wasn't his mother lying on the bed but another old woman. She was wearing an eggshell-colored dressing gown made of a coarse fabric and something that looked like a surgeon's cap on her head. Her eyes were closed, their lids like two big shells. He wanted to run away, but his heart wouldn't let him. He stood looking at her impatiently, and it seemed to him that she had something she wanted to say to him. He bent down, but she only held his hand with her thin fingers and mumbled his name. When he turned his face away Geula was gone.

This was in the summer, when she was still married to David Roizman. But the affair itself began later, by accident, one day in winter.

All night long it rained, and the rain went on falling at intervals throughout the day. A heavy cloud covered the sky, settling on the roofs and the high treetops, and a cold gray light filled the low space. In the early evening, returning from Shaul Kramer's funeral, Uncle Peretz found himself walking next to her. He walked with his hands in his coat pockets and stared at the sky and the bushes and didn't know how to begin. At the same time they left the others and walked by themselves on the muddy loam path. The ground and the grass gave off an unpleasant chill and the air was heavy and damp. In the end he said something about Shaul Kramer and how death had snatched him unexpectedly, before his time.

"Nonsense," said Geula abruptly. "Everyone dies at his time." and she pulled up a green stalk of grass and stuck it between her teeth.

"Yes," Uncle Peretz agreed, and suddenly he realized that he didn't really understand what she meant.

"And he'd been dead for a long time already," Geula continued. "In his whole life he didn't have a single thing to regret or reproach himself for or long for, not even at night, before falling asleep."

"You knew him well?"

"Yes. A nice guy," she said scornfully and fell silent.

It started raining again — a fine, irritating drizzle.

"It's raining," she remarked, as if to herself, and then she suddenly asked, "Why did you hit David Roizman?"

"What?"

"He told me that you hit him."

"Yes. It was a long time ago. I was drunk."

"But why him?"

"God knows," replied Uncle Peretz and wrapped his scarf around his throat. They walked on in silence, and suddenly he added, "We were friends. I liked him better than anyone else, and I still do. No, I really don't know why. And I've never raised a hand to anyone else in my life. The next day I apologized. It was quite horrible."

The rain fell harder.

"Should we take shelter?"

"Don't you like walking in the rain?" asked Geula and fixed her tired eyes on him, amber-colored eyes with a tiger slumbering in them.

Uncle Peretz smiled with his lips, but inside him something tensed fearfully. He looked at her and wanted to say something, but he was tongue-tied. Again he saw her, the woman who was now walking beside him, with her thick lips and hard chin, tall and shapely, sufficient unto herself and wide open to the world, in her brown leather coat trimmed with black fur on the collar and cuffs and hem, and the Russian hat, it too made of black fur, set jauntily on her head. In her coarse, broad face there was a combination of youth and overblown maturity, and something fierce and desperate that defied definition.

Afterward his tongue was loosened and he spoke, feeling all the time like someone delivering a dull, stilted sermon, but however hard he tried he could not stop and the words rose trembling from somewhere in his chest and tumbled out of his mouth like chaotic columns of refugees. And it went on until they reached the limestone hills.

Down below, at their feet, stretched the sea — gray and brown with fraying ribbons of murky white. It raged and hurled its waves noisily at the deserted shore. The horizon dissolved in the thick fog coming closer and closer. The rain poured down in silent sheets. It fell on the water and the sand and the eroded hills and the black huts and the Moslem gravestones and veiled the distant houses, which receded even further. Everything came closer and receded into the distance. Uncle Peretz wanted to run away, but he went on standing there, rooted to the spot, and the heavy drops of rain came down and bathed his brown face, and a slight shiver ran down his spine.

"Look how beautiful the sea is," he said.

"There's no need," said Geula quietly and pressed her body lightly to his. Her face now looked pure and sad. The fair hair escaping from her hat was soaked with water, and it fell onto her forehead and her shoulders in a tangle of snakes, like the hair of a mermaid rising from the sea.

"Come," she said.

Where to? Uncle Peretz wanted to ask.

Geula went down first and Uncle Peretz followed on her heels. The path was steep and dislodged stones rolled down it. But Geula almost ran, and when she reached the end she leaped onto the strip of sand, where the waves suddenly sprang up and pounced with a roar. A gray cloud of spray floated in the air.

Where to? Uncle Peretz wanted to ask and put his hands back in his pockets.

They set off side by side, but a little apart, their shoes in the wet sand and the water of the sudden waves and the piles of heaped-up shells. From time to time Geula would bend down, pick up a pebble and fling it gaily into the sea.

Uncle Peretz turned his head and looked back. The world had vanished into a vague endless void. There wasn't a soul to be seen and it seemed that nothing existed any more in this murky emptiness but for the eroded hills, the gray sky, the sea, and the unremitting roar.

It's getting late, thought Uncle Peretz and stole a glance at Geula. The chill grew sharper and sank into his skin.

They approached the harbor fence. Geula walked up to the sea and stood at the waterline. Her face hardened and grew ugly. There was something panic-stricken in it. Uncle Peretz stopped a few paces behind her and looked at her. He was tense and his eyes were burning, and the severe chill in the air and the wetness in his shoes and clothes made him feel uncomfortable and sullen. Cold shivers ran down his spine, and something tightened and fluttered in his chest and choked him.

"We should start back," said Uncle Peretz to almost to himself. "It's getting late."

"Are you afraid of it?"

"No," he blurted out and took a step toward her. His face was burning.

"It's frightening," said Geula and came and stood next to him. "It's cold."

It seemed to him that the sea was running toward him, and then that the shore was sliding into the sea, when he placed his lips fearfully on hers and kissed her. He gasped for breath, and only his arms were strong and hard in their embrace, as if he wanted to crush her to him in a vice.

"Be blind," murmured Geula and kissed him passionately on his eyes and on his forehead and his temples and his throat, and pressed herself to him as if she wanted to enter into him and find shelter in him, "Be blind and old," and her face grew blurred.

The wind blowing from the sea slapped their skin like wet sheets. Slowly and languidly Uncle Peretz stroked her damp hair, but the chill and the grains of sand sticking to his fingers made him feel sullen again. He opened his eyes and looked at the darkness and thought that it must already be late.

The way home lasted forever.

"To sleep," mumbled Uncle Peretz to himself after parting from Geula. "To sleep." and he made his feet go faster, treading stealthily as a thief. It seemed to him that he had parted from her too abruptly, and the thought upset him.

He entered the house on tiptoe. In the kitchen the lamp burned with a low flame and his supper was waiting for him on the table. He drank the cold milk and went to take a shower. The jet of water took his breath away. It was cold as the blade of a knife. But nevertheless he went on standing in the dark cubicle and let it wash over him again and again.

Aunt Yona was invisible. She had merged into the darkness. But her feathery breathing, innocent as a baby's, hovered in the room.

"She's sleeping," thought Uncle Peretz in relief.

A warm feeling flooded him. Now he wanted to be as good as he possibly could to her.

"It's late," she said.

"Yes. I was at a meeting."

And as he stretched out on the bed he compassionately placed his hand on the quilt covering her shoulders and lay down beside her, his heart full of goodwill and his eyes wide open, but his spirit insisted obstinately on roving back to Geula and the sea.

"No," Uncle Peretz swore to himself and moved closer to Aunt Yona.

"Is anything the matter?"

"No. Go to sleep," he said and turned over onto his side.

The next day he went to the Party. He was apprehensive, but the comrades greeted him as usual. Accordingly, his apprehensions were dispelled and he felt full of happiness and gratitude. But the meeting dragged on and on, and his mind kept clouding over and his thoughts wandered far from what what was being said there and attached themselves to the figure of Geula rising up before him in his memory, and he followed her.

I'm tired, thought Uncle Peretz to himself, and he tried to imagine what she was doing now. *She's probably sleeping*, he said to himself and felt a certain sense of relief. *It's already late*. And he tried to rouse himself and shake her off.

In the following days Uncle Peretz resumed his normal way of life. He went on studying Plekhanov's essay "On the Role of the Individual in History," but from day to day he felt himself sinking deeper into a foggy absentmindedness. He was obliged to read clear, simple sentences over and over again, word by word, sometimes aloud, before he was able to take them in. And then he would discover that they were dull and flat and awoke no echoes in his mind. But he kept on reading stubbornly, grim and haggard, even though by the time he reached the end of the page he had already forgotten what was at the top of it. If not for Aunt Yona sitting on the edge of the bed in front of him, he would have closed the book and left the house.

Five days later, Uncle Peretz saw Geula in the street. She walked past in her brown leather coat and Russian hat, crossed Ahad-Ha-am Street and turned into Nahalat-Benyamin. He wanted to rush after her, but he stayed where he was and watched until she disappeared. The next day he went to her house.

When Uncle Peretz climbed the stairs he was overcome with anxiety, and he felt like turning around and going home again. He knocked gingerly on the door and waited. There was no answer, and he hoped that she was out. After a moment he knocked again.

"Why did you come?" said Geula, having just gotten out of bed.

Uncle Peretz smiled in embarrassment and mumbled something and fell silent.

"I knew you'd come," Geula softened and took the hat off his head, saying, "What a funny hat," and put it on her own head, saying, "No?" and put it back again. "I was afraid you wouldn't come," she said suddenly, in a different, serious tone and seized his hand and held it tight. "I dreamed about you," and she leaned her head on his chest as if she were afraid.

"This is a nice room," said Uncle Peretz, letting his hand rest on her neck for a minute.

The room was small — nothing to write home about. It had four high, yellow walls and a tall, barred window. Nearly half the space was taken up by a double bed made of iron, which was in a state of total disarray. On the pillow lay an open book, upside down. Opposite the bed were two plain chairs, and a square table pushed against the wall. In the corner stood a water jar.

"Sit down," said Geula and tidied the bed.

"Who's this?" asked Uncle Peretz, pointing to the photograph lying under the glass covering the tabletop.

"My father."

"He looks young."

"Yes. He died young," said Geula with a smile and glanced at the photograph and at him. "Don't run away," and she went out of the room.

Uncle Peretz sat down on the edge of the bed and picked up the book. Geula came in and stood combing her hair in front of a little mirror. She saw his head bowed over the book in the mirror and she said with a sad, mocking smile:

Once upon a midnight dreary,
    while I pondered, weak and weary,
Over many quaint and curious volume
    of forgotten lore —
While I nodded, nearly napping,
    suddenly there came a tapping,
As of some one gently rapping,
    rapping at my chamber door,
'Tis some visitor,' I muttered,
    'tapping at my chamber door —
Only this and nothing more.'

"Go on," said Uncle Peretz.

"I don't remember any more," said Geula, pulling the book out of his hands and throwing it onto the bed.

"What a pity."

"Never mind. Come on, let's get out of here," and she took her coat off the peg.

Uncle Peretz glanced at the window and saw that everything was already dark.

They went outside and entered a little restaurant. A yellow light illuminated the walls, which were painted halfway up in green oil-paint and hung with portraits of the leaders of the Yishuv. Uncle Peretz chose a corner table and sat down with his back to the street. He ordered two salads and two portions of fried fish.

"If you love me, eat your egg," said the woman sitting near the counter to the little boy. He refused and burst into tears.

Geula laughed. She ate with relish and with slow movements of her hands. She had slender wrists and long fingers. Uncle Peretz looked at them and glanced occasionally at the owner of the restaurant, who was leaning on the counter and reading a book. From the bulb hanging right over his head dangled a brown ribbon of sticky-paper, covered with the flies that had fallen into the trap.

"That's horrible," said Uncle Peretz.

"They're flies," said Geula argumentatively. "Why shouldn't we kill them?"

"Let's go," said Uncle Peretz after they'd finished drinking their tea, and they stood up and put on their coats.

It was a clear, cold evening. They walked up Sheinkin Street, turned into Rothschild Boulevard and went out into the vineyards and virgin fields. What Uncle Peretz really wanted was to say goodnight and go home.

"Oh, what a night," said Geula and opened her arms, with a kind of reckless, desperate gaiety in her tired eyes.

The white, metallic light of the moon filled the landscape. Everything was still, with a delicate, misty radiance in the air. Sounds receded into the distance, as if they were happening somewhere else, behind transparent barriers. Here and there trees loomed up, like frozen puffs of smoke spangled with a harsh, silvery glitter.

The ground gave off a chill and sharp smell that mingled with the warm smell of her coat.

"Slowly," Geula implored, "slowly," and the expression on her face, which was wild and distraught, gradually gave way to a trance-like concentration, very still and dreamy and relaxed, which spread through her entire body.

"Don't leave me," begged Geula. "Don't leave me."

"I won't," whispered Uncle Peretz firmly and tightened his embrace, and as he did so he felt everything focusing and thrusting inside him, and afterwards he went limp and felt nothing but emptiness and weakness. And after that he grew calm, and he wrapped her in his coat and she rested her head on his chest.

The gray light of morning came in at the window. Aunt Yona lay in bed without moving. She lay on her back and slept, and only her head, which was sunk in the pillow, peeped out of the quilt. Her eyes were hidden beneath her large, closed lids. For a moment it seemed to Uncle Peretz that she wasn't breathing, and he bent over her. Her eggshell-pale face seemed very tired to him and old.

He took off his clothes and threw his shoes into a corner. His perspiration dried and the chilly air in the room made him shiver. He longed to lie down and sink immediately into a deep sleep. The room made him angry. And so did Aunt Yona. And Geula.

Aunt Yona opened her eyes and turned to face him. A feeling of hostility overwhelmed him. He was seized with a desire to tell her, to smash everything in one harsh sentence, and to go away.

"Your food's on the table," said Aunt Yona quietly, closed her eyes and pulled the quilt over her shoulders.

He paused for a moment, and then went up to the window, stepped into the kitchen, came back into the room, turned over Plekhanov's book, and went back to the window. Then he sat down carefully on the edge of the bed and took Aunt Yona's feet, which were always cold, between his hands in order to warm them, and all the time the sentence went round and round in his head and trembled on the tip of his tongue.

The light outside grew a little brighter, and Grandmother's doves cooed. Strange birds flew past his tired eyes, and dark lumps floated in seas shrouded in a cold mist.

It has to be done, Uncle Peretz exhorted himself, an immense weariness, like that of a hangover, making his body heavy and stupefying his senses. In the end everything was swallowed up in this weariness, except for one word that kept going round and round in his head without stopping, *Geula, Geula.*

Genia's baby began to cry, and Uncle Peretz opened his eyes and glanced at his watch, and got up and went into the kitchen, and made himself a cup of tea, and put on his white house-painter's overalls, and went to work, closing the door quietly behind him.

Winter departed and spring arrived. Next to the kitchen window the castor-oil plant bloomed, and in the Friedmans' yard the Persian lilac bloomed and gave off an overpowering scent. Aunt Yona put the thick feather quilt and the winter clothes out to air, and Uncle Peretz was beside himself.

Immediately after work he would change his clothes, grab a bite to eat, and go out. Aunt Yona would watch him until he disappeared between the houses. Only then she would turn back to face the empty room and examine it for a moment with a puzzled look. The table was littered with the socialist books and pamphlets that he had not looked at for weeks and that she did not dare return to the bookcase, or even move aside to make room on the table.

With a hurried or perhaps frantic air, Uncle Peretz would trudge through the sand, walk up King George Street to Allenby, go down Nahalat-Benyamin, turn into Herzl, and then wander aimlessly up and down streets and alleys with his hands in his pockets and his eyes straying over the pavements and the walls and the passersby without coming to rest on anything. From time to time he would glance at his watch, which Aunt Yona had once bought him for his birthday.

The time passed tortuously between desires full of anxiety, thrilling fantasies, and reluctance. He longed for Geula and at the same time he hoped that she would not be there, until he heard her voice behind the door and he saw her, and she was afraid and aban-

doned herself without any reservations, like a solitary ship with all
its sails unfurled, borne along unknown currents, buffeted by strong
winds, seeking shelter. Her sensuousness, her sensitivity and painful,
bitter despair together with her sudden bursts of joy captured his
heart like deserted courtyards, old stone houses, ancient palm trees
and places that lay beyond the sea. There was something touching
about her, and everything held a mystery and the flavor of a different freedom.

They sat in little restaurants and wandered in narrow, deserted
streets. Geula would link her arm in his, rest her head on his shoulder, and keep step with him. Sometimes she pulled him toward the
boulevards, but Uncle Peretz preferred her room and the fields and
dunes and orange groves. There he would sing and warble and whistle and hug Geula and kiss her. Once he gave her a lecture on the
differences between the idealist and materialist approach, and the
importance of human praxis, and freedom that was the recognition
of necessity. She made an effort to pay attention to what he was
saying, like a little girl at school, and he asked her if history and the
future of the world and the Yishuv in Eretz Israel interested her.

"No," said Geula and snuggled up to him.

"Never mind," said Uncle Peretz and smiled.

"Mayakovsky committed suicide," she suddenly remarked gaily.
"Would you commit suicide with me?" she added provocatively,
and when he remained silent she continued to insist, "Well, would
you?" and her face grew very serious. "Would you?"

Uncle Peretz laughed lightly and placed his hand on her head.

"Why?" he said gently. "Life is good, isn't it? Don't think about
such things."

"You're wonderful," said Geula and laughed. "In any case we're
dead already. Just twitching a little."

Uncle Peretz kept quiet.

"Will you marry me?"

"Yes."

"Then now. Not tomorrow. Today," said Geula and looked at him expectantly. After a moment, she added, "Oh, if only you were old. Very, very old."

When they were in the fields she liked to gather white snails and try to coax them out of their shells. She would go on urging them until they poked their transparent horns into the air of the world. Usually she would lie on the grass, with a stalk between her teeth, and she could lie there like that for hours without moving. But most of all she was drawn to the sea, especially when it was dark. The darkness of the sea and the noise of the waves held her spellbound, calm and full of awe.

Sometimes they would go to the Eden or the Gan Rina cinema, and Uncle Peretz would maneuver it so that they went in after the lights went out.

"Are you afraid?" Geula once asked him.

"No. Why?"

"You are afraid," she said, and gave him a hostile look. "But you're a free man, aren't you?" she added mockingly.

"Let's go inside."

"No," she said, crushing the tickets furiously in her hand, "you can go in by yourself." And she threw them on the ground.

Without a word, Uncle Peretz bent down and picked up the tickets.

"Love me. Love me," pleaded Geula as if she were pleading for her life, and she buried her head in his chest and wrapped her arms tightly around his neck, as if hanging on to him so as not to be swept away into the abyss. "Love me. However you can, but love me."

Summer came. Geula took off her coat and sweater. Her long arms grew tanned, and her hair bleached in the sun. They spoke of marriage.

Uncle Peretz knew what he had to do, he did not doubt it for a moment. In actual fact, he felt that he was no longer the master of his fate, and apparently had not been so ever since meeting Geula, and this feeling made him happy and gave him the authority to do what had to be done. He was only waiting for the right moment, and at the same time he was also hoping for a miracle, of whose nature he himself was ignorant, but which would let him off the hook.

The days went by and the miracle tarried.

Aunt Yona asked no questions and dropped no hints. She pickled cucumbers in big glass jars and made strawberry jam and pined away with an air of nobility and reserve, busy and harassed, sewing and cooking and cleaning the house. Her slightest movements and actions filled Uncle Peretz with resentment and irritation, but he bottled them up inside him. In her presence he was gloomy and taciturn, perpetually restless and ill at ease. He seemed sunk in thought, as if he were not there but somewhere else. And then, on sudden impulses, he would bring home flowers for the Sabbath, take her to the movies, help her a little with the housework, and once he bought her a purple silk scarf. Aunt Yona's eyes shone with joy, but she hardly thanked him, and only stammered a word or two, even though she was so grateful to him. All that evening Uncle Peretz felt benevolent and relaxed, and after supper he sat and read *Marxism and Empirio-Criticism*. The text itself did not awaken any interest in him, but the mere fact of reading it gave him pleasure.

The heat increased. The fields and empty lots were covered with yellow grass and dusty thorns. Lizards scuttled between them. There was a smell of figs in the air. Geula reproached him and upbraided him, with pleas and scorn and love. She would give way to despair and rise again, be glad and miserable, passionately abandoned and estranged. Sometimes she would braid her hair and put on a new dress in his honor, and sometimes she would go about as dishevelled as if she had just gotten out of bed.

"Soon," Uncle Peretz promised, "in the winter."

"Why the winter?"

Uncle Peretz explained and promised. He spoke constantly of his love. With all his heart he desired Geula. But the words lost their vitality. Suddenly they sounded forced and brittle. A depressing atmosphere of parting began to dominate their meetings and conversations, together with a feeling of barrenness and hopelessness. They grew sullen, heavy and tortuous, like all things when people no longer believe in them but only in the power of a blatant lie. Again and again they went to the places where they had first been together, and to new places, too, but everything remained arid and even became indecent.

Only sometimes, unexpectedly, brief, dreamlike interludes occurred. Thanks to the power of desire and illusion the world would fill out around them again for an hour, and Uncle Peretz would give his imagination free reign and create the lives that would be theirs before long, after they were married.

"And we'll go to Ireland," said Geula.

Her long fingers played with his hair and stroked his neck.

"Yes," Uncle Peretz agreed, feeling joy and longing.

"You'll never do it," Geula would suddenly burst out and her eyes grew very tired.

"I will," promised Uncle Peretz imploringly and clasped her to him.

"Never. You're so careful not to come to any harm," she said painfully, "and you want so badly to be a good man and you haven't got the strength to hurt anyone or the ability to give anything up. When will you be a little bad?" And her face grew hard and ugly. He wanted to say something, but he felt that it was all useless, and slowly he took his hands off her and turned his eyes to the ceiling.

"Give us a chance," begged Geula the next minute, snuggling up to him and kissing his face and his lips passionately and desperately, as if she wanted to suck out his soul or breathe a new one into him.

Uncle Peretz recoiled.

"Come on. Let's run away."

"No. I'll do it. Soon. It will be all right. I'll leave her."

"If I wait for you, I'll have to wait until kingdom come. Oh, if only you were old."

And when he got home he would see Aunt Yona. He hated her, but on no account did he want to hurt her. On the contrary. He wished that she would die.

The first rains fell, and again the air was fresh and the sand gave off a good smell. Geula waited, but in her sleep. For days on end she lay in bed, huddled under the thick winter quilt, and slept. Even when she got up in the afternoon and went to work, or when she let him in and gave herself to him, she seemed to be fast asleep. As if everything was happening without her.

And Uncle Peretz came and went. He felt that the deed was ripe and that he could do it easily. All he had to do was lift his hand and tear the web of delicate threads in which he was trapped. At the same time, however, he recognized, however unwillingly, that something, a kind of big ball of cotton wool, was restraining him, and that somewhere, in the center of the circle, a bubble of impotence was spreading and the hour of grace was gone.

I'll do it, Uncle Peretz would swear frantically to himself, and for a while he would believe it too. He simply could not resign himself.

Now he began feeling hostile toward his comrades in the Party, whom he would frequently meet and with whom he would exchange a few tortuous remarks, and also toward the members of his family, especially his mother and his brother Akiva. He did not hide this hostility, which was only strengthened by his occasional moments of contrition. Every now and then he would drop in on Grandmother, exchange a few words with her and go away again. He hoped for a sign from her but was careful not to disclose his predicament, except in obscure hints.

"Some people jump into the sea and try to swim, whatever the consequences," he said to her once in the middle of a conversation.

"The ones who want to," she replied seriously. "But not everyone wants to."

"No. You need courage."

"You need to want to," said Grandmother in Yiddish and looked at him with eyes full of sympathy, "but you don't have to want to." And after a moment she added, "Courage sometimes means standing still and doing nothing."

"No," said Uncle Peretz, disappointed. "You need courage."

Grandmother gathered the breadcrumbs scattered over the table and pressed them with her finger and kneaded them into a little ball.

"You don't love her anymore," she said suddenly, "only the memories and what you think you could have been."

"No!" said Uncle Peretz vehemently, and he sank into a silence that Grandmother made no attempt to break.

That night he dreamed he was walking down Lillienblum Street by himself. He wanted to pee and looked for a convenient place. Suddenly he heard someone calling him from a big building in the process of construction. It was David Roizman, who was standing there and peeing. He went and stood next to him, but as soon as he began the head of his penis tore and fell off. It didn't hurt or cause him any surprise or fear. As if he had always known that it was going to happen one day. All he felt was discomfort. David Roizman offered him a handkerchief to mop up the blood and said jokingly, "He who spills his seed on the ground," and laughed.

Geula packed a bag and traveled to Tiberias and from there to Jerusalem. This was at the beginning of spring. On the door of her room he found a hastily scribbled note, "To my beloved, a good, honest man." For a moment he stood there in front of the locked door, and then he tore the note to pieces and went out to wander the streets. As he walked he made up his mind never to see Geula again, and after an hour or so he went home and stretched out on the bed. Aunt Yona gave him a glance, and without saying a word she went into the kitchen and sat down to supper alone. When Geula returned Uncle Peretz was waiting for her at the railway station. He was unsmiling, full of tension and gloom. Geula waved at him from the window and when she dismounted they stood on

the crowded platform and embraced. Then she linked her arm in
his, and he led her away.

Evening was falling. The streets were filling with shade and people, and there was a feeling of relief in the air. Uncle Peretz asked
her how she was, and Geula told him about her trip. Aimlessly they
wandered from street to street: Jaffa Tel-Aviv, Herzl, the Commer-
cial Center. Spicy smells wafted from the shops and the warehouses, cooking aromas and smoke. Geula's face was beautiful and
her spirits were high. She seemed really happy to see him, but he
was silent. He felt tired and remote.

"Did you miss me?" he wanted to ask.

A merry chiming of bells came closer, immediately followed by
the appearance of a black horse-drawn carriage.

"Shall we go for a ride?" asked Geula.

"Where to?"

"It doesn't matter," she said and waved her hand.

"To Jaffa," she said to the Arab coachman after they had mounted
and seated themselves on the soft velvet seats, under the black canopy that almost touched their heads. "Kings of the earth," laughed
Geula to the sound of the bells, and snuggled up to him.

"Yes."

When they were close to the harbor the driver stopped the
coach and asked them where to go from there.

"Go back," said Geula.

They got off at Nahalat-Benyamin, and the bells chimed mer-
rily again until they were swallowed up in the distance.

"Did you miss me?" Uncle Peretz wanted to ask.

Geula laid her head on his chest and nestled against him. As they
walked she played with his fingers and then she took his forefinger
and middle finger and passed them over her lips. Something yielded
and thawed and delicate webs were woven again in the agreeable
dimness of the evening air.

"Are you tired?"

Geula shook her head. Again he sensed how lost she was and how much she needed his protection, and he was flooded by a warm, paternal feeling.

"Like this forever," he said to himself and kissed her on her head.

They turned into the market. The main street and the alleys were deserted, and the stalls were bare as gravestones. Everything was dirty and squalid, with a pervasive stench of fish and rotting vegetables and puddles of stagnant water. Uncle Peretz wanted to turn into Sheinkin Street, but Geula pulled him in the direction of the sea.

"Look at it," cried Geula and freed herself of his embrace.

The sea lay in front of them heavy and thick as a paste of lead. But for the lapping of the ripples as they reached the shore there wasn't a whisper to be heard. Uncle Peretz laid his hand on the nape of her neck, as if he wanted to hold her back.

They went down to the beach, took off their sandals and started walking. The soft cool touch of the sand was pleasant to their feet. Geula's steps grew light and joyful. She paddled in the shallow water and laughed.

Like a little girl, thought Uncle Peretz, and at the same time he felt that her laughter was strange and no longer belonged to him, and he was seized by an urgent desire to grab hold of her and hold her tight and stroke her head.

"Come here. Feel it."

He walked next to her, a few steps apart. At times he wanted to stop and talk to her, make promises, vows, but he couldn't quite open his mouth.

"You're old," teased Geula and splashed water with her feet, "but I'm even older than you."

After the Red House, she stopped.

"Let's swim."

"It's cold."

"Never mind. Look at it. It's calm enough to walk on," she said and took off her dress. "Come on, Peretz, come in with me," and she entered the water.

"Wait."

"Come on," Geula said and waded in deeper. "The water's warm."

Uncle Peretz got undressed.

"There are rocks here."

"Come on!"

He walked into the sea and stood still. The water reached his knees and sent cold shivers up his spine. He dipped his hands in the water and ran them over his face and chest.

"Come on! It's good!" cried Geula. "There are horse stables there!" She pointed, arm outstretched, at the clouds resting on the horizon.

Uncle Peretz took a few more steps and stopped. More than that he did not dare, and perhaps he did not want to, either. In any event, he was a poor swimmer and the sea was now completely dark.

"Come on, Peretz. Let's swim," her voice came from a distance.

"Come back! There are rocks there! Be careful!"

Geula laughed out loud, but her laughter was full of pain and desperation, and fear of the fathomless dark depths of the water. Then silence fell, and Uncle Peretz stood there looking, and it seemed to him that he could see the outline of her head floating farther and farther out to sea. He waited a little longer, and then he walked back to the beach and got dressed.

One month later Geula Apter sailed for Vienna. She sailed in the morning, and suddenly everything stopped.

Uncle Peretz came home from work and his face was gray and stony. He put his tools down and went out. Like a spider blinded in both eyes he stumbled lost through the streets, which were no longer his, treading with alien feet on the skin of an alien earth. The air did not touch him and his eyes did not see the views or the people, only the dazzling mirror-glitter of the sea somewhere at the end of Yona Hanavi Street.

The following evening he went to see Grandmother. She was busy praying. "…by thine abundant mercy animating the dead; supporting those that fall, healing the sick, setting at liberty those that are in bonds and performeth thy faithful words unto those that sleep in the dust," she whispered. From the small house rose Genia's voice, singing to her baby:

"Round and round the cranes will fly,
Above the grey fields in the sky…"

Uncle Peretz waited a while and went away. Friedman's stupid dog fell on him barking, but he didn't lift a hand to chase him away. Hairy feathers whirled round in front of his eyes and sank down, and a flock of startled crows flew out of the foliage of the sycamore tree. They glided through the air cawing loudly.

A week later, when he came home from work he went up to the roof again. When darkness fell Aunt Yona came out. She waited a while, then went back inside. An hour later she came out again. Up above her stood Uncle Peretz. She invited him to come in and eat his supper, but he did not answer her or give her so much as a glance.

The next morning he came down and went to work. In the afternoon he came home and went up to the roof, and after that he hardly ever came down again.

The summer intensified and the days lengthened and grew heavy and incandescent. Lizards appeared and the scent of the sycamore trees filled the hot air, together with the smell of the smoke from the fires where cauldrons of laundry were boiling in the yards.

Uncle Peretz grew lean and his skin, burned by the sun, grew dry and hard as parchment. His blue eyes, which were wide and staring, grew increasingly clouded from the smoke and the dust and the bright, glaring light. His hair grew down on his forehead and neck like coarse sheeps' wool, tangled with dry leaves and stalks of grass borne on the blazing wind. Sometimes he would suddenly break his silence with a few parched whistles that sounded as if they were coming out of a cracked reed. Toward evening, in the slow twilight, he looked like a wicked tin bird.

Aunt Yona would emerge from the house at regular intervals and invite him to come inside and eat. She would coax him gently, in a wheedling voice.

"I'm taking flight," Uncle Peretz would finally snap in a dry, threatening voice, and Aunt Yona would say nothing and go dumbly back into the house.

If only she had said something, she thought to herself, or done something when he took her feet between his hands, perhaps everything would have been different. But she had been very tired, and besides, however much she racked her brains she could not think of anything she might have said or done then to please him.

I'm taking flight, I'm taking flight, Uncle Peretz would repeat firmly and endlessly to himself, raising his eyes to the depths of the sky. "I'm taking flight." And he still could not make up his mind if the sky was the firmament into which one flew or the abyss into which one fell.

He never saw Geula Apter again. At first he clung to obsessive hopes and her image would accompany him with a terrible pain from which he could find no escape. She accompanied him like an animal, until he could even smell her skin and hair, and he would talk to her and tell her things he had never told her when they were together. But gradually, as the days went by, her image fell to pieces, grew blurred, disintegrated, and disappeared. Now Geula remained to him only as a deed left undone. He despaired without giving in. And as the summer drew to a close and he was scorched and short of breath, Aunt Yona emerged from the house holding a bowl full of wholesome leaves and seeds. Her feet were as cold as ever, but her face was warm and there was something fresh and tender in it.

It was their wedding anniversary, forgotten and ignored for years, and from the minute she woke up she was enveloped by a feeling of freedom and festivity, like the feeling of a Sabbath morning at the beginning of spring. She opened the shutters, tidied the room, returned the books to the bookcase, spread a floral cloth on the table, put on her white dress with the red polka dots, and tied the purple silk scarf around her neck.

"Come down to eat," she said in a voice that was gentle but not meek, and looked at him standing there stiff and bitter, surrounded by silver vapors. "Come on, Peretz, come down to eat." And she held out the bowl, and even tapped it with her finger. "Look what I've got for you. Nice seeds. Come down to eat."

Uncle Peretz said nothing, but he lowered his head a little and looked at her in bewilderment, and something in his face seemed to be thawing and acquiescing in great agony.

"Come on. Come down to eat, Peretz."

His Adam's apple rose and fell.

"I'm taking flight," responded Uncle Peretz stubbornly, but there was a note of supplication in his voice.

Silence fell, broken only by the sound of Aunt Yona tapping twice on the tin bowl without thinking.

"All right, then, take flight," she suddenly blurted, in a frightened but firm voice.

Again there was a silence, in which even the movement of the warm air between the leaves on the mulberry tree was audible. The smell of the sycamores hung heavy and suffocating.

"I'm taking flight," repeated Uncle Peretz, and raised his head.

No. Don't — Aunt Yona wanted to shout. But she didn't say a word. She just stood looking at him with compassionate, wide-open eyes, eyes that saw the end.

If only she closed them for a moment, perhaps everything would go away like a bad dream.

Uncle Peretz appeared to be hesitating. Something seemed to have slackened inside him. Maybe he was still making up his mind. Only his Adam's apple pointed, sharp as an arrowhead.

Aunt Yona took a step toward him.

"Come. Let's sit down to eat together, Peretz," she wanted to say. "It's our wedding anniversary today." But at that moment Uncle

Peretz stretched and quivered slightly. Then he spread out his arms and opened his mouth wide.

The chill crept up from Aunt Yona's feet to her thighs and her back. And more than fear she felt sorrow, sorrow at the waste and sorrow at the ending. But also a kind of relief, like the relief that had filled her on that third day in the week of Passover when on their way home, before meeting David Roizman, he had sung "Over the ocean and far away" for her. If only he had said one frank word, the thought crossed her mind, or if he had done one true deed, however cruel and hard and painful, then perhaps he might have been redeemed, even if his redemption lay in sin and suffering.

But Uncle Peretz neither said nor did anything. He refused everything. Stubbornly he raised his head and fixed his eyes, in which there was no more innocence but only dust and ashes, on the empty summer sky, and his face was frantic and haggard and mean. He flapped his arms limply, and suddenly, as if pushed by a rude hand, his shadow moved and dove into the yard, which was lower than the firmament and the sycamores and the Persian lilac and the roofs of the houses and the castor oil plant, and it disappeared into the fine golden sand, which was mixed with dry leaves and dove feathers and pieces of coal left over from the fires.

This happened before the dovecote was pulled down, when a hot desert wind was scorching the land.

translated by Dalya Bilu

SMALL CHANGE

❖

Yehudit Hendel

Nobody on the street could believe he'd sold his magnificent stamp collection. They said he must have bought land, houses, shops, diamonds. There were stamps worth four carats, they said. Maybe five, they said. Afterward, when his only daughter, Ruthie, whom he called Rutchen, disappeared, they said that with one stamp she could have taken a trip around the world; and when she came back, her eyes white and her skin green — it seemed a little strange to come back like this, with white eyes and her green skin, after a trip around the world — they said maybe it was disappointment in love, maybe she went looking for a husband and didn't find one, maybe a trip around the world wasn't such a big deal. He welcomed her with a growl and Mrs. Klein, who saw her come home, said she went in without a purse, without a suitcase, her coat over her shoulders, and she suddenly seemed shorter in the shoulders, as if her shoulders had caved in. As it happened, I saw her too, hunched, wrapped up like a parcel, holding her raincoat with both hands, as if she were naked under the coat, dragging lopsidedly along the street in the wind and standing outside the house for a long time, leaning on the stone fence without going up. And then she pushed herself forward as violently as if she were pushing a freight car.

And then we heard the growling and it was clear that they weren't expecting her, that they didn't know. Afterward we kept hearing it from our window night after night — long, strange, unending, like a moan, or like the sound of his bus in the morning when it wouldn't start. We couldn't hear what he said, only Gerda's silences moving back and forth in the window all the time, while he hardly stood up, just sat there bent over with his chin on his belly and the growl coming out of his belly.

As for the true story, it broke into the street in small, low waves, accompanied by little laughs from Mrs. Borak and Mrs. Klein and Mr. "Everything Cheap" and the rest of the neighbors. By then the growling had already stopped, and Gerda — a stick-like woman who stood for years leaning against the door until she became part of the door itself — now sat at the table for hours, picking at the little pink flowers on the oilcloth. He said that soon there would be nothing left to pick at, and what she would pick at would be her fingers. Yeah, my fingers, my fingers, she yelled.

And then came the evening when all the lights suddenly went out and only her scream rose from the dark house: Small change doesn't burn, doesn't tear, what burns is a human being. That's what Mrs. Borak said, but Mrs. Klein said she screamed that it was all because of the small change, all because of the small change. To tell the truth, I was at home then and what I heard was a kind of dry crackle spilling into the darkness, and when I went to the window he was standing there, on the balcony, in the dark, grunting like an empty barrel.

Have you ever seen an owl's eyes? said Rutchen. He was cursing, that was a curse. You couldn't even make out his body in the dark, only his voice and his eyes, as if his voice were coming from his eyes. She smiled a pale smile. Have you ever felt as if someone's voice was coming out of his eyes? She smiled a pale smile again. And do you know what he said? she said. He said small change is like a human being, you have to bury it, he said, you can only finish with it in the ground. The pale smile spread over her whole face, making it suddenly look small. His eyes never moved, she said, and in the night they were white, you understand? She looked at me with her head thrown back, her hand moved up to her throat. Her face took on a stubborn look, as if trying to understand but not coming anywhere near understanding. Of course you can't burn small change, she said.

This was already after everything and after the funeral, and Gerda was already sitting on the balcony in the evening again, picking at the green oilcloth, her face the color of roasted coffee. We sat on a bench in the park at the end of the street. It was a nice evening. There were hardly any people in the park, and it was quiet, with the slow pulsing of the revolving sprinklers and the water spreading in big, expanding circles. She said: It was like him, what drove me mad was the small change. I told her that for years we had watched every night. She didn't even smile. What can you see from the window, you can't see it from the window, she said. I said that for years we had watched him wrapping the stacks and sorting. Oh, she said, that's nothing, not even the beginning. She spoke slowly, there was fear in her voice.

Yes, I said, we would watch him from the kitchen window wrapping the small change in tinfoil. Every night we saw the little columns wrapped in tinfoil.

Oh, the towers, she said, there were towers of fives, towers of tens, towers of ones. He said it wasn't the size that counted or the amount, what counted was something else, and that's what he said about the stamps, too, and about life, too, really. She suddenly drew her head and her face was suffused with dark spots like ink spots. They looked transparent, spreading into her skin like ink into paper.

She looked at me for a long time.

It's not what you think, she said.

I didn't say anything. I didn't know what she meant. She looked at me again for a long time and laughed a quiet, violent laugh that made the ink spots under her skin grow bigger. That's where I first saw the monster, she said. Her words sounded familiar and I said that everyone had a little monster in some window or other. She laughed quietly, violently, not listening. The truth is, it was there long before that, the monster was there long before that, she said and looked at me for a long time, as if looking through me at some empty, unidentified place behind the bench. I said there wasn't any monster in the window. And then I said that he was simply counting small change. When he met me in the street he said so. He said that in the morning a man needs small change.

Her laughter expanded now, making the ink spots under her skin grow even bigger.

Yes, she said, in the morning a man needs small change, every day he said that to me, when I was still a little girl he said that to me, he said that the most expensive stamp in the world was a penny stamp.

Her faced turned purple, cross-hatched like a rash of thorns. She was silent for a moment, then she laughed dryly. He couldn't have guessed, she said, he couldn't have guessed that it coiled like a snake, that it glittered all the time, it moved all the time, he couldn't have guessed, he thought that all at once the riddle had been solved.

I didn't ask which riddle.

And that's what killed him, she said. Her voice sounded depressed. You think it was my revenge, oh no, but then what was it? You think I know what it was? The depression in her voice increased. Look at the trees, she said.

I looked at the trees. There was a magnificent light on the trees on the slope, wrapping them in ribbons of radiance that broke up into a thousand coins of silver and gold, cascading in long trains down the tree trunks and the mountain, and all at once the mountain turned into a moving heap of coins, the grounds and the trees and the walls of the houses and the roofs and the car bodies and the high greenness of the treetops further down along the line of the boulevard. Everything gleamed. Everything moved. Everything came apart in one mad rush as if it was spilling out of some huge basket, and in the radiant, dazzling light all you could see were the holes of the net from which this hail of coins was pouring, a hail of silver and gold that became a molten surface, turning the mountain into a steep wall of coins, a gleaming dancing wall of faces and branches and masks and letters. It lasted a moment. Maybe an hour.

The wall swayed. The mountain shook. Above the mountain, the horizon line was sharp, rigid, petrified, and the sky was narrow, alien, compressed into a long rectangle, into a closed box, and for a moment I nearly panicked, for a moment I said to myself that I too had caught the disease. The sky looked closed, stood apart from the celebration. But the mountain was still full of coins, everything was still rushing down, everything merged, everything ran together, gleamed in wildly scribbled lines and crooked contours, everything flew. And then suddenly the gold turned to brass, the silver to lead, and the huge leaden coins came pelting down on the mountainside as at the beginning of winter, as in a terrible storm.

You see? said Rutchen. She sounded so excited. You see? she said.

It seemed to me that I understood what she meant. It seemed to me that the light waves were turning into sound waves, and I said to myself: Look, look, I've caught the disease. It seemed to me that some mechanism had broken down into vague elements, everything that belonged to earth, fire, air, and water, that belonged to thoughts and fears, and I said to myself: The mountain's full of coins, Rutchen. Oh Rutchen, how quickly the gold turns to lead, how quickly it turns to zinc. I said to myself: Of course, I saw the hail, the faces, the people, the tree trunks, the gold scales on the tree trunks, the snakes, the old letters, the old kings, suddenly I remembered her, a little girl, walking round the rooms opposite us, saying short nervous words, words without endings, swallowing the ends of words. I remembered: To go to another country, to go to another country. I remembered: And I was left naked and bare. I wanted to tell her that you couldn't just pack your things, that it was a bad idea. But it was quiet now. The light calmed down. The radiation began to shrink, became infra-red. Among the trees there was only a few matches burning now, and afterward floating on top of the mountain a small dark copper stain turned blood red.

Terrible, she said.

Her face was swollen and you could feel the slow burning blush of shame.

Yes, he loved it, she said, to see how it shone, to see it in piles, he arranged it in piles, the whole house was full of piles, he called them towers, maybe they really were towers.

I didn't ask towers of what.

That's what I understood before I left, she said.

I looked at her leaning against the arm of the bench. Now, too, I didn't ask what. The light was going down, falling on the roots of the trees, making them glow at the bottom of the trunks, at the meeting point with the earth. It was hard to tell which way the wind was blowing, if it was coming from the mountain or the sea, but you could clearly see how it was shaking the trunks right down to the bottom, shaking the grass and the tops of bushes and the leaves and the black tunnels between the bushes with a loud commotion. But we were alone there in the park. That's what I understood before I left, she repeated. She asked if I knew the story about the cat. I said that I hadn't known the cat. She said: and he blamed mother, he said that she loved the cat too much, that's why the cat took liberties and that's what happened in the end. It jumped on my stamps, he said.

I asked what kind of stamps he had collected.

She said he had collected stamps with faces, with birds of prey, and anti-Semitic stamps. Later on he exchanged the faces for birds of prey. Later on he exchanged the birds of prey too and he was left with only the anti-Semitic stamps. He had the biggest collection of anti-Semitic stamps.

I asked what anti-Semitic stamps were.

He had rare ones, she said.

I asked for an example.

She said he had a postcard with a stamp of a Nazi horse stamping on the globe and she remembered the date, he looked at the date every day, it was on October 19, 1942, and there was a postmark without an address, *Europische Post Kongress*, and he said, that was before you were born, Rutchen, but it will go on to the end of the world, it will go on as long there are people in the world.

She was speaking fast.

Those were his words, you understand? Then she said that he had a copper-colored stamp of Hitler with the postmark April 20, 1944, *Grossdeutsche Reich General Government*, and a stamp with Stalin's head, a beautiful green-black stamp, Stalin's head in the middle and on the right the English crown, on the left the hammer and sickle, and 1939 written on top of the English crown, 1944 on top of the hammer and sickle, and at the bottom it said, *This is a Jewish war.*

She was still speaking fast.

This is a Jewish war, get it? Then she said he had a bright red stamp, really blazing red, also with Stalin on the left and the King of England on the right, and he looked at this stamp too, every day, he turned that page every day, he couldn't go to sleep without looking at that page, she said. Then she added that she always looked at his hands when he was holding this page, she didn't know why she did it, but that's what she did.

She was still speaking fast.

After he sat with this stamp he closed the album and put it in the cupboard. And then he began preparing the small change.

Suddenly her eyes filled with tears.

It's just incredible, she said.

I asked her what other stamps he had.

Anti-Semitic ones you mean, she said gleefully. She said he had a stamp issued by Khomeini in honor of Sadat's assassin, and the Egyptians had quickly bought up all the stamps from all the collections in the world, the whole series, so that there wasn't one stamp like it in the world, and then he decided that he had to have one. He searched for a whole year long, and he finally found one in Canada, in Montreal, and he bought it — a black-and-white stamp, the murderer in a white robe in a window of black sky, laughing inside the black sky, and when he got that stamp he said again that it's a story without an end, it never ends, and he began talking about the English penny stamp again, the most expensive stamp in the world worth three million dollars, a penny stamp.

She rubbed her forehead, making signs as if to a deaf-mute, pressing against the back of the bench. That's it, she said, and then he sold them, he traded them for small change.

All at once her face turned white, fixing me with a glittering, violet eye, and now I clearly saw him sitting on the balcony, half naked, hairy as an animal; I remembered his strong, tyrannical hands, the wine color of his eyes, the little squares with swift horses in the wind, winged horses, naked archers shooting at the sun and birds choked by snakes, and I remembered him, a short man with a rounded head sitting all summer every summer, bent over the bright pages as if sharing in some hidden secret, as if drawing closer to the pulse of the world, and by then the Formica table had long ago been transformed into extraterritorial ground, long ago become an island in international waters. And he, as keeper of the seal, cataloging, sticking, removing, transferring, sometimes peering up close without moving, sometimes slapping his knees in excitement, and it gave off a sweet smell, said Rutchen, it gave off a faraway smell, the page looked like a big map of the sky, and bent over, without raising his head, without a word — sometimes arranging the pages by subject and sometimes by place, sometimes according to generations that suddenly seemed short-lived, the continents shrunken, Cuba next to Mecca, Titus's arch next to the black stone, and you could find Genghis Khan next to Jesus, Napoleon next to Cyrus the Great, and it gave off a sweet smell, said Rutchen, it gave off a faraway smell, and what was fascinating were the teeth and the corners, she said.

I looked at her. She too had short clumsy hands and the same wine-colored eyes, and I suddenly felt a kind of compassion. She looked at me. Her face said something about the wolf never changing his ways, and that was what I thought all the time she looked at me. She said that Gerda thought they should keep them in a safe, it was enough to steal one stamp, she said, but he said that stamps were like bread, you have to have them on the table everyday.

Suddenly she looked at me suspiciously. What were you just thinking of? she said. Her eyes were on me, empty, very close, and I told her I had just remembered the story about how some people were buying a plot of land from an Indian and he asked them, How high and how deep are you buying? She smiled painfully. I told her the Indians wrote the word Earth with a capital letter. She stared at me with dark eyes and smiled painfully again, and I told her that I had once met an Indian in Arizona near the Grand Canyon, not far from the red cave city, and he was naked and he was red, and instead of a fig leaf he had marvelous blue turquoises hanging between his legs, strings of marvelous little blue rocks instead of fig leaf, and he told the story, Earth with a capital letter, he said.

She didn't take her red, swollen eyes off me. A strange smile, more like a grimace, crossed her face. That's it, she said as if she were saying something terrible.

He was a bus driver. Since he always worked the morning shift he got his small change ready every evening. First thing in the morning, he said, a man needs small change. No one was surprised that he always worked the morning shift, and for years, at four o'clock in the morning, we heard him turning on the light in the stairwell. Then we heard him go downstairs. And then we heard footsteps in the empty street and the bus engine groaning, and then came the silence, and we knew that Mr. Shlezi had driven off. Sometimes, in the summer, when the windows were open, we also heard the bread popping out of the toaster. He always wore sunglasses, even in winter and in the rain, and I sometimes saw him trudging down the street in the rain, short, small, the two round black spots dripping on his face, walking with his hands on his stomach, his broad hands putting a strange kind of pressure on his stomach, or suddenly stretching his body, swelling, and making a dash for the huge waiting machine. He liked distances without horizons, said Rutchen, he liked to see up close, what was happening on the road up close, the telegraph pole was far enough, drivers who looked too far ahead were accident prone, he said, and to tell the truth in forty years he never had an accident. Like in the New Testament, the

innocent had to die guilty, he said, that was what happened on the
road, the innocent died guilty on the road.

But the bus no longer stood in the street then, and it was already
after he had sold the stamp collection and the whole house was
filled with small change in little stacks wrapped in tracing paper and
thin tinfoil, in all the cupboards and all the tables and all the draw-
ers and in the kitchen too. It was in boxes and in suitcases, and by
then he wasn't doing anything, only transferring the stacks, smoothing the paper and turning it over, and then closing and folding, and
then pressing it down. He smoothed the paper and pressed it down
on every stack, and then he wrote it down. He had a special notebook where he wrote everything down. The size, and the amount,
and he never counted, said Rutchen, he knew with his eyes without
counting, he could see in the dark and he knew, and nobody was
allowed to come near, she said, mother never went near, and they
didn't talk about it, she said, they didn't ask, mother never asked, she
only looked, and gradually her face swelled up, gradually her eyes
grew small and she turned blue, she said she had ants in her fingers,
afterwards she said it was the rustling of the paper that had got into
her fingers, and at night they really did swell up, she said, and they
looked exactly like stacks, round, swollen, with transparent skin the
color of silver, but he said that there was nothing to be afraid of and
it was shut up in the cupboards, it was all shut up in the cupboards,
he said.

The idea came to her by chance, of course. By chance she heard
in the street that the Israeli lira was the size of a two-franc piece,
and in Zurich there were vending machines that turned two francs
into small change. There were some Israelis, they said, who put liras
into the vending machines and got out two francs in small change.
It looked good. It was after the currency was changed, but she was
sure he hadn't thrown out the liras, she was sure even before she
went looking. And then she went home and looked in the cupboards. And after that in the linen boxes under the beds. And in the
chest. And behind the books. And in the vases. There were rolls of

half-shekels. Of shekels. In the end she found the liras. She identi-
fied them without opening the paper. There was nothing simpler,
she said.

On the first day it worked perfectly. She did it in the vending
machine of a giant department store. The store was crowded. There
were people rushing around her all the time, but there was no waiting line for the vending machine. The people rushing around apparently didn't need the small change, and in the evening she strolled
along Lake Geneva and ate a fat sausage with mustard. Afterward she
sat in a café on the lakeside and licked a huge helping of ice cream.
And then she went right down to the bank of the lake and sat. It
was a silvery night. It was already quite late. Swans floated on the
water, illuminated in the transparent silver light. They had no heads
or necks, only bodies moving in the water, floating quietly in a
quiet movement, like shining black coats moving over the waves.
Their silky fathers gleamed, their heads so enfolded in their bodies
that they looked the wrong way around, floating in the direction
opposite their bodies. The man sitting next to her said: There's
nothing to be afraid of, they fold their heads into their bodies to go
to sleep. He was sitting with a box of pears and she gave him a bit
of small change and he gave her a few long slender pears dripping
with golden juice, and she sat and looked at the headless swans and
ate the golden pears, and the next day she went back to the vending machine and the next day, too, there was a lot of traffic and people dragging boxes of merchandise from the storeroom and back
again, but she inserted a lira into the slot and pressed and then she
inserted another lira and pressed again, and in the end her hand was
full and sweating slightly and she put the money in her purse, but
her hand, empty now, was still sweating. The purse suddenly felt a
little heavy on her shoulder, dragging her shoulder down, but she
inserted a lira into the slot and pressed and instead of a faded old
lira, her palm was full of small change again, pretty shining Swiss
money, really pretty, only her palm was a little sweaty and she
thought perhaps she should stop. Perhaps she was a little tired and

she would go and buy herself something to drink. She opened her purse and put a little scent on her sweaty palm and emerged from the corner where the vending machine was and two women came walking very quietly on either side of her, coming very quietly closer to her body until she almost felt their bodies pressing against her on either side and said excuse me I'm in a hurry and they squeezed her body a little and said please come with us and pushed her slightly forward with very slight pushes toward the walls which were painted a quiet pale green color and the air in the long quiet corridor was warm and pleasant and there was pleasant music playing and she wanted to ask where they were going, what they wanted, but she didn't ask, urged forward by the slight pushes of the very quiet women who didn't say a word and pushed her slowly with little movements of their elbows into a side room at the end of a corridor. A nicely furnished room that was also painted a quiet pale green color with an executive desk and an executive chair with a lightly rocking man on it whose head turned in all directions as if he was a strange gigantic doll and the two women said please sit down. But they didn't wait for her to sit and they sat down with little movements of their elbows with the same light, imperceptible movements of their elbows with the same light imperceptible pressure on a pale green leather chair and remained standing very quietly on either side of the chair, leaning on her lightly, on her body, and isolated voices were heard here and there in the long corridor and the sound of very pleasant music reached her ears.

It was very pleasant music, she said.

There was a pause. I waited for her to go on but she was silent, staring right into my face. Her voice was pale, monotonous, as after years of silence, the sentences more and more unfinished, more and more erratic, more and more absurd, and it was impossible to tell if her story was about to end or had just begun. Her face, which was white, looked thin now, and she held her head pressed hard against the bench, elongated, thrust rigidly backward, like a person standing with his back to the wall.

After all, she said in a loud sudden voice, without continuing.

Now too there was silence. I didn't ask her after all what. She said: And then I remembered the packets in the hotel, the stacks rolled up in tinfoil with a twist at the top, the way he did it.

The corners of her lips rose as if to smile, but instead of smiling they twisted into an ugly grimace, stubbornly examining my face. Her own grew sharp and venomous.

Suddenly I understood, she said.

She looked at me again, still examining my face.

I mean I thought I did, she said. Her speech was still sudden, abrupt, as if a petrified stratum of memories had suddenly been jolted.

Now too there was silence. The two of us were alone in the park. Lines of fire were still running over the lawn, down where the air had reddened on the snakeskin at the bottom of the tree trunks. Then a wind blew up, tossing among the dark bushes. There was a strong smell of grass and wilted blossoms, a smell of cut-down trees and gouged trunks, of rotting roots. Then the air turned into smoke creeping over the ground. The backs of benches were the color of marble and behind every bench stood a barrel of dynamite. Rutchen did not take her eyes off me, examined me suspiciously. Her pupils dilated with a solemn light, the kind of light where everything suddenly splits open the world splits open, is torn apart inside, lit low down like a low fire, full of patches and ropes and pieces of iron, and in every voice a mighty orchestra sounds. Suddenly I remembered how in Nesher, in the factory, I once brought a huge thermos to my uncle, my father's sister's husband, on the night shift. It was a hot night, and he was standing in the furnace room, covered with dust, leaning on the iron bar attached to the furnace, barefoot in the heaps of iron, his curly black head a pile of dust and his face too, slowly opening the thermos and slowly gulping down the cold lemonade and explaining something about life to me between gulps, and that life is like an iron bar, at first the bar gets hot but it doesn't glow, its rays are infra-red, when the temperature rises it begins to glow, at first the glow's dark red, then light red, then yellow, then it turns white-hot and after the white comes the blue, the violet comes at the end, what comes after the violet is invisible, its like the stars, he said, red stars are cold, and I'm an electrician, he said, I'll die of electric shock. He died of an electric shock.

I told her. She asked me why I had told her. I said I didn't know. She studied me suspiciously again.

Naturally, she said. She asked me what his name was.

I told her.

She asked me what he was like.

Nice, I said.

So was Papa, really, she said. She asked me if I knew his name.

I said no.

She gave me a shocked look.

Naturally, she said again. Then she asked what we called him.

Shlezi, I said.

She said: That's a pet name you know.

I said that we were fond of him.

She gave me a shocked look again. Mama never called him by his pet name, she said.

I didn't ask what she called him.

Can you understand that? she said. Her eyes, which looked tired, suddenly filled with blood, as if there were nothing left there but a scar, like a brand, and after a minute she went on with her story, speaking at the same rhythm as before, as if she had never stopped. The man on the executive chair asked her where she was from. She said from Israel. He said he knew. She felt she had said something wrong. Close to her, very close, on the chair revolving next to her, rocked a women whose face was in different places all the time, not looking at her but sticking into her from different places all the time, and someone from somewhere at the side said: *Ja, aus Israel.* The woman on the swivel chair, whose face kept revolving in the air, sniggered: *Ja, aus Israel,* and then she sniggered again, and her snigger grew smaller and smaller, narrower and narrower, the wider

the revolutions on the giddy chair. The man whose voice was coming from somewhere on the side said: *Ja, immer aus Israel, das wissen
wir schon,* and the woman on the revolving chair sniggered an even
smaller and narrower snigger, revolving on the chair in the same
monotonous and merciless rhythm that slightly twisted her lips,
and Rutchen kept watching her lips, saying to herself, She has dark
narrow lips dead lips. That was what she kept saying to herself over
and over: She has dark narrow lips dead lips, and from the crowded
department store came the sound of doors opening and pleasant
music. She tried to reconstruct what had happened but she was
absolutely unable to reconstruct what had happened. There was a
sound of movement from the executive chair facing her and she
said to herself: He's talking to me he's asking me something, but
she heard only the sound of doors opening and the pleasant music,
she felt the soothing pale green of the walls touching her skin the
quiet steady vicious hatred and a kind of absolute emptiness inside
her body inside the deep memory of her body, but opposite her
on the chair the revolving head kept on with the *immer aus Israel*
and she heard her own voice asking how long it would take. The
man's voice coming from somewhere on the side said: That we
don't know. Next to her, close to her, very close to her, in the air
next to her, the woman's head revolved, decapitated, floating in the
air above the soothing pale green of the chair and the soothing
pale green of the walls and the absolute emptiness inside her body
inside the deep memory of her body, and still it was all just a bad
joke but already she heard her own voice in a low terrified shriek:
How long? She shrieked in terror and close to her even closer to
her pressing even closer to her body, the woman's decapitated head
went on revolving on the chair in the same slow monotonous
merciless rhythm and the man's voice coming from somewhere on
the side said: That we don't know, the decapitated head was revolving right in front of her now and she terrified she shrieked again:
But how long? The man on the executive chair repeated with his
quiet smile: That we don't know, and by now she couldn't see him

either, only his face floating detached over the chair as if in a horror movie, and the quiet steady vicious hatred, the absolute emptiness inside her body inside the deep memory of her body, and she
had no time to think yet but time enough to feel the fear, light,
and weightless, sinking her body.

They asked for her purse. She put it on the table. A moment passed.
The man waited. Then he opened it. Then he turned it upside down
on the table and the small change piled up on the table, gleaming
Swiss coins, coins of ten and coins of twenty. He counted them in
silence. He asked if that was all. She said that was all. He asked for
her shoulder bag. She gave him her shoulder bag. Her hands shook.
A sound stirred on the chair opposite and she sensed her hands
shaking and the man on the chair looking not inside the bag but at
her shaking hands. She looked at her hands too. They looked big,
they looked bigger every minute, shaking as if they had Parkinson's,
like her father's father shook with Parkinson's and they couldn't
stop the shaking till he died. She saw him lying on the floor shaking after he died. She saw it clearly now. Suddenly her hands looked
to her like his hands. She remembered them shaking alive on his
corpse. Suddenly a terrible idea struck her, it struck her forehead
and pierced her skull and came out the other side like a savage drill
boring into her head deep down inside her skull. She couldn't stop
shaking.

The man held her shoulder bag and looked at her hands.

Ja, he said and overturned the bag.

First the folding umbrella fell out. The little make-up bag. The
red comb. The packet of colored pencils she had bought there that
day. The round green mirror. And then there was a clattering sound
and a pile of one lira coins fell out.

The man in the chair opposite her didn't move. He raised his eyes.
Then he dropped his eyes. Then he put the coins down one by one
on the table and counted aloud. There were twenty-one. He asked
if that was all. She said that was all. He asked what she was doing
with them. She said her father collected coins. He asked why her

father collected coins. She said she didn't know. He looked at her. He waited.

That I don't know, she said, sitting without moving, the Parkinson's hands on her knees. She lifted them into the air, so that they wouldn't be stuck to her knees, but they went on shaking in the air alien, big, almost gigantic, detached from her body, immense uncontrollable hands, like two long swollen stuffed hands hanging there on her body. She tried to stop the shaking, which only increased the wild twitching. Suddenly she remembered inserting a coin into the slot and then the click. And again the coin and the click. And the metallic chill on her palm and the sweat.

The man in the executive chair kept his eyes on her Parkinson hands all the time. He asked again why her father collected coins.

He said that a man needs small change she said.

She didn't know how she said it. She felt as if a horse had kicked her when she said it.

Natürlich, said the man on the chair.

He spoke to me without turning his head in my direction and he was very quiet all the time, he didn't look at me to hear what I said, and I didn't hear what he said only his voice and afterwards a different voice, in the opposite direction of his voice and when I turned around the voice stopped talking and the hunt began.

And maybe I didn't turn around, she said.

Suddenly she fell silent.

My head aches, she said.

I said maybe we shouldn't talk about it.

She looked at me in astonishment.

What? she said.

I said maybe tomorrow.

Oh no, she said, pressing her eyelids as if she had only just realized that there was a terrible pain there. Her eyelids were inflamed. The things I dream, she said. I said everybody dreams. She said: And the places I go. I said everybody does, everybody, the sense of falling, the giddiness, the monstrous roads, and I said that everybody

runs into steep tunnels, hangs from cliffs, and the birds of prey. She
said: What do you mean, the birds of prey? I said that last night, for
example, I dreamt there was a bird of prey on the lintel of our door
behind the wall. I saw it clearly coming out of the wall and I wanted
to scream: There's a bird of prey in the house, there's a bird of prey
in the house, and then the wall closed up.

She looked at me in astonishment.

Last night? She said. She asked if I'd read about it. I said that once
I read that contrary to what most people thought they didn't fly
swiftly when hunting their prey, the hunting was done in slow flight,
and I told her that I'd read the most impressive hunting method was
the one where the prey was caught in mid-flight, in the middle of
the sky, in this hunting method the prey was totally exposed, it had
no place to hide and nowhere to escape to. The hawk, for example,
I read, was good at pursuing birds in open spaces and it fed on songbirds, so it was very active early in the morning, because that was
when songbirds were found.

She looked at me in excitement. Songbirds? She said. There was
passionate desire in her voice. She asked me about the speed. I said:
Three hundred miles an hour. The golden eagle, for example, dove
on its prey at a speed of three hundred miles an hour. She asked
about the vulture. I said that the vulture, which fed on carrion, cir-
cled its prey like a huge butterfly. It advanced in hops with its shoulder feathers bristling and its wings spread as its thick beak prepared
to tear the skin.

She was still looking at me passionately. You've forgotten that Papa
collected stamps with birds of prey, she said in excitement, stealthily
wiping her eyes, and then pressing her eyelids hard, examining me to
see if I was listening. He had a wonderful collection of birds of prey,
she said. Her white face was now illuminated by the light from the
lamp that had gone on behind the bench — thin, childish, very like
the face I had seen for years in the golden light of the room facing
our window. And for a moment the years were wiped out, the dra-
mas, catastrophes, screams and fear, the lost albums, and all that was

left was a little girl sitting alone in a room illuminated by lamplight, asking about birds of prey, staring at me and saying: Songbirds? Songbirds? Lifting her little girl's face, looking out of the window. And the courtyard was swarming with pimps, prostitutes, respectable lawyers, respectable businessman, swarming with cats and dogs, shoe-shop owners and furniture-shop owners, groaning, coming, going, buttoning, unbuttoning, and I wanted to say to her: Yes, at a speed of three hundred miles an hour, Rutchen, three hundred miles an hour. I wanted to say to her: Vultures, Rutchen, because of the wind are attached to mountainous regions and they have very keen sight, eagle eyes, they can locate a carrion thirteen miles away, from thirteen miles away their eyes can trap a dead bird.

They were waiting for Herr Zutter. It took time. The man in the arm chair laughed contemptuously. He said: How slowly the wheels of justice turn. The woman in the chair laughed too. Just then Herr Zutter came. His eyes were alert and he looked straight at the table. Her shoulder bag was lying there, open and empty, and the money was in a neat pile. He asked something. She repeated that her father said a man needs small change; in the morning, he said, in the morning a man needs small change. Herr Zutter sniggered. Then he said that she must be careful, she should be careful because from now on everything would be written down. She didn't answer. He waited a minute. She didn't answer. Her feet were sweating in her shoes, but she sat still, frozen without moving. It seemed to her that she heard the sound of footsteps dragging slowly in the corridor, but nobody in the room said anything and nobody moved and only the quiet soothing pale green walls began turning round and round as if powered by a machine. She felt she had to stop the machine, but the heads on the chairs were also turning round and round, her own gigantic hands, the backs of chairs, the curtains, the ashtrays, the comb on the desk, the pile of coins, and the other hands in the other corners of the room, other walls behind the chairs. She pressed her hands hard against her knees. Anyway, anyway, she said. She said it in Hebrew, frightened because she said it in Hebrew, and suddenly the walls stopped turning, the emptiness in her body gripped like a vice, the pale green color quieted down, the man in the arm chair opposite turned up the volume of the radio, smoking, and she felt the light touch of terror, sitting, as if in a dream, sliding silently and surely into the abyss. And then she heard Herr Zutter. He said she should hurry up, it was late and it was a long drive, and she should really hurry up.

It was raining, she said, but my throat was full of dry crystals like beads of hail.

And we drove in the police car, behind the iron grill, she said, and it was a really long drive. When they stopped she got out. There was a big house. They told her to inside and hurry up. Everything happened in a hurry. She hurried up. There were long corridors with doors and more corridors with doors. The corridors were empty and you could hardly see the walls only the doors and they opened a door and led her in. Herr Zutter asked for the bag. She gave him the bag. He told her to get undressed. Then he told her to wait. Then he took the bag and went out and locked the door. There was a chair and she got undressed and sat down in the chair. Time passed. The room was empty. The cold of the chair burned her skin and she sat and looked at her body as if at some strange animal.

Time passed. She went up to the door. The door was locked and she went back to the chair. Again time passed. Her hands stopped shaking. Now they were small, unnaturally small, almost like a child's hands. She felt a terrible shame, sitting in the empty room, on the chair, looking at her own body, feeling something, she didn't know what, turning into a concrete, meaningless thing. Her father appeared in a flash. She heard him say: The disgrace, she saw him from the depths of her back. Oh no, it's different, she said. Her skin prickled. Time passed. Again time passed. She felt her body becoming hollow, felt his weakness and wildness and idiocy in her blood. Everything whirled in a crazy vertigo, the stupidity that had led her

astray, and the disgrace, from here it would begin again, the disgrace, humiliated, humiliated, the terror that made her jump, the
hand griping her shoulder — it was a policewoman who made her
stand up and felt her all over her body, felt her skin, in every corner, all over her skin, as if she had coins hidden under her skin.
Then she ran her hands over her once again, groping and turned
around without a word and went out of the room and after that
another policewoman came in and told her to get dressed and take
off her watch and her rings, and earrings, and she took them off
and put them in a heap on the chair but the policewoman said: The
watch, the watch too, and she took off her watch but the policewoman said: And the little ring too and she pulled the little ring
but it wouldn't come off and she said: I've had it since I was a little girl, but the policewoman said: Everything, everything left on
the body, and she brought soap and rubbed and then Herr Zutter
came and said they were leaving and they got into the armored car
again behind the iron grill again in the rainy streets in the evening
coming down on the beautiful bustling city and the gleaming lights
in the grand shops and cafés and she said: Everything's open, its still
early, and Herr Zutter said: Yes we have to be there before four because the examining magistrate leaves at four and she said: I haven't
got a watch, they took my watch away. He didn't answer. The rain
hit the roof of the car. She asked where she was. He didn't answer.
She asked where they were taking her. He didn't answer. And she
said: Oh God it's not rain it's a storm, it can't be anything but a
storm and would Herr Zutter please turn around just once. He
didn't turn around even once.

What shall I do, she said.

He didn't turn his head.

Sign a confession. Here in Switzerland you have nothing to fear.
When someone confesses and repents we let him go.

She said she was afraid.

He said: Here in Switzerland you have nothing to fear. This is a free country. What we hate is a lie. Nobody in Switzerland has ever been punished for the truth. What we can't forgive is a lie.

She shivered.

What our judges hate is a lie.

She shivered.

He said: If you tell lies you'll rot in jail. For the truth we send people home here, understand?

I remember his back, she said, he didn't turn his head, what I remember is his back. He had a brown leather jacket on and I remember his voice coming out of the leather jacket. That is what I advise you to do, he said. He had a soft voice, actually, a woolly voice. It seemed to me that his leather jacket was made of wool.

You should know that the law is always right, he said and smiled, looking at her now obliquely, a look that spread like threads over her body, sticking to her like a spider and tightening in threads around her body.

Have you ever seen the way a spider works? That was how his eyes worked, she said. And then the fear came back to her, pressing on her throat.

I hope you haven't got any more on your body, he said. And then he said he hoped she didn't have any more in the hotel. She said she didn't. He didn't ask the name of the hotel. She said he didn't. He didn't ask the name of the hotel, and only his eyes spreading around her body, and then the crazy idea came to her, then she asked if they had already passed the square where the gold was buried. He asked what gold. She said: the Paraden Plaza, where the safes were, her grandfather had one too. He asked where her grandfather was. She didn't answer. He said he was sorry, Switzerland only looked after the gold. He asked what the connection was. She said there wasn't one. He laughed a little. And it's impossible to open of course, that's the code, the secret, he said. Again he laughed a little. You have to understand, the whole world understands, he said. He turned around slowly to face her. And you stole from the Swiss government, you simply stole from the Swiss government, you'd better remember that, he said. And besides, I know that they changed the currency in your country, he said, and you came with the old money. His eyes glittered when he said this. I only want your own good, you must understand that, only your own good, he said.

After that there was a long corridor with only the other person sitting in it a strange hulking boy with strange wild eyes making savage noises. He had a shirt painted in shining colors, all peacocks with their tails open, and peacocks tattooed on his wrists. He asked her what she had done. She didn't answer. He laughed a mean laugh.

You didn't kill anyone, he said.

She didn't answer.

He said: You stole something in a supermarket, you stole panties in a supermarket.

She didn't answer.

For panties in a supermarket you rot in jail here, he said. The Swiss hate it when you take panties from their supermarkets. It's a big deal for the Swiss, panties in a supermarket — just don't lie, they'll tell you.

He fixed with his eyes and the mean laughter burst out of his whole body which shifted nervously in the chair.

And they took me in, she said. The clock on the wall said four. The Examining Magistrate said he was supposed to be home at four-fifteen and his wife didn't like him to be late. He would have to phone and tell her he was coming late. Of course, said Herr Zutter, and the Examining Magistrate phoned his wife that he'd be ten minutes late because he had a little problem here. After that he said something and typed on a typewriter. She didn't hear what he said, only the typewriter, looking first at his typing hands, and then on the wall above him, with posters of Klee and Mondrian and a still life with a guitar by Braque. The Examining Magistrate typed rapidly and she answered the questions and said *Yes, yes* looking at the Braque guitar all the time. He said they would have to get it over quickly and she understood that if they got it over quickly the little problem might grow even littler, and in the window the blue was cobalt and she said to herself that soon she would be lying on her bed in the hotel and looking at the ceiling and tomorrow she would get on a tram and ride and ride and ride all day. The cobalt blue became ultramarine. Silence fell. Again she repeated to herself what the Swiss liked was the truth and what they hated was lie, and Herr Zutter said say *Yes* and she said *Yes*. Repeat after me, said the Examining Magistrate. And she repeated after him. He asked if she had anything to say. She didn't answer. You have nothing to say, he said and asked if it was necessary to translate because he was in a hurry. She shook her head, no there was no need to translate, but the Examining Magistrate said it wasn't enough to shake her head it was a written report and she had to say *Yes* to go into the report and she said *Yes* to go into the report. Her jaws were swollen. Her cheekbones hurt. And she felt her neck swelling and its volume expanding every time she said *Yes*. She tried in vain to stretch her neck, holding a block of wood between her head and her shoulders, a block of wood full of sawdust getting thicker and thicker. *Yes*, she said, feeling the block of sawdust go from her neck to her chest, and from her chest to her stomach, and down to the pit of her stomach and something hollow and heavy moving around on her body. The Examining Magistrate gave her the paper and told her to sign it. She took it, looking at the Braque guitar and signed. The Examining Magistrate said *Ja*, he was already five minutes late, his wife didn't like it at all when he was five minutes late, and showing signs of panic he slipped into his coat and snatched his umbrella and ran, and Herr Zutter told her to wait because it was already late and the Examining Magistrate had only written a report without deciding anything definite and in Switzerland it had to be definite, and he told her to go back to the corridor and she sat down again next to the boy with the brightly colored peacocks and the mean laugh but now he didn't look at her he just sat there stinking of tobacco, and then he let out a meaningful grunt and began voraciously scratching his hands. The corridor was brightly lit. In the big window red and yellow gleamed and the ultramarine turned into indigo. She stretched her legs. The boy with the mean laugh made a peculiar noise again, looking at her from his seat, and then the policeman came and said let's go. Where to, she asked. For a ride, he said and told her to get in and pushed her inside and she sat down and they drove through the streets with the trams and the shops and the lamps and the people with the plastic bags, and then they turned into other streets and it was quiet and it was raining. A procession of priests walked past in the rain. She listened to the rain beating down on the cobblestones. The streets smelled exciting and she looked at them, squinting with wild desire. The streets raced. The trams raced. The cars raced. There were sounds of traffic in the streets sounds of traffic in the air and bells rang for prayer, bells of glass and iron of branches and trees. She listened, squinting wildly, wanting wildly to be joined to the racing world, the real running racing world, to be joined to the windows, the blinds, the neon signs, the black revolving glass doors. In the café entrances magic lights and red lamps flickered, in this direction, in that. The noise increased. The car bumped forward and backward and she was thrown forward and backward and they stopped and told her to go get out and she got out and someone pushed her lightly and told her to go in and next to the counter they asked if she had anything else on her and she said she had nothing on her, nothing, nothing, she said, but the man behind the counter didn't look at her and didn't answer her, and two policemen came and started marching fast down corridors of nailed metal walls between nailed metal doors. The block of wood was already inside her feet and she marched slowly, unable to lift her feet, and they pushed her and shouted *weiter, weiter.* She asked where to but they shouted *weiter, weiter* and took her down in a metal elevator to a huge a metal room and sat her down in a metal chair and turned her head and snapped and snapped again and after that they told her to press her thumb and she pressed her thumb and they told her to press the palm of her hand and she pressed and they moved her palm on the plate and turned the chair around and put her palm on the plate again and she said: They told me that if I signed I could go home, and they shouted *weiter* and marched her down the nailed metal corridors with the nailed doors and she shrieked wildly that they told her she could go home and she wouldn't go with them, I want to know where I am, she shrieked, and they caught her by both hands and dragged her along the iron floor down the long corridors of the huge prison and she shrieked I won't go I won't go, and two huge men held her both arms and dragged her along the floor and they reached an iron door and opened the iron door and pushed her inside and shut the iron door. And I was a prisoner, she said.

I don't know much about the jail. She said little and what she said was confused, the way people talk about a time that resembles an hallucination or a nightmare, trying to report the facts but afraid of showing her hands, as if playing for stakes that were too high, and when I try to reconstruct the story it sounds more or less like this: She beat against the iron door with her fists. A voice answered, thunderous like drums. She beat again, with both fists. The iron thundered, coming back other walls and answering countless doors along the corridors, hitting the floors above and the floors below with a renewed metallic clang. She heard footsteps on the corridor. The footsteps approached. Then they receded. The iron voice died away. She beat again, savagely, raving. The shrill swooping shrieks of a mighty flock of cymbals answered. She went on beating with clenched fists, furiously, feeling the blood pouring from her fists and streaming slowly down her arms. She felt the dampness on her arms under her sleeves, but she went on beating, hopping up and down like a little animal. The footsteps approached and receded and approached and receded again. She stopped for a minute, listening. Muffled voices came back from the empty spaces and the corridors, voices drawn out in a long low trumpet call. She began beating again, demented, hitting her fists on the iron door, hearing the iron orchestra answer, zigzagging down the corridors, breaking somewhere down below and coming back and coming back with every new blow of her fists. She went on, beating, beating, she felt enormous strength in her hands and opened her bleeding hands. For a moment she looked at them, astounded, but still she felt enormous strength in her hands and opened her fingers and began to beat with her palms, with the delicate skin of her palms, which was immediately scratched and burning, but still she felt enormous strength in her hands and she turned her fingers around, beating with the hard side of her fingers. She felt a fierce pain in her fingers, in the skin and the little joints, and that her fingers were breaking, The footsteps in the corridor approached and receded and approached and receded. The cymbals suddenly grew low, children's cymbals, almost toy cymbals, and she lifted the wounded palms of her hands to her eyes, examining the raw exposed flesh, the pink flesh of a fresh burn. The madness intensified and she began beating with her forehead, feeling her forehead deep in the bones of her temples. Thin trickles of blood dripped into her eyes, and she closed her eyes which were full of bloody tears. She wiped the reddish liquid from her eyes, feeling in the depths of her face the two painful balls hollow like two invented pockets. The reddish liquid went on flowing, dripping onto the balls of her fingers, and she pushed her fingers into her hair, drawing them backwards, wanting to wipe the balls of her fingers as she tried to stand still for a minute, but on both sides of her face two enormous ears protruded, growing bigger from a minute to minute, growing more remote from her face and more alien. She moved her head to one side, then to the other, but the enormous ears moved somewhere far from her head, heavy, full of strange sounds of tools, and hammers and saws and grating sounds of shattering glass, and she pressed her back to the iron door, beating now with her back. The hammers stopped and so did the saws, the cymbals and the trumpet, and now she heard only the grating sound of shattering glass. The scraping sound of fingernails on hard stone, the sounds of things moving and rustling. She went on beating her back against the door, trying to raise her hands, feeling the thin muddy trickles making warm little pools in her armpits, and she want on slamming her back on the door, but the blows now reached her ears dimly, like the muffled bellow of a wounded animal. She began to scream, raving, beating alternately with her forehead, her skull, her back, hearing the sounds of her thudding body coming back to her from the walls and from the corridors surrounding her like a vast barrel. The pain in her hands grew piercing, and she lifted them and pressed them to her face, tightening her face, and then she felt the terrible chill spreading through her body.

It was already dark in the peephole when she saw a crack and in the crack stood a warden. He asked if she was the one banging. She said she wanted them to inform the consulate. He smiled kindly. He said: What consulate? My country's, she said. He smiled again, kindly. He said that a prisoner had no consulate, and pushed her back inside. She said that she demanded a lawyer. He smiled again, kindly. He had small round glasses with pale steel frames, and he raised the glasses a little, smiling. What you can do is rot here, he said smiling and pushed her inside so hard that she fell on the floor. Her face was bleeding and she wiped the blood with her skirt.

The cell was all stone, yellowish-gray, and looked like a tomb, and there was an iron door in the tomb, and a bed and a lavatory and a light bulb hanging from the ceiling. And maybe not a tomb, maybe something like a dog's kennel, only higher, she said.

And then the nightmare began, when she sat down on the bed.

Her face was blank when she told me this, leaving her at moments with an expression of shock, as if something sudden had fallen next to her face which was very pale, burning with a sickly pallor. She looked at me now in silence, not taking her eyes off me, eyes glittering but cold, an iron cold, blue-gray, a steely cold, and I thought that perhaps she could still hear the chords and metallic sounds here in the park, at a lower octave. For a moment it seemed to me that I could hear them too, and the closed echo zigzagging. She went on looking at me, her face faintly illuminated by the lamp above the bench, which lit small, rather chubby hands, almost a child's hands, and suddenly I remembered the wide illuminated trams, the sausages and mustard, the long slender pears, the fruit rotten at the core and the hard winter I had spent in Zürich roaming the long street, standing at night in empty stations, freezing in my little Israeli fur, leaning against the walls of the houses with the statues of monsters, of lions and tigers, looking for a pair of wings to shelter me, looking for a God to pray to, and a man standing next to me at the empty tram station, an elegantly dressed man with an umbrella bent over me with his umbrella. You shouldn't look at the empty tracks, Madam, he said, anyone who looks at the empty tracks will die, Madam.

You were thinking about something, she said.

I denied it. I said I was listening. Her mouth twisted in an embarrassed grin, and for a moment she crossed her hands behind her back, then she put them back her knees, stretching her legs and looking up at me intently, her head lowered, stubbornly examining my face again. Of course you were thinking about something, she said. I denied it again, ignoring the signs of violence in her voice. She moved her shoulders, shuddering for a moment as if an electric current were running through her body, and went on as if there had been no interruption. Well, she said, and then I noticed the fresco.

The nightmare began when she sat down on the bed. Then she noticed the fresco on the walls, a huge colorful fresco of names and writing and huge swollen penises were drawn on all the walls, red penises and green penises and black penises and white and yellow and upside down and cut-off and squashed-up penises, drawn with thick shining crayons and charcoal and chalk and iodine, as well as coffee and soup and blood. Most of them weren't joined to any body or coming out of any body, but hanging from a little hairy triangle, which looked like medallions for hanging bathroom towels or kitchen towels, and only here and there they were sticking out of tiny little flattened out bodies, like cartoon bodies. She looked, frightened, stunned, trying to read the names that were written in

huge clumsy letters in Arabic and English and French, making out
something like Abdalla or Hafez, or Charlie, or John, and trying to
decipher the writing, but the monstrous penises swelled emerging
from the walls advancing on her, on her body. She began to shake.
The hundred-headed monster came apart and the wall suddenly
filled up with gigantic lizards covered in sticky hairy skin, and she
heard the terrible swarming, she felt the hairy skin in her mouth
and a revolting nausea. She went on sitting, clinging to the railing
of the bed, but the hundred-headed monster came apart again. The
lizards turned into snakes, and she saw them clearly advancing on
her, on her body, slimy, hissing, closing in on her and climbing up
her and coiling around her neck and crawling into her throat and
filling her mouth and her throat and choking her inside her throat.
She felt the bundles of flesh and blood, she felt gaping jaws and
tongues and teeth swelling without stopping, attached to gigantic
bladders swelling without stopping, turning into frightening tumors
covered with hard animal skin. She gazed terrified at the infinite
expansion, gripping the railing of the bed, trying to get up and failing. The monsters moved, clinging to the wall. Then they crawled
out of the wall. Everything whirled in a crazy vertigo. The nausea,
the terror, the snakes and dragons, the throttled birds, the handles,
and the axes, the soft flesh and hard animal skin, and she felt a terrible pain in her stomach and heard a growling in her stomach and
the gigantic penises writhing inside her stomach and she jumped
off the bed, trying to stand and leaning against a lavatory. But all
around her strange black wings moved with slender bones, moved
with nails and claws and she saw the ceiling getting lower and narrower, she smelled burning rubber and charred tires, the smell of
the yellowish liquid in the lavatory bowl. She began a frantic jig.
Her stomachache grew worse. The demented arabesque moved up
and down up and down whirling in a carousel in the narrow illuminated den with the ceiling getting lower and narrower all the
time and now she could see the letters clearly, the coats, the capes, the
hooks and the axes, she could see Ahmed and Hafez and Muhamed

and Salah and Charlie and John and she felt a terrible force digging
into her eyes ripping her eyes from her head. From the corridor came
a vicious laugh. After that there was a scream. The gigantic penises
swelled choking her throat and she vomited her guts onto the floor.

No, I can't talk about that night, she said.

The light bulb on the ceiling burned all night. She tried to wrap
herself in the blanket but there was an appalling stench coming from
the blanket and she lay frozen, wide-eyed, looking at the light bulb.
From the neighboring cells, she heard tapping. She didn't answer.
The tapping was repeated. She didn't answer. Fear tuned her body
into a petrified lump and she could hardly turnover or lie on her
side, staring wide-eyed at the light bulb on the ceiling. She asked
herself if it was raining. Perhaps there was a storm. Yes, there was
surely a storm. And she was here. What misery, what wretched misery, and she would die here, alone, misjudged, and forgotten, alone
and forgotten, and no one would ever know, no one would ever
look for her, even when they began to worry at home and Gerda
would say: Where's Rutchen what's happened to Rutchen why
doesn't she call, and he would grunt or growl something into the
green oilcloth.

This is where I'll remain, this is where I'll be buried, she said and
sat up in a panic. The bed was high, and she sat, sweating, in the
freezing cold, not connected to anything, in the air, at a great height,
at terrifyingly great height. The tapping on the walls was repeated,
tapping from the neighboring cell, from the corridors, from the
elevators, from the iron doors. She tried to think who was here yesterday who was locked up on the other side of the wall tonight. She
thought she heard the murmurs on the other side of the wall in the
neighboring cells, the murmurs of murderers, thieves, rapists, scor-
pions, and nails. Her hands were frozen and she tried to warm them
in vain, saying to herself that there was nothing to be afraid of, no
murmurs were coming from the neighboring cells, no noises could
penetrate these walls, no blows no hopes no fears. She felt a mo-

mentary relief, protected. From the frescoed wall opposite she heard a loud tapping, getting faster all the time. She listened. For a moment it seemed to her that she understood. The tapping was repeated more slowly, almost gently, almost warmly. It seemed to her that there were groans coming from the other side of the wall and someone on the other side of the wall was crying or singing. She listened intently, shaking all over. Somewhere in the distance a church chimed three chimes. She said: No, not chimes, it was eagles flying, three eagles flying. Now she remembered Herr Zutter saying something about a hurricane and she said: No, there aren't any hurricanes at home, why did he ask about a hurricane? No, its the rain, its a storm, there's a storm blowing, the trees are going wild outside, everything's flying outside, there's lightening outside. Suddenly she remembered how everything had happened, the empty bag gaping wide and being dragged down the corridors like a rabbit, like a little animal. She pressed her eyelids hard, searching for a snapped thread of lucidity. Her heart beat like a drum and she inclined her head to the wall next to the bed. But it was silent. Everything gradually froze. Everything was death. And she would remain here. She would be buried here. She tried to revive her hands.

But that's impossible, of course, I won't be buried here, she said. There was a moldy smell in the cell, a smell of damp earth, of flesh and bones, a smell of unknown, decomposing bodies, and she said to herself: These must be the prisoners who died here, people must have died here. The saliva turned into a thick paste between her teeth and she clamped her teeth together. These are the prisoners who died here, she said, this is the smell of the prisoners who died here, the ones the wardens found here dead in the morning, hanging on the gigantic penises in the morning, on the bundles of snakes on the empty jaws on the sheets on the strips of flesh. She trembled, bracing her arms at the sides of her body, trying to sit, but suddenly she jumped up and stood, suddenly she saw herself running, she was quite certain of it, she saw herself running in the corridors, in the empty courtyards, she was quite certain of it, in the windows and on the walls, flat against the walls and running, running, crushed in the carousel with the gigantic whirling penises, plummeting in the muddy air in the gaping barrel stuffed with lizards, the snakes, the networks of canals, the names and the eyes, the dancing demons, the cartoon bodies, the sour stench, and the writing soiled with excrement. She felt such terrible nausea that she was forced to cling to the wall, pressing hard against the huge swollen maleness, and suddenly she felt that she was bleeding, it wasn't her time yet, but she was bleeding, suddenly she felt the blood dripping dirty from her body between her legs as if from an open belly. She moved her legs. Everything was sticky, her panties, her skirt, her stocking, everything was full of the thick stale mud and the sour smell of blood. She raised it to her face, sniffing, feeling it hot on her skin. Her dirty, superfluous blood poured out of her interspersed with little lumps of glue, always too early always too late, and how life had stupefied her, and it was dark outside, outside the wind raced, the air was full of ink, and how thin her naked knees were, how strange, what short legs full of thin trickles of blood and red sweat, and she was a bleeding animal, that's what she was, an animal bleeding between its legs, that's what I am, she said. She had on a black skirt and she took it off. There was a big stain of black on black. The smell was unbearable. The skin between her legs was chafed and she thought she would get undressed and sit naked, but the cold was terrible, the writing on the wall grew bigger and so did the shiny colored penises embedded in the walls and passing through the walls and she felt their presence inside the walls and inside the floor opening the belly of the floor felt the hair in her mouth the smell of urine of yesterday and Abdalla and Hafez and Charlie and John none of them bled, not from their legs, and she bled, that's what she was, an animal bleeding between its legs, she said.

She felt a weakness in her knees, in her feet and toes, with a prickling in the toes, and said to herself that the blood wasn't reaching her legs, she tried to lift her legs sitting high up on the iron bed.

But they dangled, dropped, resisting her efforts, as if they were strapped down. Suddenly she felt a passionate desire to touch the floor, and she jumped on the floor, hearing the thudding of her feet on the floor. Her feet were hard. The echo was strong. And she felt something strong some invisible force coming from the floor and going straight into her feet. Again there were footsteps in the corridor. The light bulb burned like a little sun and she realized that it would never go out, it would go on beating on her eyes forever, and she didn't know which was worse, the darkness or the light. She climbed onto the bed, she stood on the bed, trying to reach the light, but it was fixed onto the ceiling, and she heard her own footsteps in the cell, with no day, no night, no watch, inside some eternal calendar. The silver ball opposite her eyes blazed, and something like laughter writhed inside her body, struggling in her stomach like an animal inside a sack. Suddenly she remembered reading stories in the newspapers about Israelis rotting in jails all over the world, in Amsterdam, Stockholm, Munich, New York, for taking drugs, selling drugs, and she, coins, coins — she made small change.

And still it was something without substance, without meaning. She stretched out her hands, as if freeing herself from a trap, and looked at me intently, with a sudden strength pulling in the opposite direction. There was a desolate expression on her face, as if something had happened, as if she had suddenly sensed the slow dissolution of time.

That's it, and then it happened, she said, then she felt her whole body like tattoo, she felt the ink inside her skin and the smell of stale herring in her skin. Her hands were blue. Her body long. And long snakes with tiny heads crawled in the ink on the long body, rustling like paper butterflies, Oh God, paper butterflies, and she stared and stared, the two empty balls hurt her deep inside her face but she stared and stared and the little sun that would never, Oh God, never go out again burned above her. The cell was white. The fresco passed in procession. Quiet. Moving with an imperceptible tremor and

white as white could be, it too illuminated by the light of the little
sun that would never, Oh God, never go out again, and she was here,
Oh God, she was here alone and there was no God, no coins, no
father, no people in the world no sound came from anywhere no
living soul and only the trumpet imitating the sound of weeping. A
new fountain of vomit spewed from her throat. She screamed. Someone tapped on the other side of the wall. The snakes reared to the
ceiling. The tattoo netting on her body burned like an inflamma-
tion. And then it came to her, the demented desire to write on the
walls, she said. She looked at me, blinking her eyes as if they were
out of her control, as of now too she felt the ink netting her body.
She asked if I knew what she wanted to write. I said I didn't know.
She laughed quietly, shocked by her laughter. She said: For example, what's the connection between lie and die, that was the first
sentence. She asked if I knew what came after that. I asked what.
She laughed, again, quiet, shocked by her own laughter. There was
this one verse stuck in my head, she said, it simply flew onto the
walls like soul flies. I looked at her. I didn't ask what. There was a
kind of passion of revenge in her voice, but her face was completely
blank and expressionless and only her eyes darted over me, now
shining, almost radiant, as if held by two silver tacks.

She laughed nervously.

You'll never guess, she said laughed nervously.

Her words became more and more confused, and from the few
confused words I understood that first she searched for an eyebrow
pencil and undid her pockets and linings, but there was nothing in
the pockets and nothing in the lining, and she turned the lining inside out and stuck her fingers into the seams but there was nothing
in the seams either, and then she tried with her nails but it didn't
come out with her nails, and then she wrote in her blood, opening
her legs and dipping and she wrote it big, round, the width of her
finger, you know it, she said. She fixed me with the two silver tacks
again. You know it, she said again. Her face was very white now and
only her cheeks burned like two painted poppies. She coughed dryly.

Now too I didn't ask what. She still coughed dryly. You'll never guess, she said again, casting nervous glances over her shoulder, as if she was sitting high above the floor like then, and that solitude, that loneliness, was still groaning in the stifling sourness, the words running through the air around her, smearing, big, round, the width of her finger, smearing, and I WAS LEFT NAKED AND BARE, that's it, you'll never guess, she repeated for the third time, big, round, the width of her finger on all the walls, what a celebration, AND I WAS LEFT NAKED AND BARE AND FOR THESE THINGS I WEEP AND I WAS LEFT NAKED AND BARE AND FOR THESE THINGS I WEEP AND I WAS LEFT NAKED AND BARE AND FOR THESE THINGS, you see, I'm not right in the head she said. Her face was green and she held her hands so tight against her face that it looked as if she had nails on her face. There, between the giant colored penises, between Abdalla, and Hafez and Asad and Charlie and John, AND FOR THESE THINGS I WEEP, do you think I'm crazy, she said.

The lamp above the bench shed a sandy color on her hair and she pushed her feet into the damp sparkling grass. Then she tucked them up on the bench. There was a silly smile on her face, a horrifying, almost imploring smile. She was silent for a moment, gathering her strength. And I wanted to write something else, she said. Again I didn't ask what. And again the same silly, almost imploring, almost horrifying smile spread over her face. She said: Something like the Golem, to run raving in the streets like the Golem, to lie here raving like the Golem, to break the walls, raving, like the Golem, a lifeless formless man. She spoke now without looking at me and I felt the words gnawing her, and that solitude, that loneliness, looking for the tattoo on her body. You can never reach the end of the snake, she said. She was still holding her hands to her face. I wanted to write about *their throat is an open sepulcher too*, she said, you know what I mean.

There was a silence. I didn't know what to say. She smiled. Of course, you know, she said. I didn't know what to say. I said yes, I knew what she meant. But you were thinking about something

else, she said. I said yes, I was thinking about something else. She
didn't ask what. It isn't true, you were thinking about *their throat is
an open sepulcher*, she said. She was still speaking without looking at
me. Every woman knows it she said. I didn't know what to say. I
said yes, every woman knows, and I suddenly saw the fresco in yellow in black in raspberry red moving on the trees, on the back of
the trunks, on the barrels and the damp grass, I saw the snakes rearing, the blind birds, the immense swollen maleness, the forest of
black beams, the black cylinder, the total darkness eclipsing thought.
I remembered the story about my friend in the Brooklyn subway,
how she had once gone down at night to the deserted station and
three little black demons had jumped out of the corners and pushed
a sweating black fist into her mouth into her throat and thrown
her down onto the platform of the deserted station and raped her
one after the other with the fist in her throat and a train came and
stopped and went away and came again and stopped and went away
and the three little demons went on the fist in her throat and ran
away leaving her in torn clothes and torn legs, torn between her
legs with her throat an open sepulcher.

She looked at me. Her voice blazed.

I heard there are a men who make a women do it in the throat,
she said.

I said I didn't know.

You never read about it? she said

I said perhaps, I didn't know.

I knew a woman like that, she said, all her life she walked around
with an open sepulcher. She never ate, only vomited.

She looked at me again, very concentrated.

You vomit in your soul, she said.

Sometimes, I said.

Her face turned the color of ink.

In your soul, she said.

Sometimes, I said.

She laughed a cold, bitter laugh.

Oh no, there in the cell, with the fresco, and what was crawling over the floor, what was crawling from the walls, from behind the walls, they couldn't have known there was a woman sitting there, but they knew, they sensed it through the walls, they masturbated through the walls, Abdalla, and Hafez, and Asad and Charlie and John, I felt their gigantic penises poking through the walls and the spittle and the terrible smell, I saw the holes come alive. Suddenly she was silent, shrinking on the bench. I couldn't even eat; it jumped at me from the filthy coffee from the dreadful soup, she said. She looked at me desperately. Oh, no, she said. Now her face was completely expressionless with big beads of sweat breaking out on it like drops of hot rain.

About birds of prey, she said suddenly. Her voice sounded strange, a whistling sound, and she pressed her back up hard against the bench again. There's only one bird of prey, she said, your thoughts.

And it was she of course who lit the fire, a few days after her return. How long she spent in jail I don't know, and how she got out she told me only afterward, when we were sitting on the concrete wall next to the house. The air was so still that we heard Gerda's soft moans coming clearly from the balcony, high-pitched, with a shrill sound like a tin whistle. Rutchen pretended to be deaf. She was always a wheezer, even when I was a child, she said. She didn't turn around to look through the window, although the head bobbing in there was visible from where we sat, and the whistling through the cracked pipe didn't stop. She said: How she swings there in the window. It really looked as if the head were swinging, hanging on the gathered pink curtain from a scrawny pink neck, its jaws sticking out like a skull. I remembered that she was once a beautiful woman with beautiful high cheekbones and how I liked watching her when she stood at the window. The shrill whistling went on, monotonous, irritating. It was hard to listen. Through the nylon curtain two deep holes of despair poked out and then you could see the pink fabric flapping as if torn and the two holes of despair sinking into some dark pit. Gerda had apparently turned off the light and sat down. Rutchen looked at me, perhaps reading my thoughts. You see, like a skull, she said. There was an open hostility in her voice. She said: Oh no, he won't leave her, he'll haunt her after death, he won't leave her. From behind the window the lifeless mask went on swaying down low and the tin whistle wailed. Rutchen looked, hard. Oh, no, he won't leave her, she repeated he's like the rain, like the wind, he won't leave her. She stood for a moment, listening. Suddenly she turned to me. She'll still feel his hands, she said.

The sight in the window was rather unnerving. Again Gerda popped up, shaking her head as if trying at long last to fly out the window. Rutchen asked again if I knew the story about the cat. A passing car lit her face in a sudden wash of brightness. She blinked both eyes. Then she returned to the subject of the jail, but how long she spent there I couldn't begin to understand. What I understood was only that they let her out on the day she had a plane ticket home. And that was my luck, she said. It was Herr Zutter who explained it too her. He said that the Swiss government didn't want to waste a plane ticket on her. It was early in the morning. They opened the cell door early in the morning and Herr Zutter was waiting for her below. He asked if everything had been returned to her. Then he asked what she had had. Here's the parcel, check and see, he said. She said it was all right. But Herr Zutter said: No, it's not all right, you must check, and she checked. The ring was there, and the watch. In her purse everything was arranged the way it was before, the bundles of small change too, and rolled up in a little bundle was the shame. That was what she said to them when she came home. In tinfoil, wrapped and twisted on top, only she didn't remember if it was in the bundles of tens or fives, and it was then that he cried, quietly, quietly, she said, it was then that he cried, and she said: And in the seams of the skirt that I undid, and in the lining, and he cried, and she turned lining inside out and then she turned the pockets inside out, and he, his fingers were crawling over his face, but she repeated it, and how I tore at the pockets, she said, how I tore at the pockets, how I came back, you

see, Papa, with the small change, the small change, that's what I
brought, the small change and he cried and she said: You're falling
asleep, Papa, you're fast asleep, Papa, why are you keeping your fingers on your face, Papa, and his face, to see his face, crumpled like
crumpled paper but she kept on: And what did you write on your
sick chart, Papa, and what did you write on your sick chart, and he,
suddenly lean, sharp-eyed, his hair on end: What sick chart? Your
sick chart, Papa, your sick chart, you were a driver, Papa, have you
forgotten that you were a driver that you were always looking at
the road, that you had eyes, you remember that you ran over dogs
on the road you ran over cats, you drove over squashed bodies, and
he didn't move, and where are you looking, where are you looking, Papa, and he didn't move, he said: Nowhere, I'm not looking
anywhere, and he wasn't crying anymore.

Suddenly she was silent.

Yes he wasn't looking anywhere, she said. She asked what time it
was. Her voice was wooden. I forgot that they gave my watch back,
she said. I listened to her wooden voice. She was silent again. You
think the watch is holy? she said and was silent again. She looked
weak, tired and stupefied, as if she was still hearing her own voice
and how that cruel conversation went day after day. The silence
lengthened, and I saw him suddenly, his face really crumpled like
crumpled paper, opening the empty albums, fingering the empty
cellophane paper and turning the pages, turning the pages, and the
evil spirit haunting the house, and him turning the pages, turning
the pages, I remembered Rutchen's wild laughter and Gerda: Stop
it, that's enough, take pity on the child, but he kept on turning
the pages, turning the pages, and Rutchen, inside the bubble of
light, looking, and in the huge department store the people peering behind her back ran, heads with parcels ran, the slanting little
television screens on the ceiling ran, the dent in her father's chin
ran, the cellophane pages in the empty albums ran, the rolls of tinfoil the monstrous figures clinging to the walls, the strong hands
carrying her — You think the watch is holy? she said again. Now

her voice too was dry. That's it, that's what it all adds up to in the
end, she said.

The cat's name was Pudding, but Shlezi called it "The Inheritance."
The Inheritance is hungry, he said. Or: The Inheritance is wailing
again. Sometimes he said: The Inheritance is waiting. He, at any
rate, was not going to leave any cats to his daughter, and he was
going to write it in his will, too, he said, it would be written in his
will. And sometimes he added: I'm changing it next week, you
know. And when neither of the women showed any curiosity he
repeated: Yes, yes next week. But Gerda was crazy about the cat, the
one he ran over later on. She really had inherited it from her
mother, who really did leave it to her in her will, and in fact, that was
the entire will, because when she died she took everything with her
except for the cat, which had a name as sweet as pudding and also
had a yellow body and a flabby belly that Shlezi hated. In its yellow
body were two yellow eyes that drew Gerda, bewitched her, and
this too Shlezi hated, and although Pudding was always guzzling it
had a look of permanent hunger and you could say that Shlezi
hated this too. He said that Gerda, like the cat, had a look of permanent hunger, and what was it she lacked, what was it she lacked,
always leaning against the door, always silent, never answering. She
really did lean against the door, pressing her cheek against it hard,
and it was impossible to tell from her face if she heard. The only one
she talked to sometimes was the cat, who followed her wherever
she went, to the street, to the kitchen, to the store, or lay next to her
pressed against the door, looking at her with that hungry look, a
look that tore her soul to pieces, and this too Shlezi hated. But more
than anything he hated when it jumped onto his stamp album. It
jumped on my stamp album, he yelled, raving, his eyes meeting as if
he had one eye under his forehead.

People told a lot of stories about the cat, especially how once,
when it jumped onto the stamp album, Shlezi tied it up and ran
over it. Then he drove backward a bit. After that he drove forward a

bit again. After that he left the mangled lump of flesh on the road and went inside. He jumped on my stamp album, he said. There was another version of the story, too. Mr. "Everything Cheap's" version, for instance. He said he simply smashed the cat in half, he bashed and bashed it until it popped. Only the head, whole, flew to the electricity pole, cut right along the seam. He saw it with his own eyes, how the head flew to the electricity pole. He trembled with excitement when he told it. Aiming the wheels like that, he said, aiming the wheels of a bus to cut like a kitchen knife, right along the seam. Because Mr. "Everything Cheap" suffered from asthma he had to take a deep breath, and he took a deep breath and calmed down. Incredible, you could actually see its yellow eyes jumping out and spinning round, he said after he calmed down. But Mrs. Klein told it a little differently. She said that he took an orange crate and tied the cat up inside the crate. Then he tied the crate to the tree and started the bus. They heard the tree creak and after that the dreadful howl of the cat, and then he drove backward a bit, and after that forward a bit again. She liked adding that he left a few oranges in the crate and they stayed whole next to the crushed body, only their color was no longer orange. She also liked adding that Gerda, pale as death, made some dry little sounds, but Shlezi yelled: Yes, he jumped onto my stamp album, can't you see? And Gerda went on standing there, paralyzed, her neck twisted backwards and her jaw dropping. She couldn't understand what he was talking about.

That's what Mrs. Klein said, said Rutchen. She asked me if I hadn't heard. I said I hadn't heard. She shrugged her shoulders. That's impossible, she said. Then she said that Mrs. Klein also liked adding that he had run over her over too, over Gerda, crushed her slowly without a bus and without a road, on the chair, sitting up. He had put her neck in the plaster cast right from the start. Yes, that's what Mrs. Klein said. She asked if I hadn't heard that either. Nasty, she said, but a fact. She waited a minute, as if something important had slipped her memory. And my father did that, she said. He was quiet man. He was even a good man. He had always worried about

her a lot. But it was after that that Gerda stopped talking. She said
this quietly. There was a kind of horror in her voice. She asked if
he had told me the story about the cats that ate each other. I said
he hadn't told me. She said: Really? Really? And, smiling incredulously, repeated the story about the cats that ate one another alive
leaving only their tails behind them. She smiled incredulously again.
He can't possibly never have told you that, she said. Her upper lip
quivered slightly. She said: Papa loved that story. He was always
telling it to Mama as a joke, but she never laughed at the joke. She
looked at me incredulously again. He can't have never told you that,
she repeated. Then she said that one he brought Gerda some cheese
with a picture of a laughing head of a cat and after that Gerda never
ate cheese again. Her face burned when she told me this, and she
stared at me with pale sweating, almost yellow eyes, and bent over
the stone wall beating on the stone. After that Gerda never ate
cheese again, she repeated. The simple words sounded strange in
her mouth and she went on hitting the stone. Can a wall give
grapes? she suddenly said. Her face was still burning and there was a
strange ring in her voice. Walls don't give grapes, she said wildly
and burst out crying.

I looked at her. It was a soft whimper, a kind of whine uncon-
nected to time or place or any particular event. Upstairs the telephone rang and went on ringing. Gerda didn't answer. She was still
standing in the window, still swaying as if she wanted to fly out of
the window. Since the room was dark her face was brightly lit, casting a long, vultures shadow. Her hair was tied wildly around her
head and you could see it falling sideways against the window frame
and her neck moving heavily in the plaster cast. Rutchen swallowed
her tears, sinking into her place on the stone again. It seemed to
me she said something, but I didn't hear what she said. Low clouds
came down on the street, after that the figure emerged inside them
and a clearly legible word appeared. After that the figure disappeared
and only the word remained, hanging in the air in the low dense
mist, but it was hard to read the word. Rutchen said something

again, but again I didn't hear what she said. A young man walked
down the street whistling a very pretty, merry tune. She raised herself and watched him heading away. He was wearing a shining black
coat and his steps were very soft and so was the merry tune receding into the distance. In the meantime the decor change and the
sky suddenly grew high, opening into the high air, full of disem-
bodied stories creeping over the balconies and above the roofs. Then
the mist like a soft sponge blotted out the roofs. The streets looked
like deep crevices. The mountain was full of wind, and the air was
shaken by a mighty voice, whose source was heard to tell. It's going
to rain, said Rutchen, and she turned toward the window where
Gerda's head still loomed whitely, but now she seemed amazingly
calm, standing in some distant time in some alien existence. Her
face looked very big and very white, emphasizing the coal black of
her hair, and even in the darkness you could see her look of permanent hunger. Rutchen watched her with keen attention. Papa
used to say that once people used to have funerals in the evening,
for the air, she said. Her voice was almost compassionate and her lips
trembled like the lips of a sick child, as if she wanted to cry her heart
out. She stiffened again and turned sharply toward me. Her mouth
twisted wryly. That's it, what's left is the small change, she said and
rubbed her hands as if they were stained with her own blood.

The young man in the shining black coat came back again,
whistling the merry tune. She mumbled something, wanting perhaps to get into conversation but he apparently didn't notice us sitting on the stone fence, and she watched him move away in the
opposite direction, her eyes fixed on his back in the shining black
coat, repeating, slightly off-key, the tune that sounded even better
off-key, enriched with a grotesque melancholy sound. It was clear
that somewhere, behind her, in the window, the silence deepened,
and she turned her head slowly around to face the window, where
Gerda was till standing with elongated limbs and a face of wax.
Her hands were spread out, holding onto the window frame, making the shape of a cross in the window. It seemed as if behind the

cross, in the darkness, there were other, invisible windows, and other hands multiplied there, holding onto the frames. Rutchen turned around, still whistling off-key, swaying slowly and pensively in time to the tune. In the meantime the telephone stopped ringing and it was silent inside. She asked if I had ever been to jail. I said no. Strange, she said. A couple coming down the steps from the house passed us in the street, deep in conversation. The man spoke quietly to the woman. He said: The orchestra began playing and they hanged him and the ropes broke and they brought another rope and it broke again and they hanged him again and the orchestra went on playing. We wouldn't talk, we said we'd walk without talking, said the woman. Rutchen apparently caught only the last words. Her face was now burning like fire. With Mama it took years, the madness of not talking, she said.

She lit the fire, as I said before, a few days after her return. They weren't in the house, of course, or more precisely they were at the other end of the house in Mr. "Everything Cheap's" flat, having their weekly game of cards. It was a boring game and Shlezi was particularly apathetic, brooding and withdrawn and not his usual self. He was wearing his working clothes, although he was no longer a bus driver, and they looked as if they weren't his, hanging clumsily on his body. He forgot to sweeten his coffee and drank it bitter, letting it get cold, pulling a face with every sip as if he were drinking poison. His remarks were mean, his face sour, and whenever he threw down a card he sank absentmindedly into the armchair, as if the pile of cards was disintegrating in front of his eyes, which were bleary and half-shut. The he got up and left before the end, and of course Gerda followed him. The two flats were joined by a long passage, and already in the passage they could sense something suspicious and a charred smell, and Gerda thought the toaster element had burnt out. It had already happened several times before that the toaster element had burnt out, usually causing a shock and blowing the lights in the house. But there was no short. The passage was even brightly lit, and apparently so was the flat, as they could see even through the closed door, and when they opened it Rutchen was sitting on the floor, her hair pinned around her head, the ends singed. Her sleeves were rolled up and there were little round marks on her arms. There was a dead cigarette in her mouth and her torso swayed slightly forward, bending over the flickering pile of charred tinfoil and burnt tracing paper that gave off a smell of hot metal. On her knees was her leather purse, gaping and empty, and she was staring with glassy eyes at the flame. Shlezi stood still in the doorway, stunned, and Gerda, alarmed, let out a little shriek. Rutchen raised a puppet hand in gesture of reassurance. It's nothing, she said, just a bit of small change. Her look was cold with triumph. There's nothing to worry about, she said, it didn't burn. Only the paper did.

Shlezi didn't move. He looked at her fearfully. His face was bloodless and he stood, petrified, hardly comprehending what was in front of his eyes. The air around him was very bright and trembling with lots of the charred tinfoil, swarming like little black worms. At the bottom of the pile the coins lay quietly, faded and lusterless. Rutchen went on sitting there, looking alternately at the two people frozen in the doorway and the dream writhing on the floor. Her face was damp and now two white diamonds were shining in it, and Shlezi looked at her dumbly. A terrible heat ran through him and he went out to the balcony, looking at the illuminated building surrounding him, suddenly understanding that he had never understood anything. For a moment he knew what he wanted to say with a clarity he had never known before. He felt grace, and something new, cool and mysterious, touching his body and enveloping him in a soft robe of silk. He tried to breathe deeply to fill his body with the touch of silk, and then he felt himself shrinking, becoming too small for this new understanding. He stood still, too frightened to budge from his place, not remembering what he had understood a moment before. The terrible heat pierced his chest in the direction of his arms and through the bones to the depths of his back, and he felt a terrible pain splitting his back. He moved his head in terror. The head moved, alive. He heard the blood pounding in his neck and he stretched his neck for a minute, feeling the aorta with his fingers, seeing clear pale sky surrounding him like a river. Again he stretched his neck, floating up again, but something in his stomach plunged and he began treading on the spot, already sensing he was treading on nothing. Big cold drops fell onto his eyes and he raised one hand and wiped the sweat from his forehead, stumbling into the room. Rutchen was still sitting there next to the fire and he stood gazing at her in horror, parting his lips to say something but not hearing his voice. He opened and shut his mouth a number of times without managing to say anything, and went on standing, gazing at Rutchen in horror, trying for one more minute to suck his daughter's eyes into himself, feeling her face coming close to him perhaps for the first time, and he clearly saw the black line dividing it down the middle, the bird-like movement and the hostility wiping away any other expression off her face; he clearly saw the crack opening in the floor and the yawning pit. The cold climbed to his neck, his head swayed slightly and he licked his lips as if he felt a terrible thirst.

The funeral took place a few days later, because it happened on a Thursday and they needed time to get the notices in the paper and let the drivers know, so that there would be drivers at the funeral. On Sunday the cemetery was full so they couldn't find a good time, so they put it off to Monday, although Gerda didn't like Mondays. Luckily the hospital didn't put any pressure on them, because the refrigerator wasn't full and one more corpse didn't bother them. But the truth is that he had a small funeral, only a few neighbors and a few drivers, who whispered together throughout the ceremony. Mrs. Klein said he died of sorrow, and Mrs. Borak said it was because he couldn't live without small change, and the man who eulogized him said it was true, he was a first-class driver, always on time and never short of change, he always had enough small change. He prepared it in advance. He was always prepared. He was very loyal to the job. He understood the job. He understood that driving a bus was no laughing matter, and he loved it. He said he was the type of person who enjoyed serving others. Mrs. Klein tittered and Mrs. Borak whispered something and Gerda stood without moving, with the plaster cast around her neck making her seem even more mummy-like. The sun began sinking early. Weeds grew on the surrounding paths and a wind blowing from the sea shrouded her tall silhouette and its look of a skeleton standing erect looking at the fresh earth. Rutchen too stood very still. She bent down and placed a small stone on the grave. Then she turned around, walking slowly, receding slowly toward the main path and walking along the path, keeping to the side with the light, like a person laboriously crossing a plain. Afterward she went up to the groups of beggars and pushed the pile of small change she had in her pockets into their tins. Afterward, Gerda's silhouette sat at the window, as on every evening, frozen, and Rutchen stood on the balcony, her sleeves rolled up, looking at her hands, and I saw her cautiously stroking one hand with the other, as if fingering the non-existent tattoo, perhaps feeling the ink swelling in her veins, slowly but steadily poisoning her blood.

Afterward she brought her mother food, and from her balcony I saw her bending over Gerda, who was sitting and picking at the green oilcloth with the little pink flowers crumbling on the table like roses. All evening long they did not exchange a word.

It was a clear night with low stars. The wind changed to a hot wind passing nimbly, without a sound, from the mountain to the balconies in the courtyards below, and the sense of evening came down early on the courtyard which always looked particularly beautiful in the evening, the sinking light enveloping it like a huge coat with gigantic sleeves full of resonant air still echoing *earth to earth ashes to ashes dust to dust*. For a moment it seemed that the twilight was permanent and the plunging ball of fire would never sink. The air was full of pensive sweetness. The gigantic sleeves waved madly. Then all at once an ominous darkness descended, Rutchen's nervous giggle was heard and she could be seen bending over her mother saying something in a lowered voice. But Gerda did not move. The beam of light from the opposite window crossed her tall silhouette and from my balcony I saw her back tensed against the chair, as if she were tied to a pillar.

Late at night, when I stepped onto the inner balcony, the tired neighbors were still clustered closely around Mr. "Everything Cheap's" table, enclosed in the ring of their own consuming curiosity, and there was still a question hanging in the air, as if someone unknown had been temporarily defeated. Mrs. Klein said that when all was said and done it was a sad story, and Mrs. Borak said that all the stories were sad. And let's not forget, she said, that it was an easy death and that's blessing, that's definitely a blessing. She seemed to like the sound of the word "blessing" very much, because she repeated it a third time: That's definitely a blessing, she said and added that they mustn't forget that there was still small change, too, which was confirmed by Mr. "Everything Cheap," who had more detailed information about the bundles in the closets and the beds and even in the storage space above the bathroom and above the kitchen. He expressed the opinion that it was because of this that the funeral had been postponed, because of the shroud, because they must have wanted to sew deep pockets in the shroud, and he licked his lips, making a little sucking noise when he added that it would take very deep pockets indeed to hold the piles of small change. If it was bank notes, it would have burnt, said Mrs. Klein. Mrs. Borak was silent, and Mr. "Everything Cheap" remarked that he certainly knew what he was about, hoarding that small change, a remark that gave rise to a peculiar hilarity, which he immediately made a conspicuous effort to control out of respect for the dead and the recency of his demise. But the timing turned out to be unlucky, and one week later the currency was changed again. Mr. "Everything Cheap" was the first to hear the news and he hurried to pass it on to Gerda, with the same peculiar hilarity, hinting with exaggerated concern at the stacks of coins in the closets and the storage space, and giggling irrelevantly a little. Gerda didn't answer. She straightened up,

as if his voice was reaching her from a long way away. Now too her
face was long, smooth and empty, and she thrust her body forward,
throwing herself onto the air. Late at night she was still staring into
the empty street, then into the opposite house, then up into the sky.
Mr. "Everything Cheap" heaved a tender, commiserating sigh, and
added that they would have to start going to the bank, and Mrs.
Klein, with an expression of pensive sweetness on her face, said they
would need a bus for it. Back to the bus, she said.

As for Rutchen, they said she shrugged her shoulders, and they
said she even breathed a sigh of relief, smiling blandly and not react-
ing. From my balcony in the evening she could be seen, sitting very
still. The bus, as I said before, was no longer standing in the street,
and it was a long time since Shlezi sat in the window. But sometimes, in the evenings afterwards, I too saw him, sitting and counting small change. Then I would say to myself something I learned a
long time ago, that just as life includes death so death includes life,
and that must surely be what Rutchen thought too when she said:
You see, he's still sitting in the window, arranging the small change.
The two silver tacks inside her eyes burned erratically as she said it,
flickering like a failing battery, fluid with invisible tears, repeating
fanatically: Every day, arranging the small change. It seemed to me
that I could actually hear the sentence, said out loud, like a conversation continued in the next room or behind a tree, as if the words
were coming out of her body. Now her face was netted with tiny red
veins and it bore an extraordinary resemblance to her father's face,
as if there was nothing between them now but the short distance at
the end of the road. She covered the veins with her hands crushing them slightly. Every day, every day, she said.

translated by Dalya Bilu

MY BROTHER

Benjamin Tammuz

Here's a picture of hell: about a half an hour ago the sun set behind the orange groves. Darkness caresses the yard, bearing the scent of orange blossom. Pollen floats through the air. Silence flows in from the tunnel of acacia trees in the empty street and invades the area of reddish sand between my house and the large, two-story house that belonged to my late brother. Every evening I sit by my window and wait for the sound of the car. I can hear it from a distance, coming closer down the street, stopping next to the gate, where the engine dies. It always seems to die suddenly and every evening my heart is pierced by a slight stab. Afterward, in my mind's eye, I follow the American geologist getting out of the car and entering his flat, and immediately I see the light going on in the ground-floor kitchen of the large house. From the window I raise my eyes to the kitchen window on the second floor, where the light will go off in another minute or two. Now I close my eyes, for what there is to see I have already seen. From now on my imagination will take over and show me what I know: Luscinia is walking down the inner stairs, the supper dishes in a basket in her hand, and her face is glowing with the radiance of longings fulfilled, for this is the moment she has been looking forward to all day long. In the doorway to the ground-floor kitchen stands the American geologist; he takes the basket from her hand, bends down to kiss her cheek, and they sit at the table to eat.

For about half an hour I hold my breath, gazing into the darkness of the yard until the light goes off in the geologist's kitchen. A few seconds later the light will go on in his bedroom and a moment or two later it will be switched off again. Then it will be dark until the early hours of the morning, when the light will go on again in the bedroom for a while. Luscinia will go back upstairs to her flat, and I know that she'll go into the children's room first. Perhaps she'll straighten their pillows, or she'll kiss them in their sleep, and then retire to her bedroom.

I greet the sunrise with burning, half-closed eyes and prowl around my room until noon. Then I sit down to write. I'm writing now.

About forty years ago, after our parents died, my brother went to Italy to study agriculture. I was already working as a teacher in the colony school. When my brother came home three years later we agreed that he would live in our parents' house, while I would build myself a house at the back of the yard, slightly removed from the street. There was no need to uproot the eucalyptus trees bordering our land, but we pulled up the trees growing in the middle of the yard so they wouldn't separate us from each other. The space between my house and our parents' house was covered with reddish sand that absorbed almost all the winter rain, and when we crossed it to visit each other we hardly ever tracked mud into each other's houses.

When my brother married, he added another story to our parents' house. I, who never married, am still living in the little house I built for myself. Which now looks like a kind of servants' lodge attached to a large manor house.

When my brother returned from Italy, a certified agronomist, he brought with him the nickname that stayed with him for the rest of his life. His real name was Kalman, but in Italy they called him Camillo, and the new Italian name stuck and superseded the original, and everybody began to call him Camillo. Even his wife.

I met the girl my brother married before he met her himself. When he was studying in Italy a new teacher came to the colony and joined the staff of our school. Everyone — even the women — agreed that such exquisite beauty had never been seen in our parts before, and it was doubtful if you could find its match anywhere else, either. There were some who said, "Why should she want to come to a godforsaken place like this? She could have the whole world at her feet!" But the new teacher, whose name was Sophie, a gay, lighthearted, almost childishly mischievous creature, said that she was delighted to have obtained a teaching post at our school and that she had hoped to strike roots among us and become one of us.

I told her that my father was one of the six founders of the colony, and she looked at me and burst out laughing. "So why are you a teacher and not a farmer?"

"My brother's studying agriculture," I said, as if trying to justify myself. And then, to make things even worse, I told her he would be back, with a degree in agronomy, in about six months' time.

I spent most of the next six months looking for some way to erase the impression of my first conversation with her. There was no doubt I had aroused her curiosity about my brother, and in the end I saw that she was looking forward to his arrival not merely with curiosity but with tense anticipation. Things reached such a pass that as his return date approached she would begin coming up to me in the staff room and imploring me to tell her the exact day of his arrival the moment I knew it.

My brother came home at the beginning of winter. The following spring, just before Passover, they were married.

I'm writing now. At about noon, I try to overcome the webs of sleep sealing shut the lids of my burning eyes. I know that the American geologist has driven south to the oil wells hours ago, while Luscinia's children are at school and she herself is secluded in her bedroom, hugging the memories of the night to her as they dissolve into a sweet morning slumber. She'll get up when the children come home from school and sit down with them to lunch, and after that she'll begin cooking dinner for herself and the American geologist.

When I see them before me in my imagination — each of the rooms where my hellfire burns — I sit down to write the story of something that might have been my life, or that might have been the lives of other people. And where the borders lay between my life that was only a dream, or a reverie, or a nuisance to the lives of the other people living in our yard. My brother married Sophie just before Passover and immediately set out with her to Galilee. They intended to spend two nights in Tiberias and three in Safad. I was asked to make sure that the building materials for the new second story arrived on time and that the construction men were ready to begin work immediately after the Passover holiday. In addition, my brother instructed me not to miss any meetings of the local council, to which new members were about to be elected, so that I could report back to him on his return as to which way the wind was blowing in the colony. So I was unable to join in the holiday excursion to Jerusalem and the seminar being held there by the Teacher's Federation, although I had been preparing for it all year long and had even made notes for a speech. I said nothing to my brother about the excursion and the seminar, so that he would not think I was trying to get out of helping him and possibly ascribe my motives to jealousy.

I took part in all the council meetings and when it came to electing the new council head I cast my vote according to the dictates of my conscience, but my brother was chosen regardless to head the new local council for the next four years. I also saw to it that the building materials arrived on schedule, and when the newlyweds returned from their honeymoon they found everything shipshape and ready for their comfort: the floor of our parents' house newly washed, the pantry stocked with fruits and vegetables, flour and honey. I even went to the trouble of getting the curtains laundered so that they would be as fresh and bright as they were on the day our parents came to live there.

The second story soon began rising into the sky. The ground floor, like the little house I built for myself on the edge of the yard, consisted of three small rooms, which was all that farmers could afford in the early days of the colony. But now my brother extended the foundations of the second story by adding a kind of portico with a wide entrance to the facade of the house, supporting two more rooms in addition to the three resting on the roof of the original house. So they ended up with a spacious five-room apartment, not counting the three rooms already on the ground floor.

In the end they went to live upstairs and the ground floor filled with unused furniture, the rusty remains of my father's antiquated agricultural implements, and other kinds of old junk. Once my brother announced, at a council meeting, that he intended turning the ground floor into a museum of the early days of the colony. So he said, but he never kept his promise. And in all the decades that have passed since then, the ground floor has been used for very different purposes.

A year after his marriage my brother was chosen as a delegate to the Zionist Congress, but he refused to go on the grounds that there was danger of a plague of locusts in the summer, and he was not prepared to abandon his brother farmers in their hour of need, when his professional skills might help minimize the damage.

The real reason for his refusal was different. In those days he started an agricultural journal, which he intended using as a means of influencing public opinion. Soon after it was founded the journal obtained official recognition from the Farmer's Federation, and my brother was appointed its editor, with a salary. His wife began helping him, typing articles and dealing with the correspondence, and after teaching all day at school, she would sit up until late at night, working on the journal. Later on, she reduced her teaching hours by half and went to work full time on the journal, and the

Farmer's Federation paid her a salary too. When Sophie became pregnant with her first child she went on serving my brother faithfully, both in the house and the kitchen and on the journal, and all this in addition to her part-time job as a teacher in our school.

My brother, on the other hand, was so busy with all the weighty tasks he had taken upon himself that in the end he hired a secretary to work with Sophie, while he traveled almost every week to Tel Aviv and Jerusalem, sitting on committees, and making speeches at all kinds of conferences and public meetings.

He was frequently away from home for one or two days, and the circumcision of his firstborn son had to be postponed for twenty-four hours because my brother had promised to attend a meeting of the National Committee in Jerusalem.

Sophie explained to all their guests that her husband was in a position of public responsibility and that it was their duty to understand and assist him in the performance of his tasks.

The first time I saw tears in her eyes was early in the second winter of their marriage. I pretended not to have seen anything but Sophie could tell that I had and that I was pretending not to. Today I know that at that moment a kind of bond was created between us, the nature of which became clear to me later on.

How long can a man sit at his window and look at what's happening outside? If you asked me, I'd say about forty years. And it's not over yet.

Forty years ago I sat at the window in the evening and watched the lights going on and off in the upper story my brother had built. I learned the rules of the game of lights then, and in my imagination I saw, then too, the embarrassment and shy smile and desire of Sophie's face when they switched off their bedroom lights in the first year of their marriage. From the same window — in the second year of their marriage — I would watch the lamp burning in the living room, where Sophie slaved for her husband on the journal, and a few hours later I would see the light going on in the bedroom. And sometimes I knew she was there alone, crying into her pillow.

As I write these lines forty years later, I now look out from the very same place at the dark square of the window in the American geologist's bedroom, and I know that Luscinia is lying there in his arms. And from the reign of Sophie to the reign of Luscinia most of my days have passed without anything changing in my life. The changes took place in the lives of my brother, Sophie, of Luscinia and her daughter whose name is also Luscinia and who is now my brother's widow, performing in the geologist's arms the only rite that allows her to distinguish between life and nonexistence.

And I sit by my window. And the story I wish to tell is not really my story at all. It is the story of other people. And even though I have no story of my own, it surely cannot be possible that I never even existed — for I am not a parable, after all, but flesh and blood. What then is the story I wish to tell?

Even today, when our colony is no longer a colony but a municipal council, there are a still a few old-timers left who like telling tales about me behind my back. Their favorite is that all my life I have wanted whatever my brother wanted, and that all my life I have envied him and tried to imitate him.

I have no intention of defending myself against these slanderers, and am even prepared to admit that in certain cases there may have been some truth to what they said. But as far as Sophie is concerned, it's a downright lie, since I, of course, knew her before my brother had even heard her name, and I fell in love with her at first sight. Not that there's any wonder in that. Everyone who saw her fell in love with her, but I was perhaps the most devoted of all of her suitors. And the fact is that it was my brother who married her — in other words, she stayed in the family. I don't know how to explain it, but it seems to me that in a certain sense she belonged to me too, right from the beginning, even let's say, as my sister-in-law. Which implies a certain degree of relationship at least.

During the first years of his marriage my brother made a point of being home on Friday nights, and I was almost always invited to the festive Sabbath meal. My brother was not observant, but Sophie — from the day their first son was born — used to light candles and say the blessing with lowered eyes and a quick, apologetic smile. My brother would demonstrate his disapproval of the ceremony by staring at the ceiling while she whispered the blessing, and the minute it was over, he would demand impatiently, "Well, can we eat now?"

She never replied and when her eyes met the sympathetic looks I sent in her direction she would become so flustered and nervous that the soup would spill from the ladle onto the tablecloth. She was terrified that her husband might see that I noticed the rudeness with which he treated her. To the spilling of the soup my brother would react with grim silence and a look far worse then any reprimand.

Once Sophie asked me to help her compose a circular to the subscribers of the journal. At the same time she told me that her request must remain a secret and that my brother must never know that she had asked for my help. After this, I took the initiative in becoming her regular assistant. I saw that she was collapsing under the weight of all the different jobs she had taken on, and I told her that my time was my own and that after I had finished teaching in the mornings, my afternoons and evenings were quite free, not to mention my nights.

Today I still do not know whether it was due to absentmindedness or a deliberate oversight on Sophie's part that I found all kinds of private notes in the bundles of papers she gave me. In any case, I kept coming across things that may have been diary jottings, or brief notes to her husband, and that for some reason had found their way into the files of the journal correspondence. I could not bring myself to mention her mistake — if it was a mistake — since the last thing I wanted was to embarrass her. The things I saw were not meant for the eyes of strangers. And since I was silent, Sophie's carelessness, deliberate or otherwise, persisted.

One day, in the middle of her second pregnancy, she gave me a bunch of papers to take care of. When I sat down at my desk to work on them that evening, I found the following note:

My darling, tell me how have I offended you? I want to do whatever you want me to, whatever will please you and make you happy, but you won't tell me what I should do. All you do is sulk and scowl and wound my heart. Please, my love, give me a sign.

It is written in the Bible, "Honor thy father and thy mother." But nowhere is it written, "Honor thy brother." And when God upbraids Cain, "Where is Abel thy brother?" Cain replies, "Am I my brother's keeper?"

When I read the note Sophie had written to my brother on that distant evening, a string snapped in my soul. Not only — I shouted through clamped lips, banging on the desk with my fist — not only did you take my beloved from me by force, not only did you conquer her body and soul, but you have to torment her and humiliate her as well?

What I did immediately afterward I did out of temporary insanity. But today I think that I know the reason for my actions. When you want to take revenge, to strike out against someone and destroy him, you should never keep your anger bottled up inside you. If you do, it will explode, and that will be the end of you. You have to act. Never mind how. You have to hurt the person you hate. And if this is beyond you — then hurt someone or something else, as long as you get rid of the rage that is driving you out of your mind.

What I did was to put the note in an envelope, with a postscript of my own: "Your letter got mixed up with the papers by mistake, and I am returning it to you."

And I sent it to Sophie.

Like many others in the colony, my brother had a revolver that he used to take with him when traveling in areas populated by Arabs. It was a big American Colt, which was usually kept under the mattress in their bedroom, and Sophie may not even have been aware of its existence. In any case, I began to be haunted by the fear that Sophie might get hold of it in a moment of mental distress or despair. I therefore said to myself that it would be better if the weapon were kept in my house, and if my brother needed it he could come and get it. I said to him that it would look very bad if the British police caught a man in his position, the head of the colony council, in possession of an illegal weapon. With an ordinary schoolteacher, on the other hand, things would not be so serious.

My brother agreed with me and shamelessly allowed me to endanger myself because of a weapon that wasn't even mine. And the revolver was transferred to my house.

Sophie did not react to the return of the letter. But her behavior toward me changed. If up to now, she had treated me like a brother-in-law with whom she had some little secret in common, she now treated me like a brother. Her trust was henceforth complete, and all reservations and wariness disappeared. As if she had stopped feeling any shame in my presence. A sister need not be shy of baring herself before her brother — although things never, of course, reached that point between us. Except if the nakedness in question be that of the soul.

What happened in those first years is veiled in mist. There are some things I remember clearly and others that have completely slipped my memory. I would be hard put now to say exactly when the last barriers of strangeness and pretense between me and Sophie were breached. I remember that the process began in all kinds of little signals that we sent one another. It was I who opened these moves by returning that shocking note to her. The first sign I received back from Sophie was the announcement that from now on my brother's secretary would work only three days a week in their house, spending the other three outside on various jobs for the journal. I understood that in my brother's absence I was now being invited to assist her in her home. And the very first time I presented myself in their living room, Sophie asked me — after saying nothing for over a month — whether I had read what was written in the note I had returned to her.

I was silent.

"In other words, you read it," she said.

I lowered my eyes.

"I wanted you to read it," she said.

"But you're going to have two children now," I blurted out, as if I had heard some daring proposal in her words.

"I'm not sorry," Sophie whispered, "and I'm not giving up. Help me."

"How can I?" I asked. Not in astonishment, but as a hired hand might ask for detailed instructions from his employer. I might have cried out, *Sophie, I love you. I've loved you from the first day I met you. It's not too late! Let's go away. Run away with me. You're miserable with him!* Instead I asked, "How can I?" — and Sophie immediately unveiled her plans.

Her idea was absurdly childish and had no chance of success whatsoever. She suggested that I sing her praises to my brother and remind him of how she had chosen him, out of love, from all the many suitors surrounding her, some of them richer than my brother and others just more important. She also muttered something to the effect that I should hint to my brother that if he went on treating her so badly, she might seek consolation in the arms of another man.

"Tell him it's all your idea, just what you imagine might happen," she warned me quickly, alarmed a her own boldness.

Then she started crying. She buried her face in her hands and sobbed as if I weren't sitting there opposite her. At this stage of our relationship I did not even allow myself to comfort her with words, let alone give way to the powerful desire to put my arm around her shoulders and stroke her hair. I simply sat there in silence.

But our relationship was beginning to change. And as we spent more and more time together a pattern of behavior was established between us that we began, as time went by, to take for granted. At the beginning of the summer their second son was born, and when I volunteered, this time openly, to help with the journal, my brother was only too glad to accept my offer. Since there was no longer any need to hide from him the fact that I spent my leisure hours working with Sophie, my visits to their house became a daily event. There was now a clearly marked path in the reddish soil of the yard, its breadth and direction determined by the soles of my shoes: the path led in a straight line from my front door to the back door of my brother's house, and from the kitchen I would go straight into the living room.

If there was anyone else in the house I would be greeted in the usual way. But if Sophie was alone, she would bow her head and rest it on my shoulder for a second or two, and sigh. This was as far as we went and nothing more ever happened between us, until the end.

There are a number of things to my brother's credit that must be recorded here.

When our parents died we did not divide the property between us, each taking his share in the usual way, but as proof of the complete trust we had in each other preserved our entire inheritance intact — the vineyards, the orange grove, the vegetable plots, and the family shares in the colony winery. My brother, who was a qualified agronomist, took care of all of the complicated professional aspects of the plowing, pruning, irrigating, spraying, harvesting, and marketing of the crops. It was he, too, who arranged for transporting the fruit to the Jaffa port, and he who burned the midnight oil at the meetings of the winery board. I would never have succeeded in doing even one of these things on my own. And nevertheless we divided the profits equally between us, although my brother had a family and I was a bachelor with only myself to support. Moreover, if we had lean years when frost attacked the orange grove or phyloxera destroyed the almonds and there were no profits, my brother never failed to ask me if I was short of money. My brother always had extra sources of income — whether from his work as an agricultural consultant or from his position as a director of the Agricultural Bank and his other public activities. And I would always reply that my salary as a teacher was sufficient for all my needs and even to put something aside for a rainy day.

And there's something else I have to put on the record. Once I fell ill with typhus, an extremely contagious and dangerous disease, and I had a high fever. And my brother refused to allow Sophie to look after me; for over a week he devoted himself to me entirely, calling the doctor twice a day, cooking the rice gruel that he prescribed for me, and changing the cold compresses on my head, day after day. At night he slept on a mattress on the floor next to my bed and every hour he got up to soak the cold compresses in ice water and ask me how I was feeling. And when the doctor suggested transferring me to the government hospital my brother told him that he knew the English government hospitals and he knew that anyone going into them was lucky to get out alive what with the filth and the negligence and the stupidity of the ignorant orderlies. "I'll never let them get their hands on my brother," I overheard him say to the doctor. And thanks to his firmness and his devotion, I returned to the land of living — for which I will always be grateful.

In those days my brother Kalman, or Camillo, was the only person in the colony and perhaps the entire country who was fluent in Italian. Since he had no opportunity to use the language he loved in conversation he got into the habit of reading Italian literature. Little by little he accumulated of volumes and prose and poetry that he would order by mail until he had a whole shelf full of Italian classics, as well as a number of books by unknown modern writers. I loved looking at the spines of the Italian books standing on the shelf and would pronounce their names to myself in a whisper, intoxicated by the mere sound of the words, like cow bells tinkling over valley pastures. Camillo would read these books on the nights he spent at home, and he would always take a volume or two with him on his travels. At night he would keep Sophie waiting forever until he was finished reading. She could not understand his passion for these books, but although she got nothing out of them but rejection she did not dare complain. She saw quite clearly that everything that enthralled my brother's senses served as a barrier between them, and she did not know how to reconcile her admiration with the hostility that began accumulating in her heart toward the secret worlds in which my brother's spirit soared.

One night, a stifling summer night, it was nearly three o'clock in the morning and I was sitting in the dark at my window and looking at the light burning in their bedroom, when the kitchen door of their house opened and my brother came out and hurried in my direction, as if there had been some kind of accident and he was running to me for help. In a moment or two I heard him knocking on my door. I found him standing there with a book in his hand.

"You have to hear this," he almost shouted in my ear. "I'll read it aloud and translate it for you. It's fantastic!"

There were tears in his eyes and he pushed me inside, pointed to a chair, sat down opposite me and began to read. First in Italian and then in a Hebrew translation, verse by verse, from Canto 12 of *Jerusalem Delivered* by Torquato Tasso. The passage described a duel that took place in Jerusalem during the First Crusade between Tancred and an anonymous knight in armor. Both knights are mortally wounded by the other's spear. And then, just before the anonymous knight dies, Tancred discovers that his opponent is not a knight at all, but a heathen female warrior, the beautiful Clorinda. And even as Tancred stands dismayed at the thought that he has slain this delicate maiden who lies dying before his eyes, she makes a last astonishing request: a request that shook my brother's soul to its depths and caused him to jump out of bed in the middle of night and come running to share his emotion with me. Clorinda, the beautiful infidel, asked Tancred to bring water from a nearby spring and baptize her before she died. And the passage concludes with the following lines:

> He saw and recognized her, and remained speechless,
> And motionless. Alas the sight! Alas the knowledge!
> He did not die yet but gathered all of his strength
> At that moment and set his heart to guard it;
> And restraining his grief, turned to give, with water.
> Life to her whom he had slain with his sword.
> While he recited the sacred words,
> She was transfigured with joy, and smiled;
> And in the act of dying seemed lightly and happily
> To say, "Heaven is opening: I depart in peace."

With intense emotion my brother told me that the last time he had heard those lines was at his graduation ceremony in Bologna, where a small orchestra with three voices had performed Monteverdi's *Combattimento di Tancredi e Clorinda*. Even then, my brother told me, the beauty of the work had stunned him with terrible power, and ever since he had longed for the "exalted heights" to which such music and words raised our souls.

"Every day of my life I remember that while I'm wallowing in some futile insignificant little swamp, the words of Torquato Tasso and the music of Monteverdi are alive and leading a life of their own; a life separate from my life, superior to my life, disdainful of my life, and even indifferent to it. And I want to return to that moment in Bologna, the moment when the heavens opened up to me. I, too, want to depart in peace."

I knew that he was not speaking of any longings for the Christian religion, but of longings for that "other life," the life beyond the reality of the colony and the winery and the bank; beyond my school too. The life that I yearn for night after night as I sit at my window. Could it be that he who had won Sophie was not happy either? What, then, were those "exalted heights" for which my brother longed from the groaning depths of his heart?

"I understand" I said to him.

"I knew you would," said my brother. Then he closed the book carefully, smiled at me apologetically, stood up and turned to the door.

We said goodnight and each of us returned to his place.

My brother returned to Sophie's bed and lay down beside her, and I imagine, went on longing for something that he had lost in the days of his youth in Italy. And I returned to my window, and I was probably closer to Sophie at that hour than my brother was or ever had been.

And at that same dark hour before the sun rose I consoled myself with the thought that you could only be deprived of what you already had. What you did not have, nobody could take away from you; and therefore Sophie would be mine until the day I died.

As I sat by my window, gazing at the big house looming eerily out of the dim green light of the impending sunrise, I reflected upon that other possession — dreams — that is also ours in perpetuity, and that can never be stolen from us. A man dreams when he is alone. And what does he dream of? Of crying out for someone to come and save him from his loneliness, so that he will never be alone any more.

Early one afternoon, in the middle of the seventh year of Sophie's marriage to my brother, I found a note from him on my desk:

> Please do me a favor. You know we've been looking for a new nurse for the colony ever since Manya died. Well, now we've found one, with excellent references from Dr. Oplatka and Dr. Binyamini, and everything's settled. There was one problem I wanted to look into before taking her on, but I didn't have time and now it's too late because the Council has already committed itself. The problem is that the new nurse has a child, a little girl, and we have no information about whether she

is a widow or a divorcee. I hope to God she's a widow, otherwise there
may be some question as to her moral character. In any case, it's all set-
tled, and the favor I want to ask you is to go to Tel Aviv and fetch her,
and help her with her luggage and any other arrangements necessary
for the journey. I am enclosing an address where you'll find her wait-
ing. Her name is very strange and the devil knows where she got it
from. In any case I know her family comes from Russia, just like ours,
so there's no need to worry on that score. Bring her to our place — I've
already cleared a room on the ground floor for her. If she likes she can
stay there and if not she can find somewhere else. I'll be back on Tues-
day. In the meantime you can tell her the rent will be 80 grush a
month — next to nothing, out of consideration for the modesty of her
salary as a nurse and the fact that she's got a child to support. Please
don't let me down and go and fetch her. I can only hope and pray that
everything will be all right and that we haven't made the wrong choice.

The woman's name was Luscinia Megarinsky and the name of
her little daughter was also Luscinia. The child was about six years
old and would be able to enter the first grade of our school.

Seven years earlier, when I first met Sophie, before she married my
brother, she had been a gay, laughing creature, even a little coy. Her
behavior toward me, in any case, was tinged with a certain mis-
chievousness. In the course of the years her laughter was subdued
until almost all that remained of it was the occasional flicker of a
smile. My brother crushed her with his indifference, his frequent
absences, and the cruelty with which he ignored her protests,
which grew weaker from year to year. At first her protests had a
faintly coquettish air; she still had the effrontery to believe in her
own power. Later on they were sad, reproachful, and almost mute;
and in the end they were confined to stifled sobs with which she
wet her pillow at night, and nobody knew anything about them.

This being the case, it was surprising, and even alarming, to see
the violent objections and bursts of rage with which Sophie greeted

the installation of nurse Luscinia and her daughter in the ground-floor room.

When I brought Luscinia Megarinsky and her daughter to the house and began dragging their luggage into the yard, Sophie came down from the upper story and drew me aside and whispered wildly into my ear, "What's all this about? What's going on here?"

I realized my brother had not told her about his note to me, or seen fit to consult his wife before renting the room to the new nurse. My brother, by the way, had not yet seen the woman and her daughter. It was only his sense of responsibility as the head of the colony council that had prompted him to offer her shelter in his home, in return for a symbolic rental. (The monthly rental for a room at that time was more than a pound a month.)

I briefly explained the situation to Sophie, hoping the guest would not sense the resentment she had incurred in the mistress of the house.

"Over my dead body," she hissed into my ear and stormed back up the stairs to her apartment. I was flabbergasted. I had seen her depressed, I had seen her weeping, I had seen her in despair, but never had I seen her, like some other members of her sex, as a lioness ready to bite and claw.

I had never seen this aspect of Sophie's personality before, and I was never to see it again. This was the first and last outburst of its kind, before she sank into irremediable dumbness and despair.

On Tuesday my brother came home. He came in the morning — when the new lodger was at her clinic in the hospital building — and went straight upstairs. Sophie received him with a raging fury the likes of which he had never witnessed in her before, as he himself told me afterward. Without even greeting him she said, "You'll take that woman and her child and her baggage and you'll throw them out. You can dump them wherever you like — but not in my house. And if you don't get rid of them today, I'll throw them out myself."

My brother — as he told me later that day — nearly hit her. The shock and the cheek of it (that was the word he used: cheek) made his blood boil to such an extent that he almost lost his head. But he restrained himself and said, "I'd like to see you do it," and immediately turned his back on her and left the house without even having a cup of coffee in the kitchen.

He met Luscinia Megarinsky and her daughter for the first time early that evening, when he went downstairs to ask how they were settling in and whether there was anything they needed. He assured them — so he told me — that his wife would be glad to do whatever she could to help them settle into their new home.

For a week Sophie did not come down from the second floor, and I don't know whether she occupied herself with the work on the journal or whether she kept to her bed. The Arab maid looked after the children. Sophie's two little boys soon made friends with little Luscinia and they all played together in the yard.

The first meeting between Sophie and Luscinia took place one evening soon afterward. When Luscinia came home from her work at the clinic I went over to help her fix a shutter that had come loose from its hinges.

Luscinia was a quiet woman, who spoke in a tone barely above a whisper and whose brown eyes seemed too big for her round face. When she looked at you she seemed to be caressing you with her eyes, but she was not at all flirtatious. On the contrary: there was something apologetic about her, as if she was asking you to forgive her for bothering you by the mere fact of her existence.

This humility was something she had brought with her when she came, for none of us had done anything, God forbid, to offend her; and as for the anger to which her arrival had given rise in Sophie, she knew nothing about it.

I had my own guesses about what I saw, and in the course of time it turned out that I had not guessed wrong. The reasons for her apparent timidity I deciphered correctly. But the true nature of the woman evaded me completely. I thought her a weak and docile creature, whereas events were to prove just the opposite. But we will speak of this when the time comes.

Luscinia was holding the shutter while I turned the screwdriver, when I saw Sophie approaching out of the corner of my eye. She stood a few paces away, watching us silently. Luscinia had not yet noticed her. I finished the work as quickly as I could, and then turned to Luscinia and said, "Look, here's my sister-in-law, Sophie. Your landlady." And to Sophie I said, "Our new nurse, Luscinia Megarinsky."

Luscinia took Sophie in with her brown eyes, silently observing the beauty that was already beginning to fade, but whose signs were still very much in evidence. Luscinia seemed to be aware of what Sophie was going through. Her eyes expressed pity and even sympathy. This, in any case, is how I interpreted her look.

Sophie examined Luscinia with an avid, almost impatient curiosity, which was quickly appeased. Like me, Sophie did not interpret what she saw correctly. She too apparently concluded that what we had before us was a humble, timid creature, eager to be properly grateful for anything we did for her.

Sophie spoke first:

"If there's anything you need, please tell me. I'll try to help you if I can. You're a stranger here, after all, with a little girl as well."

"You're all so good to me," replied Luscinia. "I don't know how I'll ever repay you. You're such good people."

Sophie's sons and Luscinia's daughter now came running up, scuffing the sand with their feet, and stood in front of us. Sophie put her hand on the little girl's head and said, "What a sweet, pretty little girl. What's your name, dear?"

"Luscinia," said the child.

Sophie raised her eyebrows. "Your name is the same as your mother's?"

"Yes," replied Luscinia senior. "I decided to name her after me."

"Not a Jewish custom," pronounced Sophie, to my surprise. "What a strange decision for you to make."

"I made it nevertheless," said Luscinia, almost in a whisper. And the baldness of the statement, without explanation or apology, led me to think that this woman might still surprise us.

It was Sophie who apologized: "I didn't mean to criticize. I was only asking… I'm sorry."

Luscinia left it at that and did not react. She lowered her eyes, crushed her dress between her fingers, and forced Sophie into further apologies by her silence. After which she repeated her offer of help, then took both her sons by the hand and headed back up to the top floor.

"Excuse me," said Luscinia and went into her room.

That night, when my brother returned from Tel Aviv, I told him how the two women had met. For some reason, I felt like a despicable informer, as if I had disclosed a secret that should never have passed my lips. But who I had betrayed was not clear to me.

About a month after Luscinia and her daughter came to stay in our yard Sophie shut herself into the kitchen with me and told me in alarm that my brother's behavior toward her had suddenly changed. Recently he had remarked that she hadn't bought herself a new dress in a long time, and he had forced her to go with him to the dressmaker and order two of them; and suddenly he had forbidden her to wash the dinner dishes, washing them himself despite her protests. He said she looked tired and pale and that she had to rest and think about her health.

"My heart tells me that it bodes no good," she whispered and asked me what I thought. "How can I explain it?" she said.

My heart told me something, too, but I welcomed its foreboding. For the first time, there was — perhaps — an opening for me to hope that Sophie would be mine in the end. I knew my brother. He had a conscience, and qualms of conscience that drove him to prove to himself and the whole world that he was a fair, honest man who paid his debts down to the last penny, a man whom nobody could accuse of depriving anyone of his due, or of meanness, or callousness. God forbid! He would accumulate a fund of good deeds to his credit to stand him in good stead in his hour of trial or crisis. How well I knew my brother!

There was only one thing I didn't understand: when had he managed to fall in love with Luscinia? In what circumstances had it happened? Where did they meet? From my window I had seen nothing that might suggest an answer. Could it be that Luscinia was still unaware of my brother's plans for her? That was a possibility. He was farsighted — and the keenness of his desire to seize hold, without delay, of whatever it was that had enflamed his imagination was matched by the self-control he was capable of exercising if it would bring him the desired victory and conquest.

It was well within the bounds of possibility that although he had not yet said anything to Luscinia, his conscience was already troubling him and he was compensating his wife for what he was going to do to her.

Was it my duty to help her understand the situation now? Or did I owe it to myself to keep quiet and allow the blow to fall; so that when Sophie found herself abandoned and betrayed she would fall into my lap like a ripe fruit — the fruit of my brother's blindness? For all of his cleverness he had a weakness — a romantic weakness, let's say — for things that came from far away. A plebeian weakness, to tell the truth, that made him despise the familiar and admire the foreign just because it was foreign to him. Anything that came from far away captured his imagination and seduced him like a siren's song into jumping immediately overboard. So it was when he went to study in Italy, simply because Italy was overseas, and so it was when he fell for the beautiful Sophie, because she came from outside the colony trailing the mystery of distances — even small distances — behind her. And so it was now: Luscinia came from outside and brought mystery with her in the shape of her fatherless daughter. I myself had already solved the mystery, but my brother preferred the mystery to the solution. And when he solved the mystery he would already be inextricably trapped in the snares of his love, and he would make Luscinia's life a misery and torment himself with jealousy that would drive him out of his mind. But Sophie would be mine.

These thoughts, and others like them, churned feverishly around in my brain, as if they spoke of a reality that had already come to pass. My imagination raced, and the facts lagged behind. But not far behind. Very soon, the inevitable overlap occurred between what could not be stopped — given the natures of the various protagonists — and the chain of catastrophes generated by sin.

I don't remember how much time elapsed between Sophie's confession of the embarrassing attentions showered upon her by her husband and the day my brother burst into my kitchen with the force of a tornado and demanded, "Where's my revolver?"

I offered him a cup of tea, and he fell into a chair and stared at me in astonishment, as if to decide whether I was worthy of his trust before saying any more.

"I gave it in for repairs," I lied. "It was rusty."

"Good," muttered my brother, "very good... It's better that way."

And his next remark made it clear that his feverish imagination had carried him beyond anything that had occurred to me in my wildest dreams.

From the moment he first set eyes on Luscinia, my brother informed me, he knew he had reached his goal. "Her brown eyes will be the last shore on which the ship of my life anchors" — no more and no less. The head of the colony council, the bank director and editor of an agricultural journal, was suddenly sprouting poetry. In my opinion, things had taken a dangerous turn.

This respectable gentleman, this down-to-earth businessman whose shoulders were bowed under the weight of public office, was crowned with a jaunty garland of grace. His name was not Kalman but Camillo — an insouciant souvenir of his student days in Italy. And this aura of youthful charm cast a spell over all who crossed his path. And now he was aiming his spear, or rather his battering ram, at Luscinia and her daughter, who were living in the ground floor of his house for eighty grush a month. And what songs he was singing.

"My wife," he said, "has never understood me." (What originality! Pushkin, no less!) "My wife," he said, "is always rebelling against me. She always has her own ideas about things and all kinds of demands and complaints. All day and night I have to listen to her complaints. If I had only once, once in eight long years, heard one single word of gratitude. But no! All I hear is nagging and carping. Not a moment's rest. And I'm a busy man. I work hard, I have duties and responsibilities. You'd think I was entitled to a little gratitude somewhere in this world. And if not gratitude, then at least to be left in peace. But no. She doesn't give me a moment's peace."

Who and what was he talking about? I stopped him with a blunt question: "Kalman, are you talking about Sophie?"

"What do you think?" he exclaimed angrily. "Who do you think I'm talking about? Catherine the Great? The Queen of Sheba? Of course I'm talking about Sophie."

"And so?" I asked him.

And so, in Luscinia's brown eyes, which he now compared to warm pools, he had found "an island of stillness and tranquillity." And he went on to tell me about the first visit he had paid to her room. She had made him a cup of tea and with the tea she had offered him a plate of cheap, miserable cookies — the kind of cookies bought at the colony grocery store and served at meetings of the agricultural workers' committee. For Luscinia had not yet acquired an oven, nor did she have enough money to buy anything better. Poverty shrieked from every corner of her room. The clothes she wore were plain but clean. She gave off a fresh smell of laundry soap (such was his enthusiasm that I was afraid he was about to accuse Sophie — as opposed to the new goddess — of not washing, or something to that effect). He went on holding forth about Luscinia's grinding poverty, about the wretchedness crying out from every corner of the room, as if extolling virtue, charms, and temptations that were impossible to resist.

It was only later that I realized what he was driving at: he felt sorry for her; and pity was only one step away from an almost fatherly sense of responsibility. And a father, naturally, protected his children, even if they were stepchildren. And if the stepchild happened to be a daughter — a daughter who in this case happened to be a grown woman — the father soon discovered the woman in her. And from then on the way was open to celestial love.

On that very first night (my brother told me) he had made a vow to rescue Luscinia from her wretched poverty. First of all he resolved to buy her an oven, so that she would be able, like any other housewife, to prepare tasty meals for herself and her daughter, and bake cakes for her guests. Then he had taken note of her miserable apparel, so unbecoming to the beauty that was driving him crazy, and begun bringing her finery from the city. And a sewing machine, too, since she was a competent seamstress. The gratitude this poor woman had shown him, my brother assures me, was beyond anything I had ever seen — and perhaps, said Kalman the poet, "there was nothing to compare it to in the entire world." He was still speaking in a whisper, although I was afraid that at any minute he would break into shouts of exaltation. And then he confessed something else: his love for Luscinia had brought about such a revolution in his whole way of thinking that he suddenly felt he owed Sophie something too, and that she too deserved some sort of compensation, especially in view of what the future was about to bring. And so he now took care, for every present he brought Luscinia, to bring two to Sophie, who was the "mother of his children, after all" — he added, with lowered eyes.

After describing a number of gifts he had bestowed upon each of the women in his house, he finally came to what was apparently the point of his visit — the revolver.

First he asked me if I had noticed that Luscinia had a daughter. He realized, of course, that I had seen the little girl, but he wanted to know if I had noticed how like her mother and how touching she was.

In which case, my brother inquired, how had it never occurred to me to wonder how this little girl came to be born? Of course, everyone knew how children came into the world, but in that case where was the father? "Have you ever thought about it?" my brother pressed me. He, apparently, had thought about it a great deal and asked himself the relevant question; and since he had not succeeded in coming up with the right answer out of the two possible alternatives — whether she was a widow or a divorcée — he had had no option but to address his question to the party concerned. At which point it had transpired that there was a third alternative, which he was now prepared to share with me: Luscinia had borne an illegitimate child!

And from here it was one short step to the revolver. Once my brother had conquered Luscinia with the ardor of his passion, and once she had yielded to him and allowed him to taste a love such as he had never known before — and he doubted if there was any man in the world who had ever known anything like what he had experienced in that poor, mean room, etc. — once she was already his, "body and soul," as he was kind enough to hint to me, in order to make sure that I understood exactly what he was talking about (lest anyone think my brother an utter fool, I should point out here that when it came to physical affairs, financial transactions, property deals, and so on, he was a shrewd, skilled, and ingenious operator), he felt he was entitled — even obliged — to know the truth about the private life of the woman who had just become his forever. He therefore asked her — and Luscinia burst into tears. The warm pools brimmed over, her tears wet the pillow, and the cat jumped out of the bag: Luscinia had a "friend." In the terrible loneliness of the big, strange city of Tel Aviv she had surrendered to the blandishments of this man of superior education and experience, and he had thrown all kinds of hints and promises, and even spoken of divorcing his wife as soon as his children were a little older;

and she, Luscinia, had made a mistake. The worst mistake of her life. Actually, it would be more correct to say that she had been the victim of something that could almost be called rape. Not the kind of rape you could complain to the police about, but a kind of spiritual rape, which had led to the other terrible thing — the fatal mistake.

"At first," said my brother, "I felt sorry for her. I embraced her, wiped away her tears, and told her she was the victim of shocking cruelty and injustice, and that I understood… But a day or two later I said to myself: what, exactly, do you understand? The woman simply made a whore of herself with the first man she came across… And then I was ashamed of calling her a whore. Why a whore? She was simply a girl who was ignorant of the facts of life… And then the ugly thoughts came back to buzz in my head and would not let me work in peace."

And a detailed description of my brother's torments followed, leading up to the great revelation that he was simply being eaten up by jealousy. His love for Luscinia was being consumed in the flames of his jealousy. There were moments when he wanted to kill her, but them he immediately recovered and said to himself, "What exactly is she guilty of? She didn't know me then… She didn't owe me a thing." And in the end, after weighing up the pros and cons and giving every aspect of the matter his serious consideration, he had come to the conclusion that he had to kill the man who had seduced Luscinia. She had no idea of his present whereabouts, the whole tragedy having taken place some seven years earlier. Nor did she have the least desire for my brother to meet him, since there was no need to conjure up the ugliness of the past.

But my brother had delivered his verdict and felt that only the execution of his sentence would afford him relief and enable him to return to Luscinia with an easy heart. In any case and with, however, an uneasy heart, he had returned to her already and saw her almost every day, at all kinds of odd hours made possible by complicated juggling about with his various jobs and duties. And let there be no mistake about it: in spite of everything he had said they were very happy together. Only from time to time the blood rushed to his head, and in a burst of blind jealousy he said harsh things to her and even abused her. And Luscinia wept bitter tears and was ready to kill herself to atone for her sin, but he begged her to forgive him for what he had just said, and promised her that he would stop tormenting her. But then — immediately after making love, as if the two things were connected — the blood would rush to his head again and he would start persecuting her all over again. But he always asked her to forgive him afterward, and she always forgave him. She was simply an angel, too good for this world. How could she bear his attacks on her was beyond his understanding. But the facts were undeniable: they loved each other as no one had ever loved before. Exactly so. Although he agreed with me that it might sound strange. Even though I, of course, had said no such thing.

In short, he was in big trouble, but also at the very heart of a great and terrible happiness. And sometime soon he would address himself to the final solution. He would treat Sophie with the utmost fairness and respect, since it was clearly not her fault that her character had not made it possible for them to build a happy life together.

But before he performed the necessary surgery and set about building his new life, he had to execute the sentence he had pronounced. Without this, nothing else was possible — but he wasn't sorry that the revolver was being repaired, because his plans had not yet matured, and there were still a few details that required further thought, in order to avoid unpleasant complications. Only I, his brother, flesh of his flesh and bone of his bone, would know. And it would remain a secret between us forever. Luscinia would know only that the villain had received the punishment he richly deserved.

Why had I not seen what was going on in the house across the yard, although I spent most of the night sitting at my window? For the simple reason that they often met during the day, when I was at school. And if they met at night, they didn't switch the light on. Nor did they make noise, because of the child.

And since they did not switch on the light, how should I have known? My expertise was confined to interpreting the appearance and disappearance of the lights going on and off in the house opposite my window.

When my brother told me his story, Sophie already knew where her husband spent his time after he came home from work and before he climbed the stairs to the second floor; but I did not know that she knew and once more — not for the first time — I felt I was betraying her by not telling her what I knew. I explained my silence to myself as my duty to my brother. Weaklings require rationalization for wrongdoing, and without a righteous explanation a weak man finds it difficult to be a villain, too.

I was rescued from my predicament — if that's the right name for it — by Sophie. When we were alone together working on the journal, she suddenly pushed the papers away and dropped her hands into her lap, like lifeless bars of lead, and for the first time I saw what despair could do to a woman's eyes. They were still the same dark blue-gray shade, and their shape was the same as always — fanning out and up, like a swallow's wing, from the bridge of her nose toward her temples. But the light had gone out of their windows. That was what her eyes would look like, I imagined, when she died. And that, indeed, was what they looked like when we found her dead body some years later.

"The first time I saw the avenue of acacia trees leading to your house," said Sophie with her hands lying in her lap, "I knew that if I could not be the queen of this house, the wife of the owner of this house, I might as well be dead… Can you guess what I'm trying to say? I never had a home of my own. From the day I arrived in this country with my parents they changed houses every year. Every year a smaller and cheaper flat. At the beginning we still had the money we brought with us from abroad, and afterward we lived on what my father earned as a salesman in a fabric store and what my mother earned from baking cakes for shops and for rich people. At home, my father owned the biggest fabric store in town, and my mother had baked cakes for the guests who came to play cards in the evening and to dance to the gramophone. But in Tel Aviv we moved from flat to flat, and every time we moved we sold another piece of furniture, because there was no room in the new flat. In the end we were left with a table, four chairs, two beds, and a wardrobe. And right from the beginning I told myself I would escape. All my parents' friends were new immigrants who had all lost all they owned, and they were all embittered and full of resentment and complaints. And in the school library I read stories about the farmers in the colonies, the orange groves, the early pioneers, and I said to myself that I would go and find then and join them. From the beginning I wanted to escape from the miserable malcontents who lived with us in Sheinkin Street and the Artisans' Center, and I always knew that in the end I would find the people who really belonged to this country, a unique breed of gentleman farmers, our own landed aristocracy. I pictured them as tanned, strong, and passionate, and I knew that they lived in houses made of sandstone and plastered over with pink or mustard-colored stucco, which I had seen in pictures, standing in the middle of orchards and citrus groves. And as soon as I qualified as a teacher I came to your colony and I saw the avenue of acacia trees leading to your yard, to the old house, to the giant eucalyptus trees and I knew that I had found my place. And then you told me that your brother who was coming back from his studies abroad to be an agronomist, and I fell in love with him before I had ever set eyes on him... And how wonderful it was to know that you were the sons of the founders of the colony, and that I would be transformed, like Cinderella, as if by the touch of a magic wand, from the daughter of immigrants into the wife of a founder's son, living in a house with an avenue of acacia trees leading up to it, in a dark shady courtyard with soft, hot sand beneath my feet... Are you laughing at me? It's the truth. I was overjoyed when he agreed, when he even seemed to have fallen in love with me at first sight. I thought it must be because I was so young and beautiful. But what did it matter why? In the end he would see that I was devoted to his way of life with all my heart and soul and he would love me truly... And what happened? Look what happened..."

I wanted to shout, *Sophie, run away from him, leave everything and run! It's still not too late. Come with me. Be mine. I'll give you all you dreamed of. I've loved you from the day you walked into the school staff room eight years ago...*

I wanted to, but I didn't. For one difficulty after another loomed up before me: how would I extricate myself from my little house? Would my brother be prepared to give me cash in exchange for my half of the inheritance? And if he refused — where would I take Sophie, even if she fell into my arms? Would we go on living in the colony? And would I go on teaching in the school? And what about her children?

"He doesn't even realize that I'm unhappy," continued Sophie. "On the contrary, he says I nag him, that I've got too many demands. What demands? That he should smile when he comes home at night? Stop keeping silent for days at a time? Shout, at least. But he's suddenly started giving me presents instead — dresses, handbags, shoes... I told you... And now I know why. And I don't even know myself what I want. Sometimes I wish he would be mean to me like before... I think I must be going mad. My head's full of crazy ideas. Whenever he offers to buy me something I know that it's to compensate me. I'm sure of it — and the more expensive the present, the uglier the betrayal that preceded it. That's the way his mind works, in simple equations. If he decides to divorce me and marry that...that woman, if that's what he decides, he'll offer me enormous compensation — a lot of property, perhaps a vineyard or an orange grove with a monthly income... He'll be fair, straight as a ruler, and that's why I haven't got a chance. I've already lost, because how can you beat a decent, honest man in a fight or an argument or a court case? And I won't fight or argue or go to court… He's already beaten me and he knows it. Tell me, you're his brother, perhaps you can explain where I went wrong? You've seen for yourself, all these years, every day you've seen how loyal and devoted I was and how I tried to make it easy for him to get what he wanted and realize his ambitions… All his ambitions were outside the home — but not any more. Now he's got ambitions right here at home, but on the ground floor. I know everything. Perhaps I should have been stronger at the beginning and refused to give in. But I can't fight him. I love him… And I'm frightened, too… Sometimes I wonder if it really was love — or perhaps only a kind of ambition to become part of the colony elite. Perhaps what I want isn't to devote myself but to conquer. Or perhaps devote myself in order to conquer? Maybe that's the sin I'm being punished for…? What do you think? Does that make sense? Or am I so crushed and humbled that I'm looking for some explanation to justify my situation, justify your brother? Maybe all I want is to clear him of the charges I accuse him of in my heart. Perhaps it's a kind of need to smear all the dirt on myself. Could it be my own character that's made him grow sick of me? That's made him feel only pity and revulsion toward me now — which are almost the same thing? Tell me. Haven't you got anything to say to me?"

And I remember that I kept thinking: *Where will I take her if she agrees to go with me? Will my brother agree to give me cash for my part in the inheritance? Will we go on living in the colony?* Like a stuck record my sickly thoughts went on turning around in my head and exempted me from thinking or answering her question.

Armed with evidence of my eyes and ears, I sat at my window at night and waited for the thunderbolt to strike our yard. I was sure — with a young man's impatience and the urgent desire to see the upheaval that would bring Sophie, almost in spite of herself, running into my arms — that a terrible scandal was about to bring everything crashing down around us. Perhaps Sophie would do something desperate and bring things to a head, perhaps my brother would lose patience and announce that he was leaving her with no more ado. Perhaps Luscinia would take flight at the upheaval she was causing and retire from the stage by running away one night with her daughter, leaving a letter behind her, like something from a Turgenev novel. The latter possibility seemed to me that most probable of all, because I did not yet know what Luscinia was really like, and I too had been taken in by her meek appearance and soft caressing gaze.

But none of the things I expected happened. Like the history of mankind, the pattern of individual lives, too, is determined by unforeseeable factors: things we cannot predict because of our lack of comprehension and, especially, our fear of facing up — even in our thoughts — to the compulsions under which we operate, compulsions imposed upon us against our will.

This unforeseeable element usually lies deep within our innermost personalities, where one might imagine that we would familiarize ourselves with it before turning to suppositions, guesses, and fantasies. But our innermost personality is a frightening place, sometimes a very desolate place, and which of us is brave enough to gaze into the heart of darkness? And so it happened that Sophie did not create a scandal but accustomed herself to the new situation as a person accustoms himself to a crippling injury sustained in an accident. And Kalman — Camillo, the eternal playboy — was in no hurry to complicate his life as long as neither of his two women forced him to decide one way or the other. As for Luscinia, she borrowed patiently and steadily away, keeping her voice low and waiting for the right moment to make her version public.

What had initially been a secret, involving deception, cheating, and pretense, was transformed within a few months into a permanent arrangement accepted by all three actors in the drama, with each one knowing what he knew, keeping quiet about what he kept quiet, and watching to see what the other two would do. I said three actors, but I should have said four. As the months went by and turned into a year, and then years, Luscinia the daughter moved into the center of the stage. The child who had arrived among us at the age if six, soon grew into a girl of ten, eleven, and twelve years old. And when she reached the age of Juliet she found her Romeo. My brother — naturally. At first he was a kindly father, upon whom she fawned with understandable hunger, with all the passionate adoration and dependency of a fatherless little girl. But later on, both her mother and my brother sensed that little Luscinia had turned Camillo into a kind of lover. Sophie was particularly sensitive to what was going on, and she was the first to draw my attention to it. Luscinia the mother noticed a little later, and immediately packed her daughter off to an agricultural school for girls in Nhalal. Two weeks later she ran away and came home. And then the heavens finally opened and the stormy season began.

My excitement — a poor explanation — has made me precipitate again. Before going any further I must say something about our lives during the first six years that Luscinia and her daughter spent in the ground floor of my brother's house.

The rumors began in the school where we both taught, Sophie and I. In the breaks between classes the teachers would gather in the staff room to drink tea and chat. From the day that Sophie married my brother the two of us would sit close together in the staff room and whisper to each other. Everyone knew that I had courted her from the day she had first appeared in the school and that my brother had taken her away from me. And they probably saw our whispered conversations in the staff room as some kind of compensation for the love that had been lost. As time went by, it did not escape my colleagues that Sophie's eyes were often wet with tears when she spoke to me, and the first suspicion that all was not well in her married life entered their hearts. The teachers sitting closest to us in the staff room would tactfully move their chairs to enable us to pour out our hearts without being over-heard. For a number of years they showed consideration and understanding. But when the nurse Luscinia came to live in our yard our colleagues' attitude changed. In the course of time I found out how the process had begun: one of the women teachers had gone into the grocery store exactly when Luscinia was coming out. Upon which the grocer had told the teacher in a whisper that the nurse's bills were paid by the head of the colony council, Mr. Camillo.

The gossip spread through the staff room like wildfire, reinforced by the results of certain inquiries that the teacher had addressed to the milkman. He, too, told her that Camillo paid him every week for the milk he delivered to the lady on the ground floor and her little daughter. Lately, said the milkman, he had been ordered to bring them cream and eggs, too.

About a year after Luscinia came to live in the colony an anonymous letter arrived at the office of the colony council saying that the new nurse was corrupting the young girls by her example and demanding that they put a stop to the scandal immediately forthwith. Camillo tore up the letter and threw it into the wastepaper basket, but not before the secretary who opened the correspondence every morning had read it. And the story took wing and soon spread so far that there was no point in trying to stop it.

In the meantime, Sophie had resigned herself to what was going on and that very Saturday, with the gossip in full spate, she was to be seen shepherding her sons and Luscinia's daughter — to the colony swimming pool and watching over all three of them with a maternal eye as they splashed about in the water. And people whose business brought them to our yard at the time went home and told everybody — in the synagogue, at meetings in the community center, and while strolling down the main road and taking in the evening air — that Sophie and Luscinia were sitting side by side and chatting amicably as they cut noodles, sorted lentils, and hung out their wash. Some said it was a shame and disgrace, but others marveled at the extent of Camillo's powers.

And so Camillo was crowned — in addition to all his other crowns with the crown of extraordinary sexual prowess: a kind of

Don Juan, a mysterious, superior being beyond the reach of the law — for what did we have here if not a blatant case of bigamy?

There was a certain amount of grumbling and resentment. Some of the older farmers demanded his dismissal from the bank, and others threatened to cancel their subscriptions to the journal. But it never went beyond talk. And in the meantime my brother's fame grew until it shone like a halo around his head, and children would run away when they saw him coming down the street, for they knew that this man was not like other men.

And in the double-storied house, life settled into a more or less regular pattern. Two nights a week Camillo slept downstairs, setting out again early in the morning as if he had never come home the day before. He would leave Luscinia's room before his children got up to go to school or kindergarten. They all showed the greatest concern for the children's welfare: Camillo abandoned Luscinia's bed well before seven in the morning. Sophie kept watch at the window until she saw her husband leave, and only then did she let the children go. Immediately after that, Luscinia would take her daughter to school and then cross the road to the clinic. As far as little Luscinia was concerned the censorship was not quite so strict; perhaps because her origins had accustomed her to unconventional situations.

On the nights that Camillo spent with Sophie, the arrangements were a little different: all the children, Sophie's and Luscinia's, left for school together.

When Camillo slept at Sophie's she would bathe her eyes so they would not be so red, tie her hair back as he had asked her to do when they were first married, and cook his favorite dishes for him, although some of them were not so good for his health. And if he was tired she would be considerate and encourage him to sleep and rest as much as he liked, since he worked hard and his life was not an easy one.

Camillo accepted Sophie's kindness with a stony face. Sometimes, he suddenly remembered that he had brought her a present from Tel Aviv and extracted a necklace of glass beads from his leather bag. Sophie did not remind that she already had a number of such necklaces. She thanked him, closed her eyes, and smiled blankly.

I, too, took part in the process, in my own way and according to my own needs; the minute I knew that my brother had entered Luscinia's room in order to spend the night there, my hand would shoot to the light switch in my kitchen, which faced her window. In a frenzy I would switch the light off and on, off and on without stop for about a quarter of an hour. This was how I voiced the cry of protest choking in my throat. I was not unaware of the absurdity of my actions; the worse my brother treated his wife the closer it brought the day when Sophie would "fall into my arms like a ripe fruit," as I wrote in my diary — so why should this shameful behavior make me angry? On the other hand, I felt compelled to take Sophie's side and protest on her behalf.

My brother did not have such an easy time of it with Luscinia. Right from the word go, when their love was still a hole-in-the-corner affair, she had manipulated him into promising her that he would divorce Sophie when the children grew up. But lately she had been asking him to name a date. Different people had different opinions about the ideal relation between the age of the children and the timing of their parents' divorce. Some said, the child is old enough to understand his parents' reasons for divorce even at the age of nine. And some said eleven. The most conservative held out for a minimum of thirteen. What did Camillo think, asked Luscinia.

He reminded her that she was bringing up her daughter without a father, which disqualified her from discussing the subject. Her own child — from the beginning of her life, from the day she was born — had been like the child of divorced parents, since she was born out of wedlock, in other words, illegitimately (he preferred not to use uglier words such as "sin" or "bastard"). And accordingly she had accepted the situation, whereas his own sons had grown up in a natural — not to say moral, if she would forgive him for saying so — atmosphere, and for them things were different. They had to be given more time to adjust themselves.

My brother would tell me about these discussions, demanding my understanding and sympathy for the difficulties of his situation, but it was perfectly obvious to me that he was, in fact, proud of his situation that was, for the time being, highly pleasurable, confidential (as far as the children were concerned!), and not too burdensome (for Camillo).

Until the day Luscinia took an unexpected step. When my brother went upstairs to the second floor, it being Sophie's turn, Luscinia knocked at my kitchen and asked if she could come in.

She came straight to the point. "Everyone knows you're in love with Sophie. You want her, don't you? As long as you don't deny it, there's something for us to talk about. With your permission, I'll continue."

Those caressing brown eyes impaled like two cold needles. How the color brown can be cold is a question in itself, for everybody knows that the color of ice is bluish white; but I saw brown ice.

Luscinia came to me very well prepared indeed. She appeared to have made a thorough investigation of everything that had happened to us since the first day that Sophie came to teach in the school. I imagine that both Sophie and my brother answered her questions frankly, since they could not have guessed the use to which she meant to put the information she was gathering. When she came to my kitchen Luscinia had a vigorous plan of action, the end result of which would be to throw the abandoned Sophie into the arms of the devoted lover who was her true and natural mate: me. And how did Luscinia propose to bring about this miracle? Her plan was as follows: I, for my part, had to emerge from my silence and my shameful passivity, I had to speak to Sophie and tell her what I felt for her. A woman could not live on hints, guesses, and suppositions. It was up to the man to state his case loudly and firmly. At the same time, I had to bring home to Sophie the utter

hopelessness of her relations with her husband, Camillo. And in order to disabuse me of any possible doubts, Luscinia went on to des-
cribe the strength of Camillo's passion for her, the depths of his
jealousy of her daughter's father ("to the point of planning to murder him" — she confided in a whisper), and the extent to which
they were already committed to one another; they were to marry
the moment the children were old enough. All this I was to explain
to Sophie, while at the same time making a concrete proposal to
her. And here a number of possibilities were open to us. I could take
my share of the inheritance in cash and move elsewhere, with
Sophie and the children. We could also go on living together for a
while, on the understanding that it was a temporary arrangement. In
this case, all that would have to be done was to move a few pieces
of furniture and enlarge my apartment. My house could easily be
enlarged by adding a second floor or by taking a bit of land from
the yard and adding a couple of rooms to the ground floor. Luscinia
would take of this too, and she promised that there would be no
objections from Camillo. On the contrary.

I lost my temper and took a tone uncharacteristic of me. "Madam," I said to her, "are you speaking to me as a woman in love or
as a real estate agent?"

I expected her to be offended, but she answered calmly, "A woman in love is capable of surprising people, especially men. They
would probably like a woman in love to be an innocent lamb, pre-
ferably a virgin, prepared to wait for them until her hair turns white.
But things don't always happen that way."

"I know that a woman in love can be a tigress," I stood my ground,
"but I didn't know that she could be a trader in the market place."

"You don't think, then, that the market is a place where people
can be devoured and killings can be made?" inquired Luscinia in a
philosophic vein, and I was covered in confusion.

As soon as I fell silent she returned to the attack and asked me
whether I was sure that I understood the advantages of her proposition.

In those days, I still saw people as divided into two separate camps. There were honest men and villains, good men and bad. My work as a teacher, too, had helped to reinforce these clear and well-defined categories, since such simple distinctions made it easier to explain questions of right and wrong, morality and duty, to my pupils. Today I know that the pupil forms the teacher no less than the teacher influences his pupils. But whereas the pupils grow up and become adults, the teacher grows more infantile every year.

My encounter with Luscinia did something to save me from this occupational hazard.

Today I have no doubt that Luscinia loved my brother with a passion that was incomparably greater than the hesitant and flickering flame that sustained Sophie's feelings for her husband. Both women were afraid of losing the man they loved, and although they had different reasons for their fears, both lived in the shadow of the fear of being left alone. It was the difference in their reactions to this situation, however, that opened my eyes. In the course of time I also learned what any ten-year-old pupil could probably have told me from his physics lessons: that there is no light without shade and no shade without light. And the havoc wrought by these two forces is the story of our lives.

When Sophie discovered my brother's infidelity she tried to utter a cry of protest ("If you don't get rid of them today I'll throw them out myself!" in the words of her empty threat when Luscinia and her daughter made their first appearance in our yard), but her shriek of pain soon subsided into sobs (mainly on my shoulder), and her sobbing gave way in turn to full complicity with her husband and his mistress. Sophie appears to have instinctively taken the advice of an ancient piece of Talmudic wisdom: "A man was once walking along the road when he saw a pack of dogs, and he was afraid of them. What did he do? He went and sat down amongst them." Very shrewd and practical advice, as far as it goes. But far from offering a long-term solution, since it leads only to a temporary situation that will have to be escaped in the end.

Luscinia did not take the advice of the Talmud. She attacked with tooth and claw. It is not unheard of, after all, for a man to overcome a pack of dogs and chase them off. On condition, of course, that when he is walking down the road and sees a pack of dogs he is not afraid of them.

I am not trying to argue here that superior courage is a proof of greater love. Or vice versa, for that matter. Today I am no longer interested in any kind of argument whatsoever. All I want to do is tell a story. A story that I don't understand.

Sophie may have cried on my shoulder, but she never whispered in my ear, "Let's run away together." If she had, I should have had to answer her and perhaps even do something about it.

Luscinia, on the other hand, did not pour her heart out to me but proposed taking action that, logically speaking, would solve each of our problems. But since when has logic spoken to the heart? All those years I had been burning in the torments of my love for Sophie, but when a plan of action was set before me I rejected it. And my brother, who had boasted me ad nauseam of his love for Luscinia: when he was presented with the opportunity of holding on to her, did he take it?

But I am charging ahead again. Let us return to chronicling the events as they occurred.

I did not reveal my love to Sophie, nor did I warn her of the catastrophe about to overtake her. As usual I waited. What was I waiting for? In those days I imagined that I was waiting for the gods to intervene in my favor and see that justice was done. Today I know that I was waiting for punishment and retribution, since that was what I deserved. In the depths of my heart I knew exactly what I was worth and what the future held in store.

Twelve years passed; twelve whole years vanished, dissolved, melted into thin air and came to nothing while I waited. Camillo went on dividing his week between Sophie and Luscinia, Sophie pined away in her self-imposed silence, increasingly convinced that all the blame lay at her door, since she had not come with a pure

heart and clean hands to Camillo's house but with the overween-
ing ambition to escape her fate and force her way into the aristocracy of the old established colonies.

As for Luscinia, she despaired of me and the glorious future she
had envisaged on my behalf and waited for what time would bring
on its black wings. And in the meantime she tried to fight the danger that was becoming more real from day to day. Little Luscinia
— whose anonymous father Camillo had once wanted to kill with
his revolver — was no longer so little. She was seventeen. Almost
eighteen. And she had long ago crowned Camillo as her true father,
but Camillo was a strange father. The presents he showered on her
alarmed her mother. Things reached such a pass that he was buying — and choosing — her underwear for her, her stockings, and
the bras with which she covered the budding breasts that jiggled as
she walked. And Camillo stared, and Luscinia the mother saw the
way he stared, and sometimes she saw the way he caressed this
adopted stepdaughter of his, and her heart thudded in dread. And
when the seventeen-, almost eighteen-year-old Luscinia retired to
her room at night, Camillo sat on the edge of her bed and told her
stories, just as he had done when she was six. And from then on he
had never stopped. And so little Luscinia fell asleep holding his
hand, a five-foot-seven baby. The first attempt to send her away
from home had failed, and there was no point in trying again. But
one day Luscinia the mother saw Camillo and her daughter parting
early in the morning, before the girl set off for school, and having
seen what she had seen she came to a decision. A decisive woman,
Luscinia.

She took Camillo aside and announced that the girl was older
than her years, and that if they did not want her to get into trouble they should marry her off as soon as possible.

How, exactly, they made their hasty choice I don't know, but
soon after Luscinia junior graduated from high school she was married to a young man from the colony, the manager of a packing

plant in one of the railway station warehouses in which my brother owned 51 percent of the shares. He bought them a small apartment not far from where we lived, and the problem seemed to be solved. Camillo's problem, in any case, was solved: from now on little Luscinia was all his.

Whether Luscinia senior and Sophie knew what I knew would be difficult to prove. In my opinion, they both knew that Camillo was in the habit of sending his packing plant manager to Tel Aviv on business whenever it was convenient for him and that the pair of them had agreed upon this arrangement in advance. And while Camillo's errand boy was busy in Tel Aviv, Camillo himself was busy in the love nest of the newlyweds.

During this period I was a witness to the way Luscinia senior succumbed to the same fate that had overtaken her rival Sophie: she began to cooperate in her calamity and resign herself to her fate as the victim cooperates with the murderer in a stage tragedy.

This time, too, the irresistible, the omnipotent Camillo pursued his lusts and gained his object with impunity.

Whether I hated him then, or admired him, or simply envied him, I do not know. It was probably a mixture of all three. But above all I saw myself as a participant, however passive and silent, in events, playing my part in my own way — mainly from my window, at night. And it was at this time and in this context that I wrote the following morbid passage in my diary:

Ability leads to action. Inability leads to thought, understanding, and sometimes knowledge.

When a man is able to lift a stone in the field he lays it on top of another stone and builds a house, a wall, a tower, a fort, a town.

When a man is unable to lift a stone — on account of its weight, for example — he discovers the law of gravity, invents the lever, and acquires the ability to build a wall, a house, and a town. And the circle closes.

The ability to love leads in time to the erosion and loss of love.
The inability to love leads to reflection on the nature of love and the
understanding of its mysteries; and this understanding cannot be
eroded. Only action erodes. Understanding endures forever.

This is what I wrote in my diary when Camillo was making
love to the three women in his life while I looked on, paralyzed,
as Sophie lay dying. And during that same period I also wrote:

This colony of ours, where everybody knows everybody else, and
where every deviation from conventional morality is greeted with cries
of outrage and abusive anonymous letters — why is this colony of
ours silent now? As if some oppressive guiding hand has imposed a
heavy silence on my brother's love affairs. At the bank nobody says a
word, at school nobody so much as drops a hint. There are no signs
of disapproval, or even signs that anybody knows. If they knew per-
haps they would do something. But a leaden silence prevails, and in
our yard abomination rules the roost.

Camillo's voice rose scoldingly in the night from Luscinia's
ground-floor flat and in response I heard strangled sobs, the sobbing of a woman who had stuffed her fist into her mouth to choke
back her screams. Later on I understood from what Camillo told
me that his jealousy of the anonymous man, little Luscinia's father,
far from subsiding, was growing more and more intense from day
to day. He could no longer sleep, and when he was in bed with
Luscinia at night he tortured her with his questions. He wanted to
know if the kiss she had just given him was like the kisses she had
given that man; he tried to force her to admit that that man, too,
had elicited similar moans of passion from her lips. And if she burst
into tears he accused her of putting on an act. Sometimes the
words "trollop" or even "whore" escaped his lips, and then Luscinia
froze and was unable to utter a sound. She whimpered for hours on
end, driving him mad, according to him — but he could not over-

come his curiosity. He wanted to know all the details. Did she ever take that man's organ in her mouth? How many times a night did he enter her? How many times a week? And what were the words she used when she wanted to be nice to him? Weren't they exactly the same words she was using now, with him? And if that was the case, then how could he be sure that she really loved him, Camillo? Perhaps it was all only a ritual she performed for the benefit of any man who got into her bed? She had to admit the truth. Her denials would not convince him, and he didn't believe in her tears. Tears were tantamount to an admission of guilt. If she was innocent she would rebuke him. But instead of rebuking him she cried and held her tongue. And this he refused to tolerate. He wanted a definite answer; besides, who had ever heard of a decent, self-respecting woman getting herself pregnant and giving birth to his child? What did she need it for? Why didn't she have an abortion? Perhaps she wanted a baby from the start and took a strange man into her bed in cold blood, as part of a calculated plan to get pregnant? Did her cynicism extend that far?

As I sat by my window at night their voices would reach me in bursts of sobbing and angry complaints, breaking against the closed window of their room and floating across the sleeping yard to beat against my ears like drops of water in Chinese torture.

The idea of murdering that man had been abandoned by my brother long ago, and he no longer came to ask me for the revolver. From now on his retribution was directed against Luscinia, who became the target of his wrath and the source of his madness. Camillo blamed Luscinia for robbing him of what was his by right and could not forgive her forcing him to marry her daughter off to that stupid oaf from the packing plant.

In the depths of his heart Camillo knew he was torturing and punishing her not for the sin she had committed with that man but for the loss he had suffered on her account. But even he did not have the effrontery to blame the mother for keeping her daughter from his bed.

"Believe me," Camillo said to me. "I don't care about the money I spent on buying them an apartment. But why did I have to get involved in that madness in the first place? Tell me, why?"

A few months after Luscinia's marriage to the packing plant manager, as I sat by my window early one morning listening to the muffled sobs and recriminations coming from the ground-floor flat, I fell asleep. If I had not given way to my weariness, if I had listened to the vague premonitions knocking at the threshold of my consciousness, perhaps I might have obeyed the command implicit in the brief and terrifying dream I had between the moment of falling asleep and the moment of waking to the sound of children's screams. In this dream, which could not have lasted more than a few seconds, I saw Sophie sitting up in bed and holding her arms to me, crying my name and calling me to come to her.

I awoke to the noise of children running downstairs and knocking on Luscinia's door. Whether they knew their father was there, or whether they wanted to summon Luscinia's aid, I don't know. Camillo opened the door in his dressing gown; he was in the middle of having his breakfast before leaving for work.

The children said that their mother was lying in bed with her eyes open, but she wouldn't speak or answer their questions.

We found Sophie lying on her back, with a surprised expression on her face and her arms lying limply on either side of her body.

Luscinia prepared several dishes of food, baked cakes, and put two kettles on to boil. After the funeral the mother and her daughter served the people who climbed the stairs to the second floor to console the widower, or sit with him in silence over a plate of food, in accordance with the custom of the colony. Although I was the brother-in-law of the deceased, the laws of mourning did not apply to me, and so I, too, helped them serve the food and pour the drinks. Camillo listened to his guests' condolences with a blank face, answering only the most important of them — the bank managers, heads of the Farmers Federation, and party leaders — with a nod of his head and an inclination of his ear as if he did not want to miss a single word of what they said.

In the end the visitors left and Luscinia the mother, who saw that Camillo wanted to be alone with me, stroked his hair and retired from the scene. Her daughter contented herself with a handshake and the promise that she would come back in the morning.

"Do you think she killed herself?" Camillo blurted out the moment the door closed behind them. "Did you notice anything unusual about her behavior recently?"

Idiot, I wanted to say to him, *Who do you think you're bluffing?* But I said, "It's better this way. What kind of a life did she have?"

"Do you blame me for her death?" he asked humbly.

I was silent. He too remained silent for a whole minute, and after a deliberate pause for reflection, as if he were the head of a commission of inquiry, he pronounced, "Luscinia and I are to blame for her death."

I wanted to say to him, *Which Luscinia, the mother or the daughter?* But instead I asked, "What's Luscinia got to do with it?"

"She took me away from Sophie," he said sulkingly, like a child complaining that he had been tempted from the straight and narrow by a piece of candy, and should not, in all fairness, be punished. "Didn't you see how she had me under her spell?" he added, to make his case stronger.

I said that I was tired and wanted to go to bed. At that moment I was sorry his revolver was in my house under my mattress. If he had had the revolver with him now — the fantastic thought occurred to me — he might have put a bullet into his head. But even as the thought crossed my mind I knew it had no basis in reality. Camillo was not the man to make himself pay for his sins. He was more likely to shoot Luscinia. The mother, of course; not the daughter, God forbid.

And without even looking at him, I callously turned my back on him, descended the stairs, crossed the yard, and went home. This time I did not sit at my window but went straight to bed, buried my head in the pillow, and spoke to the woman who could no longer hear me. And that must have been why I spoke to her and said everything I had been wanting to say for the past fifteen years.

Camillo was an honest man: I've said it before and I'll say it again. And since we've already buried Sophie, and I've already said a number of things in her praise, I shall now say something about my brother. Being an honest man, he was always scrupulous about paying debts of honor. When Luscinia began to hint discreetly that the time had come to settle their matrimonial status, he explained that first of all he wanted to guarantee her economic future, and since he had sons of his own and wanted to prevent her being left out in the cold after he was gone, he intended signing the ground-floor flat over to her immediately.

Luscinia was deeply moved by his generosity, but at the same time her lack of self-confidence led her to suspect that behind this chivalrous gesture Camillo was up to no good; she therefore tried to argue — with some justification — that there was no need to transfer the ground floor to her name, for two reasons: first, who said he would die before her? It was perfectly plausible that she'd be the first to go or that she would die of grief immediately after he departed this world. And second, even if he died first, half his property would be lawfully hers anyway, so why should he go to all this trouble over the ground floor now?

Camillo replied that he was the best judge in matters of property and money, and she had better leave all such decisions to him and occupy herself with things more becoming of her sex.

The version he presented to me (and from the day Sophie died, I became his almost daily father confessor) was slightly different: the version of a decent, guilt-stricken man. He knew he had murdered Sophie and that Luscinia's hands were not innocent of the dead woman's blood, either; and this being the case, he could not face the thought of going down to the ground floor and sharing Luscinia's bed. In the meantime he could endure his abstinence. How long he would be able to keep it up — time would tell. Did I understand how he felt, he asked me. And there was something else, too: from the day of Sophie's death he had suffered a certain change of heart, felt the need to search his soul anew. Perhaps he had made a grave mistake? Perhaps Sophie had been more than he gave her credit for, suffering up there in her loneliness. These were my dear brother's words: "suffering up there in her loneliness." And as he spoke them he lowered his eyes and passed his hand over his head as if he had a headache.

"For God's sake, Kalman," I said to him. "What's the point of all this talk? It's too late now."

"And besides," my brother continued, "I'm no longer sure… Perhaps I was wrong all down the line? You're right that we can't bring Sophie back to life, but there's no need to make things even worse than they already are… Hast thou killed and also taken possession? That's what hurts me…do you understand?"

Hypocrite, vile hedonist, heartless animal! I wanted to yell at him; but after having held my peace in more important matters, I let it go this time, too. "Naturally," I said, "I understand you very well, and I'm sure that you'll find an honorable and dignified way out. I can trust you for that."

And so all Luscinia's hopes came to nothing. Sophie's death, instead of giving my brother good reason to marry her, gave him an equally good reason to refrain from marrying her. For a while, it even led to a total estrangement between them. But not for long. After about two weeks my brother was no longer able to maintain his abstinence. For how could a man like Camillo — a real man, a superman, the man of every woman's dreams — abstain from sex for longer than a fortnight? And so my brother returned to Luscinia's bed, and the desperate and despairing Luscinia opened her arms while her heart trembled with foreboding.

During the period in question the nocturnal sessions at my window began to bore me, and I would retire to bed. Now that

Sophie was all mine I would speak to her for hours before falling asleep in the hope of seeing her in my dreams. But Sophie refused to come to me in my dreams. She appeared in my brother's dreams instead, and he told me about them in detail:

"Last night, when I fell asleep in Luscinia's bed, I saw Sophie. It was almost dark and she was walking down the street, holding one of our children in her arms. I know that she was already dead, and I was seeing her after her death, after she had come back from the dead, as it were. She looked fantastic, as beautiful as she used to be in the best days of her life. She pretended not to see me, and although she was sad she pretended to be happy and whispered to the child. Then she took a piece of paper, wrote something on it and put it in an envelope, which she dropped into the mailbox. She did everything with an air of indifference, as if I didn't exist at all. I thought to myself that if I were to open the envelope, I would probably find that it contained some unimportant technical communication. I had the feeling that Sophie was putting on this whole act for my benefit, to show me that she wasn't interested. When she turned away from the mailbox her step were as light and quick as a young girl's. All to show me — although she pretended not even to see me. I thought I was going to explode from sorrow."

Two days later I received another report:

"She came to me in a dream again when I was with Luscinia. This time I saw her in Tel Aviv. I was returning from some meeting, and when I wanted to cross the road, at the corner of Allenby and Bialik Streets, in the middle of the day, I heard a voice calling me, "Camillo, Camillo." I turned around and saw that Sophie — Sophie who was already dead — had come back to life again and was sitting at a sidewalk table at an outdoor café with some woman she knew. It seemed to me it was not Sophie but her friend who'd called my name. And this hurt me very much. I thought that Sophie was prepared to watch me walk past without even having me stop. I went up to the table, intending to greet her friend first, so I'd be free to kiss Sophie afterward. I patted the friend on the shoulder and turned immediately to Sophie, bent down and kissed her on the cheek. Sophie did not return my kiss, embrace me, or even smile. But she did not show any sign of displeasure either. What a good thing, I thought, that I had found her here with a woman and not a man. Still, I knew it was very likely that she was waiting for some man to turn up. Again she was as beautiful as she'd been at her best. Her face was as serene as an Acadian goddess, and she looked at me as if I were a stranger, but politely and with a kind of neutral sympathy. She froze my blood. I knew she would never come back to me, that she was lost to me and already belonged to a different orbit where I had no part. The presence of another man seemed to hover over our meeting, and her exquisite beauty, her quiet, mature beauty, was perhaps disturbed only by my presence. Something else was going on here and I was in the way. But Sophie behaved politely and patiently and showed no signs of annoyance. A terrible pain rent my heart. I knew she was lost to me, and that if I was still standing here, close to her, it was only a temporary thing. Soon this, too, would vanish. And then I woke up. And when I woke I went on thinking about what I had seen in that meeting. I remembered her eyes, her skin, and noticed that the beauty spot on her cheek had grown a little larger. Then I thought, When the body rots and ceases to exist, where does the soul go? Sophie's soul is now inhabiting my dreams. But what will happen to it when I die, I thought. Perhaps the children will remember for a while and then they'll forget, and that will be that."

A few days later my brother spoke to me again of Sophie and of what he'd seen in his dreams:

"For two days I didn't dream about her and I thought, this is my punishment. It's not enough that she's dead, she doesn't even want to visit me in my dreams. But last night I saw her again. I met her at a party with crowds of people. The party was taking place on the second floor of a house standing in exactly the same spot as the café table in my last dream. Sophie belonged to someone who was with her at the party, someone who had taken her away from me.

But the two of us had agreed to go back to each other. She allowed me to caress her and kiss her when no one was looking. But from time to time she warned me not to be so demonstrative, so as not to attract the attention of a man who had caused our separation. We had to bide our time and wait for the moment when we could declare our love in public. And the fact that Sophie was imposing underground conditions on our relationship — while her ties with the other man were free and open — depressed me profoundly. And suddenly a fuse blew, darkness descended on the hall, and she disappeared. When the lights came on again I looked for her. At first I searched only with my eyes, but then I began to call her name aloud. And then someone said she was there, and there was no need to shout. Perhaps she's down there, I said, and pointed to the street below, meaning that they had thrown her out the window and killed her. I ran downstairs shouting, "Sophie, Sophie," and I saw that the lights in the upper story had gone off, and then a man approached me, walking along the right-hand sidewalk, exactly where the table had been standing in the previous dream, where Sophie had been sitting with her friend. And the man came closer and threatened me with something that looked like a sword. I slowly backed away, still shouting, "Sophie, Sophie," and the man advanced menacingly and I could already sense the terror of the descending blow, and I woke up screaming. Dreading a return of the nightmare I tried to stay awake. But I fell asleep and dreamed again, only I can't remember the dream."

In order to spare myself the intolerable ordeal of hearing any more of his dreams, I told my brother that I was taking a vacation and going to a guest house in Galilee. And there, in a strange room and unfamiliar surroundings where I knew no one, I asked her over and over again, Sophie, why don't you appear to me? Why to him, and not to me? Don't I exist at all? Can it be possible that I am only my brother's dream? If so, then it's only natural that you don't appear in my dreams, because a dream cannot be a dreamer.

God knows, in my jealousy when Sophie was still alive I prayed more than once for my brother to disappear… But my jealousy was never so intense, so bitter and so suffocating as when Camillo told me about how Sophie appeared to him in his dreams; for the Sophie who appeared in my brother's dreams was *my* Sophie — the Sophie who in life had treated me with polite indifference and tolerance: tolerance, the most humiliating of all ways a woman can relate to a man.

In the Galilee guest house I made up mind to take a sabbatical. I wrote and told my brother about my decision but did not go home. I made all the necessary arrangements with the Education Department by telephone and correspondence, and when everything was settled I returned to the colony one morning, packed a few personal belongings, locked up my house, left a letter for my brother, and set off.

The year turned into two, then three. Once I spoke to my brother on the phone and apologized for not writing to him. He didn't sound too upset about it.

In the fourth year I was offered a post as a Hebrew teacher in Bogota, Colombia, and two years later I was appointed headmaster of the Hebrew School there.

What happened to me during these years is irrelevant to our story, and the truth is, nothing happened to me. With food I kept body and soul together, and with the help of a few friends and well-wishers I preserved my sanity.

When I returned to the colony after about seven years, it was late in the morning. My brother was presumably in his office and Luscinia at the clinic. I turned the key in the lock and opened the door to my house. A smell of mold stood in the air, the floor tile and the furniture were covered with a layer of reddish dust, and there were vestiges of dusty cobwebs hanging from the corners, where the spiders had apparently died long ago and stopped spinning them.

Using a broom and a damp cloth I restored my house to its former appearance, and at the end of several hours I dropped into the

armchair facing my window. And then I saw Camillo emerging from the ground floor with a man I didn't know, exchanging a few words with him, and parting with a handshake. The man got into his car and drove off, and Camillo went back into Luscinia's flat. He appeared to have aged considerably — in any case, his face was pale, gloomy, and angry. He did not notice me. He had always been self-absorbed, and why should he pay any attention to the fact that the window that had been shuttered for seven years had suddenly opened under his nose, and that his brother, his flesh and blood — the brother he had not seen in all that time — was now sitting at the window not five yards away, looking at him?

Afterward, Luscinia's daughter came into the yard and entered her mother's flat. She had grown a little plumper, a little heavier — a mature, thirty-year-old woman glowing with health and even a certain sprightliness. She must have noticed me, for she immediately came out again, accompanied by my brother, and pointed in my direction.

Camillo crossed the yard, almost running, fell on my neck, and burst into tears. I was thunderstruck. His head rested on my shoulder, his arms embraced me tightly, and he sobbed without restraint. God almighty, I said to myself, does he really love me so much?

Luscinia was dying. The doctors said she had at most six months to live. Her body was eaten up by cancer, but her face was almost as I remembered it when I left the country. She had fallen ill about a year before, and ever since my brother had been neglecting his affairs and spending day and night in her flat with her. When he was on the verge of collapse, two nurses came to take his place, and after a week he would return to his post, sitting by her bed most of the day and sleeping in the armchair in her room at night.

Since nothing had yet been settled regarding my return to teaching at the school, I told my brother that I was willing to stand in for him most of the day in taking care of Luscinia's needs. I urged him to go back to work on the journal and in the Farmers'

Federation. I know that these two things constituted the basis of the position he had acquired for himself, without which he would lose his self-image as a powerful, successful man.

Camillo jumped at my offer and thanked me fulsomely, in terms such as I had never heard from him before. It seemed that some hard core inside his soul had softened and melted. Tears would come into his eyes with embarrassing frequency. In the middle of a sentence he would suddenly stop, as if listening to a voice calling his name, a voice only he could hear. I was astonished at the change that had come over him. If I had not seen it with my own eyes, I would never have believed that the leopard could have changed his spots to such an extent.

A few days after I came home, my brother informed me that he was marrying Luscinia at the end of the week and that I was to have the honor of participating in the prayer quorum at the ceremony.

When the day came we sat the bride in the wheelchair in which she was taken to the bathroom for her daily toilette; her daughter brought a white lace dress, and in order for her to put it on my brother and I had to lift her from her seat. She doubled up in what was apparently a severe attack of pain, then she gave a hollow laugh and mumbled hoarsely, "So I'm going to be married at last."

The nine other men invited to the wedding ceremony were Luscinia's doctor, the secretary of the editorial board of the agricultural journal, two department managers from the bank, and five members of the colony council, as the old-timers still referred to it, although the colony had already been promoted to municipal status.

Camillo broke the glass under the canopy, put the ring on Luscinia's finger, signed the marriage contract, sipped the wine, and kissed his bride on the cheek. The look in her eyes — which never left my brother's face, as if she was afraid that he might suddenly disappear — was one of inexpressible yearning. It was a look that not only blinded me with its terrible sadness but deafened me with a kind of shriek. Joy and despair, the gladness of meeting and the dread of parting struggled with each other in her eyes, and Camillo did not dare look at her. He kept his eyes on the ground or let them wander over the faces of the guests. And when the rabbi concluded his blessings, Luscinia put her hand — which had so shriveled that her skin was as dry and glittering as a scab — on Camillo's and said to him, "My love, don't be sorry, we had happy times, too… Long ago, at the beginning… We loved each other truly, my darling. Tell me it's true, tell me…"

Camillo put his face down to hers and whispered something to her, and she smiled, as far as a person can smile on the brink of the grave. She lifted her hand slightly and stroked his pale face. Stroked his face and closed her eyes. The occasion had exhausted her and we hurried to put her back to bed. She drank a little water and the doctor allowed her to take a spoonful of the painkiller she was only supposed to take before she went to sleep at night. After that she sank into a kind of slumber. Camillo led the guests to the living room and Luscinia's daughter and I served food and drink. The guests drank without making any toasts and ate in silence. Then they all left at once, shaking my brother's hand. When we were left alone Camillo sat down on the sofa and burst shamelessly into tears. Luscinia's daughter cleared the dishes off the table, and I went to the window and looked at the deserted yard and at my little house standing opposite.

Soon a car drove in to the yard and Camillo's two sons emerged with their wives. Their father had asked them not to come to the ceremony, and they came when it was over to drink tea and inquire after the patient's health.

During the last three months of Luscinia's life I spent every day from seven-thirty in the morning till three or four in the afternoon, when Camillo came home from work, in the patient's room.

On the first days of my return from abroad Luscinia did not react to my presence in her room at all, as if I had never been away. But after a few days she placed her hand on top of mine, pressed it as hard as her failing strength would permit, and asked me to forgive her for depriving me of my freedom by her illness. Without tears in her weeping eyes she thanked me for volunteering to alleviate Camillo's suffering; she spoke as if it was agreed between us that Camillo was the sick and suffering person in that house. She told me how devoted he was to her and how many sacrifices he had made for her sake ever since she had fallen ill. A few days later, she asked me to forgive her for interfering in my life and trying to push me to action back when Sophie was still with us.

"In those days, I still thought Camillo was turning his back on me because he was jealous of my daughter's father," she said. "I was too young to understand and I thought the reason for his withdrawal was jealousy. Today I know that it was his lack of great love that caused the jealousy, not the other way around... If he had loved me with the kind of love he's capable of...in other cases...if he had loved me with all his heart and soul, he would have overcome his silly jealousy... He's capable of great love... But I was young and tried to force the issue... Don't be angry with me. I believed it was possible to achieve happiness through effort, through action...but I was wrong, of course. Happiness comes of its own accord, and love comes of its own accord... They knock loudly at your door, they almost beat it down. All you have to do is get up and open the door and drink in the happiness as long as it's pouring out... Happiness and love can't be hurried along by action and initiative...I was wrong and I paid a heavy price for my mistake... And I hurt your feelings, but you understand now and you forgive me."

I assured her that she had not hurt me at all and I tried to calm her down, hinting that it was bad for her to talk too much and that she should rest and perhaps try to sleep. But Luscinia did not stop. Almost every day of the three months before she died she told me something about her life with Camillo. She often mentioned Sophie, too, and sometimes she even tried to instruct me in the ways of the world and give me good advice about how to win my beloved. This advice, of course, related to the past to the days when

Sophie was still in the land of living. Apparently Luscinia was un-aware of the absurdity of these lectures, although I tactfully tried to point it out to her. She went on talking about the past:

"Sophie, of course, loved Camillo in her way… Her love was a true love, it came from the heart, but Sophie, poor girl, burned on a low fire… It was a feeble flame, and it could have been di-verted… Her relations with Camillo caused her so much suffer-ing. If only you had asserted yourself then, she would have come around. She was thirsty for love, but her thirst was modest… You could have offered her the cup and she would have drunk from it… And you loved her so much… I think you would have en-joyed her gentle warmth. You would have been a happy man with her, because you would have been able to feed the relationship with your own great flame, and then it would have seemed to blaze like a bonfire… Yes. I'm sure of it."

If Luscinia had been healthy, I would have reprimanded her for her words and entered into an argument with her. I would un-doubtedly have defended my love and tried to bring the shaky edi-fice she constructed down like a house of cards. But since she was lying on her deathbed I held my tongue and allowed her to go on settling her accounts and coming to terms in her own way with the life that was now passing before her eyes, the life lived by four of us in our yard.

One day, in the last month of her life, she spoke to me about her daughter.

"You've noticed my Luscinia hasn't got any children," she said. And again her face twisted on the grimace that was supposed to be a smile and was actually an admission of final defeat. "You know why she hasn't got any children…? Because Camillo forbade her to give birth. Camillo forgave me for making him marry my daughter off as soon as she graduated from high school… You know, after Sophie died I begged him to marry me, and he refused. The reason he gave was a lie, of course, perhaps because he him-self didn't know the truth… He said that he didn't want children from the same womb that had given birth in sin… That's the way he spoke to me in the beginning… Later on he realized that he was lying, and he knew that I realized it too, and so he stopped abusing me. He also stopped talking about this jealousy of Luscinia's father… The only pity is that it happened after I had already taken the blame on myself, and seen myself as a loose, weak, sinning woman who had besmirched her life with folly… I saw myself as deserving the punishment Camillo inflicted on me. It was already too late to reconcile myself with my conscience. Camillo had convinced me and broken my pride… But both of us knew what he really wanted and neither of us said anything about it. There was only one sign of what we both knew — the fact that he forbade my Luscinia to have children…to have children with her husband. Camillo wants children of his own, the children Luscinia will give him… Did you know? Tell me, did you know?"

I did not reply.

"You knew…" said Luscinia. There was not enough strength left in her lungs to allow her to sigh, and there was a certain dryness in her repeated assertion: "You knew… In any case, you know now. And from the leftovers, the margins of his love for my daughter — something came my way, too. There was something about me that he really loved, and that was apparently the resemblance between us…What he loved in me was Luscinia's mother… Like a journey backwards in a time machine…That's what must have happened… I myself was not enough… My daughter is the one he wants, the one he'll marry and have children with… I resigned myself to it long ago. I was only afraid of feeling his impatience every day, of sensing how he couldn't wait to see the last of me… But from the day I fell ill, and he's known for a year already that my fate was sealed… From the day I fell ill Camillo has been a different man, a good man, capable of godlike charity, of granting his grace freely, without asking anything in return… We haven't lived as man and wife for over a year now, and see how devoted he is to me, how he's ruining his health, abandoning his health, abandoning his career for

me… Do you think he's changed? I don't think a man his age can
change. He's simply reached a higher plane of his original nature
— which makes me think he was always the same, but there was
some obstacle preventing the revelation until now… I've never
seen him really suffer, until I got sick… And for me it's as if he
loves me at last… I know that it's pity, too, but pity caused by suffering is like love, don't you think…? I feel as if there's a kind of
light and I'm going into that light, which sometimes I can actually
see shining…"

In the last days before she died — when Camillo took her to the
bathroom in her wheelchair, after emptying her bedpan, and washed
and dried her — he would walk back along the corridor with tears
pouring freely down his cheeks. Luscinia no longer seemed to
notice. Perhaps she was no longer even aware of her own pain. She
was dazed from the morphine now being injected into her body
two or three times a day, and her eyes were dead. But even in those
last few days I seemed to notice brief moments of lucidity, when a
grieving yearning flickered in those dying eyes, a passion that broke
through the boundaries of old insults and recriminations and bore
her on her last breath toward her beloved.

How I envied my brother then! I envied him, but I loved him,
too, perhaps in the hope that by virtue of my love I, too, would
share in this wonderful thing that would never be mine.

When Luscinia died my last chance of entering that charmed circle, from which I was always being ejected, seemed to die with her.

A few days after her death my brother showed me a letter she
had left in the drawer of her bedside table: "I want my name to be
inscribed on my tombstone as follows: Luscinia Megarinsky."

My brother looked at me, waiting for my reaction. I knew that
he was very hurt by Luscinia's renunciation of the right to bear his
family name, the right he had given her by marrying her. I imagined that he expected me to express this insult to the family name
on his behalf. But all I could think of at that moment was this: if my

brother died before me, I would order one word only to be inscribed on his tombstone: Camillo.

She died, and her predictions began to come true with a speed and accuracy that reminded me of French farce.

I don't know when my brother opened the divorce proceedings between Luscinia's daughter and the packing plant manager. It is entirely possible that the divorce was an integral part of the marriage contract signed a dozen years before. There can be no doubt that the husband knew what lay ahead, just as little Luscinia knew. As compensation for twelve years of loyal service, the packing plant manager received 25 percent of the plant shares, and less than two months after the divorce he married the woman with whom he'd been waiting patiently all these years for his mother-in-law's death. Camillo and Luscinia junior were married soon before their first son was born. The second son was born a year later, and this concluded the second and final cycle of heirs to my brother Camillo, the ideal man, the real man, who at the age of sixty was enjoying the favors of a woman of thirty, to whom he was father, husband, and romantic wish fulfillment all at once. Luscinia loved him passionately. I never saw them together without her holding his hand, or stroking his sleeve, or fawning on him and kissing his cheek. And my happy brother began to blush in his old age whenever his young wife lavished these youthful tokens of love upon him.

Suddenly he didn't know what to do with his hands, he didn't know whether to stop her or join her in these cheerful demonstrations. I watched him in those days with a certain dismay, as a son might watch a father making a fool of himself in his dotage.

I'm not sure he grew any wiser as he grew older. One day he suggested to his young wife that they should go and look for her father and make themselves known to him. His jealousy had vanished, to be replaced by the desire to impress Luscinia by his chivalry. He would find her real father, and if he was in need, Camillo would be happy to help him.

Luscinia said that she was not particularly curious about the man who had never taken the trouble to find his daughter, if he knew that she existed at all. But she would not stop Camillo from going to look for him, if that was what he wanted. And that was indeed what Camillo wanted — he wanted very much to be a knight in shining armor, a man so manly that he forgave those he hated, especially when he had stopped hating them long ago. And so he set out, like a young Perseus. He hoped that he would find the object of his search in dire straits and that he would be able to rescue him. Luscinia would be impressed in spite of herself and admire the magnanimity of her noble husband.

And in fact he wasn't far wrong. The man lived in an institution for the handicapped. He was paralyzed from the waist down and unable to speak. His son and daughter-in-law came to visit him once a week, with his two grandchildren, a home-cooked dish and cookies. They would stay with him for an hour or so and then go home again. His wife had died long before and the institution was paid for by his pension fund. There was not much that Camillo could do, but he insisted on being allowed to pay for a motorized wheelchair. He gave the paralyzed man — who seemed perplexed by the whole affair — a pat on the shoulder and went home, proud and happy, to present his report to Luscinia.

When he told me about this heroic exploit, I couldn't control myself. I said, "It's too late for Luscinia's mother, too little for Luscinia's father, and completely superfluous for Luscinia your wife."

"You should have been a politician," my brother replied with tolerant affection. He was too happy to be provoked. He looked at me humorously and concluded, "Your epigrams are worthy of a British member of Parliament."

From the day little Luscinia returned to our yard to live with my brother on the second floor of his house, far-reaching changes took place in my life. First, the ground floor of the large house was cleared out and reinstated as a storeroom for old furniture and agricultural tools. It goes without saying that no lights went on in the ground floor at night; and from the observation of the lights going on and off in the upper story apartment I derived neither enjoyment or misery, so that there was no point in continuing my nocturnal vigils at the window.

The second change resulted from a decision made by Luscinia. She informed me that it was out of the question for a man to occupy himself with cooking, washing his underwear, and other women's work. "From now on," she announced, "you'll eat lunch and supper with us. And you'll bring your laundry to me to do in our washing machine. And our maid will clean your house twice a week. And I don't want to hear any arguments."

When I tried to utter a weak protest, Luscinia stated firmly, "The least I can do for someone who looked after my mother the way you did is to perform such little services for him for the rest of his life. Besides which, you're Camillo's brother. So don't talk nonsense. From now on, things will be the way I say."

To tell the truth, the only bold and assertive thing about Luscinia's personality was her way of speaking. In all other respects she was gentle, mild, and quick to perceive weakness in others. But unlike most people, who are only too eager to perceive weaknesses and mock them, Luscinia would immediately submit to the same weakness herself. With the humble and the timid she would behave with astonishing meekness; and if she came across someone crying, she would not hesitate to weep with him, even if it was only a child grieving for an escaped bird.

She idealized Camillo. If he praised a well-seasoned salad, or expressed satisfaction with a pair of socks she had bought him, she would be beside herself with joy. And if he frowned because she had forgotten to call the plumber, she would beg him to forgive her and promise that she would never, never do such a thing again. And Camillo would be obliged, in the end, to wipe her tears, apologize for criticizing her, and call himself a tyrant, a brute, and a bully. To which Luscinia would respond with vigorous protests, kissing him on the cheek and declaring that she had never met anyone so kind, understanding, considerate, and forgiving, and she doubted if there was another love as sweet, darling, and precious as he in all the world.

I would watch these cloying scenes with wonder and increasing irritation. I wondered how Camillo stood it and why he had not grown sick of it long ago. For a while I hoped that all this was no more than the obligatory billing and cooing of newlyweds, transports that would vanish with the passage of time. But a year went by, and then two and three, and nothing in Luscinia's behavior changed. She would chirp like a cricket and skip like a grasshopper whenever Camillo smiled at her; and she would get into a panic and mope and weep if it seemed to her that she'd displeased or angered him. And as she continued to behave this way, my initial reaction to her underwent a transformation. My impatience changed to wonder; and the wonder transformed into admiration. And from then on it was but a short step to all the other things that can happen to people in general, and between a man and a woman in particular.

In the end I got the message that my senses had at first refused to translate into words: if Luscinia had behaved that way toward me, instead of my brother, it is extremely unlikely that I would have turned up my nose or been disgusted by her adoration.

Not long afterward I wrote in my diary, "Little Luscinia is the Priestess of Love, the keeper of the eternal flame in our accursed yard."

For six years life in our yard ran smoothly, for the first time since Camillo's return from Italy more than thirty years before. During those six years his affairs prospered; he employed four full-time workers on the journal, the bank was incorporated by one of the biggest financial institutions in the country, and he was made a member of the board of directors, with no obligations except to attend two or three meetings a year. In summer he left his children with a nanny and took Luscinia to Switzerland. Once they took a cruise around the world and came back two months later laden with souvenirs, art objects, and presents. My brother gave me an antique English barometer that had stopped working a hundred years before, and Luscinia brought me a kind of morning robe from Peru, a woolen cape with a hole on the middle. Into this hole I was supposed to insert my head, at which point the garment fell about me and covered me completely until I looked like an umbrella. It was called a poncho. And since it had come from the hands of Luscinia, I tried it out in the winter and found it rather warm and luxurious. Extraordinary how ingenious these primitive natives are.

Luscinia was an excellent and inventive cook, and her dishes were inclined to be rich. No wonder, then, that both my brother and I put on weight; and this was especially obvious with regard to my brother, who in addition to becoming round as a barrel, became pale and puffy in the face, even his forehead growing so fleshy that the wrinkles on it looked like heavy folds of fat. He did not look well in the sixth year of his marriage to Luscinia the second; but in the depths of her affection for him — which was still strong as ever — she did not notice that anything was wrong until I pointed it out to her and suggested that she get him to see a doctor.

The diagnosis was not encouraging.

My brother was instructed to rest regularly and forbidden to eat most of his favorite dishes, with his menu in the end restricted to a few lettuce leaves, a tomato, and a cucumber. Luscinia stopped cooking and shared the diet imposed upon her husband. I, obviously, stopped eating at their table and went back to preparing my own meals in my kitchen.

Camillo lost weight, but his skin now hung on his face and arms like flabby gray rags. His belly dropped and sagged into his trousers and his shoulders seemed to slope wearily toward his arms. He stopped going out and spent most of his time in an armchair under the eucalyptus trees in the yard. From time to time Luscinia would bring him a glass of cabbage or kohlrabi juice. She herself hardly

ate at all, but her thinness added to her charms and detracted from
her years until she looked like a fourteen-year-old girl. She looked
so young now that my senses sometimes deceived me; time seemed
to stop, or to go backwards, until I found myself expecting Luscinia
the first to suddenly emerge into the yard and call her daughter to
come inside. Even their voices would sometimes echo in my ears
and bring, or so I imagined, a foolish smile to my lips.

When I came home from work I would go to my brother, if I
found him sitting in his armchair in the yard, and engage him in
conversation; for the most part, however, we would sit together in
silence. Once, after Luscinia had placed the glass of juice before him
and covered his shoulders with a woolen shawl, and gone back into
the house to take care of the children, my brother said to me, "This
happiness isn't mine. It's an inheritance I came into... Sophie taught
me to love Luscinia's mother, but apparently I didn't learn enough.
Afterward Luscinia the mother taught me to love her daughter...and
at long last I grasped what I should perhaps have known a long time
ago... I learned to be happy."

"Little Luscinia is the Priestess of Love," I quoted what I had
written in my diary to him, but I didn't finish the sentence.

"Yes," said my brother and the wrinkles on his face gathered
around his mouth in a smile. "You put it well. The Priestess of
Love... She can do no other... She's the essence of the longings
of generations...generations of women who wanted to live but did
not have the opportunity. Their men weren't worthy of it. But my
Luscinia found it. The only pity is that we met so late... It'll all be
over with me soon."

And after a few moments' silence he went on, "You know that
before she died her mother commanded me, actually commanded
me and made me promise to marry her daughter? Didn't I tell you?
Well, it's the truth. She didn't even cry when she said it. She looked
at me seriously, but not sadly, and made me promise. She said that
it would be like a continuation of the love between me and her. I
don't know why I never told you that before. You must have judged

me harshly… But now do you understand?" And after an additional
silence, he said, "How come you never got married?"

I laughed. "Now you're asking me," I said.

"You're right. I should have asked you long ago," he said. "But I
didn't ask. Maybe because I knew the answer… Do you hate me?
Tell me, don't be shy."

I got up and made a great effort to put my hand on his shoulder, even on the shawl in which Luscinia had wrapped him, but I
couldn't do it. I looked at the reddish sand of our yard and told my
brother that he was in a strange mood and was saying strange things
that didn't make sense.

He replied with a smile and even tried to wink, but it was more
like an involuntary twitch than the mischievous gesture he intended.
I turned toward my house and went into the kitchen.

In the night I was awakened by voices in the yard. I leaped out
of bed, stuck my head into the hole in the poncho, and went outside. An ambulance was parked at the gate and two people were
carrying a stretcher. Luscinia — wrapped in a dressing gown —
was holding Camillo's hand as he lay with his eyes closed and his
face contorted in pain. When she saw me she said, "Please go
upstairs and reassure the children. We're going to the hospital. I'll
phone you from there as soon as I can."

I have never been able to relate to children too young to speak or
think logically, perhaps because I had never had any children of my
own, and perhaps because I am incapable of developing human
relations on anything but a minimal level of thought.

When I went up to the second floor I found the children
Luscinia had given my brother huddled in their beds; they were
frightened and looked at me with wide open, questioning eyes. I
told them their father wasn't feeling well and their mother had
taken him to the hospital and that she would soon call us on the
phone. In the meantime I suggested we all go back to sleep, and
that I would stay with them until their mother came back. And if

necessary, I would give them breakfast and send them to school in
the morning. I told them I was a great expert at making omelettes
and pancakes and that if they went to sleep right away I would surprise them in the morning with dishes the likes of which they had
never tasted in their lives.

I was full of admiration for my newfound talent in making contact with children and persuading them to do what I told them.
They fell asleep, once I had promised to make them something
sweet for their breakfast.

I remember that on those hours in the dead of the night before
the sun rose I was mainly preoccupied with the sudden friendship
that had blossomed between myself and the children. Before this I
had hardly spoken to them. If one of the children in our yard had
had a birthday, I brought a book as a present, tasted a piece of cake,
and retired to my room. And suddenly, in the circumstances thrust
upon us in the middle of the night, I had succeeded in establish-
ing an immediate and even pleasurable rapport with them. A man's
thoughts leap over the obstacles of logic and morality, and gallop
full speed ahead like bolting horses. That night I saw myself appointed the guardian of Luscinia's fatherless children. At first I won
their hearts with cute culinary tricks, with presents and other
forms of bribery. Later the relationship grew into one of friendship
and trust, until they came to see me — after various processes had
taken place — as their father in every respect. In my fantasies
Luscinia played a rather passive role at first: she watched how I won
her children's hearts. In the end she would come to her own conclusions. I relied on her natural proclivities, too: hadn't we agreed,
Camillo and I, that she was the Priestess of Love? Moreover, nothing was dearer to Luscinia than the need to devote herself to anyone who took the place of the father she never had, to any man
who was ready to play the role of a father bringing up children in
her life and thereby restore her loss to her — the loss in whose
shadow she was to live all her life.

Early in the morning the telephone rang: Camillo had suffered a stroke and was paralyzed in half his body. The doctors said that many people in his situation recovered and returned to lead a normal life. She asked if I could send the children to school, so that she could stay with Camillo until noon. I promised I would take care of the children and expounded on the omelets, pancakes, and sweets I was going to prepare for them, as well as telling her, in detail, about the conversation that I had held with them in the night, and how they had listened to me and gone back to sleep. And they were still sleeping now. For a while there was a silence on the other side of the line. Luscinia was apparently too taken back by my blathering to reply. But she soon recovered and thanked me for my readiness to help out.

It was only after I put the receiver down that I realized how garrulous I had been; and I had even forgotten to ask her to give my best wishes to my brother or to ask for details of his illness. I hoped Luscinia would attribute my peculiar behavior to the shock of the calamity that had overtaken us.

After sending the children to school I too went to work. At noon I phoned Luscinia's apartment from school and found her at home. There was no change in my brother's condition, she informed me. I promised that as soon as I'd finished work I would go to the hospital, after which I'd be able to look after the children again until the next morning, freeing her to be with her husband. I could do this every day, I told her, and all she had to do was be with the children at lunch time to give them food I'd prepared the night before.

When I arrived at the hospital they told me my brother was sleeping. I looked at him from the door of his room and saw that his face was pale, his eyes closed, and his mouth open.

It was only at night, when the children had fallen asleep and I lay down on the couch, that I was suddenly struck by the thought that with my brother's death, I, too, would die; for I was nothing but a kind of shadow, a kind of dream that my brother had dreamed. And when the dreamer died the dream would be over. And all the fantasies that had filled my head the night before — about the children and Luscinia — disintegrated and turned to dust blown in the wind. The sound of laughter screeched and mocked in the wind and died away into a dark emptiness.

We were at the end of September, with the brief, deceptive autumn appearing and disappearing almost at once. During this elusive season my brother fell ill and was taken to the hospital, where he remained for about a month. In the early hours of the afternoon I would come home from work and go up to the second floor, to free Luscinia and let her go to the hospital. Our daily contacts lasted no longer than the time it took me to enter their apartment and for her to say "Thank you," slip out the door, and hurry off down the stairs. I would run after her and call down to the ground floor, "How's Camillo?" And she, before slamming the door, would reply, "There's no change." Afterward I would hear the engine of her car starting and I'd return to the children.

In the meantime I devoted my efforts to consolidating my relationship with her offspring. The rest will come with time, I said to myself, quite consciously, without making any attempt to suppress my fantasies. I spent the month of my brother's hospitalization bringing my secret thoughts from the basement of my soul to the attic, as the psychology books say. These books were now having a heyday in my heart, after years of neglect during which I'd found no use for them in my life. A reference to the teachings of a famous psychologist can justify almost any mental process — especially when the process in question is nothing to be proud of from the standpoint of ordinary bourgeois values. Why wonder, then, if a man who has long despaired of certain theories calls on their support when they serve his purpose and justify his deeds — or even his desires? And what, after all, separates the wish from the deed? Only the realization: that is, the descent from the exalted world of dead to the base world of action. Is so contemptible a process really worth letting influence our lives?

To believe in the visions appearing in my rosy dreams, I was forced to muffle my sense of judgment. And what could better serve to cloud the issue than the cunning of learned sophistries?

My brother died in the middle of October.

My first reaction was to freeze on my chair and listen to what was happening inside me, as I waited for the first signs of life draining from my body.

No signs appeared, and I stood up and walked about the room, at first slowly and cautiously, afraid I might begin to fall apart; then charging from corner to corner to test my strength; and in the end, prevented by the smallness of the room from breaking into a run, prancing about in something similar to a dance. I needed proof that I was alive. That my life was not over. That it had, perhaps, only just begun. That perhaps I had just been born. All these sensations made me giddy, and not for a moment did it occur to me to wonder at the complete absence of any sorrow or grief. But after capering about in my room a bit, until I was out of breath and my heart began to pound, I froze in place again — this time standing up — and suddenly had a vision of the world without Camillo. A world in which a place had been vacated. A void had suddenly yawned, a vacuum had to be filled. I was going to fill it; already I was expanding, swelling, almost rising above the ground, growing light, floating. Happy? Perhaps. I was certainly serene. Looking forward to the future. An heir.

Luscinia did not speak. From the moment I was notified of his death until the morning after the day of the funeral I did not hear her say a single word. I therefore kept a close watch on all her movements so as to gauge the right moment to introduce a remark or two into the silence in which she had wrapped herself.

At first big tears streamed from her eyes, trickled down her cheeks, and dropped onto her dress. She didn't bother to wipe them away. When the fountain of tears dried up, the whites of her eyes were red, and she stared silently into space. She stroked the heads of her frightened children without uttering a single sound, glancing at them from time to time as if trying to remember who these children were and where they had sprung from. She didn't look at me at all, even though I was there circulating among the visitors most of the day and night, serving coffee and dragging chairs from the dining alcove into the living room. In the morning I went out to buy all the newspapers, in order not to miss a single one of the obituaries published by the banks, the local authorities, our municipal council, the Farmer's Federation, and the Publishers' Union. The condolence letters we received, too, were from institutions, not individuals. For a moment I was on the point of drawing Luscinia's attention to this significant fact, but I immediately thought the better of it. I imagined she would notice it for herself, and it would be better for such comments not to come from me. And as I wandered around the apartment, shaking hands and serving coffee, my mind swarmed with plans. Once I even caught myself examining the possibility of making architectural changes on the second floor so that I could have a room to myself, a kind of library and study combined. My little house we would be able to rent, thereby increasing my monthly income, which in any case couldn't compare with my late brother's. At the same time, Luscinia and her children would now be coming into property that had once belonged to my parents, and it was only fair that I, too, should share in the benefits. Eventually, Luscinia would inherit my property, too. There were about thirty years between us.

The seven days of mourning passed without an opportunity for me to speak to her. At the end of the mourning period Luscinia opened her mouth and thanked me for all the help I had given her during her husband's illness. She said I had done my duty faithfully and that she would never forget it. She also said that she no longer would require my help and that from now on I was free to go about my business. "You must have neglected a lot of things at home," she said. "Now you'll be able to put everything straight again." And to make certain I understood her correctly, she took my hand and as she shook it she steered me firmly toward the door.

The shock was so great that all I could do was mutter something about always being at her service and go away.

It was only when I sat down on a chair in my kitchen that I felt the rage flooding me. I rested my elbows on the table, held my head in my hands, and tried to remember when, in fact, I had begun to think about Luscinia. For a long time, perhaps the whole day long, I sat there, until in the end I came to the final conclusion that I had never fallen in her net, and I had certainly never been in love with her. When all's said and done — I said to myself — she's nothing but a mixed-up little girl, who was brought up by a wild, reckless mother and without a father; her first marriage was imposed upon her and only increased the confusion of her deluded mind and crazy character. In the end she married my brother, who could have been her father, if not her grandfather. And now she's gone out of her mind completely. There's no reason for me to feel insulted. On the contrary, I should be glad that I wasn't swept up into that madness; an infantile, almost retarded child in the body of a woman approaching forty. I should congratulate myself on my good fortune at having escaped the fate of my brother, who had made a laughing stock of himself and fathered two grandchildren in his old age. He even brought about his own death by carrying on like a man of half his age. God help the man who refuses to reconcile himself to growing old. Old age has to be accepted for what it is, with all its pain and loneliness. A man should be grateful to life for offering him friendship and love in the days of his youth and in his prime. When he grows old, he should be satisfied with memories.

At that moment, sitting in my kitchen, I forgot that I had no memories. Or rather, my memories were not mine.

Luscinia, however, surprised me. Less than a week after she had thrown me out of her house, I found a note on my door: "Shalom. You know I cook for myself and the children anyway, and it would be no trouble at all if you joined us every day for supper. Please let me know."

Aha, I said to myself, the Priestess of Love! Nature was beginning to take its course. But I was in no hurry; I had time. I wrote back: "Thanks for the offer. For the time being I prefer to eat at home."

After which I heard no more from her, either in writing or otherwise, apart from "good morning" and "good evening" whenever we bumped into each other in the yard. Sometimes I was almost tempted to ask her if she needed advice or help with the formalities of my brother's death or in moving the furniture. But I checked the impulse and held my tongue. I hoped she would take the initiative. Women like her, I said to myself, don't beat around the bush, and in the end I would be sure to hear what I wanted.

And so the days passed and turned into months. Then, six months after Camillo's death, something did happen in our yard.

At first I read about it in the newspapers: when the British army evacuated the country, in 1948, there was a rumor that the British Mandate government had begun drilling for oil on the south, without completing their explorations. Now our own government had decided to take up where the other had left off. The rumors gave rise to hopes, and some people even spoke of a speedy solution to all our economic and military problems, of making instant fortunes, of a new era in the Middle East.

If Camillo had been alive he would surely have known whether it was wise to buy oil shares. But Camillo was dead, and Luscinia made do with her pension and did not bother her about shares. As for me, I went to see my bank manager and asked him if he thought I should invest. From him I learned that a crew of American oil drillers led by a well-known geologist was coming to stay in our town within a matter of days and that he meant to consult this geologist himself. After that, he'd be in a better position to advise me.

A few days after my interview with him, the bank manager called and asked if the ground floor of my late brother's house was available for rent. The American geologist had arrived and was looking for somewhere to stay; if we had anything to offer him, we would not lose on the deal.

I leaped at the chance and went over to speak with Luscinia and advise her to rent the ground floor flat to the American geologist. As usual, my tongue ran away with me, and I told her about the chances of finding oil, the shares, and the inside information I was about to receive from the bank manager.

Luscinia said she had no objections and that, in fact, she had been thinking lately that an addition to her monthly income would come in handy.

The next evening the bank manager arrived with the American geologist, who graciously consented to come and live in our yard while I waited patiently for his verdict before deciding whether to invest my money in oil futures.

In the meantime I helped Luscinia drag some of the old furniture and junk from the ground floor flat into one of the rooms in my house, since one room, apart from the kitchen and bathroom, was enough for me as long as I lived alone.

Two members of the drilling crew delivered the geologist's few possessions and he followed them in his car, which we gave a permanent parking place between the two eucalyptus trees at the entrance to the yard.

On the day he moved in I invited the geologist to have supper with me in my kitchen. He was about fifty, fifteen years younger than I, with a thatch of tough gray hair growing closely over his head that looked like a silver crown over the dark beaten bronze of his tanned face. His eyes were blue, very light and round, and their whites were veined with red, like his nose — both indications that he indulged in various alcoholic beverages. He was a talkative fellow, with clumsy but hearty manners, and a level of general knowledge — outside the limits of geology and the bituminous layers in the bowels of the earth — identical to that of a child of ten brought up in a family of peasants.

We soon discovered that in addition to English we had another language in common — Spanish. The geologist had worked for years in Latin America and even spent some time in Colombia. Our memories, however, had very little in common. I had lived in the Jewish community, above a synagogue, while he had lived with a Catholic woman who was separated from her husband and accordingly treated her lodger with remarkable friendliness. He explained that the ideal accommodation for a peripatetic geologist was in the home of a divorcee or widow, since such a woman longed for the delights that they had already tasted but were now denied. And if the lodger knew how to treat a woman right, he would be amply rewarded in the end.

And the geologist winked at me with his pure, glassy eyes and cocked his head in a gesture at once guilty and coy.

It transpired that he had no idea of the family connection between Luscinia and myself, which accounted, no doubt, for the uninhibited tenor of his conversation. That supper he shared with me in my kitchen was our first meeting and could also be called our last. Afterward, when he'd heard (apparently from Luscinia) that I was her late husband's brother, our relations were confined to polite greetings.

Early in the morning he would return from his work in the south and park his car between the eucalyptus trees next to the gate. Lazily almost in slow motion, he would extract his long body — tightly clad in blue jeans and a red, white, and black striped flannel shirt — and before locking his car door he would bend down and remove the presents he had brought for Luscinia's children: long thin cylinders of rock drilled up from the depths of the earth as samples of the geological strata. Every evening he would bring these samples back for them. The children would shriek with delight when they caught sight of him from the second-floor window, where they had already stationed themselves half an hour before to wait for him and his daily offerings. They would charge down the stairs, prance around him, and tug at his sleeves. But I was their uncle, their father's brother! Why should they bestow their love on this briber and seducer, who turned their heads with worthless bits of rock? There was something perverse, cruel, wrong, and unnatural about the whole affair. How had things come to such a pass?

And I, from my window, looked on. I too — following the children's example — made a habit of sitting at my window before the sun set and waiting for the geologist's return.

The first weeks of his arrival amongst us coincided with my retirement, and a more or less logical chain of association led me to consider writing Luscinia a note in the following terms: "I accept your offer and will come to you for supper." But I put it off day after day, until in the end I realized that the circumstances were inauspicious.

I do not know if it had been agreed between them in advance that in addition to the room he rented on the ground floor he would also receive — in return for extra payment, I hope — his dinner, which he would eat with Luscinia and the children. In any case, this is what he began to do. From his car he would go to his room to shower, and then he would go upstairs to dine with them in their kitchen.

From my window I saw that they spent a long time over their meal, but as soon as it was time to put the children to bed the geologist would retire to his room downstairs. The light would go on for a while in the children's room and soon go off again. Afterward the light would go on in Luscinia's bedroom, without going off in the geologist's bedroom on the ground floor. He was busy classifying the finds of the day's drilling and typing his reports, and Luscinia — what was she doing? The light was on in her room, and that is all I know.

Gradually the clouds gathered on the horizon of my life. I would not be swallowed up instantly by terror and extinction, but drop by drop, as far as my mind was able to absorb the poison step by step, in regular doses and amounts insufficient to kill me on the spot.

At first I saw and understood that Luscinia and the geologist were becoming close friends. The nomadic geologist had nobody here — or perhaps in the whole world — but this temporary landlady, the young widow; and Luscinia, too, had nobody to talk to in our colony apart from her lodger. Her lodger and her children.

At this stage in my awareness of what was happening in our yard I kept going back to my fantasies: whether they found oil or not, the time would come for the geologist to go home, or to move on to some other country. And then Luscinia would gladly come back to me (come back to me? or just come to me?). And it would be I who went upstairs in the evenings to sit at her table with her children, who listened eagerly to my stories, my instructions, my advice, and my guidance. And after supper, after Luscinia put the children to bed, she would return to the kitchen, where I would be sitting and waiting for her with a book in my hands, ready to read her some tender, moving passage that spoke to the heart and prepared it for intimacy and reconciliation.

That was what I fantasized during the first stage, as I sat at my window and observed the sequence of the lights going on and off in the kitchen, the children's room, his room, and Luscinia's bedroom. Just before midnight all the lights would go off and I, too, would retire to bed.

And then came the second stage, less than two months after the geologist arrived in our yard.

One day he drove up in his car at sunset, the children greeted him exuberantly, he presented them with the smooth pretty stone cylinders and went into his room. But this time he failed to emerge from it. He stayed in his own flat. *They've had a row*, I said to myself. *Tomorrow she'll chase him out of the house.*

And I sat at my window and imagined Luscinia coming to me, crossing the reddish soil of the yard and approaching my window. "It's so long since we were alone together," she would say to me. "Isn't about time for you to come up and have a serious talk with

me? We've got so much in common. After all, you're my late husband's brother, and it's high time for us to get together, talk things
over, thrash out whatever needs thrashing out, and come to the
logical conclusions." Thus I put words into her mouth, words that
made sense and hinted deliberately at what I was only too ready to
understand. I immediately acceded to her request and went upstairs with her to her apartment.

And even as I was choosing the right words to say to her, I saw
something that at first I was too stunned to take in and whose sig-
nificance I perhaps only comprehended after two or three days. It
was the children's bedtime. The light in their room went on and
after a while went off again. Luscinia was putting her children to
bed. Instead of the light going on in her bedroom, however, it went
on again in the kitchen; but only for a short while. And then the
light went on in the stairwell. I heard her footsteps. She was going
downstairs to the ground floor. The geologist was standing in his
doorway. He was ushering her into his flat, and the door was closing behind them. But before it closed I saw the pot and the basket
of food in Luscinia's hands.

The light now went on in the geologist's kitchen. Were they sitting down to eat? I don't know. I can only guess. Two days later I
knew that I had guessed right. They were sitting down to eat. For
about a half an hour I held my breath, gazing into the darkness of
the yard. And then the light went off in the geologist's kitchen. A
few seconds later it went on in his bedroom, and a moment or two
after that it went off again. I sat at my window and in the early
hours of the morning I saw the light going on in his bedroom, and
a moment or two after that it went off again. Luscinia went up to
the second floor and the light went on in her bedroom. Went on
and off again immediately.

Within the space of two or three days everything becomes clear:
the lights go on and off and tell their story, and my staring eyes see,
and my mind refuses to grasp what they see, and the eucalyptus
trees in the yard do not shudder. The sky does not fall and the soft,

fragrant summer evening breathes with divine insouciance. Not a creature, not a bush, not a star sympathizes with my agony.

And so it goes all summer long, and then the brief autumn comes and the first rains, and the winter, and they have not yet found oil in our parts, but neither have they despaired of finding it. And the bank manger has still not decided on the right advice to give me with regard to the shares, and consequently I do nothing. I wait.

My daily routine does not change. In the morning I am still at my window watching the geologist: he emerges from his room with a broad, slow step, like a movie star in slow motion, and as he walks over to his car he puts his hand in the back pocket of his jeans and pulls out a bunch of keys. Very slowly, as if he takes some special pleasure in this insignificant daily routine, he passes the various keys before his eyes, like a Moslem rolling his prayer beads between his fingers. Finally he lights on the car key, which he handles with absurd, irritating care, as if it were some precious, fragile object. For a split second, as he inserts the key into the car door, his face takes on a solemn expression. He looks at the opening door like a man witnessing a miracle. I would almost say, like a man watching a baby emerging from the womb of his beloved wife. But all it is is a car door opening. What, I wonder, can he be seeing in that crude, limited imagination of his? Memories of the night, perhaps, from which he has just parted, rising from his warm bed with the smell of Luscinia's body still clinging to its sheets.

His tall body, supple as a panther's, bends over the car and he slides into the driver's seat and disappears. Now all that remains is to wait for the sound of the engine, then the wheels leaving the sand of the yard and meeting the gravel of the private road leading from our house to the street. And then I stand up, sip a glass of cold water from the kitchen tap, and go to bed. Most of the day I sleep, which is my great good fortune; for there are some people who are unable to sleep at all. But I can sleep, and I sleep until noon, make myself a snack, and then go back to sleep again, this time with the help of a newspaper or a book; and if necessary I take a sleeping pill. Late in the afternoon I get up to prepare myself for sunset. I sit at my window and wait for the sound of the car. It makes itself heard from a distance, comes closer on the road, stops next to the gate; the engine dies. It always seems to die suddenly, and my heart is always pierced by one slight stab, every evening. Afterward I follow the geologist in my mind's eye getting out of his car and going into his flat, and immediately I see the light going on in the ground-floor kitchen. From my window I now raise my eyes to the kitchen window on the second floor, where the light will go off in another minute or two. Now I close my eyes, for what is there is to see I have already seen. From now on my imagination will take over and show me what I know, Luscinia is coming down the inside stairs, the supper dishes in a basket in her hand, and her face is glowing with the radiance of longings fulfilled, for this is the moment she has been looking forward to all day long. In the doorway to the ground-floor kitchen stands the American geologist; he takes the basket from her hand, bends down to kiss her cheek, and they sit at the table to eat.

For about half an hour I hold my breath, gazing into the darkness of the yard until the light goes off in the kitchen. A few seconds later the light will go on in his bedroom, and a moment or two later it will be switched off again. Then it will be dark until the early hours of the morning, when the light will go on again in the bedroom for a while. Luscinia will go back upstairs to her flat, and I know that she'll go into the children's room first. Perhaps she'll straighten their pillows, perhaps she'll kiss them in their sleep, and then she'll retire to her bedroom. I greet the dawn with burning, half-shut eyes.

After a while I watch the geologist walking sleekly to his car. As if performing the steps of a dance.

Lately I haven't been sleeping in the morning but prowling around my room. Afterward I sit down to write. I'm writing now.

★

It's winter. Sometimes it rains all night long and drenches the earth not with drops but with rivers of water. That's the kind of rain we sometimes get in these parts. And torrents of water pour down on my windowpane, distorting my view of the outside world. The light in the opposite window is no longer a light but a fire, a flame flaring up and dying down, leaping and whirling, playing tricks, mocking me gaily. And even the torrents of water pouring down my windowpane have something evil about them. The water tries persistently to break into my life, and only the windowpane stops it from carrying out its plan. But it won't give up, as if this were some deliberate and maddening show of hatred. Sometimes the rain is so fierce that I can see the sand in our yard refusing to soak up any more, and a glittering puddle spreads before my eyes. The light in the opposite window is reflected in the puddle. Now I have two lighted windows, as if one weren't enough. If you still haven't gotten the hint, says the rain, here's another window for you. Now do you understand?

Sometimes lightning brightens the yard. A short flash, and immediately the sound of thunder rolling beyond the orange groves. And in the brief moment of absolute white light I try to take in the sights that the lightning is, perhaps, trying to show me. As if the lightning can make the walls transparent. As if the lightning wants to tell me that a dark window does not necessarily mean everything has come to a stop and gone to sleep. Behind dark windows lusts blaze and bodies writhe and cries escape, says the lightning. And the thunder deafens the pain a little. And the stillness in its wake, with the gurgling of the water in the drains and the pattering of the rain in the puddles and on my windowpane — all these bode me no good.

I stare into the windowpane that is dry inside and drenched outside, and my thoughts whirl: water thoughts, accompanied by watery sounds, wet and cold. The bodies of the dead I think are exposed to this water, which ultimately seeps into their graves and washes their white skeletons. From where I sit, from my window

and yard, it percolates below our little road, flows into the subterranean channels underneath the main street, turns right and reaches
the old cemetery. Sophie and Luscinia are there, and my brother is
not far away. My mother and father, too. Only I sit here alone in
the land of the living, a solitary witness to the revels in which the
skeletons of those who are not yet dead dance. And they do not
only dance: they clutch at each other in fierce embraces, they give
vent to passionate cries, as if in a frenzy they perform the rites
incumbent upon them in this world — copulation, a fleeting cry
of joy, which is no more than a shriek of terror in the face of certain death.

For a while the warm beds withstand the cold, menacing water,
flowing without cease. In the end the water will seep into the
shrouds and make them moldy; it will rot the flesh and purify the
white bone, until it reverts to chalk in the earth.

And I, who do not know what part I have to play in this process
— since all I do is sit at my window and watch — I, who have been
appointed to observe, momentarily rebel. In my stupidity I rebel,
in the terrible sadness that seeps through me and empties me and
annihilates me. And instead of being proud of the nothingness that
has revealed itself to me, chosen me out of all creation to reveal
itself to me; instead of being grateful, I rebel. And in my rebellion
I fall very low, which is the fate of all rebels who lack the intelligence to accept the divine order and submit to it. I rebel and de-
grade myself and dream:

Oil is not found in the south. The geologist is sent packing. And
Luscinia — our Priestess of Love, who personifies the tumult, who
worships the transient and the perishable — crosses the yard. There
is a basket of food hanging from her arm, and all the teachers who
used to sit drinking tea in the staff room with me see her crossing
the yard and approaching me with a basket of food on her arm. She
lays the table in my kitchen. And then we go to bed. The rain can
beat against the windowpane as hard as it likes; the wet and the dark
can reveal themselves in a sudden flash of lightning and disappear

again in the roll of the thunder, and she and I will refuse to read the writing on the windowpane. She and I will be oblivious. This gift of sweet oblivion we shall seize from the jaws of the void, so that we may possess a single hour of what I have never known, of what geologists, bank managers, and the heads of local councils call by the name happiness.

The plan took flesh.

When the light went off in Luscinia's children's room, and then in her bedroom, and the sun was about to rise, I stood up and went into my room and removed my brother's revolver from its hiding place under my mattress. From the weapons training of my youth, I remembered everything I needed to remember. I dipped a rag in the sunflower oil I use to make my salads and I oiled the barrel and the trigger. The magazine was full of nine-millimeter bullets. One of those bullets from the barrel of an American Colt would not only kill, it would smash to pieces. Knock its victim to the ground with its force.

A dull gray light rose from the east. The rest of the sky was dark black, with rivers of water washing the earth, trickling down the window, and making the surface of the puddles shudder. In the flashes of lightning the huge raindrops looked like a veil of lace separating me from the house opposite. Hostile, dancing lace that refused to tear and disappear.

You can come out of your room now, I said to my geologist. *Go on, come out, put your hand in your back pocket and play with your keys to your heart's content. I'm ready for you.*

I stepped out of the door and stood in the entrance alcove, hidden from the rain but with a good view of the yard and the place where the car was parked. From where I was standing to the car was less than ten meters away. And I'd been a good shot when I was young.

As the sun began to rise the rain increased, and the lightning splitting the air revealed nothing new to my eyes. Light within light, I said to myself, brings no benefit. Only the thunder in its wake interrupted the monotonous swishing of the water dripping from the clouds. A filthy morning. But I — so close now to the hour of my longings — refused to submit to the elements. Suddenly I was girded with heroism and arrogance, and it's quite possible that I may even have hummed a bar or two of some song to myself.

The door of his flat opened, and he stood in the doorway looking up at the sky, as if he'd just realized it was raining outside. Surprise was on his face. He dropped his eyes to the ground, as if selecting islands of dryness among the puddles over which he could hop to his car. *Hop to your heart's content, geologist,* I said to myself. *Soon you'll hop into your grave you thieving swine. Of all the yards in the world you had to choose ours?*

My excitement reached fever pitch. After all, I'm not a professional killer. I've never so much as swatted a fly on the wall.

He began to jump over the puddles, the lightning flashed and the thunder thundered, and the whole thing took on the aspect of an operetta, with the hero dancing to the strains of the orchestra. I watched the spectacle with amazement and almost burst out laughing.

When he approached the car and put his hand into his back trouser pocket I realized that the moment of decision was almost upon me. It was now or never. I slid the bolt back and inserted a bullet into the barrel. I raised my arm and aimed.

When he bends down to open the door he'll get it, I said to myself.

There was a flash of lightning followed by a thunderclap. And since one noise leads to another — this, it seems to me, was the reason for what I did then — I squeezed the trigger prematurely. My arm jumped with the force of the blast.

Now he was next to the car, examining the keys in his hand. At last he found the right key. Now he bent down to the door. I shot again. I heard the shot but the geologist, who was standing about ten meters away from me, did not seem to hear anything. I saw him inserting the key into the keyhole. I shot a third time. He got into his car, easing his tall, lithe body into the seat, and shut the door. I listened for a moment to the sound of the ignition, which coughed a couple of times before the engine started. The car moved off and drove out of the yard.

I burst out of my hiding place and ran after the car, shooting bullet after bullet until the magazine was empty. I stood on the gravel of our private road, a tunnel enveloped by acacia trees, and looked after the receding car. At the bend of the road he turned right onto the main street and disappeared from view. I stood where I was, my wet clothes clinging to my body, the empty revolver in my hand, following the car in my mind's eye. I saw it passing the old cemetery, and its driver didn't even know who lay buried there in our red soil. He sped southward, crossed the borders of our town and turned onto the highway going to the desert. In an hour or so he would reach the drilling site.

Luscinia turns over in her bed, murmuring something into the silence of the dim room. Remembering, no doubt, the touch of his catlike body, returning to his embraces in her sleep. And the geologist, no doubt, before stepping out of his car and beginning the day's work, raises his hand to his nose and breathes in the smell of her body clinging to his fingers.

I walk down the road in the rain, the revolver hanging from my hand. At the bend in the road I turn right and drag my feet along the old cemetery wall. On both sides of the wall the rain beats down incessantly. I go to my dead and they do not come back to me. In this regard the ancients were right.

What was I trying to do? What was I trying to prove? And what would have happened if I had succeeded in my designs? I have no solutions. Luscinia — if she so desires — will be able to have her say. But Sophie never said anything; and neither did Luscinia's mother. And even my brother never took the trouble to explain. Once he asked me why I never married. But he immediately added that he knew the answer.

So why didn't he tell me, too? I was standing in the rain with the revolver in my hand. I looked at it, raised my arm, and hurled the revolver over the wall into the cemetery. I heard it falling onto one of the tombstones, the sound of the steel hitting the marble. Then I turned around and started walking home. I walked slowly, letting the rain wash over me.

The rain would go on falling for a long time, I thought. The sky was charged with black clouds, swollen with water. The rain must be deluging the whole of the south too. But since the oil drillers delved into the depths of the earth, the rain would not stop them from doing their work. Soon, perhaps, they would even find oil, and my bank manager would come to me with a proposition, perhaps.

But whether they found oil or not, in the end the geologist would be dismissed. He would probably go back to Latin America. And another love would come to dwell in our yard; the love that perishes only with the body, and what the body hides within it. Something that, when all is said and done, I apparently know nothing about.

translated by Philip Simpson

IN THE ISLES OF
ST. GEORGE

❖

Aharon Appelfeld

IN THE COURSE OF HIS WANDERINGS, Chohovsky arrived at the Isles of St. George. These little islands south of Italy were once inhabited, and the name they were given, although its origin has long been forgotten, bears witness to the certain sanctity attributed to them. For years they have been devoid of human dwelling. The sparse vegetation lives its humble life under the sun.

Many years ago oil prospectors came to try their luck. They drilled and went away again without finding anything. And ever since then, the place has been abandoned to its silence. Not even tourists and adventurers go there anymore. The desolation of the islands is well known throughout the area.

Chohovsky was tired of his wanderings: only solitude would be able to absorb the poison of the years from his body. He embarked in a simple rowboat. He wanted to leave his fate behind, his stupefying weariness. He didn't expect to find anything but infinite emptiness, infinite sunshine. He would sleep a long sleep and let the ripening of time do everything, as it were, without him.

Early in the morning the old fisherman plied his oars and the calm, late summer sea stretched before them.

"To St. George," said Chohovsky, and the old fisherman understood that a tourist with money to spend had fallen into his net.

The fisherman did not speak much, but his very silence seemed to endow the little he did say in his rather curious dialect with an importance over and above its contents.

Chohovsky felt the uneven progress of the boat drawing him into the heart of the sea. At first he felt a slight nausea, which gradually gave way to sleepiness and then to a kind of elation, as if his life were approaching some exalted end. But he wasn't sure about the nature of this exaltation, for in his time he had also pursued sin with the same elation. He knew, though, that this time it would be different. He imagined some long seclusion, perfectly pure, that would purge his heavy body. In the depths of his heart he believed some kind of atonement was awaiting him. In his mind's eye he saw the figure of a man who would recount one evening, in a hut or cave, the miraculous events of his life — a benevolent monk perhaps, to whom he could reveal his guilt. He knew this would not atone for his sin, which was too deep for any human hand to eradicate, but he hoped that the unknown distances held some listening presence to whom, and to whom alone, he would be able to reveal his guilt, and to him alone.

For a moment he felt he was already free of himself, that he was no longer running away but about to surrender himself willingly, and everything to do with financial speculation and the police was already behind him.

The night before he had still not decided whether to give himself up or flee. Until midnight he had walked the streets of the drowsy little town, wondering at the tranquility and the country smells. It was a rural scene, bringing a familiar memory to mind — the village of his childhood, which had been destroyed long ago and did not even survive in his heart. He walked on, glad of every sight that greeted his eyes — brown-skinned children running about half naked, pregnant women, men in the café. The police looked half asleep in their faded uniforms, like low-grade municipal inspectors too dim-witted for any other job. The police station was housed in a shed. It looked like a kiosk keeping its cold drinks hidden from the heat. An electric light bulb shone dimly from the recesses of the room.

The idea of announcing his presence here to them seemed idiotic. A few tourists strolled through the town. In their light, foreign hats they stood out in the crowd. Ideas of escape did not preoccupy him; he had no plans. All roads seemed possible to him. The tension and oppression were already behind him. His thoughts were like a reel, mindlessly spooling out yards of film and quickly winding them up again. For a moment or two his thoughts would evaporate and then a rapid movement would fill his head with the grating rhythm of the reel.

The fisherman rested his hands on the oars. They were far from shore, with water all around them. "We'll be there by evening," said the fisherman, trying to gauge this passenger and his intentions.

The locals were used to strange visitors. Over the past few years they had seen adventurers, embezzlers, people whose madness drove them where it would. Ever since the rest home had been built in the hills of Fiarte, the little town had been roused from its slumbers and quietly attached to the beaten track.

What does he want in that wilderness? thought the fisherman. Chohovsky read his thoughts.

Always, ever since he was a boy, he had been able to guess the right direction; even though he never saw it clearly, he always had some intimation. And thanks to this obscure knowledge he always arrived at his destination. Now he was far out at sea, the boat advanced, and you could scan the distance without straining your eyes. For the moment the islands were anonymous shapes shrouded in mist.

The full sunlight suffused everything, down to the tiniest drop of water. It was hard to believe in the existence of darkness, but the dense mist enveloping the islands showed clearly enough that at night the clouds would come and the light would dim. He trembled at the thought that at night he would remain there alone. Only now, it seemed, did he realize the meaning of what he had done. The speculator in him came to life, the days when he had faced danger defiantly, navigating his transactions through narrow straits. Daring, and perhaps even madness, had guided him then.

"Perhaps you'd be so kind as to tell me something about these islands?"

"Haven't you been here before?" asked the fisherman, as if his venerable age gave him the right to a rude reply.

"Never."

"It's empty, they say, right down to the lowest level of hell."

"But from a distance they look beautiful."

"Emptiness can be deceptive — people have already been tempted by the thought of treasures buried there. They dug and dug and found nothing. And you, sir, if you don't mind my asking, is this a pleasure trip?"

"Something like that."

The fisherman asked no more questions, but it was clear he felt there was something odd about his passenger and his purpose. The fear of God was on him. Chohovsky thought about all the times he'd been on the run. His whole life after the war seemed like one long flight, whose end he imagined he now saw in the misty shapes looming up before him.

At first he was in Vienna. Deals with American soldiers — the army surplus trade, they called it — flourished, reaching heights undreamed of by the boldest speculator. But it meant walking a tightrope, and the tightrope snapped. Like music, commerce, too, sometimes reaches heights only the spirit can attain. Too subtle to grasp, he always sought, as if in some godlike game, to bring his speculations to his secret summit, a tower too high to support its own height. Everything moved inevitably toward the collapse he could not prevent, although he had often tried to.

He was forced to flee to Italy. His previous experience and old contacts proved useful. He recovered, changed his name, lived under two false names, quickly adjusted to the Italian climate and mentality, and soon felt as much at home in Rome and Naples as he did in Vienna: just as familiar with the alleyways where money and goods changed hands.

And again his dealings rose to dangerous heights. For a moment everything appeared stable, and then it all collapsed. With only a small amount of cash, he had arrived in Israel, destitute. In Israel, too, he could not rest. As soon as he arrived his mind began to race, and it found plenty of scope. Only this time he knew exactly how things would end, and he watched the tower closely as it built toward its own downfall.

Again he escaped to Italy, knowing that this time he would not get away. Wherever he turned he met a trap.

"Where did you learn Italian?" asked the fisherman.

"I know Italy well. I lived here for years."

"Greek?"

"No, Jewish."

Never before had he revealed his identity to a stranger, although all the names he'd adopted had been Jewish. He preferred not to be explicit about his origins, for even in the remotest hamlet Jews were regarded with suspicion.

The fisherman was taken aback and swallowed his reply, but politeness obliged him to respond and he said, "You don't look it." And after a pause, he asked, "Do you want me to take you back to the mainland this evening?"

"No," Chohovsky said firmly.

The noonday sun stood high in the sky, an autumn sun whose rays were harmless even in the middle of the sea. The tarpaulin the fisherman had spread out shaded his head. The mild sunshine caressed his shirt.

"We're making progress," said the old man.

It was plain that his peace of mind had been disturbed. He rowed through the water as if he wanted only for the voyage to end.

Among other things, these poverty-stricken regions engendered legends of their own about the Jews. For years no Jew had lived here; but travelers, especially Armenians going south in search of a living, had casually sown stories and sayings about the origins and ways of Jews, which the southern imagination endowed with dimensions of its own. The old man was apparently having difficulty accepting the idea that he had a Jew for a passenger in his boat. But they had already gone halfway and retreat was out of the question. Besides, the stranger had treated him generously, paid him in advance, and more than he had any right to expect. But this very generosity now presented itself to his simple mind as an act of temptation. In the end he recovered himself and said, "Pardon me for asking, but what are you going to do there?"

"Nothing."

Now he knew there was something wrong about this voyage.

"I'm afraid," he said and rested the oars. "I'm an old man. I'll give you back your money, but please don't make me go any farther. I had a bad dream. I'm afraid to go any farther."

The old man's expression was helpless. His terror was palpable and expressive, stiffening his face into cold, unnatural lines.

Chohovsky hung his head. He was overcome with a kind of self-pity, as if it was only now that he realized what this voyage meant to him.

The old man looked at him, sobbing, and said nothing.

"You're afraid," said Chohovsky. "If you want to turn back I'll buy the lifeboat off you — for the full price."

The old man had not expected this. For a moment common sense, or fisherman's sense, battled with superstition and overcame it.

"I'll pay you extra," said Chohovsky, to encourage common sense, "and I promise that nothing will happen to you."

The old man put out his hand, examined the notes, and put them in his pocket, as if the money were a recompense he had coming to him.

Chohovsky realized that it would now be best to reveal the truth, but this truth refused to be put into words. In the end he said, "You've gained my confidence. I'm prepared to tell you the truth."

The fisherman laid down his oars, as if surrendering to powers greater than he. Those tough fishermen, who treated their wives roughly at home, could be as gullible and obedient as children.

"I'm on the run from the authorities," said Chohovsky.

The old man's eyes lit up. He now looked at Chohovsky as if only the most trivial misunderstanding separated them. It seemed that his whispered confession was close to the old man's heart.

"So that's all," he said. His muscular hands suddenly looked younger. "If that's all it's about, you can be sure I won't leave you to your fate." There was a childish glee in his eyes. There was nothing the people in these parts understood so well as being on the run. No fugitive had ever been handed over by them.

The fisherman lit a cigarette and began plying the oars vigorously, and Chohovsky saw from the expression on his face that some deep fear had been dispelled. The sun dropped and a cool wind blew over the warmed tarpaulin. And Chohovsky felt that his end had receded and he still had days to come, but what they held he did not know. All he knew was that his financial speculations were behind him, like something that had cut itself off from him in order to go on living its life independently. The relief of nakedness. He had always sensed that it wasn't for himself that he was accumulating capital. The laws of acquisition and accumulation require deliberation, patience, steadiness. He had always reached out for risks, compelled by his own nature. He had known moments of supreme enjoyment — one might even say exaltation — for even financial transactions in their higher reaches, like any other real risk, can exalt the human spirit. Although it was a risk that was bound to land him in trouble in the end, he proceeded on the strength of the contempt he felt for the small-mindedness of the bureaucrats, the pettiness of his business colleagues.

He had always known that his chosen path would end in failure and disgrace, and everything he did only brought the failure closer and precipitated the end.

The fisherman, a practical man, from the moment that his initial fears faded, began to calculate what he might gain from this voyage, and now he asked, "How long will you stay on the islands?"

"A long time," said Chohovsky.

"So we'll have to say good-bye?" said the old man, imparting a sentimental tone to his words in order to hide their real intentions.

"You'll come and visit me," said Chohovsky, with something of his old courtliness.

The mists rose higher and an azure radiance, distilled from the blue water, enveloped the islands. For a moment he felt as if he were being borne home. For years his home had cut itself off from him, and only the dream ship appeared from time to time. His longing for home had not faded, not even in his deepest dreams. Sometimes he felt like a messenger sent to this world against his will and that one day his mission would be over and the dream ship would come to take him home. How much he would have to tell them then about his extraordinary adventures and experiences! How many people, after all, were given the chance to undertake journeys like this?

A moment of exaltation descended on him, the grace that God bestows on his creatures so that despair will not engulf them.

"Tell me something about the islands," he said to the old man, as if he were saying sing me a song, bring some dormant rhythm in me to life.

The old fisherman, sensing the tenderness in his voice, said, "What is there to tell? The islands are deserted. Years ago they tried to drill for oil but they found nothing. There's nothing there but stones and more stones."

"And now no one lives there?"

"I don't think so. Years ago, I remember, we used the place as a stopping point. We were young then. We used to take our catch to the north. We got a good price."

The old man clung to his distant memory. And Chohovsky felt that his own life had been irretrievably lost, swallowed up somewhere along the way by his ambitious dealings. His life was gone, and he was left behind.

The old man's excitement faded. He took out the food he had brought with him and bit into a blackened piece of bread, thinking, no doubt, about his extraordinary passenger. For Chohovsky he was a messenger leading him into an unknown land, and his voracious appetite a sign that there was still an outer skin to life. He gave him a few extras pennies in order to see the trembling hand outstretched, adding penny to penny.

"Will you come visit me?" asked Chohovsky, as if suddenly conscious of the approaching separation.

"Sure," said the old man. And it was impossible to tell if he was trying to console him, or merely making a promise he had no intention of keeping. They were still far from the islands. The sun was low in the sky, the light had softened. Weakness after long weariness overcame him.

He knew that in a little while he would be abandoned to the night. The old man's words were as meaningless as the words spoken to a condemned man on his way to the guillotine. But he felt no resentment. The fisherman seemed to feel a need to entertain and counsel him, and he told him that in the thirties he, too, had run afoul of the authorities and had been forced to remain in hiding in the north until the war broke out. The charges had been forgotten, the files burned, and in the end he had returned to find that his sons had grown into men and his wife was an old woman.

Chohovsky listened without taking in the implied moral.

He wanted to tell the fisherman about his adventures in commerce, or what in other spheres was called commerce, but he knew the old man wouldn't understand, or even believe him, and so he repeated his previous question, but this time with a note of skepticism: "Will you really come?"

"Of course, and I'll bring you food, too."

Chohovsky remembered that he had once had the same kind of conversation in similar circumstances, but he couldn't remember where. His childhood memories had been pushed aside by his speculations but they went on glowing dimly, like the eternal flame, somewhere in the depths of his soul. Sometimes it was the only whisper he heard there. But he didn't know who it was that was speaking to him so gently.

The sunset was triumphant. Above and beneath them it played with fire. Their eyes could not take in the splendor.

"Where were you born?" the fisherman asked. Something important was missing, and his primitive eyes groped for it with the same expression they must have had when scanning the water in his fishing days.

"Blishik," said Chohovsky, without realizing that this would mean nothing to the fisherman.

"I've never heard of that country before."

"It's not a country, it's a town."

"I've heard that Jews have no fixed place in the world."

"True, but they're born in a particular place, and that place goes on calling them all their lives, even if they're far away, even if they never go back."

Chohovsky felt he had retrieved something for himself, too. For years he had not uttered the name of his town. And he had never replied the way he had now. It was a wonder to him that he'd replied as he had.

The mists parted. Towering rocks spread their arms toward the sea like mythical creatures frozen in screaming postures. And the blue in their gaping mouths was frozen too.

"We're getting close," said the fisherman. All the ships had sailed into open sea, the boats had disappeared over the horizons. They were exposed to the approaching night.

If only a miracle would happen. So his heart had often cried before, but always with some definite aim in view. Now his heart cried out for a miracle without asking for anything but the miracle itself. Something in him wanted to break through the long corridors of common sense and logic, but his mind was well armored against any breakthrough, trapped in consciousness.

He dropped his eyes and saw that the boat was full of cases of food. The night before he had made provisions for his journey. This time, too, his thoughts had raced on ahead, old scouts sniffing out the lay of the land. Always they anticipated future events and took care of their rear as well. Now, though, it was only the advance they provided for; there was not the slightest possibility of retreat.

The boat entered shallow water. They felt the ground beneath them. The cliffs greeted them like sleepy sentinels guarding a town that had fallen into ruin long ago and whose gates stood open to all comers.

It was already night. His arrival was simpler than he had imagined, without any kind of ceremony at all. The fisherman carried his cases onto the shore. In the interior, darkness reigned.

All that remained was to say good-bye. He was afraid to stay behind. The lights on the other side were so far away he could hardly make them out and a deep murmur came from the sea.

"Why don't you stay with me tonight?" he said, feeling his own weakness speaking. Now it was really him. All his many names were forgotten, even the name his parents had given him.

"I'll pay you," he added.

"How much?"

"A fair price"

The old man agreed. They pulled the boat up and spread the tarpaulin. The rapid movements exerted his muscles and restored some hidden source of energy. He thought, This may be the last person I'll ever meet. But the thought no longer bothered him. They lit the hurricane lamp and drank coffee. It reminded him of the days in the forests, when they were being hunted. He did not know then that similar days awaited him in the future. In days to come the old sights would surface again, in even greater perfection, and they were still running through his mind one after the other.

The old man received his reward. He sat and reminisced about the days of his youth when fishing was his trade and the nocturnal fishing expeditions were accompanied by singing and their happiness in the morning was as bright as the sun. Chohovsky listened as if he wanted to submerge himself in the monotonous rhythm of the old man's words, but he couldn't because he was flooded by the sound of himself, murmuring like the waves of the sea.

How many years had passed since he had escaped to the forests? Twenty, if not more. A young boy in many forests. And hadn't that flight ended yet?

The old man fell asleep and left him to himself, so that he could accustom himself to other days, days without a living soul. The fire died down, and little flames flickered among the embers. How silly his request had been, like a child afraid of staying alone in the dark. And perhaps all his risks and tricks had been just that: a way of evading terror. The speculations had collapsed, the terror had remained.

The wind blew through his shirt. How amazing, how wonderful his last transactions had been in Israel. If only it hadn't been for that man, that woman. A thousand tiny gold watches. Boxes within boxes, false bottoms within false bottoms. Who had informed on him? But for the informer they would never have been found out. But there was always a weak link in the chain, a faint heart who prevented his plans from coming to fruition. Suddenly everything collapsed; exposure seemed to come of its own accord. Who were the informers, the spies, the petty self-interested ones who brought his bold projects down in ruins?

It wasn't he who asked, but a different Chohovsky; something inside of him asked these questions.

His transactions in Israel were brief — brief and bold. In Israel he had met his old business acquaintances from Vienna. But they had married, had children, bowed their heads to honest toil.

Sometimes he would say to himself, soon I'll get married too, but then the idea for some new venture would present itself, firing his imagination and tying his hands. And there were moments of exhilaration, of exaltation. The ship docked, the goods arrived, and at night when he switched off the lights the gold glittered.

With a belated sense of surprise, he remembered that his name was not really Chohovsky. In any case, he wouldn't be using names here. It was in Vienna, when the first refugees arrived and speculation flourished. He needed identity papers. A passport. A man called Chohovsky had died. His parents were Austrian citizens and after the war they restored all his rights. A young man, about twenty-five years old. He jumped naked into the Danube. Someone got hold of his papers and sold them. Since then he had been called Chohovsky. He had had many names and this one he hung onto as long as circumstances permitted. Sometimes he thought it was his real name. But sometimes, at night, he heard the sound of his own name and then he would cry out indignantly: I'm not Leibel, I'm Chohovsky!

Leibel Gustman was his name. This particular combination had died a long time ago, in the forests, when he called himself Yanosh for fear of the Gentiles. The old fisherman poked his head out of his coat and said, "Morning," as if he were telling him in his sleep that morning had come. There were no signs of morning yet in the sky, but an early breeze whipped the sea into waves.

The old man promised to return. Chohovsky did not believe him, but he doubled his pay anyway. "I'll be seeing you," he said. Skeptically, as if to say. You think I don't know? It was the language of his business days, a vestige of the past, a rusted tool.

"So you're a Jew?" The old man stood there for a moment with a bewildered expression on his face.

"A Jew."

"I heard they were all killed in the war."

"Not all of them."

"I imagine the best survived." Something awed and pious made his thick lips tremble.

The old man set sail. The sun rose from the sea. And Chohovsky felt that something had been taken away from him, from his body. His eyes wandered. The little boat sailed away in a big sea, a low murmur drifted over the waves. "St. George," he whispered.

Only now did he hear the solitude. An infinite solitude. The years had led him to this place. The language of his business dealings

drained away and left him with a mute terror. Gaping spaces, looking for something to take hold of, speechless and violent.

Something drew him toward the interior. It wasn't curiosity. A
burning thirst gripped him and compelled him to follow it. He
responded as once he had responded to the call of speculation.

He climbed a low hill. Endless time in the shape of the sky flowed
above him. He paused, as if he had just realized there was no need
to hurry. He gazed at the sky and his head spun.

When he reached the top of the hill a startling sight greeted his
eyes. The plain was covered with huge clumps of upturned earth,
testimony to a holocaust not long past. Unearthed rocks leaned pre-
cariously on each other, suspended in thin air. A force not of this
world seemed to have ripped them out of the ground. The silence
was more absolute than any he had ever known, as if this was its
true home. The recently unearthed rocks did not look like inanimate objects. They looked different, raw, as if they had not yet had
time to die. He remembered hearing that prospectors had drilled
for oil here, but he had not imagined the extent of their excava-
tions. All his calculations vanished; his thoughts stood still as in
dreamless sleep. Weariness descended on him, the heaviness of the
autumn sun. If only he could have spread the tarpaulin over his
head, it would have afford him some relief. He had never in all his
life felt so tired. The years of his youth had climbed indefatigably
upward, measured countries and continents, always presented openings for escape, ways of cheating the world, the police, the militia,
the border patrols and customs guards. It had happened many years
ago. He was with his father, traveling in a convoy to Sadigora, near
a river. All the way they sang and sang. Gentile children threw
stones at them, but they went on singing; drunks fell on the convoy, but they went on singing, as if they wanted to prove that it was
possible to go on and possible to sing. Then he did not yet know
that it was a contest, just as he did not know that business was a
contest. Victory went to the strong.

He had always known it would end, but not that it would end

like this. He had pictured harsh prison sentences, beatings, but a prison like this he had never imagined.

His provisions lay below; he had purchased them a day or two before. The short stay in the little Italian town seemed remote to him now. Even the fisherman had grown insubstantial. Hunger reminded him of the food.

"They're looking for Chohovsky," he said to himself as he ate. He felt a certain satisfaction at having cheated them again, but it wasn't like the happiness of the forest. Then they were happy. Now the long-drawn-out game seemed senseless to him. He did not cry "I give up," but in his heart he surrendered.

He saw a picture that opened the doors of a dream. The reality of the dream was flimsy and insubstantial, and he stepped carefully so as not to disturb its flow. He came to a river and stood beside it. The water runs on, he said, wondering at the silent flow. Willows bent their boughs to the rhythm of the water. The sound of a mill reached his ears. For many years he had not heard the sound of a mill, but now he heard it clearly. His feet were light, and he wondered at this lightness carrying him forward. The dam was full, the world spun around. Carts loaded with sacks surrounded the mill, and because the horses were asleep he passed beneath their legs as if they weren't horses. Inside the mill Gentiles were assembled; he remembered them but not their names.

Suddenly the heavy darkness grew white. The Gentiles spoke and spewed flour from their mouths. Their wives stood with flour flying from their hair. They were talking to each other and trying to beat each other down. Next to the scales stood his father, trying to shake off the flour blowing from all the funnels.

Chohovsky rose and said, "A dream." For a moment the word hung in the air, and then it dissolved into the murmur of the waves. He felt he had been far from his present self, deep in the years of his childhood. The sun retreated, and a cold wind blew through his shirt. On the horizon, little boats seemed to be standing still on the water.

He remembered that he had arrived here only the day before. An old fisherman had brought him in a rowboat. The doors of the dream closed behind him and left him with the sea, the endless sea, a hill behind him and two cases of untouched food lying on the sand.

He rose to his feet, conscious of the many sights buried inside him. He had stolen them on the roads, at the railway stations, in all the hiding places where he had taken refuge. A strange joy flooded his heart. "My secret," he whispered to himself. It wasn't faith, but a kind of happiness to hear the whisper rising out of his innermost being. A soundless voice whispering, There is a way out, it exists within you.

And when he woke in the morning the sun was already up. The dream pulsed in his temples. He washed his face in the sea water and consciousness returned. "I must hurry," he said to himself, but immediately he realized that his speculating days were over, there was no need for him to move. He remembered that on the other side of the hill the earth was all churned up and rocks teetered in the air. But still his legs bore him in that direction, and he did not try to stop them.

The autumn sun rose higher and its rays grew weaker; delicate clouds crept over the sky, heralding winter. He was wearing light summer clothes. He walked slowly and stepped carefully.

Opposite him was a ruin with two holes in its walls. He smiled at this sign of human presence. A dense, heavy smell of rot and excrement rose to greet him. For a moment he felt the fear of a human hand. Inside and out the ruin was covered with graffiti. The writing told him that a band of smugglers had camped out here not long ago. The ashes of a fire, empty cans, crumpled cigarette packs. The sight filled him with disgust. For some reason it re-minded him of a deserted railway station, and he was overcome with giddiness, as if the train had just left.

A few steps away sparse vegetation, eroded rocks — all the shapes fashioned by the hand of nature — lived their lives undisturbed.

Small sights came to gladden his eyes. A flowering bush, a rock, a blue thorn. For a moment he gazed at this mute movement.

Something came back to him. If anyone had been there, the flood of warmth inside him would have broken out into words. He wanted to kneel down and pray, confess. Since he could find no other person and no words in his heart, he sat down to rest. Suddenly he felt he was being drawn back into yesterday's dream.

He came to the riverside and stood next to the pools of water. Because he knew what had happened inside the mill, he started walking home. Reb Simha, the cattle dealer, came toward him, and his beard was white as his father's. A herd of cattle followed him. How could they not know that he was leading them to the slaughterhouse? They walked behind him, kicking up dust as if he were their shepherd. The animals knew him, but he didn't know them. They cried "Moo, moo," and the sound of their lowing was like the sound of the wind. Reb Simha walked behind them, sunk into himself. "Reb Simha!" he called.

Reb Simha walked on without hearing him. Only the cattle answered, "Moo, moo." He wanted to warn them of Reb Simha's intention, but because they were cattle they didn't understand his human voice and they went on following their herdsman.

Reb Simha's son, who had studied with him in heder, came out and called, "Moo, moo." He had been studying for all those years, had even learned the language of the birds and the beasts, but he had remained as small as the last time they'd seen each other. "Yudel!" he called. Yudel, with his quick mind, understood that he was Leibel who had changed his name to Chohovsky and said, "Don't call him Leibel, call him Chohovsky." And he began reciting verses from the Torah and the Prophets until he came to the verse "Unto slanderers let there be no hope," and he stopped. The cattle turned their heads as if they understood everything that was being said.

Reb Gad the melamed sat in the women's gallery and taught the little children. He read the verse "Unto slanderers let there be no hope" in a singsong. And when he finished he said, "Don't call him

Leibel, call him Chohovsky," and spat, and all the children with whom he had gone to heder spat after him.

He wanted to climb up to them, but all the openings were as small as ant holes and so was the staircase. Because he couldn't climb up he said, "I'll go to the river and when the time comes I'll go back home." When he came to the river he heard a voice calling from the water and he understood that the real Chohovsky was calling him from the waters and he wondered how he came to be in the Prut when everyone said he had drowned himself in the Danube, and he remembered the verse "For he hath founded it upon the waters." Which meant that everything was water and there was no division between water and water. And he said, "I hereby declare that I am willing to give you back your name. I have many names." But although he wanted to give the drowning man back his name he felt that the name was clinging to him, and he couldn't get rid of it. The young man floated like a fish on the water and disappeared.

The morning light woke him. He was far away from his cases. "So I'm here." He said to himself. There was solid earth under his numb feet.

He felt as if he had been drawn up from the depths of the years but had remained himself, just as the boat had discharged him onto these shores. His summer clothes were crumpled and shapeless. If he didn't meet someone soon he would surrender to the temperature of his dreams and one of these days he would freeze to death in their snows. And perhaps his frozen body would go on dreaming for a long time afterward.

He longed for the sight of a human face. He dreaded falling asleep. He remembered Jerusalem, the neighborhoods of Geula and Sha'arei Hesed. That had been a time of relative peace, except that his thoughts kept turning to the goods at sea and the goods in the port, and the people who were supposed to hand them on. Once or twice he said to himself, I have been granted the privilege of seeing Jerusalem. But it was only a phase. Sometimes he met the friends who had been with him in the forests, and he wondered at their composure and their petit bourgeois manners and began avoiding them. Sometimes he felt that something was burning, burning without being consumed. Sometimes he looked out and said, "Those are the mountains of Moab." And in Meah Shearim he would stand listening to the women talking and marvel and say, "They're talking Yiddish." All the sights of Jerusalem came to him bathed in a tender autumn light, sunk into him as if distilled.

How many days have I been here already? He shook himself. There were boats on the horizon. The noonday sun rested on the water. Weakness dragged him back to sleep. Dreams came. He was back home. All the years led back home.

His father was sitting next to the table and his face was white with the flour the Gentiles had spewed at him.

"I'm Leibel," he said.

"Don't we know your name is Leibel?" said his father.

"People don't recognize me and they call me Chohovsky, after the young man who threw himself into the Danube."

"A man must examine his own deeds."

"All my life I will be called Chohovsky."

"I heard that in Israel you were called Tushinsky."

"I bought that name for next to nothing. From the same Jew. He had lots of passports. He looked like me — look, look."

"Who is this Tushinsky that my son is called after?"

"He died long ago."

"You took the names of the dead in order to live."

"I needed that passport to cross the border."

"And you went to Rome, with all the beggars."

"The seashore was full of refugees. They wanted to conquer the world with commerce. Fantastic deals were made there. I remember one fellow, the son of the Rabbi of Katmtchuk, declaring, 'The gates of heaven are open,' but no one took any notice of him because he was mad, quite mad."

"They say you were in Israel."

"I had no choice, my affairs came to a dead end. They told us Israel was the only place where we could find a refuge."

"Oranges and wine from Rishon Lezion."

"I was in Israel, believe me. I was there. I didn't get to Zefat or Meron, but I was in Israel. I was busy."

"Busy with what?"

"In Vienna, in the transit camp, they told us that from now on God had given business to the People of Israel, and that being the case we said, 'Thy will be done.'"

"Hush."

"And I have to tell you, and please don't think I'm bluffing, there were marvelous moments. Goods came in from the south and the north, the east and west. Everything was wide open. We saw that luck was on our side. And there were fantastic profits, undreamed of."

"An illusion, my son, magic and witchcraft."

"But we didn't know it was witchcraft. I know I shouldn't say so but business was fantastic. In Vienna we bribed the governor; the army provided us with surpluses. All the borders were wide open."

"And couldn't you see you were under a spell? Weren't we given signs to distinguish truth from illusion?"

"Business was big. It was bigger than we were."

"I heard you were seen in Jerusalem."

"Autumn in Jerusalem. There's nothing else like it."

"I don't believe you."

"Do you think I'm lying to you, father?"

"I don't believe in magic spells."

"I traveled the length and breadth of Israel without seeing that I was in Israel. If I'd stopped to look I wouldn't have had time for my speculations. Isn't that astonishing?"

"The ways of witchcraft are astonishing."

"It was wonderful speculating in Israel."

"And aren't the wicked burned there?"

"But in autumn, father, the sky comes down over the mountains of Moab and from the observation post in Talpioth you can see the blue of the sky resting on the mountains."

"I am not allowed to believe you."

"There's only one thing I'd like to ask. Was it really just an illusion?"

It was dawn, and low winter clouds were gathering over the Isles of St. George. A boat approached. He was afraid of being cut off, with the fear a man feels on winter nights when the snow clings to his feet. He knew that something had been revealed to him in a dream, but he didn't know how to interpret the signs. His soul thirsted for a human sight, a human face, human words. For years he hadn't spoken to people. His dealings had required secrecy, withdrawal, mobility. Even in Jerusalem he had often changed his room so as not to stay too long in one place. And when he did meet someone the meeting was conducted in haste, in the allusive, disjointed language of smugglers.

That night the sign came. To the far right of the island a light flickered; he saw it from the hilltop. Low-lying mists covered the upturned rocks on the plain. Like a human hand the light guided him toward it. If it had a voice it would have called to him. His eyes were wet with tears.

He no longer felt guilty. His guilt had sunk into him and become part of him, transmuted into something it was no longer possible to call guilt. And his deed, too, was gone.

He wanted to return to human society. Not in crawling or cravenness. Like the feeling of a bird for its own species, like a man drawn to the face of a man. At that moment he did not say to himself, What kind of man does this light belong to? He understood only that it had been lit by a human hand in darkness.

Loneliness had laws of its own, like a drug that modifies the behavior of an organism. Once he would have said, a thousand dollars. Once he would have fingered gold coins. Once he had sat and planned his escape routes. How remote all this seemed to him now, as if it was not he who had done these things.

He stood and contemplated the light, calculated the distance, worked out ways of approach. The old talent for calculating risks, appraising dangers, foreseeing trouble, came unconsciously to life in him again.

Sleep fell away from him completely. He could see everything in the light of logic. Something like the feeling that had come to him a few days before the liberation returned to him now. In the forests they believed that when the war was over life would return.

As soon as day broke he set out. Again that extraordinary land-scape greeted his eyes. It was like the first days after the liberation, before news of the catastrophe, when army songs filled the forest and streams of people marched to their rhythm. Rocks greeted his eyes. Scattered blue thorns. It seemed that this was their last hour of blooming. He stood and listened to the wind rustling in the thorns.

Now he saw the empty cans and rubbish on the paths. Years ago people had walked here.

Slowly he made his way back toward the world of human beings, as if there was nothing to be afraid of.

He was surrounded by a wall of rocks. They showed signs of having only recently emerged from the darkness of the earth. Lumps of soil still clung to their sides, but like the other inanimate objects they had already grown gray and taken a protective coloration. Even the hut at the edge of the plain seemed at first like just another shape in the wilderness.

There was a man standing in the doorway. For a moment his eyes focused and made out a hairy face, then the colors blurred and merged. He saw a faded pith helmet, khaki trousers, a silver beard.

"Who is it?" cried the man, and the words hung frozen in the air.

"Me," he replied and his legs stood still.

He approached. A human creature down to the last detail, and judging from its stance this had been its home for many years. In order to quell the commotion in his heart he said, "You must be the guard here." The man turned his head as if he was about to go back to his hut. His great height, his deliberate slowness, his muscular arms all pointed to the fact that he was, indeed, a solitary guard in this godforsaken place. His face was lined. His few words, the loudness of his voice, seemed to indicate that he had not uttered a sound for years. "Chohovsky," he said and stretched out his hand.

"Vinter," said the guard.

Their eyes crossed, as if they wished to keep each other at bay. For a moment they stood hesitating.

"Jewish?" said Chohovsky, the way people used to ask once.

The guard recoiled as if some voice had invaded his space.

"Yes," he said. The Yiddish word sounded strange in his mouth, as if it wasn't a Jewish mouth uttering it.

Chohovsky felt he was disturbing the flowing course of the silence. The man seemed native to the place, as if it were only here that he could have been created.

"Jewish," repeated Chohovsky. "I'm on the run from the authorities, looking for a hideout on the island. A big deal that didn't come off."

"Aha," said the guard. These were evidently words from his lexicon.

"The sea, maybe the sun, made me long for human company again. Longing stronger than hunger, thirst, or fear."

They went into the hut. A bed, a mattress, a sooty kettle, the temporary things a man takes with him on a journey. Years ago he had hired himself to the oil prospectors as a guard. For two years they had drilled without stop until it was clear beyond a shadow of a doubt that the inside of the earth here was as empty as the outside. The drilling machinery had been left behind, he had stayed on to guard it. It had already rusted. The owner did not want to abandon his machinery — or perhaps he had abandoned it long ago, but the paycheck kept coming. Every month a messenger arrived with money and food supplies.

Words lose their sounds in the open spaces. A man grows used to listening to the wind, the rain, the thunder of the rocks, the shrieking of the birds. The guard sat and his eyes were still. The words were torn from his mouth in a stammer, and when Chohovsky spoke he listened as if to sounds coming from a distance. For a moment it seemed that he had forgotten his mother tongue, but the few words he brought up from his depths denied this.

"Those were speculations on a grand scale," Chohovsky found the right tone at last.

The guard raised his eyes. Something stirred in him. Ten years on the island of St. George had frozen him, but not deprived him of human expressions. At first he thought that after a few years he would return to town and open a textile business, but with the passing of the years his plans had lost their substance.

"A textile business," said the guard, and the word had a different meaning, an imaginary creation of the Isles of St. George.

Suddenly it was clear that there were two realms, the world and the Isles of St. George, which the sea tried unsuccessfully to join together. Textile. The guard's pronunciation showed that his word had been created here, for his father's textile business had long ago been obliterated from his memory.

Beneath the heavy tarpaulin lay the corroded machines. The tarpaulin itself was rotted; it was only a pretense. The sun ate everything. Even the rocks could not withstand it.

The earth had been disemboweled, the rocks thrown aside, but the curse of St. George had triumphed. Nothing had been found in the wilderness. Soon there would be no evidence that men had once drilled the earth here, and all traces of their efforts would be lost. Just as no one remembered anymore that the place had once been a prison. Everything ran its course here, in accordance with simple, elemental laws. If the guard had only had the words, he would surely have told what had been revealed to him here. But the words had frozen. Other expressions came into play, which had nothing to do with the words.

Chohovsky looked at him as if contemplating his own secret.

The guard uttered a few sounds. His strong body, hardened by the years of his vigil, stood still as a rock. A creature of the place. In the end the sounds joined into words, and he said, "You and I come from the same parts, Chohovsky." A kind of radiance flooded his eyes.

That night Chohovsky slept in the guard's hut.

He had forgotten everything that had happened in the war. Or perhaps with practice and effort he had made himself forget, so that he could go on living here. He didn't say this to Chohovsky, but Chohovsky suddenly sensed that he was trespassing on private ground, and that he'd best be moving soon. And when the guard sensed his intention, he told him that when winter came he could find shelter with him. Not everything had rotted; in the garage there were still sacks and tarpaulins. He could sleep all winter long.

The guard's eyes filled with the same cold brilliance. And Chohovsky was sorry for having disturbed him.

Before dawn he set out on his way back to his cases on the shore. The guard did not say "Till we meet again" or ask him which way he was going. He only repeated that when winter came Chohovsky could take shelter in the garage. For a moment he stood with his back to him, and then he returned to his hut.

Once more Chohovsky stood opposite the hills, the dull sun and the smell of the sea. He knew that he had met someone and he did not know whom.

The man was stranger to him than the sea and the rocks. Weariness settled on his shoulders again.

His cases had faded. The food had staled. He knew that he had come within the orbit of a person close to him. And he had been rejected.

On the Isles of St. George a man had to serve his sentence without human company. So that he would plumb his sins to the depths, as far as a human hand was capable of reaching.

During the course of his wanderings over the island he came across a band of smugglers. They used the island as a halfway point on their way to the mainland. There were four of them, all small and thin, and one of them was a Jew. He bought canned food and cigarettes from them. They were on their last trip before the winter. In winter they stayed home. The Jew told him that for a year now he had been with them. Twice he had been caught and escaped. There was a warrant out for his arrest on the mainland, and still he had to go back. Chohovsky, with the practiced eye of a businessman, saw that the man was small fry and that one day he would be caught. A kind of pity welled up in him for the Jew who would be caught one day without anyone to save him.

The first rains started coming down. They pulled their boat up to the shore. And Chohovsky was glad for these people he could sit with until the rain stopped. He hospitably opened the cans he had bought from them and they sat and ate. They made their trips once a week. The man who ran the show on the mainland exploited them and threatened to hand them over to the police. Chohovsky remembered his own dealings. He had conducted his business from a distance, but these men, with their bodies and simple wooden oars, plied their way back and forth week in and week out.

The Jew spoke plaintively about his troubles, about the endless weekly trips. He was married, and his wife demanded money. Years ago he had wanted to go to Israel with all the other refugees, but he had married instead and stayed behind. And Chohovsky told him that he himself had escaped from Israel not long before because he had sailed too close to the wind and his speculations had collapsed and reached a dead end.

They sat and spun their stories. And in the end they returned to the years in the forests, when they had to move on every day without leaving any traces behind them.

There was a lull in the rain. The Gentiles played cards, fought, and made up over a bottle of vodka. They were drunk, but they wanted to set out. Between curses the smugglers dragged their boat into the sea.

Chohovsky watched them as if something was being torn out of him and was sailing away. His speculations had always led him into hidden territory, into the secret at the heart of the mystery.

When a man abandons his affairs he admits defeat. There was something he had wanted to say to this Jew, but the Jew was a prisoner among the Gentiles and he said nothing.

Evening fell. The compassion of the creator descended on him. All the roads he had traveled were inside him. He wept, and there were no tears on his cheeks. A distant chiming of bells rang in his ears. Sounds that only his silence could make so clear. At first he thought the sounds were coming from the mainland. When the pealing grew louder he realized they were the bells of the monastery of St. George. The ringing became measured, rhythmical. Six o'clock hung for a moment in the air.

All his life the sound of church bells had followed him, and now it had reached him here too. Now he knew that once again all his roads had come to a dead end. He threw his two remaining cases into the sea. Not far from here Vinter sat in his hut. But he did not have the right to go to him yet. Perhaps when winter came, and perhaps never. Only Vinter in his speechlessness would be capable of sensing what his mouth was unable to utter. Only Vinter.

Unthinkingly his feet drew him toward the pealing bells, making a detour around Vinter's hill and valley so as to keep out of his range of vision. From now on he would see nothing but Vinter's eyes.

Once more he came across the debris of civilization. Empty cans and cigarette packs. The island was uninhabited, but not completely deserted.

The monastery stood at the top of a hill. The gates were open. Smooth stone floors absorbed his footsteps. The walls were high. He called and no one answered. The neatness of the place bespoke the care of a human hand, but this hand was hiding.

He drew water from the well and drank. He was tired, with a hopeless, despairing fatigue. All he wanted was to collapse into the warm dark web of sleep. But he was exposed to the sky and the searching rays of the sun illuminating the world from one end to the other. Even in this secluded courtyard there was no escape from it. Arches led into another courtyard, and then into another. The world narrowed here into a series of rigid squares.

Many times he had sought refuge in monasteries, but the monks had rejected him. This time it seemed he had not come to seek refuge, but that his legs had carried him of their own accord. He remembered his speculations like a worn-out adventurer with nothing left but his memories to comfort him. How exhilarating his moments of happiness had been. No more so, certainly, than in some intoxicating game, and still — would the drunkard refuse a drink?

He remembered his two old aunts in Jaffa. He had paid them one short visit and that was all. They sat and spoke, he sat and listened, led into the unknown realms of himself. Every detail was preserved in their old memories. He told them about his travels, but not about his transactions. But in their concern for him they felt something was not right and they said, "Let it be, let it be." He did not go again. Every day he thought of going and telling them some great news. But he didn't go. Perhaps they were still alive, speaking his name to each other with a sigh.

He heard footsteps; a monk was approaching him. He rose. They were dwarfed by the high walls. "You are welcome," said the monk and the greeting sounded glib, as if this was how he greeted every stranger.

Chohovsky made no request at all. He said, "I'm just passing through. I'd like to see the monastery."

For some reason the tall monk reminded him of Vinter. It was only a superficial resemblance, apparently the climate and environment stamped their likeness on all the creatures here.

He seemed an observant man. He must have perceived that it was no accidental visitor standing before him but a life story worth listening to. Good manners obliged him to say something about the monastery. But first he wanted to discover something about the man.

Chohovsky responded to his questioning look, held out his

hand, and said, "Chohovsky's the name." Suddenly he realized that this was his standard procedure when introducing himself to officials he wanted to bribe. It had a rather pompous, self-important tone, and here, in these different circumstances, it sounded affected.

"I'm glad to meet you," said the monk, and indeed it seemed that Chohovsky's words, spoken in a foreign-sounding Italian but a firm tone, had made a good impression.

"Where are you from, if I may ask?"

"Hiding out from the authorities," said Chohovsky in the same tone as before, but immediately he sensed that a different tone was called for and he added, "I've been wandering around the island for a month now."

"It must have been a misunderstanding," said the monk, as if he was expressing not himself but the code he was expected to represent.

"No, it wasn't a misunderstanding," said Chohovsky, in order not to soften anything. He remembered that in the winter, in the forests, they would knock on the church doors and cry, "Have pity, Christians!" But the Christian hearts never responded. Now he did not want to make things easier, neither for himself nor for anyone else.

"I can't believe it," said the monk. His full face expressed nothing but composure and equanimity.

"It wasn't a misunderstanding," he repeated firmly.

"As bad as that."

"Business was my downfall."

The monk smiled as if to diminish the severity of this statement.

Chohovsky felt that words were coming back to him. For years they had been hiding in slogans, in hints. Now they welled up in him. Not the words of give and take, of complaint, but the words, as it were, of himself. "Business was my downfall," he said again. The monk invited Chohovsky to accompany him. The narrow door led to closed courtyards with glaring white walls. They were full of an oppressive emptiness. The sun shone brightly. They went down a flight of stairs and the light gave way to long shadows.

A large hall, indirectly lit, greeted them. The monk went to make tea. Chohovsky sat on a bench. The hall ceiling was lost in darkness.

In the days of his success, and perhaps only then, he had known that when the time came he would have to pay the price in full. A long and circuitous route had led him to the payment.

The monk emerged from the shadows, his habit trailing on the stone floor. The rough cloth made a grating sound.

"The Isles of St. George are open to repentance," said the monk, sipping his tea. "A man goes astray and opens his heart and the light of God's grace returns to him." His voice sounded hollow as it produced these glib phrases. In his heart he knew that it was more than a matter of "going astray."

The monk looked hard at Chohovsky, trying to pick up his passing thoughts.

"The police seldom visit us here," he said. Chohovsky imagined himself staying in the monastery, sweeping the floors, as he had done when he was still a boy in his sparse Ukrainian village. There was something consoling in these thoughts at this quiet twilight hour.

"Where are you from?" asked the monk in a fatherly tone.

"From Blishik," said Chohovsky, and he felt that he had betrayed something intimate to the monk. "Poland," he added.

"Your Italian is good."

"I lived for years on the mainland." He remembered hearing the word recently from the smugglers. "I came to Italy after the war."

"And where have you come from now?"

"From Israel." Again he felt he was putting something very intimate into the words.

The monk added detail to detail, understood one thing from another until he grasped who Chohovsky was, where he came from, why he had set out on his wandering, and why he had come here. A criss-crossed map spread before his eyes.

"From Israel," the monk could not contain his excitement. "From the Holy Land."

"Hardly," said Chohovsky and felt something tightening inside him.

The monk told him that in six months, maybe even sooner, he himself would be going to Israel. Or so he had been informed by his superiors. Someone else would be coming to take his place here.

Evening fell, the dusk settled on the window bars. He remembered autumn in Jerusalem. Sometimes he went to Talpioth to feed his eyes on the abundant blue. Of other places he knew nothing. He kept to the main roads, back and forth on the triangle Jerusalem-Tel Aviv-Haifa.

He was forty-five. The same age as the monk. The years had drained him to the dregs, led him to the place he had pictured in his imagination but not to himself. He remembered his last evening on the mainland, walking the streets of the drowsy little Italian town, and the fisherman who had brought him here. Many days had apparently passed since then, more than he could comprehend. And when the evening deepened and the shadows swallowed up all the light except for the light of the candles, the monk rose from his seat and his long habit hid his feet. They walked in the darkness, through the narrow doorways. A heavy silence rose from the corners, the moon shone through the clouds above them and cast a dim light on the courtyard walls. He knew that the monk would give him a bed for the night. His weary limbs longed for a bed. The monk left him to go pray and the bells pealed out again. Although he lived alone in the monastery the monk rang the bells as if calling people to prayer. The place was used to the sound, which probably reached Vinter's hut, too — the hut to which he wouldn't be able to return before winter came.

The next morning he worked with the monk in the garden. They picked the last of the late apples. For a moment he marveled at the monk's generosity toward him, but soon he became absorbed in the work and let the rhythm of the picking flow undisturbed.

And so he passed his days. Picking fruit, weeding, he bent his back to toil. And something like a breath of reconciliation touched his brow. At noon they sat down to eat. The monk told him about the plans for his trip and asked if he would be kind enough to teach him a little Hebrew. For years he had yearned to read the Bible in the original Hebrew. And Chohovsky suddenly knew that he had another language, one that he had not used in years. Even in Israel he had not spoken it. Was it a language at all? His speculations had driven him onward and left him no time for wonder. Sometimes he would lie on his bed and the music of the liturgy would play in his mouth, as if it was welling up from some hidden source that could not be stopped.

He read and the monk listened. But the words were tied to their sweet melody. The monk was surprised by this intonation, without which he could not read a single line. "That's the way we read when I was a child," he said, and he felt a blush covering his cheeks. Winter approached. Clouds settled on the Isles of St. George; at night the jackals howled. The monk learned the words by heart, and the sound of his voice pronouncing the words reverberated through the halls of the monastery. He did not dream at night. But his imagination often led him homeward, to the little house on top of the hill with the flour mill at its feet.

The monk learned the verses by heart, provisions for his journey. Soon he would be going to Israel.

And one evening when they were sitting on the terrace, Chohovsky said that if he told the story of what had happened to him in his life a stranger would probably understand the meaning of the words, but for someone who had traveled the same roads, those roads flowed like a river.

It was already the middle of winter; rain poured down without stopping. The monk cooked their food. Between the rains they went down to the garden to pick vegetables. Activity came to a standstill, their movements grew confined, the gates of Chohovsky's dreams were locked. His eyes saw what they were shown.

"Where are we now?"

"The golden calf."

"All made of gold, all made of gold."

"Their intentions were good, weren't they?"

"As good as gold."

And when the winter drew to a close and the almond trees blossomed in the garden, the monk prayed and prepared for his journey, his pilgrimage to the Holy Land. All the old terrors returned with the spring, as if they had only closed their eyes for a brief moment. Everything seemed about to begin anew, as if life was determined to repeat itself over and over again, until the very end.

Longings awoke in him for the days in the forests. But immediately he remembered that it wasn't a question of forests but of trees, every tree with its separate shadow. He longed for Vienna, but immediately he remembered the dark alleyways. Only autumn in Jerusalem stayed with him as a sight without equal. But even that was only autumn and a blue sky and a certain smell. Beyond them stood the house on the hill and the flour mill on the river below. For a moment his hand tried to take hold of them, but they vanished again like a dream.

"A man can begin again from the beginning. That is the promise of the resurrection, the promise of God's grace to man."

"But where is that beginning? Perhaps it would be better to ask where is the end? And perhaps it would be better to forget. To sit and forget year after year until forgetfulness eats you up from inside, and then to rise again. A new man. A new Chohovsky. For that reason, and that reason only, I came here. Otherwise the cancer will find many places to take hold and grow, innumerable places. Teach me the art of forgetfulness so that I can start again from the beginning... Do you know a man called Vinter?" he said and felt the ice of that loneliness. "Not far from here?"

The monk who was supposed to replace his monk did not come. The monastery was used to being without people. The monk locked the doors. Chohovsky helped him carry his luggage.

Once more he stood on the shore as on the day he had come, but not in his summer clothes this time. The monk had given him some winter clothes to cover his nakedness for the time being.

translated by Dalya Bilu

ACKNOWLEDGMENTS

SHRINKING was originally published as "Hitzamtzemut," in *Nashim* by Ruth Almog (Jerusalem: Keter, 1986). This translation first appeared in *Ribcage: Israeli Women's Fiction,* ed. Felice Kahn Zisken (New York: Hadassah, 1994).

YANI ON THE MOUNTAIN was originally published as "Yani b'Harim," in *Ratz* by David Grossman (Tel Aviv: Hakibbutz Hameuchad, 1983). This is its first appearance in English.

UNCLE PERETZ TAKES FLIGHT was originally published as "Hadod Peretz Mamree," in *Hadod Peretz Mamree* by Yaakov Shabtai (Tel Aviv: Hakibbutz Hameuchad/Siman Kriah, 1972). This translation first appeared in *World Literature Today,* 72:3 (summer 1998).

SMALL CHANGE was originally published as "Kesef Katan," in *Kesef Katan* by Yehudit Hendel (Tel Aviv: Hakibbutz Hameuchad/Siman Kriah, 1988). This is its first appearance in English.

MY BROTHER was originally published as "Ahi," in *Hazikit Vehazamir* by Benjamin Tammuz (Jerusalem: Keter, 1988). This is its first appearance in English.

IN THE ISLES OF ST. GEORGE was originally published as "B'iyei St. George," in *Kfor al Ha'aretz* by Aharon Appelfeld (Ramat Gan: Massada, 1965). This translation first appeared in *Jerusalem Quarterly,* v. 28 (summer 1983).

ABOUT THE AUTHORS

RUTH ALMOG has been an editor at the literary section of *Ha'aretz* since 1967 and is the author of more than a dozen books, among them the novel *Death in the Rain*.

AHARON APPELFELD's many works in English translation include *Badenheim 1939, The Age of Wonders, Tzili, To the Land of the Cattails, For Every Sin, The Iron Tracks,* and *The Conversions.* He is a recipient of the Israel Prize and winner of the 1987 Harold U. Ribelow Prize.

DAVID GROSSMAN was born in Jerusalem in 1954 and worked for twenty-five years as a correspondent for Israel Radio. His books in English translation include *See Under: Love, Smile of the Lamb,* and the essay collection *Yellow Wind.*

YEHUDIT HENDEL has won some of Israel's highest literary honors, including the Jerusalem Prize, the Newman Prize, and the 1996 Bialik Prize. Her publications include some ten novels and short story collections.

Of YAAKOV SHABTAI, the French newspaper *Le Monde* said that he was in "that category of rare authors whose *oeuvre* is small but brilliant and of incomparable splendor." His works in English translation include *Past Continuous* and *Past Perfect.* He died in 1981.

COLOPHON

Six Israeli Novellas has been set in Monotype Bembo, a fine Venetian old face adapted by the English Monotype Company. The great Italian printer-scholar of the Renaissance, Aldus Manutius, first used the roman for the printing of *De Aetna* in 1495. The characters were cut in 1490 by Francesco Griffo, who was later to cut the first italic type. The Bembo italic is base on the hand of the scribe San Vito and the Renaissance writing master Giovannantonio Tagliente, who practiced and taught in Venice.